The Loving Heart

A Son Who Did Not Know His Father

Assaf Sawaya

PAGE PUBLISHING, INC.
Conneaut Lake, PA

First originally published by Page Publishing 2021

ISBN 978-1-6624-1422-0 (pbk)
ISBN 978-1-6624-1423-7 (digital)

Printed in the United States of America

Abbreviations

General
c.—About approximately
cf.—Compare confer
ch.—Chapter or chapters
e.g.—For example
etc.—And so on
i.e.—That is
lit.—Literally
NT—New Testament
OT—Old Testament
v., vv.—Verse, verses (in the chapter being commented on)

I am the youngest of the growing brood my mother and father brought to life. We lived in a generously sized house by the entrance of our beautiful town Douma and strategically by the running water fountain where all the inhabitants of Douma and other neighboring towns come to fill their buckets of water; and when visitors stop by the fountain for a refreshing water, my mother will have the coffee ready, bringing it to them and welcoming them to our town. She was that loving woman; that is how I inherited the loving heart of my mother. My two oldest brothers and one sister I have not met until my early teens. I lived in Douma with my other two brothers who are older than me and our mother. Our father worked outside our town, and he came home every two months at a time. He always brought with him our supplies of food to live on until his next trip, and he paid off the merchants and others in our village; but sometimes he used to come home empty-handed and tell me to go to his rich friend in our village to borrow money from him because of his gambling habits. That was the most difficult task for me—to ask anybody for money even I was a little boy—and everybody at home was mad at him; but he read the BIBLE for me and my mother when he was home because my mother was illiterate. Despite that, she quoted the word of GOD for me by memorizing verses from the BIBLE as she attended the Sunday mass, and she used to quote the priest, explaining the Word of GOD for me. She was a devoted Catholic—always fasted, prayed, and walked barefoot in the entire month of May; she did that to humble herself for our mother of GOD, the Virgin Mary. She is very loving mother to her children and to others; I have inherited her loving heart and constant smile, and from my father, I inherited his gambling habits.

My mother raised chickens, rabbits, and goats for milk and lived off the field by growing vegetables of various kinds. My assignment was to gather grass to feed the rabbits. One day, I was at the end of our property gathering grass close to the wall of our neighbor's property of apple trees. My mother saw me from a distance throwing rocks over the property of our neighbor; she yelled at me and told me to cut a whip and come home. I ran to her empty-handed.

She asked me, "Where is the whip that I told to bring with you?"

I asked her, "Why the whip, Mom?"

"Why were you throwing rocks over our neighbor's property?"

I said to her, "No, Mom. Those were no rocks but apples falling over our property from the trees of our neighbor's, so I was throwing the apples back over to his property because the apples don't belong to us."

Immediately, she raised her arms to heaven and thanked GOD, for the way she raised us, and she hugged me close to her chest, crying and kissing me.

My mother told my story to whoever she visited in our town or abroad and always taught me to treat others the way I expect others to treat me, and that is what JESUS taught us. She is responsible for the nickname I got: GOD bless you and by GOD'S will because she always repeated these two sayings.

I have so much love and respect for every mother in the world because of my mother's love.

Two weeks after that apple story, I was in the prairies up the mountain of our large vineyard trying to climb a wall to the upper field; and as I put my foot one at a time in the area between the stones and as I placed my hands on the top, pulling my head up, I was facing a snake preparing to strike me with its mouth wide open to an extent and its tongue split into two parts with the flame coming out of it about one inch long and its head moving back and forth and our eyes communicating within three inches apart, telling me, "Go away, you eight-year-old boy, before I strike you!" Then I climbed down, and I left running back home to my loving mother; and I told her about the scary encounter with the snake. Again, my mother lifted her arms to heaven, thanked GOD, and hugged me, kissing me

6

and crying while telling me, "You are special to GOD my son. GOD saved you. GOD must have a plan for you in life."

My two brothers Anton and Majid moved to the city Amioun to continue their education, but they spent the summer vacation in our home, Douma. The majority of the inhabitants of the city Amioun belongs to a party who believes in the great Syria, its founder being Anton Saadeh in 1932. Anton Saadeh led a coup on July 1949. He was caught and shot within twenty-four hours without a fair trial. On his knees with his hands tied behind his back, he asked the executioner to remove a gravel from under his knee. His followers glorify him as a philosopher and a leader. To the point when he was facing death, he was sensitive to a minor gravel under his knee.

One of my brother Anton's classmate came to visit him in our home in Douma, and they were talking and calling one another comrades to my surprise. I did not know that my brother already joined that party. As they were glorifying their leader Anton Saadeh, my brother made the comparison that he admired Saadeh more than JESUS because JESUS, when he was at the cross, asked GOD the Father if he will pass the cup from him; while Saadeh asked the soldier to remove the gravel from under his knee as he was facing death, so he was in control. I was disappointed when my brother thought JESUS was afraid of death.

Both my brother and his comrade are Catholic, and we all attend the mass on Sunday; and yet we do not know why JESUS died for us. But if I knew then what I know now after I read the BIBLE and understand why JESUS died for us, I would interrupt my brother and stand up, saying to him in a loud voice: "You are glorifying man more than our LORD JESUS, who asked GOD the Father to pass the cup because our LORD JESUS was obeying GOD the Father to shed his blood for us, the sinners—*he* who did not sin. GOD the Father condemned all men because of the disobedience of one man, and he sent his only begotten son as a sacrifice for our salvation." Here were two people in their twenties who were devoted Christian and did not know why JESUS was crucified on the cross.

The following summer, my brothers moved to the city of Antelias, a suburb of Beirut; my brother Anton got a job, while my brother Majid continued his education and became a teacher; I was still living in our town, Douma, with my mother. One weekend, my father came home with no money! My mother was upset with him and said to him, "Did you lose our money by gambling again?" They got into an argument, and my mother started to cry. I started to cry because I loved her so much. I ran to my mother and held her, but she actually held me close to her and took me to the bedroom. My father called me to come out and go to his friend to borrow some money, so I went and spent the night with my relatives. My mother came to pick me up after my father went back to work.

After that incident, I asked my mother to move with my brothers in the city and learn a trade because I used to stutter and my classmates made fun of me. When my mother asked my older brother about my intention, he said to her, "How this boy? He is going to leave you while he still sleeps in your bed?"

Finally, I made the move down to the city and worked as an apprentice to become a tailor. I loved my trade so much I became a tailor within a short time. My brother helped me to open a shop; and in three months, I had ten people working for me, and I was the youngest of them, telling them what to do and, at the same time, learning from them.

After four years of having my own business, the sounds of war start to ring in my ears; I decided to immigrate to the USA. I was twenty-two years old when I got my immigration visa to the USA; I left Lebanon on Friday, February the 13, and arrived at San Diego, California, on Saturday the 14 in 1970. I was told it was Valentine's Day at my bother-in-law Tony Sawaya's and his family. It was a very happy day for me.

Later, I asked Tony, "How I am going to get a job?" He took me to a factory in the downtown of San Diego. I did not get the job because I did not speak English well. Finally, I got a job as a tailor on Fifth Avenue.

One day, the owner asked me if I knew how to drive to help him drive some of the distance to Las Vegas. I said yes; the next day, we drove up to Barstow, and there, he asked me to take over. I got behind the wheel and started driving. To test my driving, he asked me, "Now brake."

I answered, "Yeah."

He repeated, "Brake."

Again, I answered, "Yeah."

Now I see him hitting his head with his hands. "Brake, brake, brake."

"Yeah, yeah," I said.

By then, he realized that I did not understand the order. He said in a loud voice, "Stop, stop, stop!"

I slammed on the brake so fast his wife and daughter hit their faces on the back seats. He then took over driving to Las Vegas; no rest for the poor guy.

I was overwhelmed by the lights and the city of Las Vegas. The next day, I found a job on Las Vegas Boulevard; the tailor was French, and I was able to communicate with him. The next day, I informed my former tailor that I found a job and I desire to stay in Las Vegas; he was not disappointed at all.

I tried to make a collect call to Tony in San Diego. I asked the operator for a collect call.

"What is your name?" she asked.

"My name is Sawaya."

She replied, "I am fine, sir, but I need your name to inform Tony if he will accept the collect call."

"Sawaya."

"Sir, sir, trust me, I am fine. But I have to have your name for Tony to accept a collect call. Do you understand?"

"I have been telling you my name is Sawaya."

"Oh, okay, okay. Is that your first name or last name?"

"Last name."

"What is your first name?"

"Assaf."

"Spell it, please."

"*A* as Assaf, *S* as Sawaya, *A* as Assaf, and *F* as *friend*." And I hung up.

After I have been in Vegas for a month, I found a Lebanese restaurant where they have music and belly dancing, just like Beirut, a twenty-four-hour; it was heaven to me. I got to know the owner and the musicians. One early evening as I was walking with my musician friend to have dinner, I noticed a young girl dining with her mother with her eyes glancing at our dining table; the owner came and introduced her to us as a Lebanese.

Nina and I started dating, confessing to me. When I walked into that restaurant, her mother asked her what happened to Nina. "Mom! Mom, that is the man I saw in my dream last night."

As a tailor, I made myself a suit. One evening as we were dining together, her mother commented on the suit I was wearing, and she told me, "I am going to tell my friend about the beautiful work you do. She has all of her clothes tailor-made."

Nina and I went to the house of her mother's friend to take her measurement and her needs of a specific design, and I asked the rich lady how soon she expected her garment to be ready. "Yesterday," she said. Nina and I smiled. That evening, I went to my shop and worked all night and prepared pants for her. The next day, I drove to her house, and when she put those pants on, she looked at the mirror and said, "That is a handsome pant, Assaf. You got a job for life with me."

My shop was in front of a cleaner I sublet from the owner, and he allowed me to display my work on the wall. One of his clients was admiring a suit I displayed. "Is this your work, Assaf?"

"Yes, it is."

"I want you to make me a suit just like it," Mr. X said. "I have not worn a suit for a long time. I just got out of college. So you have your own business?"

"Yes."

"Funny business."

I had no idea what he was talking about. We got to know each other well. After I made him a several suits, we became friends.

"What nationality are you?"

"I am a Lebanese."

"So you are from Lebanon?" He added, "Your people supply lots of countries with drugs." I did not pay any attention to what he said.

When Nina and I got married, we moved to an apartment owned by the rich lady; I turned one of the bedrooms into a sewing room. Mr. X was regular at my new place, and when I was not there, he used to chat with one of my workers. After five years of marriage, Nina and I separated; and Nina, for the one year of separation, often came to spend the weekend with me, telling me, "As long as I am married to you, I will not sleep with any man."

It came to the point when I wanted to buy a house. She refused to sign with me and suggested to get a divorce; I said fine. So we got a divorce, and after the court and we went and had lunch together, then she asked me, "Why did we get a divorce?"

"Because you did not want to take a risk with me."

I did not realize the bad decision I had taken until a month passed by and no Nina came home. I used to spend the nights crying by myself on what jewel I lost; but at that time, I was not a jeweler to recognize what a jewel I had, and how many of us go through that experience because of our ignorance?

Months passed feeling sorry for myself. I started going to the casinos, created a gambling habit, and learned how to become a dealer. I got a job in the casino, bought a new house, and turned the garage into sewing room. I was making lots of money and losing all of it on the game that I love: craps. Mr. X kept coming to me for new clothes, as well as the rich lady.

Three months passed, and I did not pay my mortgage. I asked Mr. X to loan me three thousand dollars. He brought me the money the next day and said to me, "Oh, man! Either you are stupid or not of this culture."

"What are you talking about?" I said.

"The two people I had met in your place of business, your homeboys, they already made hundreds of thousands of dollars with me. And you are my best friend, and I like you."

"So what is it you want me to do?"

Mr. X said, "Don't you know anybody from Lebanon could bring heroin to the USA?"

"I will ask some people about that."

I brought the subject to a friend of mine; let me call him Mr. D. He happily said, "Why didn't you tell me that before?" So Mr. D set the connection for me in Lebanon.

I called Mr. X about the good news; he fronted me twenty-five thousand dollars to go to Beirut. When I arrived at Beirut, Mr. D told me the money was not enough. He paid ten thousand dollars out of his own, on the condition he gets a bigger cut for himself. Did I know what I was doing? Absolutely not. Mr. D showed me the powder. To test the drugs, I was told to put very little on my tongue, and if its sour, that is a good sign for a quality of that drugs.

That night, we packed the drugs in the shoulder pads of a suit; genius idea, right? How stupid it was. I put the suit in a garment bag, and I also had two other bags; I checked them all through the cargo—another stupid idea—and I did not have to carry anything on the plane. We made a stop in London, and the next stop in New York.

I collected all my bags and carried them to customs. A lady officer was tending the counter; she asked me, "Where are you coming from?"

"Lebanon," I said.

"Lebanon. Oh! That is a drugs country. Are you bringing any drugs with you?"

"Oh. *No*, Officer."

"Let me see what you have."

I placed the garment bag at her counter, and she told me to open the other two bags; she found a gold necklace, and she told me I had to pay tax for it. "Gladly," I said. I was tempted tell her, "Do you want me to open the garment bag also?" But I thought, *Don't push your luck, man. If she asked me to open the garment bag, the drugs would spill from the shoulder pads all over the bag!* It seemed that my hour did not come yet; I honestly felt bad for that kind officer, but I was happy to go through. All my thinking was to get to Vegas to play craps!

The next flight was to Vegas. When I arrived at the airport, my brother and our friend collected me from the airport. We drove to my house. I saw my neighbor Louis in front of his house; he ran toward me. We hugged halfway.

I heard my girlfriend calling me, "Assaf! Assaf!" Full of happiness to see me back safe, she ran and jumped on me, hugging my waist with her legs, and her arms around my neck, kissing me with passion. The friend who drove us from the airport—I noticed him looking at us with envy. I knew then he was no true friend; let us call him Mr. S. Dana was a gorgeous girl, an angel; we were to be married in the near future.

After everybody left, I called Mr. X, telling him I have the package. He came that night, inspecting the merchandise. After I gathered the powder from the bag, he put the powder in his special bag and reached into his pocket, handing me five hundred dollars! I was shocked.

"Are you out of your mind? I have to pay my people in Lebanon."

Mr. X told me, "I have to get the stuff to my contact in Texas. Just give me few days, and I will get you the rest of the money."

In a few days, Mr. X was arrested; I heard it on the news. I collapsed and said to myself, "My hour just came." The people in Lebanon will have me or my family killed.

After one week, Mr. D called me. "Where is my money?" I told him it was going to be delayed a minute. Three days later, he was knocking at my door, coming from Lebanon. I was shocked and scared to see him! I said to him, "Wait and listen to the news." He heard it himself that Mr. X was in jail; it was a sad news, but it did calm him down. I also calmed him more when Mr. X called me from the jail, assuring me he will send me one of his people to explain to me what was going on. The person who came to me explained that Texas contact got most of stuff, and they will send me the money. I was relieved that my hour did not come yet. Five days later, the money was delivered to my house; I paid Mr. D, and he left back to his home.

Does anyone believe this story? It is all fact!

Two months later, Mr. X called me from his prison, telling me some of his people will come to see me with a good news. His people informed me that Texas liked the merchandise and they need more of it with the same quality. Mr. X's people required a thirty-thousand-dollar cash transaction; we agreed after I received a one hundred thousand dollars in advance.

A week later, Texas sent me ninety thousand dollars as a down payment. I booked a flight to Beirut, and that night, I paid myself twenty thousand dollars to shoot dice at one of the casinos. I lost about ten thousand dollars. It did not matter to me; I enjoy shooting dice, win or lose. Then I moved to another casino; I lost the rest of the money. I went home and slept it off, and the next morning, I took my flight to Beirut.

July 1983. It was my second trip to Beirut to smuggle another kilo of heroin. This time, I got smarter; I split the one kilo into two parts and sealed them inside my boot, another ingenious idea of mine, not so. As I was walking to board the plane, I faced a checkpoint. I could not go back, and the officers were waiting for me; they padded me from head to toe. "What is this in your boot? Take it out!" I handed him the drugs, with him laughing at me. "We don't let a fly pass us anymore?" Then I knew I have been sold out! The man who came to visit my dealer when I was meeting with him was the undercover agent.

I was under arrest for the possession of illegal drugs. The officer in charge asked me, "Who gave you a ride to the airport?"

Finally, I said, "Mr. D."

"Let us go outside and look for him." The officer told me, "I am not going to cuff you, but if you try to run away, I will shoot you!"

I put him at ease. We looked all over the airport, but Mr. D already left. Two hours later, the arresting officer informed me that my conspirator was arrested. It was late at night, and another officer with three stars on his shoulders came in. The other officer saluted him and called his name, and that was more embarrassing to me because his nephew was my friend.

In the morning, four soldiers took me in a jeep to the courthouse; on the way, they were singing with joy, celebrating my arrest. I was handed to the investigator officer; in his office and on his desk, he placed a whip! He informed me that he will get the truth out of me one way or another, pointing out the whip on his desk. He started by asking me where I got the hashish.

I answered him, "I do not have any hashish!"

"You were arrested with a kilo of hashish at the airport?"

"No, sir. It was heroin."

At this point, he was so furious with me, and I was so calm and in control of myself but so stupid! When they placed me in the cell with other inmates, the first thing the inmates asked was, "What are you arrested for?" And when I told them for the possession of heroin, every one of them said, "You have no problem! You will be out of here in a few months!"

"What are you talking about? The investigator officer told me I have to spend seven years in the prison for the possession of the heroin!"

"No, no. You pay some money, and the heroin will become hashish!" I told the inmates that the investigator officer was asking me repeatedly where I bought the hashish from. Now I know why! Haha! Everybody was laughing at me. "And you call yourself a drug dealer?"

I kept telling the officer that was heroin I had on me.

"So! so where did you buy the heroin from?"

"Mr. D and Mr. F." Mr. F never was arrested. He is the supplier of the drugs in Lebanon.

"So you know Mr. F?"

"Yes, sir, through Mr. D."

"How much did you pay for the one kilo?"

"Thirty thousand dollars."

"And how much are you going to sell it for?"

"Two hundred thousand dollars."

"What is the name of the person that you are going to sell the drugs to in the USA?" I gave him the information. "And how long have you been doing that?"

"It is my second time."

"How much money do you have?"

"Five thousand dollars."

"Is that all you have?"

"Yes, sir."

"What did you do with the rest of the money?"

"I lost it all playing craps, the game I love."

"You deserve what is going to happen to you! You are going to spend the next seven years in the prison for what you have done; and you have nothing to show for the crime you committed!" I was motionless. He made a telephone call, saying, "I'm finished with this prisoner, and I got all the information we need."

I was handcuffed and moved to a holding cell, a place fit for rats; and there was plenty of them! No bed to sleep on, no bench to sit on, and no toilet, of course, purposely; and who said crime does not pay? The result of crime and its reward is to repent and stop doing the crime, then GOD will recognize you are remorseful and will welcome you back by the blood that JESUS paid for you on the cross.

I was surprise that Mr. D was already there. He started complaining why I told the authority about him. I had no choice. The investigator officer had a whip on his desk, pointing at it and saying, "I will get the truth out of you one way or another, so let us start from the beginning." Mr. D started to raise his voice. By then, I lost my temper.

We quietly started discussing our tragedy; Mr. D. reminded me when we were at Mr. F's house. That man who came to visit him! That was the informant.

We faced the matter of hiring a lawyer to defend us. The inmates referred to me one of the best lawyer in Lebanon. I had to borrow some money from two different friends as a down payment to our best lawyer; he was able to move me from the prison to a hospital for two months and then to a different prison.

I was a celebrity among the inmates, and everybody wanted be my friend for being an American and having connections into the drug market! Their question was why I had to carry the drugs myself instead of having somebody doing this mission for me. After a few days, I got friendly with the inmates, and they confided with me; one source I felt comfortable with knew one of my relatives, and he assured me he will deliver any amount anywhere into the USA and will help me get out of the prison because of the civil war that was taking its toll in Lebanon!

Within seven months, I was out of the prison and left Lebanon after a few days even when I was released on bail. Coming to my home, the USA, my first impression was how wide and clean the streets were. It was a heaven coming back to America. By my action, I lost my job, my house, and my lovely girlfriend. With all those tragedies, I moved to San Diego with my brother-in-law Tony. He helped me to open a tailor shop, but he had no idea the shop was a front for my activity.

I called Texas, and I explained to him what happened to me and that I had a reliable connection with unlimited supply. "Bring it in," he said. I called Lebanon and ordered one kilo; within two weeks, I had the merchandise. I called Texas, telling him that his white suit was ready for pick up! "You are so quick. You finish it so fast. I will send you my driver in a few days to pick it up." Sure enough, his driver arrived with a suitcase filled with ninety thousand dollars. The exchange took place; he asked me for a nice restaurant to have dinner before his flight.

I gave the ninety thousand dollars to the people from Lebanon, and off they left back home. Texas did not mention to me about the ninety thousand I lost in Lebanon, and he paid me the full amount; he also ordered another kilo for the coming month.

I started my contact and said to them my contact in Lebanon were very happy for the arrangement, and I stated to them, "When the carrier comes to the USA, check into any hotel, call him where he is at, then they will call me of his location so he will not know my name in case he was arrested." Then I called Texas to send his people to pick up the merchandise.

I was the mastermind for trafficking the drugs from Lebanon to the USA. I was on top of the world, living high, and met a beautiful young girl. She traveled with me to different places, especially to Las Vegas, my favorite city where I lost all the money I made trafficking drugs. She was pleasant and kind. One evening, she was crying.

I asked her, "What is wrong?"

She said, "You don't want to marry me!"

I was troubled, and I did not want to tell her what I was doing for a living. I let her go, big mistake on my part.

My contact from Lebanon this time came himself with other two guys through the Los Angeles airport, calling me to let me know that one of them was in the hospital. I asked him if he knew of me. He assured me that no. I told him to come to San Diego as fast as he can; he arrived with his friend! "Tell me exactly, what happened?" He and his friend came through customs, but the other one got caught. As the officer was shaking his bag, one of the hangers was broken, and the powder spilled all over the bag! He was arrested immediately; we thought by containing the powder in wooden hangers, it was foolproof! Not this time. I told the two guys, "You can't stay with me, and you can't go back to Lebanon through any airport from the USA."

I sent them through Mexico with one of my men to the Lebanese consulate in Mexico City; they met with the consular and informed him that they had no Mexican visa and were running from the authorities of the USA. The consular told them, "No way I could help you!" They threatened him by killing his family in Lebanon! It was their story.

Two days later, a drug agent came to my shop and asked me if I knew the two guys from Lebanon.

I said, "Yes?"

"Did they come to see you?"

"Yes."

"Did they have any drugs with them?"

"No, they did not? They spent the night in my place, and the next day, they left." He informed me that the district attorney would like to see me in her office. I said, "No problem."

He set an appointment for me to meet the DA in Los Angeles; I was there on time to meet with the DA. "Thank you, Mr. Sawaya, for coming. I am Marcha Clark, the assistant DA."

"It is a pleasure meeting you, Ms. Clark."

A gentleman came to her door, asking her if she got a hold of Sawaya from San Diego. To shut him up fast, "This is Mr. Sawaya."

He left immediately. "I was informed that two guys came to see you and stayed with you over night?"

"Yes, they did."

"Are you going to testify to that in court?"

"Yes, I will."

The court date came, and I was there to testify. I was called to the stand, and sworn in. "The two guys from Lebanon came to see you?" the prosecutor asked me. "Did you know them?"

"Yes, sir."

"Did they bring any drugs to you?"

"No, sir."

"What did they come to see you for?"

"Usually, when they come to the USA, they visit me because we are good friends from back home."

"Do you know the defender sitting over there?"

"No, sir."

"Did they have any guns with them?"

"No, sir. I did not see any guns."

"You step down," and he said it with an angry voice. When I saw him outside the court with the drug agent who came to see me at my tailor shop in San Diego, he looked at me with contempt and said, "You are wearing a very expensive suit!"

And before I replied, the drug agent said it for me: "He is a tailor."

The next day; with no time wasted, I noticed a trailer parked across the street of my apartment! That did not stop me from doing my daily walk by passing in front of the parked trailer; I knew they don't have any proof against me. That trailer stayed there for one month, and during that time, the telephone company's workers and the plumbing company's workers were in and out of my apartment; I still wasn't nervous.

After what happened at the Los Angeles airport with the built-in wooden hanger breaking, the guys from Lebanon used the old invention: placing the drugs at the bottom of the suitcase. That was a good way to smuggle the drugs; we had no problem with it at all until Texas sent me a new guy to pick up the drugs and bring me the money.

Now I started to get nervous; I called him and told him, "I don't feel good about this new guy!"

He said, Don't worry. He is my best friend. We grew up together since our childhoods." But I did not know until that guy recently was released from the prison serving a life sentence! Big mistake on the part of Texas.

I met a new girl, and I opened a shoe store for her in La Jolla, spending five hundred dollars and another five hundred thousand dollars on gifts; but the relation wasn't going good between us. In my other living place in Las Vegas, I met another girl, and I let her move in with me. The one hundred thousand dollars I was making every month wasn't enough to cover the gambling habits and other expenses; I had to wait for the next shipment to come to be able to go gamble in Las Vegas. I used to win twenty to thirty thousand dollars in a couple of hour and lose it back! I loved the game of craps, win or lose, but sometimes I used to win big and get paid by check and claim it as an income and paid taxes. Often, I took a flight to Vegas just to play craps for relief. On one of my flights, I was sitting next to a girl. She said to me, "I see you often play craps, you win and lose big money, but you don't show any emotion or expression? How sad that is." I told her they called me the man of steel.

Texas sent the new guy, but this time, he stayed in my house. Suddenly, I walked on him while he was on the telephone, and I noticed fear in his eyes! I knew there was something wrong; after that incident; I flew to Texas to speak to Texas about the new guy and asked him not to send me that guy anymore. I will come myself to pick up the money and let us not talk on the telephone anymore. I took the telephone number of the telephone booth he had on the comer of his store. "And any time we need to talk, I will call you, and you will go to the telephone booth to arrange our next steps." He smiled and agreed.

After Texas received another shipment from me, I went myself to pick up the money. When I arrived at the hotel to pick up the key to my room, I said, "My name is Assaf Sawaya. I have a reservation."

Immediately, that receptionist went back to some office and returned after five minutes and handed me the key to my room; I knew then there was something wrong. I got to my room and called Texas to send somebody to give me a ride to his place of business. When we were close to his place of business, I noticed a police car parked not too far from Texas's business. I asked the driver, "How come the police car is here?"

"Oh, probably are watching somebody."

I knew it was me. Also I noticed the telephone booth was not there, and when the driver dropped me off, the first thing on my mind was to ask Texas what happened to the telephone booth. He replied, "The telephone company took it!" My disturbing thoughts were *What other bad things am I going to experience today?*

In his office, he took off my mind the troubling thoughts and asked me about the cocaine's connection from South America. I said, "It is going to take some time to set it all together through my connection in Lebanon."

"We should be rolling within a few weeks," he said. "We will be averaging about a million dollars monthly."

He counted the money I was supposed to pick up and gave it to me; I put some inside my socks on both sides and the rest all over my body. The driver dropped me at the airport, and as I was taking the escalator, the money was sliding down my socks. It was a scary moment, and it showed on my face; I looked up the escalator, and a policeman was standing there.

I walked to the counter, handed in my ticket, and took a seat. Waiting for my flight, I noticed three men together consulting one another. One of them took a seat, pretending to read the paper; and the other two were staring at me and walked up to both of my sides, showing their badges, and asked me, "Do you have any drugs or any money on you?"

I answered, "No, I don't have any drugs on me."

"Do you have any money on you?"

"Yes, I do."

"Please come with us to the office."

"But, sir, I will miss my flight."

"We'll make sure you won't."

They walked me to the office, and one agent introduced himself and told me to put the money on the table. As I took out about fifty thousand dollars, then the agent said, "You don't have to take it all." I was surprised to hear that from the agent. "Where did you get all of this money from?"

"I have a client, and I make him very expensive clothes. And he front money for gambling. I am a professional gambler."

"Do you have a card that shows that you are a professional gambler?"

"No, sir, I don't. But I am a tailor, and I have a shop."

"Wait a moment, I have to talk to my boss." He came back after five minutes, no blood in his face, and with an angry voice, he told me to take the money and go! I couldn't believe it! I should have been arrested for that amount of money I was carrying.

The angry agent took me to my flight as the flight attendant was closing the door! The drug agent kept their promise as they usually do, and that is a fact; and I was on my way to my favorite city, Las Vegas, to play my favorite game: the craps.

On my way to Las Vegas, I thought I will not be able to play craps anymore, but I did; and I lost lots of money that night without blinking. The next day, I flew to San Diego and rested for a few days. I was not enjoying my time. I flew back to Vegas, and in two hours, I lost the rest of the money I had left; and I did not feel bad at all. Now I had to wait for a new order to get some money to be able to go back to play craps again.

Mr. S came to visit me in San Diego in my new house. I showed him around; he was impressed and asked me if I could do business with his brother. I thought that was odd because his brother could do business through Lebanon more than I could. I told him, "Only because you and I are very good friends. Otherwise, no way that I would do business with anybody. I don't need any extra headache."

Mr. S said, "Let me call my brother in Oklahoma. He has a connection there, and he could use one kilo immediately. And I will let you know tomorrow."

Mr. S called the next day as he promised, and his brother was ready to do the exchange. I sent my right-hand man to pick up one kilo of heroin from Texas; he was on his way to Oklahoma to deliver it. He had made the contact with the brother of Mr. S, who's supposed to be my friend, to do the exchange. His brother called me, saying, "Assaf, you surprise me! I thought that you will be coming yourself!" He was very disappointed, and so was I; and I lost fifty thousand dollars for that episode but not my freedom because my right-hand man said, "If you were there, the drug agents would have arrested you!" Then I had the flashback when my girlfriend was kissing me, and Mr. S was looking at me with envy. So much for friendship. We should be able to recognize this behavior in people; it is a lesson for all of us.

That was the second time my hour has not come yet. Another time, Texas ordered five kilos, the first time for this amount. "But wait until I confirm with you." I was so excited. I called my people in Lebanon, and they got excited as well; and within two weeks, they managed to deliver five kilos to me at one time! "I did not confirm with you guys yet. But let me call my guy, and I will let you know."

I called Texas to let him know that I had five kilos in my position. He told me, "I only could use one kilo. And that deal with the man who wants five kilos—he was shot to death by his jealous wife."

The people from Lebanon were very disappointed. I said, "You have to wait another month. By then, I will be able use another kilo."

So they waited and got their money; but they could not wait any longer, and they had three kilos left. They gave it to me, saying, "Take your time, and when you get the money, let us know."

I refused to keep the drugs in my possession; I will not take that chance by keeping the drugs. I suggested to give it to my guy. He could be trusted; I had been doing business with him for the last three years. They agreed! I called Texas and suggested to front him the three kilos of heroin and to pay me as much as he can within three months, he paid me the full amount! Believe it or not, that is the truth. For the third time, my hour did not come yet!

Sitting on the bench in front of my store in La Jolla, I was meditating about all the events that took place when I checked into the hotel and the driver of Texas took me to his place of business and what happened at the airport and the release with the money to catch my flight to Vegas; was this my hour coming now?

In the last four to five years, I had been conspiring with other bad people against GOD and the USA to smuggle drugs into my beloved hosting country, the USA. All because I created a gambling habit and all the dirty money I had was wasted on supporting my gambling urges and on girls who were younger than I was.

Traveling in a limousine with my twenty-one-year-old girlfriend through the downtown of Los Angeles at dusk time and looking at the pavement of the street covered with many homeless people—am I going to join them someday? Those scary thoughts were reflected clearly on my face!

My girlfriend held my hand. "What is wrong, my love? Tell me."

I am going to tell you. I used to design and make suits for very famous and rich people. And they walked confidently with a smile on their faces, and I say, "I made this suit for him or her." But now looking at those unfortunate people, what do I say? I sold them drugs so they could cover the pavements? And other thoughts start to stagger on my mind, from the police car parked at close distance from Mr. Texas's store to the removal of the telephone booth from the corner of his store also and the episode of the drug agent at the airport; I think my hour was approaching.

My experience in life is, whatever is about to happen in my future, I see it in a dream one or two days before. One week after I returned to San Diego, I had a dream that as I was sitting at the bench in front of my store in La Jolla, the drug agent who questioned me at the airport was going around my store, asking questions; and my dream continued where I was in the tub, taking a bath, and I had a doll stuck with pins. And I woke up sweating; I knew something bad was going to happen to me.

Two days after that bad dream and at six o'clock in the morning, I was awoken by a continuous loud knock at the door with a loud voice as well. "Open up! This is the police." I ran to open the door, and the second I opened the door, I was ordered to be on the floor. They cuffed my hands. "Do you have any guns?"

"No, sir."

"Anybody else in the house?"

By then, a cousin of mine came to the door; he also was cuffed. And the drug agent came. "Do you remember me?"

"Yes, I do, sir. From the airport."

Then he commanded me, "Give me the codes of the two safes you have in the house." So I did. Later, he came out without any blood in his face again! "Where are the drugs? Where is the money?"

"I have no drugs, and I have no money."

Then he asked me, "I only found the wraps of the ten thousand dollar bills. Where is the money?"

"I lost it on the craps table in Las Vegas."

"So why did you keep the ten thousand dollar wraps?"

"Well, sir, I figured one day, you will come to arrest me. At least you will have some evidence that I made money, but I was not smart enough to keep it. My addiction was the beneficiary."

After they checked the whole house, they only found two thousand dollars on my dresser. "Is that all the money you have?"

"That is all, sir." After the millions I earned in dirty money. "Am I arrested now?"

"You have been arrested a month ago."

My cousin asked if he was arrested also. They said no and removed the handcuffs on his hands.

I was taken and placed in the front seat of the drug agent; on the way to the MCC prison in downtown San Diego, the agent made a comment that some of the nicest people are drug dealers! That was a comforting comment.

I asked him, "Why am I arrested? While you did not find any drugs or any large amount of money in my house?"

He answered, "You put two and two together, and you will find out."

We arrived at the prison in downtown San Diego. I was assigned to a cell with one inmate only; a common question the inmate asked me was "What did they arrest you for?"

"The accusation is drugs, but they did not find any drugs or any money in my house."

"It does not matter. They must have been watching every move you made for a long time. Do you have a lawyer?"

"Not yet."

"You need a very good lawyer."

I found a prominent lawyer, and we discussed my situation. He informed me that my case will cost a hundred thousand dollars to defend me. I agreed, then he said, "I will get the indictment first and will go from there." Four days later, he brought me the indictment and handed me the heavy book, saying, "You have a plenty of time to go through it, and let me know what you want me to do for you."

The indictment was two thousand pages. As I was reading through the pages, I realized that the drug agents knew every move I made for the last two years, and the government charging me with a CCE crime (continuous criminal enterprise) will carry a life sentence. My room inmate was facing his crime, and his advice was to do what he was doing.

"What is that you are doing?" I asked.

"You have to cooperate with the government."

"What do you mean?"

He laughed at me, saying, "How long you have been doing this?" And he continued, saying, "You have to confess all your sins and tell the district attorney all that you've done—naming names and testifying in court against the ones you dealt with!"

I called my lawyer and told him I decided to cooperate with the government; he said, "I have to see if I could sale this with the district attorney for you."

I was waiting for some good news from my lawyer. As I went through the pages of my indictment, I found out the name of Mr. Texas's best friend since his childhood; he was a confidential informant and was released from prison working with the drug agents— picking up the drugs and bringing the money for me to San Diego. Also the guy who got shot to death by his jealous wife was working with the drug agents, and my best friend's brother from Oklahoma also was working with the drug agents. All those people were informants to set me up and Mr. Texas. Finally, my lawyer came back with some encouraging information from the district attorney of Dallas and Fort Worth: that he will come to San Diego to talk with me about all the sins I committed against the people of the USA.

The day came, and my attorney picked me up from the prison and took me to the hotel where the district attorney, the arresting drug agent, and the big boss who was in charge of our case from the beginning of the case were. My attorney was not allowed to be with me during the interrogation; he said, "Go ahead. Tell them everything." I sat on a couch, and the two agents sat across from me; the district attorney sat away from us, smoking one cigarette after another. The first question from the agent in charge was how I met Mr. Texas.

"The first time I met him, he came to my house with Mr. X to order a few suits, and he was happy with my work. He ordered some more. Then Mr. X told me that he was his connection in Texas. Mr. X gave me 25,000 dollars to go to Lebanon and buy one kilo of heroin. I did. I was successful in passing through the customs at the New York airport and all the way to Vegas. I called Mr. X that evening. He came, picked up the bag, and gave me five hundred dollars only and said as soon as he gets the money from Mr. Texas, he will pay me the rest of the money.

"Few days later, I heard on the news that Mr. X was arrested, and from the prison, he was calling me every day and sent me one of his people to pay the rest of the money. And that same person informed me that Mr. Texas was pleased with the merchandise and would like another kilo of the same quality. I asked for a hundred thousand dollars up front. Two weeks later, his man brought me the money, and I was on my way to Lebanon again. But this time, I was not so lucky. I was arrested at the airport in Beirut."

"What happened then?"

"I suppose to serve seven years in prison. But some drug dealers helped, and I got out within seven months!"

The agents looked at each other! "Who are those drug dealers?" I gave them the names. "And they were supplying me with the drugs every month or so."

"How many kilos did they bring to our country?"

"Oh, over twenty kilos."

"How also did you supply with drugs?"

"Nobody else. That was my only connection."

"Is that all?"

"Yes, sir."

Suddenly, the district attorney stood up and threw the ashtray so hard on the wall and said to me, "Do you think we are some kind of kids here talking to you?"

"But that was all I did, sir." The district attorney was expecting me to be one of those dangerous drug dealers. "I am just a humble man who got involved when the big boys came."

He was angry as he opened the door and called my lawyer, who was waiting outside, and said to him, "We have no use for your man!" And they left!

I asked my lawyer, "What are you going to do now?"

"I will go to the trial, and I will defend you in the best way."

"How are you going to do that after I confessed to them all that I did for the last four years?"

He told me, "They can't use that against you in the court of law! They are going to extradite you to the state of Texas, and my advice to you is not to fight it. But if you want, I could delay the extradition for about one year and take you back to the prison where you belong."

Then I said, "No, I will not fight the extradition."

I started thinking and asked myself, *Am I going to spend my entire life in the prison? Oh, dear GOD, that is too big of a cup to swallow! Help me, dear Lord, out of this one. Do you want me to spend all my life in the prison? For my stupidity? Have mercy on me, dear Lord!*

"Hey, Sawaya. Did you hear what happened today?"

"No. Tell me."

"You are not going to believe that one of the inmates was so lucky today. While he was sitting on his bed, a woman dropped on his bed from the opening of the air condition!"

"But how could that happen?"

"You know that the women prison is under our floor. That woman was desperate for the feel of any man. She climbed into the air-condition pipes and made it to his room! This happy situation continued for about two weeks until one day, the woman overstayed her welcome, and she was missed by the daily count of the inmates. And that is how the guards found out and made it stop."

I was sitting on the bench in the dorm of the prison chatting with an inmate, and a roar exploded. We looked at this man walking proudly, waving to everybody. I asked, "Who is this guy?"

The inmate sitting next to me said, "He is the big bully of the dorm. He just got out of the hole!"

"What is that?" I asked

"You mean you don't know what that term means?"

"No, I really don't!"

"When you break the society law, they send you to prison, and when you break the prison law, they send you to the hole. That is more severe punishment, and that roar was from his gang."

I had a gut feeling that he was going to bully me, and I was so right. A few days passed. He came and sat next to me, asking me lots of questions and saying, "If you need anything around here, I will take care of all your needs." I thanked him and walked away.

My girlfriend was visiting me, and by chance, he was in the visiting room as well. When we went back to the dorm, he made the comment, "How many of those girls do you have?" Suggesting I have lots of money because of my case as a big-time drug dealer, he told me to send a big number of money to his family. I walked away. Next, he sent me a message with one of his gang members not to come out of my room like what he ordered the other inmate.

The immediate time when our cell door opened, I was the first one to be at the dorm, taking turns to play pool, and the bully was there. My cell mate appeared behind me, and out of any plan on my part, he portrayed himself as a bodyguard.

The bully guy looked at me with his monstrous eyes and said to his gang, "Look at this guy with money," and one of his boys showed me a sharp object, telling me, "I am going to slice you with this."

My bodyguard told him, "You have to pass me first, buddy."

No plan of my own, but GOD the creator of Heaven and Earth, was there for me—another time since my childhood. *Ya habibi ma atibeck ya elahe*—the translation, from the Arabic language in the Lebanese dialogue, being "My beloved GOD, how delicious you are."

The extradition paper came, and I was on my way to Fort Worth, Texas. We were chained by the legs and the hands around our waist to board the airplane, and when the lunch was served, we ate handcuffed as well. We arrived at the Texas airport and transferred us to our destination, the prison. As we were guided to our penthouse, what a surprise! My friend, the drug agent boss who knew every move I made for two years, was very busy going through lots of paper. I was so happy to see him there. What a coincidence! It was not; he was waiting for me! "Hello, sir. I would like to speak to you some more."

He came to my cell, talking to me through the iron rods. "Do you have any more information for me?"

"Yes, sir. I have more details."

"I will call your lawyer, and we'll talk."

The next morning, I was moved to the Tarrant County Jail with twenty-two inmates, and everybody knew who I was because of the news coverage and the well-known Mr. Texas's famous case. The mood of the inmates was that Mr. Texas had the best team of lawyers, and he will beat his case like he did for the last fifteen years; the only thing he had against him was his right-hand man, and that man was at large. If they catch him, he probably will testify against him because he was still young and he was a player; he will do anything to stay out of the prison.

I felt comfortable among the inmates. I helped some of them financially. A new inmate came into our dorm. He was charged with murder of one of the inmates' cousin, and that cousin brought a newspaper telling me to read it with the paper as a cover to my face. And four guys overpowered the new inmate. He fought them at the beginning, but after he realized their intentions, he gave up to save himself, and he actually did. He took the opportunity to run and rang the emergency bell, and within seconds, the police was there. They saw that guy bleeding, and the officer said from the sound of the bell, they realized something serious was taking place. The police removed the injured inmate and started taking the inmates one after another for questioning, and after the questioning, I asked them what happened. They said nobody saw anything; that guy must have fallen when he was in the shower. The case was closed. The prison system is aware of the silent code among the inmates, and it can't be broken. Maybe one of these days!

That night, I had a dream, or you may call it a vision. As I was standing on the roof of our house in Lebanon, looking up to the sky, I saw an angel looking at me and smiling! I was in ecstasy, and the angel kept smiling at me and coming closer and closer with a wider smile; and my ecstasy was exaggerated a hundred times over. But I was awaken by the whistle of one of the inmates, saying, "The show is here." I walked up to him, angrily yelling at him, "You woke me from the most beautiful dream in anybody's life! I was in an ecstasy that cannot be reached in this lifetime!" He apologized so many times to me. I went back to bed expecting the continuation of that awesome ecstasy, but it did not happen. I was so sad yet so happy to know that our GOD, the creator of Heaven and Earth, was showing me his love. I am the sinner. Our LORD GOD JESUS tells us in the BIBLE, "I come for the sick, not for the healthy" [Ya habibi ya elahe ma atyabek]. And I am one of his sick children, and GOD loves me!

In the morning, I called my lawyer to ask him if there was any good news? "Yes, there is," he said. The agent called my lawyer, and he told him he will be coming to see me to go through more details about the whole operation. "So keep in touch with my office on a daily basis." So I was exactly calling his office until I reached him. By then, he gave the good news that the assistant district attorney wanted me to cooperate with the government and he will come to meet with me soon because the right-hand man of Mr. Texas was still on the loose and there was no sign of him. The district attorney decided to use me instead of him; it was GOD'S hand in my life through all my trials.

The drug agent came and pulled me out of the prison to a location to talk in detail about my operation smuggling drugs to this country. And as he talked to me, he looked me in the eyes making a tight fist and I felt he was squeezing my heart in his hand, to make point the government has a strong case against me and telling me, "We got you." Just like that! He repeated those movements several times, and every time he did that, I felt he was squeezing my heart; so I can't breathe.

During the interrogation, it seemed he wanted to enjoy his moments after he was watching every move I made for the last two years. Three hours passed for the interrogation. I was tired, and I asked the agent if we could continue that tomorrow. "No. No, we have to finish every detail tonight because I have to prepare all the information and take it to the judge to be able to set up as a star witness!"

My lawyers came from San Diego to the court date; the prosecutor and the agent—we all were in the courtroom to let the judge know about me as a star witness. A journalist was in the court, and my lawyer objected to his presence because we didn't want the public to know about me testifying yet. Then the journalist told the court with an angry voice, "I am going to get a court order."

The judge told him, "You are entitled to that."

By the time he went to get the court order, my lawyer presented our case so fast that we were done within fifteen minutes with all the secrecy. The journalist came back with the court order, and he was able to attend the rest of the motion.

After that court appearance, I was removed from the previous jail to a different prison where all the inmates were in lockdown all day, except for one hour of exercise. In that prison, I saw the famous CI (confidential informant), the best friend of Mr. Texas. I heard from other inmates that he was caught in a drug deal, and the district attorney flew to the place of his arrest to get him out of that mess and get him back into the prison for safety. That was another chance for me to testify, to secure the case for the district attorney.

My lawyer informed me that the drug agent and the district attorney will come to meet with me days before the trial, but they did not come until late the night before the trial. The guard came and secretly took me to meet with the DA and others.

The district attorney said to me, "Tomorrow, the trial will start. I want you to tell the truth. Is there anything else you like to add, like you forgot something to tell us, or any lie you told the court anywhere in this country? Tell us now. Otherwise, you will not see the light again in your life!"

"Yes," I said.

"Yes what?" The district attorney asked.

"Yes, I lied one time in a trial in Los Angeles court. When a Lebanese carrier got caught smuggling heroin through the LA airport, he was traveling with two of my suppliers."

"Tell us exactly how you lied."

"Well, when the prosecutor asked me if I knew the two people from Lebanon, I said yes. But when he asked me if they brought any drugs for me, I said no. That was a lie, but I did not lie about taking them to Mexico."

"Any other time you lied?"

"No, sir. That was all."

"Well, I am going to bring that up myself in the trial. It is better than the other lawyer bringing it up himself."

The day of the trial came, and for the first time in seven months, I got to dress up for the occasion, I felt good for a change. We got close to the courthouse, and I noticed the snipers all over the roofs of the surrounding buildings of the courthouse. I did not know that Mr. Texas was that dangerous of a man.

I was called to the stand and sworn in to tell the truth, nothing but the truth. "So help me, GOD, and my name is Assaf Sawaya."

The defense lawyer asked me if I speak good English. I said, "I speak fairly good, but sometimes I may need help to know the meaning of some words."

Then the judge asked me if I needed an interpreter? The defense lawyer objected! "Your honor. This witness—it seems he has the advantage by thinking how to answer the question while the interpreter explains it."

They all decided—the defense lawyer and the DA—that the words that I don't understand are to be explained to me.

The defense lawyer started his questions. "Do you know me, or have we met before?"

"No, sir."

"When you travel, do you use an alien name to check into hotels?"

"No, sir."

Now the DA was objecting. "Your honor, I am going to have a problem with this witness."

The judge asked me, "Do you know what *Elias* means?"

"Yes, Your Honor. It is my middle name. Assaf *Elias* Sawaya."

"No. No. *Alias.* Did you ever use a different name than your real name to travel or to register in hotels?"

"No, sir, never."

"Do you know Mr. Texas, and how did you meet him?"

"He came to my place of business in Las Vegas to make him some clothes."

"So you are a tailor?"

"Yes, sir. Actually, the suit Mr. Texas is wearing now."

"You made it for him?"

"Yes, sir, I did."

"Mr. Texas, if you please, stand up and show the label of the suit you are wearing. What does it read?"

"'Custom-made by Assaf Sawaya.'"

"Let the record show that Mr. Texas's suit is made by Assaf Sawaya. No further questions, Your Honor," as he was looking at the DA.

The DA takes the floor. "Mr. Sawaya, you testified that you sold suits to Mr. Texas."

"Yes, sir."

"Can you please also tell the court what else you sold Mr. Texas?"

"I sold him heroin as well!"

A loud noise took over the courtroom and over the hammering gavel of the judge.

"Objection, objection!" from the lawyers of Mr. Texas. "Order in the court, order in the court!" And the courtroom was quiet on the order of the judge.

The defense lawyers said, "Your Honor, we object to the witness's statement."

The judge, to the defense lawyers, said, "Your objection is noted, and it is on record."

The DA said, "Your Honor, I am establishing that Mr. Sawaya did not only sell suits to Mr. Texas but he also sold him heroin for the last four years." The judge authorized the DA to continue with his questions. "When was the first time you supplied Mr. Texas with heroin?"

"Mr. X in Las Vegas fronted me twenty-five thousand dollars to bring him one kilo of heroin from Lebanon, and he mentioned to me the money was from Mr. Texas."

"Objection, Your Honor! That is hearsay."

The judge said, "Let the witness's testimony be stricken from the record."

The DA said, "Mr. Sawaya, tell the court what happened to the twenty-five thousand dollars that Mr. X fronted you."

"I flew to Beirut, and Mr. D picked me up from the airport to spend a few days at his house until he arranged for the heroin to be delivered for us. When we received the one kilo of heroin, I place it in the shoulder pads of the jacket and then I flew back to Las Vegas. I arrived to Las Vegas at seven o'clock in the evening. I called Mr. X to come pick up his drugs. He came to my house that evening. I gave him the drugs, and he paid me five hundred dollars!

"'What is this?' I said.

"'I will pay you all the money as soon I receive it from Mr. Texas.'"

"Objection, Your Honor! The witness has done it again."

"It is stricken from the record. Continue," the judge said with his finger pointed at me.

"Well, Mr. X was arrested, and he used to call me from the prison, saying he is going to send me one of his people with the money. And he did! Mr. X's man came back again asking me if I could supply him with another kilo of heroin. I said yes, but I wanted a hundred thousand dollars up front. He told me, 'Let's find out if I can arrange this one.'

"Later, I got a telephone call from Mr. Texas himself, saying to me, 'I liked that white suit you sent me last time, and I would like to have another one suit out of the same fabric.'

"'Yes, of course, but I need to have some money first? To be able to buy the fabric?'

"'I will send you the money soon.'"

"Mr. H showed up bringing me ninety thousand dollars. I told him, 'It is going to be about two weeks to get you the stuff as soon as you can.'

"I took another flight to Beirut, July 1983. But this time, put the heroin in my boot going through the airport, I was caught, arrested, and put in prison for seven months, but was released on bail and came back home to the USA. To Las Vegas first then to San Diego to open a tailor shop.

"After that, I called Mr. Texas and told him what happened to me in Lebanon. And I met a new people, and they will supply the drugs for us any time we need. Within two weeks only! Two people arrived at my tailor shop with one kilo of heroin. I called Mr. Texas and informed him that his white suit was ready. He sent me Mr. H with the money. He paid me and picked up the drugs."

The DA said, "Now, Mr. Sawaya, did you sell to Mr. Texas other than that kilo you have sold him before?"

"Yes, sir. I was supplying him with heroin for the last four years until we were arrested."

The DA said, "Mr. Sawaya, how many kilos of heroin you believe you supplied Mr. Texas through the years?"

"About twenty-two kilos or more."

The DA said, "Through all your testimony, have you been telling the court the truth?"

"Yes, sir. I have been telling the truth all my testimony."

The DA said, "Again, Mr. Sawaya, have you ever testified in any court before where you did not tell the truth?"

"Yes, sir."

"Objection, Your Honor!" the defense lawyers yelled.

"Overruled," the judge ruled.

The DA said, "Please tell the court why you lied."

"I was subpoenaed by the Los Angeles court to testify about three people who came from Lebanon smuggling three kilos of heroin. One of them was caught, but the other two passed through customs. And they came to my residence in San Diego as they did in the past, and the DA in LA court questioned me if they stayed in my house.

"I said, 'Yes, they did.'

"'Did they bring you any drugs?'

"I lied about that part and testified, 'No, they did not bring me any drugs.'"

The DA looked at the defense lawyers and said to them, "He is your witness now."

"You have lied under oath in your own admission in the court of law?"

"Yes, sir. I have lied to protect myself."

"How much money was the DA paying you to protect yourself? About all the lies you testified against Mr. Texas?"

"No, sir, I did not lie. I have made an agreement with the DA: If I tell the truth about all the drugs I sold in my entire life, the DA promised me he will recommend to the judge for a lesser sentence."

I believe that the defense lawyer realized that I was going all the way by telling the truth, so he stopped questioning me! Then I was excused to step down from the witness stand. I left the courtroom with big relief.

My lawyer was waiting for me; I asked him, "What next?"

"That was it. You have done what you're supposed to do. Now we'll wait for the sentencing day."

Our agreement with the government will still be under the recommendation of the DA. The trial will continue for another three months, and after that, the judge will set a day for sentencing.

My lawyer came from San Diego on my sentencing day. In the court, he argued for a lesser sentence for me.

The judge ordered me to stand up, telling me, "Assaf Sawaya, I am about to pass the sentence on you. Do you have anything to say?"

"Yes, Your Honor."

I raised my index finger, asking the judge if I could have another chance at life with a choking voice and about to cry. The entire courtroom was shocked, and everybody felt how remorseful I was. My lawyer put his hands around my shoulders, asking me, "Are you okay?" And the judge called on the probation department personnel, asking them to give me a lesser sentence. Their recommendation was "If Your Honor will give him a lesser sentence, we ask for a life probation."

After the judge organized his desk, he said, "Assaf Sawaya, I hereby sentence you to twelve years in prison and life probation."

After hearing the sentence, I was disappointed! I looked at my lawyer, and the judge noticed me addressing my lawyer and said I did him a favor.

After we left the court, my lawyer explained to me, "The judge really did you a favor. He had written your sentence on a piece of paper as a twenty-year sentence before you pleaded for him in a remorseful attitude. Here is the plan for you: I already recommended to spend your time in a camp. There is one not too far from San Diego called Boran. I will put a motion for you in the court using the rule 35 to get you a lesser sentence, but you have to go to school and be in a good behavior. And that will help you to be released a lot sooner than twelve years!"

When I arrived to Boran camp, there was no fence or a wall; the place was a base for our brave soldiers! The previous base was so comfortable I did not feel like I was in prison; I got a job working in the laundry, issuing clothes and altering them for the inmates. My shift was four hours only every day; I used the extra time studying.

I started the school by basic education and then finished GED. We had a teacher coming from Barstow College, and I had special lessons by an inmate with a PhD. In math, he got me to finish trigonometry and calculus 1; also English lessons by a psychologist; and I belonged to the Toastmasters Club and finished my ten speeches. I graduated, from all my classes and got my GED diploma from Barstow College and sent them to Mr. Devil himself, whom I helped through the years to finish his college and master's degree. When he came to pick me up from the prison on the day of my release to go live with him in my house, where he lived for the three years of my incarceration, the first thing I asked him was about my diplomas. His answer was "I did not receive them"; that is why I called him Devil, but there is more to tell about his devious actions.

I was a role model for the other inmates. The math teacher gave a speech at the Toastmasters Club, and to prove his topic, he gave as an example that Assaf Sawaya, when he began teaching me math, did not know how to add or multiply fractions.

I occasionally had a BIBLE study with an inmate, preaching to me about JESUS. One day, he confessed to me about his people, preaching to him to join them because they were a majority and he has to belong to a group to survive through the prison life. But his confession was, he was still struggling with the salvation of our LORD JESUS.

Here I was, a forty-two-year-old Christian man; I had not read or studied the Word of GOD to give any encouragement to that desperate man. I felt so ashamed after what GOD has done for me throughout my life even since my childhood and, above all, saving me from a life sentence I was facing. That day, I promised myself to study the BIBLE and tell the world how GOD saved me from all my stupid actions against him and the society. I always was thinking that GOD favored me because of my loving heart, but it took me thirty years to return GOD'S favor and his love. I am seventy-two years old in the autumn of my life, but I am writing my life story.

One specific incident I would like to emphasize is on the relative Devil who was living in my house. He was going to Lebanon for the summer vacation, so I paid his air fare and gave him spending money as well and five thousand dollars to give to my brother. When he came back, I asked him if he gave the money to my brother. He said yes. For the loving heart I had and trusting people, I did not ask my brother if he got the money. Here is a lesson to learn, one I would like to share with you: that Devil was counting on the information he heard by being around us. I had my two brothers living with me at that time in Las Vegas. The three of us, that day, traveled to Los Angeles and came back in the same day without letting one another know about our trip; he was depending on our lack of communication with one another. This evil person should be a consultant in times of war.

Another incident was when I met him in New Orleans for the Mardi Gras festival. I always carry large amounts of hundred-dollar bills. He already saw the large cache in my hand, and he asked me this weird question with beggar eyes if he could carry my bundle of money in his hands for a while. I felt so sorry for this kind of a person with that weakness, and after ten minutes, I told him, "Give it to me now. You already got your fix."

My lawyer gave me the good news about the motion with rule 35 that the judge granted based on the accomplishment I made in the prison and the letter from my ex-wife. Part of what she stated was that "Assaf—he trusts people," and what she means is that I have a good, loving heart; and always when I read her letter, I used to cry.

The prison office called me and gave me the good news about my release. I immediately called my relative in San Diego and told him about my good news, but it was not good news for him. He came and picked me up from the prison in my own car. People, he is married and bought a new house. As we arrived to the house, he said to me, "This house is for you and me," because he was making the payments.

His wife came to meet me with a sad face and a black eye. I asked him, "What did you do to her?"

His answer was "Good thing I didn't kill her!"

And when I got to know her, she told me he got mad at her because she did not agree with him to buy a house in Lebanon. And she said he married her for her money, and he lied to her so many times. She also told me that he broke the kitchen door and called the police reporting a robbery of all the jewelry in his house. I immediately described all the jewelry for her, and she said, "How would you know that?"

"Because they are mine."

She was shocked. "What else is yours of here?"

"Everything you see and touch is mine, from the car to the furniture to even the forks and the spoons."

"I have one more question for you. The bedroom set where we sleep—is that for you as well?"

"Yes, it is." Because his mother told me they paid lots of money for that bedroom set, and I confessed to her that he asked me, "In case my wife asked you about that bedroom set if it is for you, please say no?"

After a few weeks, she bought a new house, and they moved to it; and I moved out of that house because I did not have the money to make the payments. His mother came from Lebanon to bail him out of the prison because of assault and battery on his wife after they moved to that new house, and they left to Lebanon.

I ask myself this question: what possesses people to behave that way? He is a thief, a liar, and a batterer; and I am a gambler. I got involved in smuggling drugs to support my bad habit. GOD saved me from a life sentence; I always believed it's because of my loving heart, but what about the thieves, the liars, the murders, and all the breakers of GOD'S commandments? GOD sent his only begotten Son, OUR LORD JESUS, to shed his blood and take our sins, he who did not sin to redeem us and save us from eternal death because GOD so loved the world.

Today I am reporting to my probation officer as a condition to my early release; his instructions were "Get a job, report your monthly earning, no drinking. And I read your file. You don't have any drug use, and keep it that way."

I got a job in a supermarket belonging to my brother-in-law Tony; I worked there for a few months. I was bored with that job, then I asked Tony to help me open a tailor shop. It is my profession, and that is what I love to do.

We found a location in the downtown area, but under the ground with a display window on the street by the trolley railroad. I did well for three months. One night, it was pouring rain nonstop until morning; I went to my shop and opened the door, and as I walked to go down the stairs, I stood at the first step looking down at the floor covered with two feet high of water. I looked at that devastating scene, smiled, and said to myself, "I wonder what GOD has that's better for me." My family cried and said what bad luck I have! But I did not because I was extremely positive, and I turned any negativity into positive; and that quality in me is GOD' gift.

I finally found a job at the clothing factory. Tony took me to it twenty years ago; they did not hire me then because I did not speak English well. I was overwhelmed with how fast they operate, producing one thousand suits every day. I was so eager to learn the other operations; I started walking around to observe some of the operations.

The manager noticed me that I was not at my operating machine. "What are you doing here off your operation?"

I answered him, "I am a tailor, and I'd like to learn how you do the mass production."

First, he gave that "You're not supposed to be here!" look. But in this case, he said, "I will show you every operation in this factory." After he realized my capability, he recommended me to the vice president to become a supervisor! God is good and good to me, and GOD loves me, I believe, because of my loving heart.

The vice president called me to his office and told me about my promotion and asked me to go through all the operations if I could find how to save the company a few pennies in some of the operations. I said yes, I will let him know as I went around the five hundred employees, learning from them and teaching them as well. I found three different operations I could save five to six seconds with and did better. After those findings, I met with the vice president and explained to him how we could save a few seconds on the operations; he called for a meeting with the other supervisors and explained to them my findings. They all agreed with me and suggested to him to implement those findings right away.

After the calculations the vice president made, he told me, "Now you earned your money, Assaf. You have saved the company over two hundred thousand dollars a year by those few seconds on the three operations only. Keep up the good work."

Thanks to the love of GOD, I knew that GOD'S hands were in my life. He saved me from a life sentence in prison; like what my mother said to me as a child, "GOD has a plan for you, my son."

I walked around as a supervisor, checking every operation and conversing with the operatives. Sometimes I ask a personal question: "How long have you been working in this factory?" Some said thirty years, others forty years; they all moved from the main factory that was located in downtown San Diego. That was the same factory I applied a job for when I first came to San Diego twenty-six years ago! I said to myself, *If I got this job twenty-six years ago and learned what I am learning now; I would met the same workers and become a famous designer, like what I was dreaming all my youth!* Something must've happened to prevent that dream of mine.

With the money I was earning now, I was able to buy a car to get to work instead of walking two hours back and forth to get home; but I didn't mind all that because I was doing my body good and taking care of GOD'S temple, and that pleases GOD. No matter what kind of situation I am in, I never complain, but I accept the fact and look for the positive side in all my situations I am facing. I believe I am blessed to accept the good and the bad because after all, it is the will of GOD. What we go through in life, if we accept it without complaint—that will please GOD. We are his children, and GOD loves us. All we have to do is to believe in him and have a loving heart; those are the two main conditions GOD asks from us.

I worked for the factory for four years, and with the knowledge I accomplished, I was able to open my own factory after my broker called me from Las Vegas. He was telling me the good news that he sold our property and had a check for me and asked me to meet him at his favorite hotel in La Jolla overlooking the ocean.

Mr. Romano, accompanied with his wife at the dinner table, told me, "You haven't being making your payments on the property for the last seven years, and that property was sold. The money was divided to the shareholders, and everybody was paid except you. The words in the contract are very clear; if you default, you lose your shares. Let me explain to you what I decided in your case." I was expecting the worst, then he reached for his breast pocket and pulled a check, saying, "This is your return on the five-thousand-dollar deposit on the property twelve years ago."

I looked at the amount of the check! The tears flooded out of my eyes when I read the amount of one hundred thousand dollars; I had never seen that amount of money given to me by a check. I thanked Mr. Romano for his gift, telling him, "You just bought me years of happiness. You are one of a kind, Mr. Romano."

I took that check and drove to Chula Vista, to the poker room where I played, usually walking around the tables. "Seat open. Assaf, get in."

But I said, "No, I am not open tonight," and left the casino. So proud of myself.

And I did not like that alcoholic man when he solemnly swore not to drink anymore. One night, he was passing along the bar building where he used to drink, and when he got to the end of the building, he said to himself, "I am so proud of myself. I have made it through without any urge to drink! Now that deserves a drink." The poor man got inside the bar, and after his first-drink celebration, he asked for a second drink, and we all know what will happen after that.

My place of business is in an industrial area located in National City, California. I spent all my check on machinery and other equipment. I designed and prepared a few samples to show to retailers, but I could not sell my product. Even when the retailers were pleased with my work, they all bluntly told me, "You are not a well-known name in the fashion world." I was thinking that was a setback for me. I turned my factory into a tailor shop, and I was surviving by making custom-made clothes. My health deteriorated. The tegument (a prescribed medicine for stomach ulcer) I was tacking to help my stomach ulcer wasn't helping anymore, and I started go to the poker room in Chula Vista. My life was a mess.

One Sunday afternoon, my pain in my stomach was unbearable. I went to my bedroom and laid on the bed, holding my stomach with my two hands to relieve the pain and started crying to GOD, "Please help me, dear LORD, and take this pain out of my stomach to be able to work. If I don't work, I won't be able to eat or survive. Please, my beloved JESUS, help me?"

While I was crying to my Savior, I saw a hand up to the elbow coming from the wall of my bedroom traveling to my stomach, holding it, squeezing it, and pulling that pain in that very second; and the arm disappeared. Then I started rubbing my stomach for about ten minutes nonstop; my stomach was healed. I got off my bed, on my knees, and started praying, thanking GOD for that miracle. Another testimony of mine that GOD is with me throughout my life. I must add that was not a dream or a revelation, I was totally awake.

The following Sunday at eight o'clock in the morning, I was driving, going to the gym to get ready for the church. In one hand,

I was holding the rosary, praying and aware of my surrounding to cross my green signal, but I saw a truck coming so fast. I figured he will stop on his red light, but did not. As I was crossing, reaching the middle street, the truck was about to hit me on the driver's side as I turned to drive with his direction. The impact was on my front wheel. My car was thrown eight yards away. I tried to move my arms. I was able to, and I opened the door! I tried to move my legs! I was able to move them as well! I walked out of my car. Nothing was broken! I got to the driver. "Didn't you see the red light?" He was so apologetic and was trying to get to his job. "You would've killed me if I wasn't praying and aware of my driving." I made him sign a document that it was his fault, but I was in pain for two weeks.

My lawyer told me, "You did a good thing by making the other driver sign that he was at fault, but you should have called an ambulance to take you to the hospital that way I would have gotten you more money."

That is another testimony of mine that GOD is with me, and I was a Catholic at that time. I was a regular at the gym, and I met a girl. She seemed to be nice. We went out on a date two times. I figured she was a gold digger, but I didn't have any gold for her to dig into. I did not pay any attention to her; and the more I did that, the more she came closer to me, and she invited me to her church. She was a born-again Christian. I went with her to her church on Sunday and Wednesday of every week and to BIBLE study. It was rewarding for me to know the BIBLE better after all. I knew that GOD is with me all my life, and it is about time to study his Word to be able to serve him and return his love.

I was baptized in the water and became a born-again Christian, and after the ceremony, one of the brothers said to me, "Now that you have been baptized, you have to follow GOD'S Ten Commandments." Oh no. I wanted to enjoy my life before I commit to anything, and that was my selfish thinking about the joy of life.

Ignorance is the root of distractions, and I did not find out about that ignorance until I was at the autumn of my life. That is why I am writing this book at the age of seventy-one years old to share with the whole world the good news about our LORD JESUS, when I missed giving my heart to JESUS, who is my LORD and Savior.

Eight months passed. I have been with that girl, and every Sunday, we spent the day going from church to another, observing the mass until the last mass was finished. And I didn't get home until eleven o'clock that night. I got tired of pleasing her and stopped seeing her. My hairdresser invited me to lunch; I thought it was because I brought her lunch every time I go for a haircut or occasional lunch break, but there was a different thing on her mind. After that lunch, she invited me to her home for a glass of wine. I was happy for the invitation. We got comfortable in front of the fireplace, drinking wine and caressing each other, and eventually undressed and were ready to commit a sin. Then she said to me, "I am on my period," and when she said that, I was so relieved. A big load came off my shoulders. That was the first time I behaved that way; other times, I never cared about that situation. I got dressed and left.

On my next haircut, I went to see her. She wasn't there. I asked, "I need a haircut. Where is she?"

"Oh, you haven't heard!"

"Heard what?"

"She has been in the hospital for a month and passed away!"

I couldn't believe what I was hearing. "What happened to her?"

"She died of full-blown AIDS!"

I drove back home. On the way, I found a church. I went inside, and on my knees, I prayed and thanked GOD for saving me another time. And this time, I was a born-again Christian. I always thought that GOD saved me from all my trials in all my life because of my loving heart, and I left at that.

I got to know GOD better, but I was still going to the poker room, losing my money. Now I was approaching sixty-two years old. I decided to take an early retirement and go live in Lebanon. I could survive on 716 dollars a month from Social Security, and that is what I have in this world to live on because of my addiction to gambling.

I sold my business for 10,000 dollars and my car for 22,000 dollars. I bought a one-way ticket to go to Lebanon for my retirement, and four days before my flight, I took the money to Las Vegas for a last chance. I came back to San Diego with two hundred dollars, and that was what I had left. I said to myself, *Another last chance at the poker room.* I lost the first hand, and I had one more hand to play. If I lost that hand, I will go to Lebanon empty-handed and I had to wait for my next check from Social Security.

For some, in the game called Texas Hold'em, my first two cards were a pair of kings; it's a very good hand to play. I raised the pot; only one player called my hand. The first three cards on the table where 2-10-ace, and those are three cards any player could use. Now my pair of kings was not favorable anymore because of the one ace on the table or what's called the flop. The other player made a bet; I had to call his bet and hope for a king to have the winning hand of three kings against two aces. The fourth card the dealer dealt was an ace; now I knew my chances were very slim. The only way I could win that hand was if I lost it! And I already lost that hand, unless the fifth card will be another ace! For my last chance to go back to Lebanon with some money, the fifth card was an ace, and that is my nickname.

I screamed with the loudest voice to the other player to show me the fourth ace. And he did. By then, every player in the poker room surrounded our table to watch; the biggest jackpot was in that poker room of 40. The 40 thousand dollars jackpot split among the players of that table; the loser of the hand will get half of the jackpot. Twenty thousand dollars was my share, and half of the twenty thousand dollars was the share of the winning hand, ten thousand dollars. The rest of the money was split among the rest of the other players.

The next morning in my flight to Lebanon, I made it to the airplane with my pockets full of money. Throughout my life, I have had the experience of when I am at the bottom of my life with no hope to get up for some reason. My LORD and Savior will lift me up, but not to the mountaintop; I always stayed in the valley. I am the sinner.

We arrived at Beirut airport late that afternoon. Going through customs, I showed my American passport. The officer was looking through the pages! "You have no visa, sir, to enter Lebanon?" Then I pulled out my Lebanese passport and handed it to the officer. He looked me in the eyes. "You are a funny guy. How long you are staying in Lebanon?"

"For the rest of my life!" I answered.

"Welcome home."

My family and some friends of my youth welcomed me home. There was a beautiful reunion. Our people in Lebanon are passionate. They show love and hospitality, until it comes to the politics; there is no passion in that area. My timing was bad; it was the parliament election in 2009, and each side wanted me to vote for their leader. I am only one vote! What is the big deal?

One time, they were arguing among themselves, and they couldn't agree on any issue. So one of them suggested, "Let us ask the American about his opinion."

Spontaneously, I answered, "I don't follow any man. I only follow and love our LORD and Savior, JESUS CHRIST. JESUS is about love, and he does not lie to us. And JESUS bought our sins by shedding his blood on the cross and saved us from eternal torment, and he who believes in him will gain eternal life in heaven."

There was a silence among everybody. One friend made a comment, "You are a changed man, Assaf."

"I will tell you how I have changed! You gentlemen all know I was facing a life sentence for the drugs I helped to smuggle to the USA. But our LORD and Savior was there for me because of my loving heart, and now I am returning his love by studying his Word in the BIBLE."

I just started to read the BIBLE at the autumn of my life, but never too late. And as I walked through our beautiful village of Douma, lots of young people welcomed me and invited me into their homes. Friends I went to school with—now they have their own children going into colleges; and what amazed me about the young generations was that they knew me through my mother! By telling them about me when I was eight years old and how I threw the falling apples over our neighbor's property because the apples don't belong to us. And how my mother held me kissed me and thanked GOD for the way I turned out.

All people were not the same. As I was passing the streets of Douma, I saw a friend of mine standing by the street in front of his house. I stopped to say hello to him and how happy I was to see him well and how I would like to visit him soon, but he hardly invited me to his house. He walked me into the front of his house without inviting me inside. He waved his hand for me to sit down, and he sat at a distance from me; and his body language was telling me that I was the bad guy! Judging me for my sins while he is a sinner as well as I am. In Matthew 7, JESUS tells us, "Do not judge, or you too will be judged. For in the same way you judge others, you will be judged, and with the measure you use, it will be measured to you."

His wife came out with some beverages, and she noticed I was uncomfortable and her husband was sitting at a distance from me. I didn't want to insult her like I was insulted. I drank my welcome beverage and got up and left. I knew she was going to say something to her husband about his behavior.

The next day, I was passing by his house; he actually was waiting for me to pass by his house to let me know he was sorry about his behavior the day before and invited me into his house. I felt good about his change of heart, and I was sure that his wife said to him about what Luke said in 6:37–42: "Do not judge, and you will not be judged. Do not condemn, and you will not be condemned. Forgive, and you will be forgiven."

Other people showed me the scorn attitude. After all, I was the only one in Douma who did this type of crime because the majority of the inhabitants in Douma were highly educated, and in some families, all of their children were doctors, lawyers, engineers, or some other high achievement.

In Douma, we have a well-known bone doctor specialist all over the Middle East. I remember him from the school of Douma when I was a child as Anton el Basha. As he took his walk, he always had a book in his hands, reading as he walked. I said to myself, *How smart Anton is and what a good future he is going to have.* And he did. They call him from all over the Middle East to save somebody's life, and he is also a good Christian. I also remember his father as the soulest in our church until he died at a long and comfortable age. Now I am seventy years old, and as I walk, I read the BIBLE to learn how to serve GOD and save people's lives for eternity when they know the Word of GOD and obey him.

After I have been in my hometown of Douma, my schoolmates forty-five years ago noticed I was overweight and said, "We thought you left Douma to the USA to become a movie star." Well, I did not pursue that career; I was struggling to survive, and it was not that easy. Now I have to exercise to lose weight, and I should know better than that. I have to implement what I learned in the fitness and nutrition classes I achieved and graduated with a diploma. I started to walk every morning from our town to the neighboring towns—two hours and part of it uphill—but I was lazy to run in order to raise my heartbeat. But that time came when it started to rain! I had to run to get home because with any drop of water on my head, I will catch cold. So I started running to get home, but it took me forty minutes. I was wet, and I thought I will be very sick! From that time on, I was running every day after fifteen minutes of walking.

My heart rate got over 125 per minute, and that is good for the heart because the higher the heart rate is as you run, the better it will be for the heart. As you're resting, by then, the heart rate should be under 72 per minute. Of course, you should consult your doctor before you start any type of strenuous exercise.

October in Douma. Winter starts. It was cold, and I could not tolerate that freezing cold. I had to leave or live by the stove day and night; it was an easy decision to make. I booked the next flight to Los Angeles and then to Las Vegas. My only income is from Social Security of 716 dollars a month only because of my early retirement. That is all I have in this world because of my gambling habits.

In Las Vegas I rented a room with an old friend for three hundred dollars a month and found a job as a tailor with a very good company and with good salary and benefits. The manager was impressed with my experience. But! Why doesn't all go well? I had to deal with one of the staffers; I am a positive person with a loving heart, and he is a negative person with a vile heart. I immediately felt he was trouble, and he did not disappoint me by showing me his hateful heart; but my loving heart showed him a different way on how to be kind to others.

He followed on his promise. One day, he walked into my work area, going through all my assignments as an excuse to pressure me, and said on his way out, "You have to speed it up." And he left fast, like a snake when injecting its venom in its prey and leaving the crime scene fast as well.

By then, I was boiled up of his hateful comment, and I followed him out to the floor where he and other sales people attend to serve the clients. By then, I lost my temper in front of the other salesmen, telling him, "You have no right to tell me to speed it up, and if you have any complaints about me, take it to your manager."

"I did not tell you to speed it up." Of course, he lied. By then, I walked to my work area. He followed me and said, "If my father talks to me that way, I will punch him in the face." And he repeated his lie! "I did not tell you to speed it up."

I called the main office and reported him; they informed me to go through the proper channels. I did as they suggested, and after I went through more channels, I came to a dead end. Satan was gaining ground in my heart, telling me, "You are a nice man with a loving heart, and he is a bad man with a hateful heart. You have to get him." I started to pray to JESUS and asked him to punish him by not making any sales. Even if he was the number one salesman in all the company, he lived from check to check. By not blessing him with any sales... By that moment, he made over 15,000 dollars in sales! When I heard that news, I slid on the floor and, on my knees, asked our LORD GOD for forgiveness for using his name in vain.

I was still disturbed by his attitude, and Satan was telling me, "You have a loving heart, and his is not." I am not capable of doing a drastic act, but I thought of it.

GOD talked to me, saying, "You pride of loving your mother and every mother in the world. Have you thought of how his mother will feel if her son got hurt or his wife? She is a mother with two angels. You also pride you love all the children in the world because JESUS loves them for their loving heart. JESUS came to earth and shed his blood for you and him. JESUS loves both you and him."

"Are you going to believe that, Assaf?" Satan was speaking.

"Go away, Satan, to where you belong—hell, that is. And your time is short, Satan. You already lost, and you were stupid to rebel against your creator. GOD is the creator of heaven and earth. And JESUS did not die for you, Satan, but for me and all the sinners of the earth. And you're not included. And you are going crazy. You had all at the beginning, but you lost it, Satan, by deceiving Adam and Eve. Big mistake, and you will not be forgiven."

I was still thinking like a human because I didn't want to get myself in trouble. I told that guy, "I don't want to talk to you anymore, not even say good morning to each other." It went like that for two months.

Our manager told me that we were most likely to renew our lease for another ten years. I felt good about that because I am sixty-nine years old and I still need that job to survive. One day in the morning, I felt the Holy Spirit filling my heart with love, and overflowing, I felt my heart about to burst. GOD himself manifested in my presence, telling me to go hug my enemy and tell him GOD had directed me to do that because GOD loves us both. That salesman came to get himself a cup of coffee in the area where I worked. I was led to him, hugging him, and said to him, "GOD directed me to hug you and show you my love and forget about all that happened between us before because GOD loves us both and GOD wants us to love each other, and I am obeying his commands."

"Assaf!" He said, "You got it all wrong. It is all in your mind."

My brother, all gone and forgotten. I was doing GOD'S will; praise his name. Two weeks after the manifestation of GOD, our manager came and sat next to me, telling me that the company decided not to sign the lease and we were moving to the new chop because they invested millions of dollars in the new place. "And guess who put in a good word for you to keep your job? Yes, your buddy, the one you did not want to talk to anymore, telling the corporate personnel that we have clients that shop at our store because of your good work."

I jumped up and said again, as I always say when GOD shows me his hand in my life, "Ya habibi Ma atyabak ya elahe" (How delicious you are, my beloved GOD).

I was standing in front of the shop of my place of work. I saw a smiling face coming toward me, uttering, "I recognize you from the church. The minute the mass is over, you don't stick around and chat with other people."

"I don't have any time to socialize, and I have other things to do." That was my response. The smiling face introduce himself; we shook hands. "My name is Assaf Sawaya."

"Assaf? Did I say it right?"

"Yes, you did."

"I would like to introduce you to my uncle. He teaches the BIBLE at the new church I go to. You will like him, and he teaches from the BIBLE."

I said, "I have been looking for someone to learn the BIBLE because I am going to write my life story as a testimony of what GOD had done in my life, saving me from all the trouble I got myself into."

One evening, we went to his uncle's house. I met the pleasant and hospitable uncle and his family. The evening turned into a BIBLE study with delicious ethnic food. I asked the preacher if I could continue studying the BIBLE with him because I am writing a book about my life story and how GOD favored me all my life. "I like to return the favor by telling all the world about GOD and his love for us." He was very happy to hear that from me especially when I made it clear to him for my hunger to learn and study the BIBLE. We met on another occasion in front of the shop where I worked, and that was it; the smiling face moved to another state, and I lost contact with the pleasant preacher.

My brother who was living with me from San Diego asked me if it was okay with me to invite some preacher to come over to preach the BIBLE to him and his daughter? "Of course. I welcome anyone who teaches the Word of GOD."

Two years passed by. I did not have any contact with the preacher. In fact, I was praying to GOD to be able to contact that preacher because I already finished the first part of my book of my personal story, and now I needed to work on the second part that related to GOD in my life.

My brother got up to answer the knock at the door. As he opened the door, the voice I heard was the BIBLE teacher that I was praying to find; GOD sent him to my doorstep. I lifted my hands up to GOD and thanked him for watching over me all my life. As he was asking my brother if he was related to Assaf Sawaya, I came to the door smiling. We hugged and told him that GOD answered my prayers and brought him to my doorstep.

We had BIBLE study that day—my brother, his daughter, and myself. We agreed to attend the BIBLE study two days a week at their church, and for one day, the teacher will come to our home for another BIBLE study. I told him I was hungry to learn the Word of God because of what GOD has done in my life, and I would like to preach to the whole world the Word of GOD and serve him through the rest of my life for the love he showed me and saved me from a life sentence and death many times over. I always believed in my heart; GOD saved me because of my loving heart.

My teacher was excited about us three people added to his congregation, and he used to come to pick up my brother and his daughter, taking them wining and dining and studying the Word of GOD. My brother and his daughter were pleased learning the BIBLE and sometimes getting out of house and going to a new church, and after the service, the preacher will take them to dinner with his family and others.

My brother and his daughter dropped out of the BIBLE study after two months without any explanation, and when my preacher asked me about my brother and why he was not coming anymore to study the Word of GOD. I told him, "He doesn't want to come anymore."

And when he realized that he lost two people, I noticed the look on his face, like he lost someone dear to him. And then he asked, "How about you, Assaf?"

I told him, "I want to learn the Word of GOD to be able to serve him for what GOD has done in my life. I am devoting my energy and my loyalty to GOD." He was pleased to hear that from me. I was a regular and never missed any BIBLE study or service attendance. I was so hungry and thirsty to learn the Word of GOD to be able to finish writing my book and announce my ministry…

One day, I received a material from a publishing house in New York, so I took it with me to the church and was very excited to show it to my teacher about how GOD was helping me to accomplish my dream to serve him. He took the booklet from my hand, glanced at it for one second only, and handed it back to me! Looking me in the eyes and expressing his dissatisfaction, his eyes were saying to me, "We don't agree with what you are doing!" I faithfully kept my attendance to study the BIBLE.

One evening after the church service, he invited me to his house for dinner. His wife is an excellent cook, and she spends lots of time in the kitchen preparing food for the brothers and sisters from the congregation. They are a family of exceptional hospitality.

At the dinner table, I told him, "My loyalty is to GOD." He and his wife looked at each other. I took that as a positive sign and felt good about that and also said to him that GOD directed me to study the BIBLE with him and GOD talks to me.

The preacher corrected me by explaining to me that was during the Mosaic time. "GOD spoke to the prophets, but GOD does not speak to the people anymore. GOD already said what he has to say and sent his Son JESUS to die for our sins."

My response was that "GOD talks to me. And one time, I was suffering with a severe pain in my stomach from my ulcer. I got into my bed and laid on it, holding my stomach to relieve the pain and crying my heart out to GOD, to take the pain away from my stomach and asking GOD to cure me because if I was not able to work, I will not eat. And while I was crying to GOD, I saw an arm come out of the wall from the elbow to the hand traveling to reach my stomach, and the hand squeezed into my stomach and pulled the pain away that second! I started to scratch my stomach as the wound was healed. I was totally awake that Sunday afternoon when that miracle took place."

My preacher's explanation was that sometimes Satan will do that to deceive us! What a rationalization! But I answered him that "I was crying out to GOD the Father, GOD the Son, and GOD the Holy Spirit, but not to Satan, as you claim. And nobody could take that away from me—teacher of the BIBLE or any theologian. My loyalty is to GOD, not to any man, and that is why I am writing my testimony to let the world know about GOD and his existence."

Another occasion I told my preacher about GOD was in my workplace. "It filled my heart with love, overflowing love, and my heart was about to burst. GOD directed me to go and hug my coworker whom I told not to talk to me anymore because of his hating heart toward me to avoid any bad circumstances.

"Two months after I told my coworker not to speak to me or even say good morning, GOD directed me to hug that guy and reconcile with him. I obeyed GOD in that second. When he came to my work area, I walked up to him like a robot unconsciously, hugging him and telling him, 'You are my enemy, but GOD manifested himself to me, directing me to hug you and tell you that you are my brother and should not show you the hatred you have been showing me.' 'Assaf, it is all in your head!' We became good friends, and he started showing me respect.

"Two weeks passed. Our manager came to me and told me, 'We have to close this location because the company is not going to renew the lease. We have to move to the new location because they invested a large amount of money in the new shop, but here is the good news: guess who put in a good word for you? Your good friend, the one you told not to speak to you anymore.' If I lost that job, it would have been a disaster for me. At that time, I was sixty-nine years old, and I had no money saved to live on." I told all that happened to my preacher and how GOD always talks to me and directs me for my benefit, and when I obey GOD, he shows me the results. "And that is why I came to you to learn GOD'S Word: to serve him by returning GOD'S love, the love GOD showed me throughout my life since my childhood."

My preacher's comment was "Well, that incident turned to your favor, but GOD does not talk to you!"

I was very disappointed with his comment. Instead of recognizing GOD'S favor in my life, he played it down.

My main disappointment was when we were discussing the journey of the prophet Jonah. He was thrown overboard the ship, and the big fish swallowed him. My preacher rationalized that Jonah survived the three days in the belly of the big fish because there was lots of air in the belly of the big fish. Now I am convinced that he was a false teacher because he does not admit to GOD'S plan and ability. Here is the story of the PROPHET JONAH.

JONAH 1:1—JONAH Flees from the LORD

The word of the LORD came to JONAH son of AMITTAI: "Go to the great city of NINEVEH and preach against it, because its wickedness has come up before me." But JONAH ran away from the LORD and headed for TARSHISH. He went down to JOPPA, where he found a ship bound for that port. After paying the fare, he went aboard and sailed for TASHISH to flee from the LORD.

Then the lord sent a great wind on the sea, and such a violent storm arose that the ship threatened to break up. All the sailors were afraid and each cried out to his own god. And they threw the cargo into the sea to lighten the ship. But JONAH had gone below deck where he lay down and fell into a deep sleep.

The captain went to him and said, "How can you sleep? Get up and call on your god! Maybe he will take notice of us, and we will not perish."

Then the sailors said to each other, "Come, let us cast lots to find out who is responsible for this calamity." They cast lots and the lot fell on JONAH. So they asked him, "Tell us, who is responsible for making all this trouble for us? What do you do? Where do you come from? What is your country? From what people are you?"

He answered, "I am a Hebrew and I worship the LORD, the GOD of heaven, who made the sea and the land."

This terrified them and they asked, "What have you done?" [They knew he was running away from the LORD because he had already told them so.] The sea was getting rougher and rougher. So they asked him, "What should we do to you to make the sea calm down for us?"

"Pick me up and throw me into the sea," he replied, "and it will become calm. I know that it is my fault that this great storm has come upon you."

Instead, the men did their best to row back to land. But they could not, for the sea grew even wilder than before. Then they cried to the LORD, "O LORD, please do not let us die for taking this man's life. Do not hold us accountable for killing an innocent man, for you, O LORD, have done as you pleased." Then they took JONAH and threw him overboard, and the raging sea grew calm. At this the men greatly feared the LORD, and they offered a sacrifice to the LORD AND MADE VOWS TO HIM.

But the LORD provided a great fish to swallow JONAH, and JONAH was inside the fish three days and three nights.

JONAH'S Prayer

JONAH 2:1—From inside the fish JONAH prayed to the LORD his GOD.

He said: "In my distress I called to the LORD, and he answered me. From the depths of the grave I called for help and you listened to my cry.

"You hurled me into the deep, into the very heart of the seas, and the currents swirled about me: all your waves and breakers swept over me.

"I said I have been banished from your sight; yet I will look again toward your holy temple.

"The engulfing waters threatened me, the deep surrounded me; seaweed was wrapped around my head.

"To the roots of the mountains I sank down; the earth beneath barred me in forever. But you brought my life up from the pit, O LORD my GOD.

"When my life was ebbing away, I remembered you LORD. and my prayer rose to you to your holy temple.

"Those who cling to worthless idols forfeit the grace that could be theirs.

"But I, with a song of thanksgiving, will sacrifice to you. what I have vowed I will make good. Salvation comes from the LORD."

And the LORD commanded the fish and it vomited JONAH onto dry land.

JONAH 3:1—JONAH Goes to NINEVEH

Then the word of the LORD came to JONAH a second time: "Go to the great city of NINEVEH and proclaim to it the message I give you." JONAH obeyed the word of the LORD and went to NINEVEH. Now NINEVEH was a very important city_ a visit required three days. On the first day, JONAH started into the city. He proclaimed: "Forty more days and NINEVEH will be overturned."

The NINEVITES believed GOD. They declared a fast, and all of them, from the greatest to the least, put on sackcloth.

When the news reached the king of NINEVEH, he rose from his throne, took off his royal robes, covered himself with sackcloth and sat down in the dust. Then he issued a proclamation in NINEVEH: "By the decree of the king and his nobles: Do not let any man or beast, herd or flock taste anything; do not let them eat or drink. But let man and beast be covered with sackcloth. Let everyone call urgently on GOD. Let them give up their evil ways and their violence. Who knows? GOD may yet relent and with compassion turn from his fierce anger so that we will not perish."

When GOD saw that they did and how they turn from their evil ways, he had compassion and did not bring upon them the destruction he had threatened.

JONAH's Anger at the LORD'S Compassion

But JONAH was greatly displeased and became angry. He prayed to the LORD. "O LORD, is this not what I said when [I was still at home?] That is why I was so quick to flee to Tarshish. I knew that you are a gracious and compassionate GOD, who relents from sending calamity. Now, O LORD, take away my life, for it is better for me to die than to live."

But the LORD replied, "Have you any right to be angry?

JONAH went out and sat down at a place east of the city. There he made himself a shelter, sat in its shade and waited to see what would happen to the city. Then the LORD GOD provided a vine and made it grow up over JONAH to give shade for his head to ease his discomfort. And JONAH was very happy about the vine. But at dawn the next day GOD provided a worm, which chewed the vine so that it withered. When the sun rose, GOD provided a scorching east wind, and the sun blazed on JONAH'S head so that he grew faint. He wanted to die and said, "It would be better for me to die than live."

But GOD said to JONAH, "Do you have a right to be angry about the vine?

"I do," he said. "I am angry enough to die."

But the LORD said, "You have been concerned about this vine, though you did not tend it or make it grow. It sprang up overnight and died overnight. But NINEVEH has more than a hundred and twenty thousand people who cannot tell their right hand from their left, and many cattle as well. Should I not be concerned about that great city?"

Anybody who reads the story of the prophet Jonah will still believe he survived by the air in the belly of the big fish? After that comment by my BIBLE teacher, I stopped attending that kind of BIBLE teaching in their kingdom hall is a place of worship. And by missing one meeting, I got a call from one of the elders; he was concerned about my absence. I clearly explained to him that I was directed by GOD to finish writing my book and announce my own ministry. Then my former teacher called me from out of town, asking me why I stopped coming to the kingdom hole. I explained to him that GOD has talked to me to be on my own, and he will direct me how to serve him. My former teacher told me that as soon as he returned to town, we'll get together to talk.

Two days after our conversation, we agreed to have dinner to talk. At dinner, he said to me, "Do you think that GOD has time for you? And you are a seventy-year-old?"

The Holy Spirit immediately uttered out of my mouth, telling my former teacher, "You have no faith in GOD. And wait and see. Within ten years, I will have a hundred million followers, and what I mean by that is they have been around for 150 years and they only count eight million, according to them."

He was speechless and asked, "When you are going to finish that book?"

"In August," I said.

And as we departed, he told me, "If you live that long!"

I got a telephone call from one of the elders asking if he could come to see me. I said, "You are welcome any time."

He came after five weeks with another elder. I welcomed them, and they opened the subject by telling me what a nice guy I am—kind, hospitable, and well liked among the congregation. I thanked him and returned his compliment, and they are nice people. My former preacher's wife fed me for the last year and six months, and I haven't lost my love for all those kind people; but their agenda was different from mine.

One of the elders asked the question, "After one year and six months, what went wrong?"

"With all honesty, I am not going to continue listening blindly any more to your teaching."

"Can you give us some example?"

"Yes, I can, and plenty of them. My intention is to learn and study the Word of GOD, the BIBLE, and write a book about my experience with GOD—how he saved me from all my transgression against GOD, and the people. But after I started questioning his teaching, I want to go on my own to serve GOD." And I told the elder about my former preacher. "One time out of the blue, and I believe he was preparing to tell me what he said for some time, 'Do you think GOD has time for you?' Well, yes, GOD does have time for me, and he knows the count of my hair.

"In Matthew 10:30–33, '"And even the very hairs of your head are all numbered. So don't be afraid; you are worth more than many sparrows. Whoever acknowledges me before men. I will also acknowledge him before my Father in heaven. But whoever disown me before men, I will disown him before my Father in heaven."'

"In Luke 12:7–9, '"Indeed, the very hairs of your head are all numbered. Don't be afraid; you are worth more than many sparrows. I tell you, whoever acknowledges me before men. the Son of Man will also acknowledge him before the angels of GOD. But he who disowns me before men will be disowned before the angels of GOD."'

"And when I used to tell him that GOD spoke to me, he said GOD does not speak to people! That was in the Moses time. And there are other occasions when GOD healed me and manifested himself to me!"

But I was interrupted by the other elder. "Assaf. That happened to everybody."

"Yes, it does, but others don't know that GOD is talking to them. I have experience throughout my life that GOD is with me, and he talks to me."

Then the other elder made the comment, "Is GOD wrong?" Here he was referring to me when one time, I told my former preacher that GOD had directed me to study the BIBLE with him. "What about this book you are going to write? How if it is a flop?"

By then, I got upset and started to speak with a loud voice. "My book will not be a flop because it is GOD'S will for me to serve him." They both were very calm; and I knew that from their teaching, they don't let anyone express their feelings until they get everything out of their heart, and then calmly they respond. Then I calmly responded, "GOD has directed me to leave you because I already passed his test by acknowledging how to discern between false teaching and true teaching, and our LORD GOD JESUS spoke of false prophets and false ideology and between our heavenly GOD the Creator of heaven and earth and between false gods."

I often watch Joyce Meyer's teaching, and one of her messages was you don't have to have a degree to write a book. Just take the first step and you will be on your way by writing what you have. And that was a huge encouragement for me. Unlike my former teacher who puts me down, no encouragement, and his teaching is to strip your personality to control you.

If Joyce Meyer was among his congregation, she wouldn't be allowed to even stand behind the pulpit. Now she teaches the BIBLE in ninety-five different languages to a hundred million people all over the world, and that is JESUS'S message to all his disciples: to teach his Word throughout the globe, and then it will be his second coming to establish his kingdom. She is serving GOD. And I reverse the cliché for her: "Behind every great man is a woman." Now I say, "Behind every great woman is a man." And that man is her husband, David. That is another example how they use the BIBLE verses to brainwash their women and others as well, and I stand behind every word I say.

I have more respect for Bill Maher when he said he doesn't believe in GOD to the whole world. That does not mean I have respect for you, Bill, but less disrespect than the group I am talking about. GOD gave you some intelligence. I don't like how you talk about my heavenly Father—you and other people like you. I am smarter than all of you because I believe in GOD, the creator of heaven and earth. You breathe because of GOD. And you probably will live on this earth for about a hundred years, but I will live forever either in heaven or on earth when JESUS comes again to establish his kingdom on earth. I challenge you to a public debate, and my education is only GED. But all my PhDs are sealed by the Holy Spirit. If you study the BIBLE, Bill, it is all historic; and there are witnesses to those facts. And please don't behave like a teenager and say, "Bite me." And GOD loves you. So are we who believe in GOD. Don't you want to live forever, Bill?

I returned a call from my former preacher, August 1st, and the first thing he asked me was "Did you finish your book? And do you already have the millions of followers? Or maybe just one follower?" Of course, he was speaking mockingly. He couldn't wait until the middle of August at least to mock me because I was blindly listening to his teaching, and he and his brood don't believe that GOD talks to people anymore. And from the beginning, I made it clear to them that my loyalty is to GOD, and I am hungry to study the Word of GOD to be able to serve him, not to learn about anybody's else agenda.

My answer to him was "I am now learning the BIBLE by watching Daystar, TBN, Hillsong Channel, and The Word, plus other channels. And I relate to their teachings by what happens to me in relation with our LORD GOD JESUS.

He said, "You listen to those smooth talkers?" While he is the smooth talker.

"No, I haven't finished my book or started my ministry, and I said to you before I will have the millions of followers in ten years, not in August." And he started to quote verses from the BIBLE, and at the end, he said that they were the only group GOD has chosen to be in heaven. The Holy Spirit uttered out of my mouth, "You portray yourselves that way, but you are not."

Then he mumbled, "Okay. Okay. Assaf, I will talk to you when I get back to Las Vegas."

Again I said to him, "No, you are not." By then, he hung up, and I was right. He never called, and he will not ever call even when he reads or hears about the success of my book in 2019.

I believe my destiny is to write about the prophet Jonah; I owe that to my beloved mother by preaching and teaching about Jonah because she always repeated his name since my childhood and how

GOD saved his life after three days and three nights of being in the belly of a big fish! And I never read about Jonah until I met my preacher after about sixty years later to learn the BIBLE because of the miracles GOD did in my life, and I want to return GOD'S love by learning and studying his word, the BIBLE. So one time, I mentioned to my preacher how my illiterate mother used to quote some of the verses from the BIBLE just by listening to the priest by attending the Sunday mass and especially Jonah's story, which I knew by heart—how GOD saved his life. Otherwise, he would be dead by being in the belly of the big fish for three days! But my preacher rationalized that because of the volume of the air in the big fish, it kept Jonah alive! I said to him, "What does the air have to do with that?" He did not answer me and occupied himself by going to the kitchen.

Well, now that was the breaking point for me to leave that kind of teaching for the staggering evidence. Any time I mention GOD' divine power in my life to him, he diverts GOD'S power to other explanations! For example, when I told him about how GOD healed my ulcer by crying to him! His explanation was that Satan sometimes does that, and it is in the BIBLE. But I said to him I was crying to GOD to heal me, not to Satan. And when I said that GOD talks to me, he explained that was during Moses's time, when GOD talked to the prophets. "Do you think that GOD has time for you?" Yes, GOD has time for me, you false preacher, and GOD knows my name is Assaf and the count of my hair as well; that is in the BIBLE too. Also when I told him about the divine interruption when GOD manifested himself and poured his love into my heart to go to my coworker and hug him after I said to him not to speak to me anymore and we became a best friends and because of him, my job was saved; the only thing he said to me was "Oh, that worked out for you!" Is that a false preacher or what?

We, the majority, know that the end is near. Nothing in this world is worth losing your everlasting life over a short time on this earth. GOD loves you all; so am I. And now I obey GOD'S Word and do what GOD says. I am the sinner Assaf Sawaya.

Now, my beloved reader, let me expand and explain Jonah's divine mission.

The word of God came to Jonah son of Amittai: "Go to the great city of Nineveh and preach against it because its wickedness has come up before me." (Jonah 1:1) "The word of the lord came"—it is a common phrase used to indicate to divine source of the prophet's revelation (also in [1 King 17:8; Hosea 1:1; Joel 1:1; Hag 1:1, 3; Zee!! 1:1, 7]).

> Then the word of the Lord came to him. (1 King 17:8)

> The word of the Lord that came to Hosea son of Beeri during the reigns of Uzziah. (Hosea 1:1)

> The word of the Lord that came to Joel, son of Pethuel. (Joel 1:1)

> In the second year of Kind Darius, on the first day of the sixth month the word of the Lord came through the prophet Haggai. (Haggai 1:1)

> In the eighth month of the second year of Darius, the word of the Lord came to the prophet Zechariah, son of Berekiah, the son of Iddo. (Zechariah:1, 7)

"Its wickedness has come up before me." (Jonah 1:2) Nineveh was the center of idolatrous worship of Assur and Estar and her evil ways and cruelty. Assyria (represented by Nineveh, Nahum 1:1) had already been destroyed Samaria (722–721 BC), resulting in the captivity of the northern Kingdom of Israel and posed a present threat to Judah. The Assyrians were brutally cruel, their kings often being depicted as gloating over the gruesome punishments inflicted on conquered people. They conducted their wars with shocking ferocity, uprooted whole populations as state policy, and deported them to other parts of their empire. The leaders of conquered cities were

tortured and horribly mutilated before being executed; no wonder the dread of Assyria fell on all her neighbors!

But Jonah ran away and boarded a ship traveling the opposite direction, to Tarshish, near Gibraltar. Seemed the end of the world. His refusal to go to Nineveh brought these pagan sailors into peril.

The Lord sent a great wind on the sea, and such a violent storm arose that the ship threatened to break up. All the sailors were afraid and each cried out to his own god. And they threw the cargo into the sea to lighten the ship. But Jonah had gone below deck, where he lay down and fell into a deep sleep. The captain went to him and said, "How can you sleep? Get up and call on your god! Maybe he will take notice of us and we will not perish."

Then the sailors said to each other, "Let us cast lots to find out who is responsible for this calamity." The lot fell on Jonah. By the lot of judgment, the LORD exposed the guilty one.

The sailors ask Jonah, "Who are you? And where do you come from?"

Jonah answered, "I am a Hebrew and worship the Lord, the God of heaven who made the sea and the land."

Jonah confessed his refusal to fulfil his divine mission to Nineveh. *"What have you done to us? And what can we do to escape your God's wrath on us?"*

"Throw me into the sea!" Jonah's readiness to die to save the terrified sailors.

Instead the men did their best to row back, but they could not. For the sea grew even wilder than before. The reluctance of the sailors to throw Jonah into the sea stands in sharp contrast to Jonah's reluctance to warn Nineveh of impending judgment.

Then they cried to the Lord, "O Lord, do not let us die for taking this man's life. Do not hold us accountable for killing an innocent man, for you O Lord, have done as you pleased." Then they took Jonah and threw him overboard, and the raging sea grew calm. At this the men greatly feared the Lord and they offered a sacrifice to the lord and made vows to him. But the Lord provided a great fish to swallow Jonah, and Jonah was inside the fish three days and three nights.

"Three days and three nights, Jonah was inside the fish." My mother repeated to me those exact words over and over through my childhood, and then I was faced with my former false teacher that Jonah survived his ordeal because of the air in the big fish's belly! That is why I refer to him as a false preacher, and I stand by what I am saying and face anyone to challenge me publicly, Assaf Sawaya.

But the Lord provided a great fish to swallow Jonah, and Jonah was inside the fish three days and three nights. The New Testament clearly uses Jonah's experience as a type of foreshadowing of the burial and resurrection of JESUS, who was entombed for three days and three nights. "For as Jonah was three days and three nights in the belly of a huge fish, so the Son of Man will be three days and three nights in the heart of the earth." (Matthew 12:40)

From inside the fish Jonah prayed to the Lord his God. Jonah acknowledged that his circumstances were judgment from the LORD. Jonah's life was threatened in every way by his water surroundings even to the point of death. Jonah found himself in the same position as the sailors: offering sacrifices and making vows. Jonah's vow could well have been to carry out GOD'S, ministry for him by preaching in Nineveh. Just as GOD calls the stars by name, so he speaks to his creation in the animal world; *And the Lord commanded the fish, and it vomited Jonah onto dry land.*

Then the word of the Lord came to Jonah a second time: "Go to the great city of Nineveh and proclaim to it the message I give you." (Jonah 3:1) A prophet was the bearer of a message from GOD, not primarily a foreteller of coming events.

Jonah obeyed the word of the Lord and went to Nineveh. (Jonah 3:3) But reluctantly, still wanting the Ninevites to be destroyed. Nineveh was a great city to GOD. The text emphasizes not only its size but its importance. With a circumference of sixty miles, it would require three days just to get around it. And the city had more than 120,000 inhabitants.

On the first day, Jonah started into the city. He proclaimed: "Forty more days and Nineveh will be overturned."

The Ninevites believed God. They declared a fast. And all of them, from the greatest to the least, put on sackcloth. When the news reached the king of Nineveh, he rose from his throne, took off his royal robes, covered himself with sackcloth and sat down in the dust. Then he issued a proclamation in Nineveh: "By the decree of the king and his nobles: Do not let any man or beast, herd or flock taste anything; do not let them eat or drink. But let man and beast be covered with sackcloth. Let everyone call urgently on God. Let them give up their evil ways and their violence. Who knows? God may yet relent and with compassion turn from his fierce anger so that we will not perish."

When God saw that they did and how they turned from their evil ways, he had compassion and did not bring upon them the destruction he had threatened. (Jonah 3:4–10)

The sackcloth is a customary sign of humbling oneself in repentance and believing GOD. This may mean that the Ninevites genuinely turned to the LORD. On the other hand, their belief in GOD may have gone much deeper than the sailors' fear of GOD. At least they took the prophet's warning seriously and acted accordingly. Inclusion of the domestic animals was unusual and expressed the urgency with which the Ninevites sought mercy.

GOD often responds in mercy to man's repentance by canceling threatened punishment. "'If at any time I announce that a nation or kingdom is to be uprooted, torn down and destroyed, and if that nation I warned repents of its evil, then I will relent and not inflict on it the disaster I had planned. And if at another time I announce that a nation or a kingdom is to be built up and planted, and if it does evil in my sight and does not obey me, then I will reconsider the good I had intended.'" (Jeremiah 18:7–10)

Jonah was angry that GOD would have compassion on an enemy of Israel. He wanted GOD'S goodness to be shown only to Israelites, not to Gentiles.

But Jonah was greatly displeased and became angry. He prayed to the Lord, "O Lord, is this not what I said when I was still at home? That is why I was so quick to flee to Tarshish. I knew that you are a gracious and compassionate God, slow to anger and abounding in love, a God who relents from sending calamity. Now, O Lord, take away my life, for it is better for me to die than to live. (Jonah 4:1–3)

A comparison of the two prophets Jonah and Elijah, who flees to Horeb. "While he himself went a day's journey into the desert. He came to a broom tree, sat down under it and prayed that he might die. 'I have had enough, LORD,' he said. 'Take my life; I am no better than my ancestors.' Then he lay down under the tree and fell asleep" (1 Kings 19:4).

To Jonah, GOD'S mercy to the Ninevites meant an end to Israel's favored standing with him. Jonah shortly before had rejoiced in his deliverance from death, but now that Nineveh lives, he prefers to die.

The Lord replied, "Have you any right to be angry?"

Jonah went out and sat down at place east of the city. There he made himself a shelter, sat in its shade and waited to see what would happen to the city. Then the Lord God provided a vine and made it grow up over Jonah to give shade for his head to ease his discomfort. And Jonah was very happy about the vine. But at dawn the next day God provided a worm, which chewed the vine so that it withered. When the sun rose, God provided a scorching east wind, and the sun blazed on Jonah's head so that he grew faint. He wanted to die and said, "It would be better for me to die than to live."

But God said to Jonah, "Do you have a right to be angry about the vine?"

"I do," he said. "I am angry enough to die."

But the lord said, "You have been concerned about this vine, though you did not tend it or make it grow. It sprang up overnight and died overnight. But Nineveh has more than a hundred and twenty thousand people who cannot tell their right hand from their left, and many cattle as well. Should I not be concerned about that great city?" (Jonah 4:4–11)

As in Exodus 34:6–7, "And he passed in front of Moses compassionate and gracious GOD, slow to anger, abounding in love and faithfulness, maintaining love to thousands, and forgiving wickedness, rebellion and sin. Yet he does not leave the guilty unpunished; he punishes the children and their children for the sin of the father to the third and the fourth generation."

It is better for me to die than to live. Perhaps Jonah was expressing the reality of breaking his vow to GOD, a second time. In Numbers 30:2, "When a man makes a vow to the LORD, or take an oath to obligate himself by a pledge, he must not break his word, but must do everything he said." Moreover, in Ecclesiastes 5:4–5, "When you make a vow to GOD, do not delay to fulfill it. He has no pleasure in fools; fulfill your vow. It is better not to make a vow than to make one and not fulfill it."

Jonah made himself a shelter. Apparently, this shelter did not provide enough shade. But GOD provided a vine to give him more shade. But Jonah waited and hoped that Nineveh would be destroyed. GOD graciously increased the comfort of his stubbornly defiant prophet. But the vine sprang up overnight and died overnight, indicative of fleeting value.

Again, Jonah said, *"It would be better for me to die than to live."* But GOD said to Jonah, *"Do you have a right to be angry about the vine?"* Jonah was angry about the scorching wind, the blazing sun, and the short-lived vine. He wanted to die again. But GOD said to Jonah, *"Do you have a right to be angry about the vine?"* A vine he did not tend to and did not make any effort to take care of; now he wanted to die.

What about the Ninevites? They cannot tell their right hand from their left, like a small children. The Ninevites needed GOD'S fatherly compassion, and many cattle as well. GOD'S concern extended even to domestic animals. *"Should I not be concerned?"* GOD had the first word, and he also has the last.

The commission GOD gave Jonah displayed his mercy and compassion to the Ninevites, and his last word to Jonah emphatically proclaimed that concern for every creature, both man and animal. The LORD preserves both the man and the beast. In Psalm 36:6, "Your righteousness is like the mighty mountains, your justice like the great deep."

But GOD takes no pleasure in the death of the wicked, but desire rather that they turn from their ways and live. In Ezekiel 33:11, "Say to them, As surely as I live, declares the sovereign LORD, I take no pleasure in the death of the wicked, but rather that they turn from their ways and live. Turn! Turn from your evil ways! Why will you die, O house of Israel?" In Ezekiel chapter 18 verse 21, "But if a wicked man turns away from all the sins he has committed and keeps all my decrees and does what is just and right, he will surely live; he will not die."

Jonah and his countrymen traditionally rejoiced in GOD'S special mercies to Israel but wished only his wrath on their enemies. GOD here rebukes such hardness and proclaims his own gracious benevolence. GOD'S plan always becomes fact regardless of any interruption, and what GOD says always will happen.

Jonah's divine mission was interrupted because he harbored hate in his heart toward the Ninevites because they destroyed Samaria, the northern kingdom of Israel, and posed a threat to Judah. The Assyrians were brutally cruel; the Samarians were tortured and horribly mutilated before being executed. Jonah hated the Ninevites—hatred for the Israelites.

Jonah knew that GOD is gracious and compassionate, slow to anger, and abounding in love, who relents from sending calamity to his children. Jonah behaved as a human. He could not forgive his enemy, while he knows for sure that GOD forgives his children when they stop doing evil and return to GOD—not only the Israelites but the Gentiles also because GOD is not for the Israelites only but for all his creation, even the animals.

Jonah disobeyed GOD, and tried to run the opposite direction to Tarshish by taking a boat, but GOD'S plan has to work exactly the way GOD planted it regardless of any interruption, even the interruption of Satan in the Paradise. All of GOD'S plan for Jonah to go to Nineveh and preach to them and proclaim the great city of Nineveh—that must be done.

The LORD sent a great wind on the sea, and a violent storm threatened the ship to break up; that was the first time the sailors experienced such a violent storm and started crying out to their gods, their imaginary gods, to help them in their trial until Jonah confessed to them it was his fault what was happening to the ship because he disobeyed his GOD, the creator of heaven and earth and its inhabitants—all the people and the animals.

Jonah wanted to die, so he asked them to throw him overboard in order for the violent storm to stop. First, they refused to kill a man, but he told them that was the only way for them to survive because of his GOD'S anger toward him. Then they realized that was the power of GOD, the creator of heaven and earth, and they offered sacrifices to the LORD GOD, and made a vow. After that, they threw Jonah overboard.

GOD provided a great fish to swallow Jonah, and he was inside the big fish for three days and three nights. Jonah wanted to die because of his disobedience to GOD, but GOD'S plan hasn't been fulfilled yet; and by Jonah, GOD is going to fulfill his plan.

When Jonah was facing death inside the belly of the fish, he cried out to GOD for help, and GOD listened to his cry and commanded the fish to vomit Jonah onto dry land. The big fish obeyed GOD and vomited Jonah on a dry land! GOD talks to animals as well as to men.

The second time the Word of GOD came to Jonah to go to the great city of Nineveh and proclaim to it the message he gave him, Jonah obeyed the LORD, and the Ninevites believed GOD. They declared a fast, and all of them put on a sackcloth. It is a sign of obedience and humiliation, and that was how they were saved from GOD' S calamity.

In Matthew 12:38, JESUS was asked by the Pharisees, and the teachers of the law said to him, "Teacher, we want to see a miraculous sign from you." JESUS answered them, "A wicked and adulterous generation asks for a miraculous sign! But none will be given it except the sign of the prophet Jonah, for as Jonah was three days and three nights in the belly of a huge fish, so the Son of Man will be three days and three nights in the heart of the earth."

The Pharisees wanted to see a spectacular miracle, preferably in the sky, as the sign that JESUS was the Messiah. He cites them a sign from history and uses Jonah's experience as a type of foreshadowing of the burial and resurrection of JESUS, who was entombed for three days and three nights in the heart of earth. "A wicked and adulterous generation" refers to spiritual, not physical, adultery, in the sense that their generation had become unfaithful to its spiritual husband (GOD).

My brothers and sisters in GOD, I had testified in court about the bad things I did in my life, and the court has my file; but now I am testifying about what GOD has done in my life to show the entire world how GOD saved me from the belly of the fish because of his love and the plan he has for his children. GOD' plan always works, no matter how much we sin against him only because of his love for us. I am the perfect witness for GOD. When I cried for him to heal my ulcer, GOD healed me before I stopped crying up to him!

Jonah cried out to GOD from the belly of the fish to save him, and GOD did save him by commanding the fish to vomit him on a dry land. And Jonah obeyed GOD, by going to Nineveh and proclaimed to it the message GOD gave him. GOD has the record for all that he has done for us, and GOD knows us by name.

My brothers and sisters, are you in the belly of a fish? What addiction do you have? Drug use, alcohol use, gambling, or any other desire of the flesh? You can't overcome a bad doctor's report, bad relation with spouse, or any other thing you can think of, and there is no one to help you? Yes, there is GOD, who helps all his children. When we cry out to him, GOD is there for us to help us and recognize his love for us, like what GOD did for me; and now I obey him and have overcome all my addictions. What was hard for me now is easy. I did it one by one and asked GOD to help me, and GOD transformed me. When I fail, I come back to him for forgiveness, and GOD tells me, "Welcome back, my child," and forgets about it. GOD is love, and he loves us unconditionally; and GOD is there for us any time we come to him.

We have to also recognize him and thank him; GOD has a record when we come to him. In Luke17:11–19,

> As JESUS was going into a village, ten men who had leprosy met Him. They stood at a distance and called out in a loud voice, "JESUS, MASTER, have pity on us!"
>
> When JESUS saw them, He said, "Go show yourselves to the priests." And as they went, they were cleansed.
>
> One of them, when he was healed, came back, praising GOD in a loud voice. He threw himself at JESUS' feet and thanked Him—and he was a Samaritan. JESUS asked, "Were not

all ten cleansed? Where are the other nine? Was no one found to return and give praise to GOD except this foreigner?" THEN JESUS said to him, "Rise and go; your faith has made you well."

GOD has a record of the ten men he healed from leprosy, but only one came back to thank JESUS. "Where is the other nine?" Well, I am the one who is thanking GOD by writing my book as a witness to what GOD has done in my life by saving me from all my the bad things I caused to myself and others. Now I am serving the LORD GOD and obeying his commandments; I am the sinner.

In John 1:1, "In the beginning was the word, and the word was with GOD, and the word was GOD. He was with GOD in the beginning." Moreover, in John 1:14–18,

> The word became flesh and made His dwelling among us. We have seen His glory, the glory of the One and only, who came from the Father, full of grace and truth.
>
> JOHN testifies concerning Him. HE cries out, saying, "This was he of whom I said, 'He who comes after me has surpassed me because he was before me.'"
>
> From the fullness of his grace we have all received one blessing after another. For the law was given through Moses: grace and truth came through JESUS CHRIST. No one has ever seen GOD, but GOD the One and only, who is at the Father's side, Has made Him known.

JESUS fulfilled his Father's plan for us to be crucified on the cross by taking our sins and the stripes the soldiers inflected on him, and JESUS asked the Father to forgive the soldiers who spit on him and caused him to bleed since they did not know what they were doing; and that is the love of GOD for his children. Our loving God has created man on his own image, a perfect man, to live forever and rule over all animals on earth, the birds of the air, and the fish of the sea, but Adam failed God and was condemned to death, he and all his offsprings; that is, all mankind.

Adam and Eve

GENESIS 1:1—In the beginning GOD created the heaven and earth. Now the earth was formless and empty, darkness was over the surface of the deep, and the spirit of GOD was hovering over the waters.

And GOD said, "Let there be light…"

And GOD said, "Let there be an expanse…"

And GOD said, "Let the water under the sky be gathered to one place…"

And GOD said, "Let there be light in the expanse of the sky to separate the day from the night…"

And GOD said, "Let the water teem with living creatures…"

And GOD said, "Let the land produce living creatures…"

So GOD created man in his own image, in the image of GOD he created him; male and female he created them.

The LORD GOD formed the man from the dust of the ground and breathed into his nostrils the breath of life, and the man became a living being.

Now the LORD GOD had planted a garden in the east in Eden; and there he put the man he had formed. And the LORD GOD made all kinds of trees grow out of the ground-trees that were pleasing to the eye and good for food. In the middle of the garden were the tree of life and the tree of the knowledge of good and evil.

The LORD GOD took the man and put him in the garden of Eden to work on it and take care of it. And the LORD GOD commanded the man, "You are free to eat from any tree in the garden; But you must not eat from the tree of the knowledge of good and evil, for when you eat of it you will surely die."

The LORD GOD said, "It is not good for the man to be alone. I will make a helper suitable for him."

Genesis 2:19.

Now the LORD GOD had formed out of the ground all the beasts of the field, and all the birds of the air. He brought them to the man to see what he would name them: and whatever the man called. So the man gave names to all the livestock, the birds of the air and all the beasts of the field. But for Adam, no suitable helper was found.

So the LORD GOD caused the man to fall into a deep sleep; and while he was sleeping, he took one of the man' s ribs and closed up the place with flesh. Then the LORD GOD made a woman from the rib he had taken out of the man, and he brought her to the man.

The man said. "This is now bone of my bones and flesh of my flesh; she shall be called woman, for she was taken out of man."

The man and his wife were both naked, and they felt no shame.

Now the serpent was more crafty than any of the animals the LORD GOD had made. He said to the woman, "Did GOD really say, You must not eat from any tree in the garden?"

The woman said to the serpent, "We may eat fruit from the trees in the garden, but GOD did say, You must not eat fruit from the tree that is in the middle of the garden, and you must not touch it, or you will die."

"You will not surely die," the serpent said to the woman. "For GOD knows that when you eat of it your eyes will be opened, and you will be like GOD, knowing good and evil."

When the woman saw that the fruit of the tree was good for food and pleasing to the eye and also desirable for gaining wisdom, she took some and ate it. She also gave some to her husband, who was with her, and ate it. Then the eyes of both of them were opened, and they realized they were naked: so they sewed fig leaves together and made coverings for themselves.

Then the man and his wife heard the sound of the LORD GOD as he was walking in the garden in the cool day, and they hid from the LORD GOD among the trees of the garden. But the LORD GOD called the man, "Where are you?"

He answered, "I heard you in the garden, and I was afraid, because I was naked; so I hid."

And he said, "Who told you that you were naked? Have you eaten from the tree that I commanded not to eat from?"

The man said, "The woman you put here with me gave me some fruit from the tree, and I ate it."

Then the LORD GOD said to the woman, "What is this you have done?"

The woman said, "The serpent deceived me, and I ate."

SO the LORD GOD said to the serpent, "Because you have done this, Cursed are you above all the livestock and all the animals! You will crawl on your belly and you will eat dust all the days of your life. And I will put enmity between you and the woman, and between your offspring and hers; he will crush your head, and you will strike his heel."

To the woman he said, "I will greatly increase your pains in childbearing; with pain you will give birth to children. Your desire will be for your husband, and he will rule over you."

To Adam he said, "Because you listened to your wife and ate from the tree about which I commanded you, you must not ear of it. Cursed is the ground because of you: through painful toil you will eat of it all the days of your life. It will produce thorns and thistles for you, and you will eat the plants of the field. By the sweat of your brow you will eat your food until you return to the ground, since from it you were taken: for dust you are and to dust you will return."

Adam named his wife Eve because she would become the mother of all the living. The LORD GOD made garments of skin for Adam and his wife and clothed them.

And the LORD GOD said, "The man has now become like one of us, knowing good and evil. He must not be allowed to reach out his hand and take also from the tree of life and eat, and live forever." So the LORD GOD banished him from the garden of Eden to work the ground from which he had been taken. After he drove the man out, he placed on the east side of the garden of Eden cherubim and a flaming sword flashing back and forth to guard the way to the tree of life.

Formed. The Hebrew for this verb commonly referred to the work of a potter who fashions vessels from clay. *Make, create,* and *form* are used to describe GOD'S creation of both man and animals. Breath of life. Humans and animals alike, have the breath of life in them. In Job 33:4, "The Spirit of GOD has made me; the breath of the Almighty gives me life."

Man became a living being. The Hebrew phrase here translated "living being" is translated "living creatures." The words therefore imply that people, at least physically, have affinity with animals. The great difference is that the man is made "in the image of GOD" and has an absolutely unique relation both to GOD as his servant and the other creatures as their divinely appointed steward. In Psalm 8:5–8, "You made him a little lower than the heavenly beings and crowned him with glory and honor. You made him ruler over the works of your hands: you put everything under his feet: all flocks and herds and the beasts of the field, the birds of the air, and the fish of the seas. O LORD, our LORD, how majestic is your name in all the earth."

Tree of life—signifying and giving life without death to those who eat its fruit. In Revelation 2:7, "He who has an ear, let him hear what the Spirit says to the churches. To him who overcomes. I will give the right to eat from the tree of life, which is in the paradise of God."

Tree of knowledge of good and evil—signifying the knowledge of good and evil, leading ultimately to death to those who eat its fruit. "Knowledge of good and evil" refers to moral knowledge or ethical discernment. In Deuteronomy 1:39, "And the little ones that you said would be taken captive. Your children who do not yet know good from bad they will enter the land. I will give it to them and they will take possession of it."

Adam and Eve possessed both life and moral discernment as they came from the land of GOD. Their access to the fruit of the tree of life showed that GOD'S will and intention for them was life. In eating the fruit of the tree of the knowledge of good and evil, Adam and Eve sought a creaturely source of discernment in order to be morally independent of GOD. Man is now charged to govern the earth responsibly under GOD'S sovereignty. *Surely you will die if you eat from the tree of life.* Despite the serpent's denial, disobeying GOD ultimately results in death.

The great deceiver clothed himself as a serpent, one of GOD'S good creatures. He insinuated a falsehood and portrayed rebellion as clever, but essentially innocent self-interest. Therefore, "the devil or Satan" is later referred to as that ancient serpent. In Revelation 12:9, "The great dragon was hurled down—that ancient serpent called the devil, or Satan, who leads the whole world astray. He was hurled to the earth, and his angels with him."

The Hebrew words for *crafty* and *naked* are almost identical. Though naked, the man and his wife felt no shame. The craftiness of the serpent led them to sin, and they then became ashamed of their nakedness. Did GOD really say, "You must not eat fruit from the tree, and you must not touch it. Or you will die"?

The question and the response changed the course of human history. By causing the woman to doubt GOD'S word, Satan brought evil into the world. Here, the deceiver undertook to alienate man from GOD. You could read Job chapter one and chapter two. In Zechariah 3:1, "Then he showed me Joshua the high priest standing before the angel of the LORD, and Satan standing at his right side to accuse him."

GOD also said, "You must not touch the tree." The woman adds to GOD'S word, distorting his directive and demonstrating that the serpent's subtle challenge was working its poison. *You will not surely die.* The blatant denial of a specific divine pronouncement. *But you must not eat from the tree of the knowledge of good and evil, for when you eat of it you will surely die.*

GOD knows. Satan accuses GOD of having unworthy motives. In Job 1:9–11, "'Does Job fear GOD for nothing?'" Satan replied, 'Have you not put a hedge around him and his household and everything he has? You have blessed the work of his hand, so that his flocks and herds are spread throughout the land. But stretch out your hand and strike everything he has, and he will surely curse you to your face.'" Moreover, in Job 2:4–5, "'Skin for Skin!' Satan replied. 'A man will give all he has for his own life. But stretch out your hand and strike his flesh and bones, and he will surely curse you to your face.'"

Satan accuses the righteous man of the same. *Your eyes will be opened, and you will be like God.* The statement is only half true. Their eyes were opened, but the result was quite different from what the serpent had promised in knowing good and evil.

And the Lord God made all kinds of trees grow out of the garden-trees that were pleasing to the eye and good for food. In the middle of the garden were the tree of life and the tree of the knowledge of good and evil. (Genesis 2:9) Good for food... Pleasing to the eye... Desirable for gaining wisdom... Three aspects of temptation. In 1 John 2:16, "For everything in the world—the craving of sinful man, the lust of his eyes and the boasting of what he has and does comes not from the Father but from the world."

They realized they were naked. No longer innocent like children, they had a new awareness of themselves and of each other in their nakedness and shame. They made a covering, their own feeble and futile attempt to hide their shame, which only GOD could cover.

The garden. Once a place of joy and fellowship with GOD, it became a place of fear and of hiding from GOD. *Where are you?* A rhetorical question. *The woman you put here with me gave me the fruit and I ate it.* The man blames GOD and the woman—anyone but himself—for his sin.

The serpent deceived me and I ate the fruit from the tree. The woman blames the serpent rather than herself. GOD "cursed" the serpent. The woman and the man were all judged, but only the serpent and the ground were cursed. To Adam, GOD said, "To dust you will return," the symbol of death itself and would be the serpent's food.

He will crush your head, and you will strike his heel. The antagonism between people and snakes is used to symbolize the outcome of the titanic struggle between GOD and the evil one, a struggle played out in the hearts and history of mankind. The offspring of the woman would eventually crush the serpent's head, a promise fulfilled in CHRIST'S victory over Satan—victory in which all believers will share. In Romans 16:20, "The GOD of peace will soon crush Satan under your feet. The grace of our LORD JESUS be with you."

Pain in childbearing. Her judgment fell on what was most unique, hers as a woman and as a "suitable helper" for her husband.

Similarly, the man's "painful toil" was a judgment on him as a worker of the soil. Some believe that the Hebrew root underlying *pains, pain,* and *painful toil* should here be understood in the sense of burdensome labor or hard work.

Give birth to children. As a sign of grace in the midst of judgment, the human race would continue. Her sexual attraction for the man and his headship over her will become intimate aspects of her life in which she experiences trouble and anguish rather than unalloyed joy and blessing.

You will eat. Though he would have to work hard and long (judgment), the man would be able to produce food that would sustain life (grace).

GOD said, "To dust you will return." Man's labor would not able to save off death. The origin of his body and the source of his food became a symbol of his eventual death.

GOD graciously provided Adam and Eve with more effective clothing to cover their shame.

Knowing good and evil. In a terribly perverted way, Satan' s prediction came true, which always results in death. In Romans 6:23, "For the wages of sin is death, but the gift of GOD is eternal life in CHRIST our LORD." Moreover, in James 1:14–15, "But each one is tempted when by his own evil desire he is dragged away and enticed. Then after desire bas conceived, it gives birth to sin; and sin, when it is full grown, gives birth to death."

Then it cuts the sinner off from GOD'S gift of eternal life. GOD banished Adam from the garden to work the ground. Before he sinned, man had worked in a beautiful and pleasant garden. Now he would have to work hard on the ground cursed with thorns and thistles.

Cherubim. Similar to the statues of winged human-headed bulls or lions that stood guard at the entrances to palaces and temples in ancient Mesopotamia. In Exodus 25:18, "And make two cherubim out of hammered gold at the ends of the cover."

To guard. The sword of GOD'S judgment stood between fallen man and GOD'S garden.

And the Lord God said, "The man has now become like one of us, knowing good and evil. He must not be allowed to reach out his hand and take also from the tree of life and eat and live forever." Only through GOD'S redemption in CHRIST does man have access again to the tree of life. In Revelation 2:7, "He who has an ear, let him hear what the Spirit says to the churches. To him who overcomes, I will give the right to eat from the tree of life, which is in the paradise of GOD."

I am furious with Adam and Eve! You don't do that to the One who loves you. GOD gave the power, the wealth, and above all, the helper; and she is the most beautiful gift of all what GOD gave you. You don't do that to the One who loves you.

We all, one time or another, got a telephone call or a letter from a scam artist, and they deceive us by telling us a part of the truth. But we owe it to ourselves to check around with friends; in this case, only GOD, before we make any deaccession.

My wife, one time, called me at work, telling me we won a trip to Hawaii; and she was very excited, so I told her to calm down and said to her, "We did not win anything. Calm down now." And I explained to her there are evil people who give false hope to others to manipulate them to their own benefit, but it will be too late when you find out about their scam.

The perfect example is Satan, the way he deceived Eve. From the beginning, GOD created heaven and earth and every living thing on earth, and then GOD created man in his own image. Male and female, GOD created them. GOD created man from the dust of the ground and breathed into his nostril the breath of life. GOD planted a garden in Eden and put the man there. GOD made all kind of trees good for food; in the middle of the garden were the tree of life and the tree of knowledge of good and evil.

The Lord God commanded the man, "You are free to eat, from any tree in the garden, but you must not eat from the tree of the knowledge of good and evil, for when you eat of it you will die." GOD brought to Adam all the beasts and all the birds of the air that he formed from the ground, like how he formed Adam, to name all the livestock, the birds, and all the beasts of the field. But for a suitable helper for Adam, GOD caused the man to fall into a deep sleep, and when he was under the influence of drugs, GOD took one of the man's ribs and closed up the place with a flesh. GOD made a woman from the rib he took from the man and brought her to the man. The man and his wife were both naked in the garden and felt no shame.

Now the name *serpent* the man gave it; it was more crafty than any of the beasts GOD made. Satan clothed himself as a serpent and said to the woman, *"Did God really say, you must not eat from any tree in the garden?"*

The woman said to the serpent, "We may eat fruit from the trees in the garden, but God did say, You must not eat fruit from the tree that is in the middle of the garden, and you must not touch it, or you will die."

"You will not surely die," the serpent said to the woman. *"For God knows that when you eat of it your eyes will be opened, and you will be like GOD, knowing good and evil."*

Now here is the deception by Satan clothed as a serpent. He told Eve a part of the truth, knowing good and evil, but the lie was by telling her that "you will not surely die." That lie was to deceive the woman, like he was deceived by imaginations to overthrow GOD, and take his place, the place of who created him. How stupid of Satan. Because GOD gave him some power, it went to his head; and also he deceived one third of the angels in heaven to follow him, and they did. But GOD'S plan for the earth will not change. Even if GOD has condemned the man to die, by the sin of one man, also GOD saved the man by the sacrifice of one man. Our LORD GOD became flesh and saved us from death because of GOD'S love for the world. As shown in Romans 5:12–21, "Death through Adam, Life through CHRIST":

> Therefore, just as sin entered the world through one man and death through sin, and in this way death came to all men because all sinned—for before the law was given, sin was in the world. But sin is not taken into account when there is no law. Nevertheless, death reigned from the time of Adam to the time of Moses. Even over those who did not sin by breaking a command, as did Adam, who was a pattern of the one to come.

But the gift is not like the trespass. FOR if the many died by the trespass of the one man, how much more did GOD'S grace and the gift that came by the grace of the one man JESUS CHRIST overflow to the many? Again, the gift of GOD is not like the result of the one man's sin: The judgment followed one sin and brought condemnation, but the gift followed many trespasses and brought justification. For if by the trespass of the one man, death reigned through that one man, how much more will those who receive GOD'S abundant provision of grace and of the gift of righteousness reign in life through the one man, JESUS CHRIST?

Consequently, just as the result of one trespass was condemnation for all men, so also the result of one act of righteousness was justification that brings life for all men. For just as through the disobedience of the one man the many were made sinners, so also through the obedience of the one man the many will be made righteous.

The law was added so that the trespass might increase. But where sin increased, grace increased all the more. So that just as sin reigned in death, so also grace might reign through righteousness to bring eternal life through JESUS CHRIST our LORD.

"Dead to Sin. Alive in CHRIST."

What shall we say then? Shall we go on sinning so that the grace may increase? By no means! We died to sin; how can we live in it any longer? Or don't you know that all of us who were baptized into CHRIST JESUS were baptized into his death? WE were therefore buried with him through baptism into death in order that just as CHRIST was raised from the dead through the glory of the Father, we too may live a new life.

If we have been united with him like this in his death, we will certainly also be united with him in his resurrection. For we know that our old self was crucified with him so that the body of sin might be done away with, that we should no longer be slaves to sin—because anyone who has died has been freed from sin. Now if we died with CHRIST, we believe that we will also live with him. For we know that since CHRIST was raised from the dead, he cannot die again: death no longer has mastery over him. The death he died, he died to sin once for all; but the life he lives, he lives to GOD. In the same way, count yourselves dead to sin but alive to GOD in CHRIST JESUS.

Therefore, do not let sin reign in your body so that you obey its evil desires. Do not offer the parts of your body to sin, as instruments of wickedness, but rather offer yourselves to GOD as those who have been brought from death to life; and offer the parts of your body to him as instruments of righteousness. For sin shall not be your master, because you are not under the law, but under grace.

What then? Shall we sin because we are not under law but under grace? By no means! Don't you know that when you offer yourselves to someone to obey him as slaves, you are slaves to the one whom you obey—whether you are slaves to sin, which leads to death, or to obedience, which leads to righteousness? But thanks be to GOD that though you used to be slaves to sin, wholeheartedly obey the form of teaching to which you were entrusted. You have been set free from sin and have become slaves to righteousness.

I put this in human terms because you are weak in your natural selves. Just as you used to offer the parts of your body in slavery to impurity and to ever-increasing wickedness, so now offer them in slavery to righteousness leading to holiness.

When you were slaves to sin, you were free from the control of righteousness. What benefit did you reap at that time from the things you are now ashamed of? Those things result in death. But now that you have set free from sin and have become slaves to GOD, the benefit you reap leads to holiness, and the result is eternal life. For the wages of sin is death, but the gift of GOD is eternal life in CHRIST JESUS our LORD.

A contrast between Adam and CHRIST. Adam introduced sin and death into the world; CHRIST brought righteousness and life. The comparison begun in v. 12 and is completed in v. 18; these two verses summarize the whole passage. These two men also sum up the message of the book up to this point. Adam stands for man's condemnation. In Romans 1:18, "The wrath of GOD is being revealed from heaven against all the godlessness and wickedness of men who suppress the truth by their wickedness." In Romans 3:20, "Therefore, no one will be declared righteous in his sight by observing the law; rather, through the law we become conscious of sin."

CHRIST stands for the believer' s justification. In Romans 3:21–24, "But now a righteousness from GOD, apart from law, has been made known to which the law and the prophets testify. This righteousness from GOD comes through faith in JESUS CHRIST to all who believe. There is no difference for all have sinned and fall short of the glory of GOD, and are justified freely by his grace through the redemption that came by CHRIST JESUS."

Physical death is the penalty for sin. It is also the symbol of spiritual death, man's ultimate separation from GOD. The context shows that Adam's sin involved the rest of mankind in condemnation and death. We do not start life with even the possibility of living it sinlessly; we begin it with sinful nature. In Genesis 8:21, "The LORD smelled the pleasing aroma and said in his heart: 'Never again will I curse the ground because of man. Every inclination of his heart is evil from childhood. And never again will I destroy all living creatures as I have done." Also in Psalm 51:5, "Surely I was sinful at birth sinful from the time my mother conceived me"; and in Psalm 58:3, "Even from birth the wicked go astray; from the womb they are wayward and speak lies." Moreover, in Ephesians 2:3, "All of us also lived among them at one time, gratifying the cravings of our sinful nature and following its desires and thoughts. Like the rest, we were by nature objects of wrath."

Sin is not taken into account. In the period when there was no Mosaic law, sin ("breaking a command") was not charged against man. Death, however, continued to occur. Since death is the penalty for sin, people between Adam and Moses were involved in the sin of someone else—namely, Adam. Adam, by his sin, brought universal ruin on the human race. In this act, he is the prototype of CHRIST, who through one righteous act. (v. 18), brought universal blessing. The analogy is one of contrast.

The *many*, the same as all man in (v.12) Isaiah 53:11: "After the suffering of his soul, he will see the light of life and be satisfied: by his knowledge my righteous servant will justify many, and he will give him their iniquities." In Mark 10:45, "For even the Son of Man did not come to be served, but to serve, and to give his life as a ransom for many."

"How much more?" A theme that runs through this section. GOD'S grace is infinitely greater for good than is Adam' s sin for evil. The gift of GOD, is salvation. Many trespasses. The sin of the succeeding generations. Reign in life. The future reign of believers with JESUS CHRIST. In 2 Timothy 2:12, "If we endure, we will also reign with him. If we disown him, he will also disown us." And in Revelation 22:5, "There will be no more night. They will not need the light of a lamp or the light of the sun for the LORD GOD will give them light. And the will reign for ever and ever."

Life for all men. Does not mean that everyone eventually will be saved, but that salvation is available to all. (v.17)

Law was added. Not to bring about redemption but to point up the need for it. The law made sin even more sinful by revealing what sin is in stark contrast to GOD'S holiness.

Shall we go on sinning so that grace may increase? This question arose out of what Paul had just said in 5:20: "Where sin increased, grace increased all the more." Such a question expresses an antinomian (against law) viewpoint. Apparently, some objected to Paul's teaching of justification by faith alone because they thought it would lead to mortal irresponsibility.

The when and how of the Christian's death to sin. In NT times, baptism so closely followed conversion that the two were considered part of event. In Acts 2:38, "Peter replied, 'Repent and be baptized, every one of you, in the name of JESUS CHRIST for the forgiveness of your sins. And you will receive the gift of the Holy Spirit.'"

So although baptism is not a means by which we enter into a vital faith relationship with JESUS CHRIST, it is closely associated with faith. Baptism depicts graphically what happens as a result of the Christian's union with CHRIST, which comes with faith. Through faith, we are united with CHRIST just as through our natural birth, we are united with Adam. As we fell into sin and became subject to death in father Adam, so we now have died and been raised again with CHRIST, which baptism symbolizes. Buried with him through baptism into death—this is amplified in Romans 6:5–7. Through the glory of the Father. By the power of GOD. GOD'S glory is his divine excellence, his perfection. Any one attribute is a manifestation of his excellence. Thus, the power is a manifestation of his glory, as is his righteousness. In Romans 3:23, "For all have sinned and fall short of the glory of GOD."

Glory and power are often closely related in the BIBLE. In Psalm 145:11, "They will tell of the glory of your kingdom and speak of your might." Also in Colossians 1:11, "Be strengthened with all power according to his glorious might so that you may have great endurance and patience and joyfully give thanks to the Father." Moreover, in 1 Peter 4:11, "If anyone speaks, he should do it as one speaking the very words of God. If anyone serves, he should do it with the strength God provides, so that in all things God may be praised through Jesus Christ, to him be the glory and the power for ever and ever. Amen."

In Revelation 1:6, "And has made us to be a kingdom and priests to serve his GOD and Father—to him be glory and power for ever and ever! Amen." In 4:11, "'You are worthy, our LORD and GOD, to receive glory and honor and power, for you created all things, and by your will they were created and have their being." In 5:11, "Then I looked and heard the voice of many angels. numbering thousands upon thousands, and ten thousand times ten thousand. They encircled the throne and the living creatures and the elders. In a loud voice, they sang: 'Worthy is the Lamb, who was slain, to receive power and wealth and wisdom and strength and honor and glory and praise!'" In 7:11, "All the angels were standing around the throne and around the elders and the four living creatures. They fell down on their faces before the throne and worshiped GOD, saying 'Amen! Praise and glory and wisdom and thanks and honor and power and strength be to our GOD for ever and ever. Amen!' And in 19:1, "After I heard what sounded like the roar of a great multitude in heaven shouting: 'Hallelujah!'" Salvation and glory and power belong to our GOD.

Our old self. Our unregenerate self; what we once were. Body of sin. The self in its pre-Christian state, dominated by sin. This is a figurative expression in which the old self is personified. It is a "body" that can be put to death. For the believer, this old self has been *rendered powerless* so that it can no longer enslave us to sin—whatever lingering vitality it may yet exert in death throes.

Paul begins by surveying the spiritual condition of all mankind. He finds Jews and Gentiles alike to be sinners and in need of salvation. That salvation has been provided by GOD through JESUS CHRIST and his redemptive work on the cross. It is a provision, however, that must be received by faith—a principle by which GOD has always dealt with mankind as the example of Abraham shows. Since salvation is only the beginning of Christian experience, Paul moves on to show how the believer is freed from sin, law, and death—a provision made possible by his union with CHRIST in both death and resurrection and by the indwelling presence and power of the Holy Spirit. Paul then shows that Israel too, though presently in a state of unbelief, has a place in GOD'S sovereign redemptive plan. Now she consists of only a remnant, allowing for the conversion of the Gentiles, but the time will come when "all Israel will be saved." In Romans 11:26–27, "And so all Israel will be saved as it is written: 'The deliverer will come from Zion; he will turn godlessness away from Jacob. And this is my covenant with them when I take away their sins.'"

The letter concludes with an appeal to the readers to work out their Christian faith in practical ways, both in the church and in the world. None of Paul's other letters states so profoundly the content of the Gospel and its implications for both the present and the future.

Has died. The believer' s death with CHRIST to sin's ruling power. Freed from sin. Set free from its shackles and power. As resurrection followed death in the experience of CHRIST, so the believer who dies with CHRIST is raised to a new quality of moral life here and now. Resurrection in the sense of a new birth is already a fact, and it increasingly exerts itself in the believer' s life.

He to sin once and for all. In his death, CHRIST, for the sake of sinners, submitted to the "reign" of sin (5:21); but his death broke the judicial link between sin and death, and he passed forever from the sphere of sin's "reign." Having been raised from the dead, he now lives forever to glorify GOD. To GOD. For the glory of GOD.

Count yourselves. The first step toward victory over sin in the believer's life (6:12–13). He is dead to sin and alive to GOD, and by faith, he is to live in the light of this truth.

In CHRIST. The first occurrence in Romans of this phrase, which is found often in Paul's writings. True believers are "in CHRIST" because they have died with CHRIST and have been raised to new life with him.

A call for the Christian to become in experience what he already is in position—dead to the sin (6:5–7) and alive to GOD (6:8–10). The second step toward the Christian's victory over sin is refusal to let sin reign in his life (6:12). The third step is to offer himself to GOD (6:13). Put yourselves in the service of, perhaps also echoing the language of sacrifice, parts of your body. All the separate capacities of your being (6:19).

Sin shall not be your master. Paul conceived of sin as a power that enslaves, and so does authority. He has, however, been freed from the law in the manner in which GOD'S people were under law in the OT era. Law provides enablement to resist the power of sin; it only condemns the sinner. But grace enables. Under grace. For the disciplinary aspect of grace. In Titus 2:11–12, "For the grace of GOD that brings salvation has appeared to all men. It teaches us to say 'No' to ungodliness and worldly passion, and to live self-controlled upright and godly lives in this present age."

The question raised here seems to come from those who are afraid that the doctrine of justification by faith alone will remove all moral restraint. Paul rejects such a suggestion and shows that a Christian does not throw morality to the winds. To the contrary, he exchanges sin for righteousness as his master. The contrast between sin and obedience suggests that sin is, by nature, disobedience to GOD.

Wholeheartedly obeyed. Christian obedience is not forced or legalistic but a willing form of teaching. May refer to a summary of the moral and ethical teaching of CHRIST that was given to new converts in the early church.

Slaves to righteousness. A Christian has changed masters. Whereas he was formerly a slave to sin, he becomes a slave (a willing servant) to righteousness.

Set free from sin (6:6). Holiness. Slavery to GOD produces holiness, and the end of the process is eternal life. Viewed not in its present sense but in its final, future sense.

There is no eternal life without holiness. In Hebrews 12:14, "Make every effort to live in peace with all men and to be holy: without holiness no one will see the LORD." Anyone who has been justified will surely give evidence of that fact by the presence of holiness in his life. For other occurrences of the word *holiness*:

- Romans 6:19. "I put this in human terms because you are weak in your natural selves. Just as you used to offer the parts of your body in slavery to impurity and to ever-increasing wickedness, so now offer them in slavery to righteousness leading to holiness."
- 1 Thessalonians 4:3. "It is GOD'S will that you should be sanctified: that you should avoid sexual immorality."

- 2 Thessalonians 2:13. "But we ought always to thank GOD for you brothers loved by the LORD because from the beginning, GOD chose you to be saved through the sanctifying work of the Spirit and through belief in the truth."
- 1 Peter 1:2. "Who have been chosen according to the foreknowledge of GOD the Father, through the sanctifying work of the Spirit, for obedience to JESUS CHRIST and sprinkling by his blood: Grace and peace be yours in abundance."

In Romans 6:23, two kinds of servitude are contrasted here. One brings death as its wages; the other results in eternal life not as wages earned or merited but as a gift of GOD. For the contrast between wages and gift, in Romans 4:4, "Now when a man works, his wages are not credited to him as a gift, but as an obligation."

Now Satan is frustrated because he knows that his days are numbered on earth, and Satan knows there will be no redemption for him and his angels. JESUS did not die for the falling angels but for the descendants of Adam; but not for Adam and Eve because we were condemned to death by the sin of one man, and GOD saved us from death by the sacrifice of one man, the Son of GOD who became flesh and took the stripes on his naked body instead of us for our sins.

Now Eve, how could you do that decision without discussing it with Adam? You are the helper, and you should not have even touched that fruit. I am furious with you; you killed me and interrupted GOD'S plan. We were supposed to live forever in paradise without any sickness and getting bold and old.

GOD'S plan is going to take place as GOD planted from the beginning and always GOD will do whatever GOD promises at all time, and there is no place for Satan among GOD'S children when JESUS comes back again to establish his kingdom on earth forever and ever. That is the promise of GOD, the loving GOD, who loves us all, but we have to obey his commandments and serve him and praise him—unlike some of his angels and their leader, Lucifer, the proud, the ambusher, the dreamer, and above all, the stupid one.

So Adam and Eve are the deceived ones, who, by their uncalculated action, were sentenced to death! I wish instead of Adam, GOD sent Job! Here is the story of Job:

> JOB 1:1—In the land of UZ there lived a man whose name was JOB. This man was blameless and upright; he feared GOD and shunned evil. He had seven sons and three daughters, and he owned seven thousand sheep, three thousand camels, five hundred yoke of oxen and five hundred donkeys, and had a large number of servants. He was the greatest man among all the people of the east.
>
> His sons used to take turns holding feasts in their homes, and they would invite their three sisters to eat and drink with them. When a period of feasting had run its course, JOB would send and have them purified. Early in the morning he would sacrifice a burnt offering for each of them, thinking, "Perhaps my children have sinned and cursed GOD in their hearts."
>
> This was JOB'S regular custom. One day the angels came to present themselves before the LORD, and Satan also came with them. The LORD said to Satan, "Where have you come from?"
>
> Satan answered the LORD, "From roaming through the earth and going back and forth in it."
>
> Then the LORD said to Satan, "Have you considered my servant JOB? There is no one on earth like him; he is blameless and upright, a man who fears GOD and shuns evil."
>
> "Does JOB fear GOD for nothing?" Satan replied. "Have you not put a hedge around him and his household and everything he has? You have blessed the work of his hands, so that his

flocks and herds are spread throughout the land. But stretch out your hand and strike everything he has, and he will surely curse you to your face."

The LORD said to Satan, "Very well then, everything he has is in your hands, but on the man himself do not lay a finger." Then Satan went out from the presence of the LORD.

One day when JOB'S sons and daughters were feasting and drinking wine at the oldest brother's house, a messenger came to JOB and said, "The oxen were grazing nearby and the Sabeans attacked and carried them off. They put the servants to the sword, and I am the only one who has escaped to tell you!"

While he was still speaking, another messenger came and said, "The fire of GOD fell from the sky and burned up the sheep and the servants, and I am the only one who has escaped to tell you!"

While he was still speaking, another messenger came and said, "The Chaldeans formed three raiding parties and swept down on your camels and carried them off. They put the servants to the sword, and I am the only one who has escaped to tell you!"

While he was still speaking, yet another messenger came and said, "Your sons and daughters were feasting and drinking wine at the oldest brother's house, when suddenly a mighty wind swept in from the desert and struck the four corners of the house. It collapsed on them, and they are dead. And I am the only one who has escaped to tell you!"

At this JOB got up and tore his robe and shaved his head. Then he fell to the ground in worship and said: "Naked I came from my mother's womb, and naked I will depart. The LORD gave and the LORD has taken away: may the name of the LORD be praised."

In all this, JOB did not sin by charging GOD with wrongdoing.

On another day the angels came to present themselves before the LORD, and Satan also came with them to present himself before him. And the LORD said to Satan, "Where have you come from?"

Satan answered the LORD, "From roaming through the earth and going back and forth in it."

Then the LORD said to Satan, "Have you considered my servant JOB? There is no one on earth like him. He is blameless and an upright man who fears GOD and shuns evil. And he still maintains his integrity, though you incited me against him to ruin without any reason."

"Skin for skin!" Satan replied. "A man will give all he has for his own life. But stretch out your hand and strike his flesh and bones, and he will surely curse you to your face."

The LORD said to Satan, "Very well, then. He is in your hands: but you must spare his life."

So Satan went out from the presence of the LORD and afflicted JOB with painful sores from the soles of his feet to the top of his head. Then JOB took a piece of broken pottery and scraped himself with it as he sat among the ashes. His wife said to him, "Are you still holding on to your integrity? Curse GOD and die!"

He replied, "You are talking like a foolish woman. Shall we accept good from GOD, and not trouble?" In all this, JOB did not sin in what he said.

When JOB'S three friends, Eliphaz the TEMANITE, Bilad the SHUHITE, and Zophar the NAAMATHITE, heard about all the troubles that had come upon him, they set out from their homes and met together by agreement to go and sympathize with him and comfort him. When they saw him from a distance, they hardly recognize him: they began to weep aloud, and they tore their robes and sprinkled dust on their heads. Then they sat on the ground with him for seven days and seven nights. No one said a word to him, because they saw how great his suffering was.

The LORD said to JOB [40:2], "Will the one who contends with the Almighty correct him? Let him who accuses GOD answer him!"

Then JOB answered the LORD: "I am unworthy—how can I reply to you? I put my hand over my mouth. I spoke once, but I have no answer twice, but I will say no more."

Then the LORD spoke to JOB out of the storm: "Brace yourself like a man: I will question you, and you shall answer me. Would you discredit my justice? Would you condemn me to justify yourself? Do you have an arm like GOD'S and can your voice thunder like his? Then adorn yourself with glory and splendor and clothe yourself in honor and majesty. Unleash the fury of your wrath, look at every proud man and bring him low, look at every proud man and humble him. Crush the wicked where they stand. Bury them all in the dust together: shroud their faces in the grave. Then I myself will admit to you that your own right can save you. Look at the behemoth, which I made along with you and which feeds on grass like an ox."

42:7—After the LORD had said these things to JOB, he said to Eliphaz the TEMANITE, "I am angry with you and your two friends, because you have not spoken of me what is right, as my servant JOB has. So now take seven bulls and seven rams and go to my servant JOB and sacrifice a burnt offering for yourselves. My servant JOB will pray for you, and I will accept his prayer and not deal with you according to your folly. You have not spoken of me."

Eliphaz the TEMANITE, Bildad the SHUHITE, and Zophar the NAAMATHITE did what the LORD told them; and the LORD accepted JOB'S prayer.

After JOB had prayed for his friends, the LORD made him prosperous again and gave twice as much as he had before. All his brothers and sisters and everyone who had known him before came and ate with him in his house. They comforted and consoled him over all the trouble the LORD had brought upon him, and each one gave him a piece of silver and a gold ring.

The LORD blessed the latter part of JOB'S life more than the first. He had fourteen thousand sheep, six thousand camel, a thousand yoke of oxen and a thousand donkeys. And he also had seven sons and three daughters. The first daughter he named Jemimah, the second Keziah and the third Keren-Happuch. Nowhere in all the land were there found woman as beautiful as JOB'S daughters, and their father granted them an inheritance along with their brothers.

After this, JOB Lived a hundred and forty years; he saw his children and their children to the fourth generation. And so he died, old and full of years.

Land of UZ. A large territory east of the Jorden, which included Edom in the south and the Aramean lands in the north.

Blameless and upright. Spiritually and morally upright. This does not mean that Job was sinless. He later defends his moral integrity but also admits he is a sinner. In Job 7:21, "'Why do you not pardon my offenses and forgive my sins? For I will soon lie down in the dust; you will search for me, but I will be no more.'"

Seven sons. An ideal number, signifying completeness. In Ruth 4:15, "He will renew your life and sustain you in your old age. For your daughter-in-law, who loves you and who is better to you than seven sons, has given him birth.'"

Seven thousand sheep. Job's enormous wealth was in livestock, not in land. In Genesis 12:16, "He treated Abram well for her sake, and Abram acquired sheep and cattle, male and female donkeys, menservants and maidservants, and camels." And in Genesis 13:2, "Abram had become very wealthy in livestock and in silver and gold." He had so many flocks and herds and servants that the Philistines envied him (26:14). All that wealth Abram was treated with was from the pharaoh of Egypt because of his wife, Sarai. The best way to know the complete story is to read and study the BIBLE, and hopefully you will make it a habit; and that will be the best thing you will do to know the Word of GOD and apply it to your lifestyle. Then you will thank me. May the LORD be with you and touch your heart.

Donkeys. The Hebrew for this word is feminine in form. Donkeys that produced offspring were very valuable.

He would sacrifice. Before the ceremonial laws of Moses were introduced, the father of the household acted as the priest. In Genesis 15:9–10, "So the LORD said to him, 'Bring me a heifer, a goat and a ram, each three years old, along with a dove and a young pigeon.' Abram brought all these to him, cut them in two and arranged the halves opposite each other; the birds, however, he did not cut in half."

Purified. Made ceremonially clean in preparation for the sacrifices he offered for them, where the Hebrew for this verb is translated "consecrate." In Exodus 19:10–14, "And the LORD said to Moses, 'Go to the people and consecrate them today and tomorrow. Have them wash their clothes and be ready by the third day, because on that day the LORD will come down on Mount Sinai in the sight of all the people.'" And in Exodus 19:12, "'Put limits for the people around the mountain and tell them, be careful that you do not go up the mountain or touch the foot of it. Whoever touches the mountain shall surely be put to death. He shall surely be stone or shot with arrow; not a hand is to be laid on him. Whether man or animal, he shall not be permitted to live. Only when the ram's horn sounds a long blast may they go up to the mountain.' After Moses had gone down the mountain to the people, he consecrated them, and they washed their clothes."

Angels came to present themselves. They came as members of the heavenly council who stand in the presence of GOD. In Psalm 89:5–7,

> The heavens praise your wonders.
> O LORD your faithfulness too, in the assembly of the holy ones.
> For who in the skies above can compare with the LORD?
> Who is like the LORD among the heavenly beings?
> In the council of the holy ones GOD is greatly feared;
> He is more awesome than all who surround him.

In Jeremiah 23:18, "'But which of them has stood in the council of the LORD to see or to hear his word? Who has listened and heard his word? But if they had stood in my council, they would have proclaimed my words to my people and would have turned them from their evil ways and from their evil deeds. Am I only a GOD nearby who declares the Lord and not a GOD far away?'"

In Revelation 12:10, "Then I heard a loud voice in heaven say: 'Now have come the salvation and the power and the kingdom of our GOD, and the authority of his CHRIST. For the accuser of our brothers, who accuses them before our GOD day and night, has been hurled down.'"

The relationship between GOD and man is not exclusive and closed. A third party intrudes, the great adversary incapable of contending with GOD hand to hand. Power pitted against power, he is bent on frustrating GOD' enterprise embodied in the creation and centered on the GOD-man relationship. As a tempter, he seeks to alienate man from GOD as accuser (one of the names by which is called *Satan* means "accuser"). He seeks to alienate GOD from man to effect an alienation that cannot be reconciled.

In the story of Job, the author portrays the adversary in his boldest and most radical assault on GOD and the glory man in the special and intimate relationship that is dearest to them both. When GOD called up the name of Job before the accuser and testified to the righteousness of this one on the earth—this man in whom GOD delights—Satan attempted with one crafty thrust both to assail GOD'S beloved and to show up GOD as a fool. True to one of his modes of operation, he accused Job before GOD. He charged that Job's godliness is evil. The very godliness in which GOD takes delight is void of all integrity; it is the worst of all sins. Job's godliness is self-serving; he is righteous only because righteousness and blessing will expose the righteous man for the sinner is.

It is the adversary's ultimate challenge. For if the godliness of the righteous man in whom GOD delights can be shown to be the worst of all sins, then a chasm of alienation stands between them that cannot be bridged. Then even redemption is unthinkable, for the godliest of men will be shown to be the most ungodly. GOD'S whole enterprise in creation and redemption will be shown to be radically flawed, and GOD can only sweep it all away in awful judgment.

The accusation, once raised, cannot be removed, not even by destroying the accuser. So GOD let the adversary have his way with Job (within specific limits) so that GOD and the righteous Job may be vindicated and the great accuser silenced. Thus comes the anguish of Job, robbed of everything of God's favor so that GOD becomes for him the great enigma. Also his righteousness was assailed on earth through the logic of the "orthodox" theology of his friends. Alone he agonized. But he knew in his heart that his godliness has been authentic and that someday he will be vindicated. And in spite of all, though he may curse the day of his birth and child and GOD for treating him unjustly—the uncalculated outcry of a distraught spirit—he will not curse GOD as his wife, the human nearest his heart, proposes; in fact, what pained him most was GOD'S apparent alienation from him.

In the end, the adversary was silenced. And the astute theologians, Job's friends, were silenced. And Job was silenced. But GOD was not. And when he speaks, he brings the silence of regret for hasty speech in days of suffering and the silence of repose in the ways of the Almighty. Furthermore, as his heavenly friend, GOD heard Job's intercessions for his associates, and he restored Job's beatitude.

In summary, the author's pastoral word to the godly sufferer is that his righteousness has such supreme value that GOD treasures it more than all. And the great adversary knows that if he is to thwart the purposes of GOD, he must assail the righteous man. At stake in the suffering of the truly godly is the outcome of the struggle in heaven between the adversary and GOD with all-encompassing divine purpose in the balance. Thus, the suffering of the righteous has meaning and value, commensurate with the titanic spiritual struggle of the ages.

Have you considered my servant Job? The LORD, not Satan, initiated the dialogue that led to the testing of Job. He held up Job as one against whom "the accuser" can lodge no accusation, a designation for one who stands in a special relationship with GOD and is loyal in service. In Isaiah 42:1, "'Here is my servant, whom I uphold, my chosen one in whom I delight: I will put my Spirit on him and he will bring justice to the nations.'" In 52:13, "'See, my servant will act wisely: he will be raised and lifted up and highly exalted.'" And in 53:11, "'After the suffering of his soul, he will see the light of life and be satisfied: by his knowledge my righteous servant will justify many, and he will bear their iniquities.'"

The accuser boldly accused the man GOD commends. He said Job's righteousness, in which GOD delights, was self-serving—the heart of Satan's attack on GOD and his faithful servant in the book of Job.

Stretch out your hand and strike. Satan, the accuser, is given power to afflict, but is kept on a leash. In all his evil among men or in nature, Satan is under GOD'S power. The contest, however, is not a sham. Will Job curse GOD to his face? If Job does not, the accuser will be proven false and GOD'S delight in Job vindicated.

Sabeans. Probably south Arabians from Sheba whose descendants became wealthy traders in spices, gold, and precious stone. Calls the Sabeans "traveling merchants" and associates them with Tema (about 350 miles southeast of Jerusalem). In Psalm 72:10–15,

> The King of Tarshish and of distant shores will bring tribute to him; the King of Sheba and SEBA will present him gifts.
>
> All Kings will bow down to him and all nations will serve him.
>
> For he will deliver the needy who cry out the afflicted who have no one to help.
>
> He will take pity on the weak and the needy and save the needy from death.
>
> He will rescue them from oppression and violence, for precious is their blood in his sight…
>
> Long may he live! May gold from Sheba be given him. May people ever pray for him and bless him all day long.

In Isaiah 60:6, "Herds of camels will cover your land, young camels of Midian and Ephah. And all from Sheba will come bearing gold and incense and proclaiming the praise of the LORD." In Jeremiah 6:20, "'What do I care about incense from Sheba or sweet calamus from a distant land? Your burnt offerings are not acceptable; your sacrifices do not please me." In Ezekiel 27:22, "The merchants of Sheba and RAAMAH traded with you; for your merchandise they exchange the finest of all kinds of spices and precious stones and gold." And in Job 6:19, "The caravans of Tema look for water, the traveling merchants of Sheba look for hope."

Fire of God (Job 1:16). In Numbers 11:1, "Now the people complained about their hardships in the hearing of the LORD, and when he heard them his anger was aroused. Then fire from the LORD burned among them and consumed some of the outskirts of the camp." In 1 Kings 18:38, "Then the fire of the LORD fell and burned up the sacrifice, the wood, the stones and the soil, and also licked up the water in the trench." And in 2 Kings 1:12, "'If I am a man of GOD,' Elijah replied, 'may fire come down from heaven and consume you and your fifty men!' Then the fire of GOD fell from heaven and consumed him and his fifty men."

Chaldeans. A people who were Bedouin until c 1000 BC when they settled in southern Mesopotamia and later became the nucleus of Nebuchadnezzar's empire.

At this, Job got up. He is silent until his children are killed, tore his robe and shaved his head in mourning. In Genesis 37:34, "Then Jacob tore his clothes, put on a sackcloth, and mourned for his son many days." In Isaiah 15:2, "Dibon goes up to its temple, to its high places to weep: Moab wails over Nebo and Medeba. Every head is shaved and every beard cut off.

The Lord gave and the Lord has taken away. Job's faith led him to see the sovereign GOD'S hand at work, and that gave him repose even in the face of calamity. Except for the final sentence, this passage is almost identical to 1:6–8. He who accused JOB of having a deceitful motive is now shown to have a deceitful motive himself: to discredit the LORD through Job.

Strike his flesh and bones (1:11). In Genesis 2:23, "The man said. 'This is now bone of my bones and flesh of my flesh: she shall be called woman for she was taken out of man.'" In Luke 24:39, "'Look at my hands and my feet. It is myself! Touch me and see; a ghost does not have nesh and bones as you see I have.'"

Spare his life. Satan is still limited by GOD. Should Job die, neither GOD nor Job could be vindicated. The precise nature of Job's sickness is uncertain, but its symptoms were painful festering sores over the whole body, nightmare scabs that peeled and became black disfigurement and revolting appearance, bad breath, excessive thinness, and pain day and night.

Sores. The Hebrew for this word is translated to "boils." In Exodus 9:9, "'It will become fine dust over the whole land of Egypt, and festering boils will break out on men and animals throughout the land.'" In Leviticus 13:18, "When someone has a boil on his skin and it heals." In 2 Kings 20:7, "Then Isaiah said, 'Prepare a poultice of figs.' They did so and applied it to boil and he recovered."

Ashes. Symbolic of mourning (42:6). In Esther 4:3, "In every province to which the edict and order of the King came, there was great mourning among the Jews, with fasting, weeping and wailing. Many lay in sackcloth and ashes." Which speaks of sitting in dust.

Curse God. The Hebrew for this expression here and in Job 1:5 employs a euphemism (lit. "Bless GOD"). Satan was using Job's wife to tempt Job as he used Eve to tempt Adam and die. Since nothing but death was left for JOB, his wife wanted him to provoke GOD to administer the final strike due to all who curse him. In Leviticus 24:10–16,

> Now the son of an Israelite mother and an Egyptian father went out among the Israelites, and a fight broke out in the camp between him and an Israelite. The son of the Israelite woman blasphemed the Name with a curse; so they brought him to MOSES. His mother's name was SHELOMITH, the daughter of DIBRI the Danite. They put him in custody until the will of the LORD should be made clear to them.
>
> Then the LORD said to MOSES: "Take the blasphemer outside the camp. All those who heard him are to lay their hands on his head, and the entire assembly is to stone him. Say to the Israelites: If anyone curses his GOD, he will be held responsible: anyone who blasphemes the name of the LORD he must be put to death. The entire assembly must stone him. Whether an alien or native-born, when he blasphemes the name, he must be put to death."

"Shall we accept good from God, and not trouble?" A key theme of the book: Trouble and suffering are not merely punishment for sin; for GOD' people may serve as a trial or as a discipline that culminates in spiritual gain. In Job 5:17, "Blessed is the name whom GOD corrects; so do not despise the discipline of the Almighty." In Deuteronomy 8:5, "Know then in your heart that as a man disciplines his son, so the LORD your GOD disciplines you." In 2 Samuel 7:14, "'I will be his father, and he will be my son. When he does Wrong I

will punish him with the rod of men.'" In Psalm 94:12, "Blessed is the man you discipline. O LORD: the man teach from your law." In 1 Peter 3:11–12, "'He must turn from evil and do good: he must seek peace and pursue it. For the eyes of the LORD are on the righteous and his ears are attentive to their prayer, but the face of the LORD is against those who do evil.'" In 1 Corinthians 11:32, "When we are judged by the LORD, we are being disciplined so that we will not be condemned with the world." In Hebrews 12:5–11,

> And you have forgotten that word of encouragement that addresses you as sons: "My son, do not make light of the LORD'S discipline. And do not <u>lose he</u>art when he rebukes you, because the LORD disciplines those he loves, and he punishes everyone he accepts as a son."
>
> Endure hardship as discipline: GOD is treating you as sons. For what son is not disciplined by his father? If you are not disciplined [and everyone undergoes discipline], then you are illegitimate children and not true sons. Moreover, we have all had human fathers who disciplined us and we respected for it. How much more should we submit to the father of our Spirits and live! Our fathers disciplined us for a little while as they thought best; but GOD disciplines us for our good, that we may share in his holiness. No discipline seems pleasant at the time, but painful. Later on however, it produces a harvest of righteousness and peace for those who have been trained by it.

The three friends of Job—Eliphaz, Bildad, and Zophar—could hardly recognize him, tore their robes, and sprinkled dust on their heads. Visible signs of mourning.

Sat on the ground with him. A commendable expression of sympathy. Their mere presence was of more comfort to him than their words of advice would prove to be (see Job 16:2–3).

Job 40:4, *unworthy*. The Hebrew for this word can also mean "small" or "insignificant."

Once...twice. See note on Job 5:19. "From six calamities he will rescue you; in seven no harm will befall you."

In the prologue to the second divine discourse, which ends at 41:34, unlike the first discourse, GOD here addresses the issues of his own justice and Job's futile attempt at self-justification. In chs. 21 and 24, Job complained about GOD'S indifference toward the wickedness of evil men. Here the LORD asserted his ability and determination to administer justice—a matter over which Job had no control. Therefore, by implication, Job was admonished to leave all this including his own vindication under the power of GOD' S strong arm.

Clothe yourself in honor and majesty. The Hebrew underlying this clause describes GOD in Psalm 104:1: "Praise the LORD, O my soul. O LORD my GOD, you are very great; you are clothed with splendor and majesty." The LORD here challenged Job to take on the appearance of deity, if he can. In Isaiah 13:11, "'I will punish the world for its evil the wicked for their sins. I will put an end to the arrogance of the haughty, and will humble the pride of the ruthless,'" the LORD describes himself as doing these things.

Despite Job's mistakes in word and attitude while he suffered, he is now commended and the counselors are rebuked. Why? Because even in his age, even when he challenged GOD, he was determined to speak honestly before him. The counselors, on the other hand, mouthed many correct and often beautiful statements, but without living knowledge of the GOD they claimed to honor. Job spoke to GOD; they only spoke about GOD. Even worse, their spiritual arrogance caused them to claim knowledge they did not possess. They presumed to know why Job was suffering.

My servant Job. The phrase is used four times in these two verses (see note 1:8).

Job's prayer for those who had abused him is a touching OT illustration of the high Christian virtue our LORD taught in Matthew 5:44: "'But I tell you: Love your enemies and pray for those who persecute you.'" Job's prayer marked the turning point back to prosperity for him. It made him prosperous again. The Hebrew for this expression is translated "restores the fortunes of" in Psalm 14:7: "Oh, that salvation for Israel would come out of Zion! When the LORD restores the fortunes of his people. Let Jacob rejoice and Israel be glad!"

Contrast 16:2 and 19:13: "I have heard many things like these: miserable comforters are you all!" and "He has alienated my brothers from my acquaintances are completely estranged from me."

Piece of silver. The Hebrew for this phrase is found elsewhere in the OT, only in Genesis 33:19: "For a hundred pieces of silver, he bought from the sons of Hamore the father of Chechem, the plot of ground where he pitched his tent."

In Job 42:12–16, "The cosmic contest with the accuser is now over, and Job is restored. No longer is there a reason for Job to experience suffering—unless he was sinful and deserved it which is not the case. GOD does not allow us to suffer for no reason, and even though the reason may be hidden in the mystery of his divine purpose—never for us to know in this life. We must trust in him as the GOD who does only what is right."

In Isaiah 55:8–9, "'For my thoughts are not your thoughts, neither are your ways my ways.' declares the LORD. 'As the heavens are higher than the earth, so are my ways higher than your ways and my thoughts than your thoughts.'"

The number of animals in each case twice as many (42:10). After Job had prayed for his friends, the LORD made him prosperous again and gave him twice as much as he had before.

Seven sons and three daughters. To replace the children he had lost earlier (see Job 1:2, 18–19).

In Job 42:14, *Jemimah* means "dove." *Keziah* means "cinnamon." *Keren-Happuch* means "container of antimony," a highly prized eyeshadow (see note on Jeremiah 4:30: "What are you doing, O devastated one? Why dress yourself in scarlet and put on jewels of gold? Why shade your eyes with paint? You adorn yourself in vain. Your lovers despise you; they seek your life.")

Granted them an inheritance along with their brothers. Contrast Numbers 27:8: "'Say to the Israelites, If a man dies and leaves no son, turn his inheritance over to his daughter.'"

Lived a hundred and forty years. The longevity of a true patriarch (see note on Exodus 6:16: "These were the names of the sons of Levi according to their records: Gershon, Kohath and Merari. Levi lived 137 years.")

He saw to the fourth generation. See Genesis 50:23: "And saw the third generation of Ephraim's children. Also the children of Makir son of Manasseh were placed at birth on Joseph's knees."

Old and full of years. See Job 5:26: "You will come to the grave in full vigor, like sheaves gathered in season." In Genesis 25:8, "Then Abraham breathed his last and died at a good old age, an old man and full of years; and he was gathered to his people."

After we read the story of Jonah, a part Genesis, and a part of Job, let me expand on those three stories and walk you through them, plus other notes from the BIBLE.

Jonah was angry against the Ninevites because of their hatred to his people and the way they persecuted them; he tried to escape GOD'S divine order by taking a ship to the opposite direction because he knew that GOD is a loving, gracious, and compassionate GOD, and GOD will forgive the Ninevites when they repent and come to him. But Jonah could not forgive them for their hateful hearts toward his people, the Israelites.

Jonah is a prophet and has a loving heart, and in this story, GOD is showing him what love is! And the Ninevites are his children as well, and he loves them as he loves all his creations. Man cannot comprehend the love of GOD; otherwise, the Ninevites and Jonah would not come to that hatred they have toward one another. And when man acknowledges the love of GOD, he will be pleased with us, and we will not get ourselves in the mess we are in throughout the history of man.

Jonah, by taking the ship going the opposite direction, thought he could escape God's plan. My beloved Jonah, Satan could not change GOD'S plan, even when he was successful in deceiving the first man. And GOD'S plan will always succeed regardless of any interruption.

Our GOD created a storm to stop the ship from proceeding its direction. As you read the story of Jonah, he was thrown overboard, and GOD provided the big fish to swallow Jonah and vomit him on a dry land after three days and three nights!

Here I'd like to point out the turning point for me: when I mentioned Jonah's story to my then preacher that since my childhood my mother always quoted the word of GOD to me because of her faith in GOD and her love for him and repeated the story of Jonah to let me know the power of GOD and his ability and his love for us. But my preacher did not give any credit to GOD, how he saved Jonah, but his explanation to me on how Jonah survived the three days and the three nights in the belly of the big fish is because its big belly contained volumes of air! Here, I started to be his preacher instead of his study! The evidence was staggering. Any time I bring GOD to what he did in life and others and especially in my life, he used to divert that possibility and explained to me by verses from the BIBLE; he was using GOD'S name in vain, and that is a blasphemy.

I stopped going to their kingdom hall and read the BIBLE and studied it on my own and watched the true Christian channels like Daystar with Marcus and Joni, Hillsong Channel, TBN with Matt and Laurie, and other true Christian channels; their teaching of the BIBLE was relating to what GOD has done in my life, not like those false teachers when JESUS warned us about them toward the end of age.

Then GOD said to Jonah go to the great city of Nineveh and proclaim it; now Jonah obeyed GOD, and he did what GOD said to him from the beginning. GOD'S plan was accomplished, and the Ninevites redeemed themselves and put a sackcloth on their heads a symbol of humility.

When GOD said to Jonah to go to Nineveh the second time, he obeyed GOD; and when GOD redirected me to leave the Jehovah's Witnesses' false teaching, Jehovah knew I was able to discern between false and true teaching and said to me, "Assaf, you are the true witness to Jehovah, that I am Jehovah. Because you knew GOD'S favor in your life and the life of others, and now you are testifying to GOD not only by speaking to others but testifying to the whole world by writing all your life story and what GOD has done in your life. And GOD is pleased with you, and GOD will be also pleased when his other children testify to his existence and power and love. GOD'S unmerited love."

I knew he was a false preacher because every time I told him about what GOD has done in my life, he'd tell me that was not GOD! GOD does not speak to his people anymore; that was during Moses's time when he used to speak to the prophets, but not anymore because GOD already gave Moses the Ten Commandments and he does not have to remind us of what he already commanded.

On another occasion, I said to my false preacher that GOD cured my ulcer when I cried my heart to him from the severe pain I had. GOD cured me in that moment! That false teacher's response was that GOD does not talk to an individual; that was probably some Satanic force. But I said to him I did not pray for Satan to cure me; I prayed for GOD to cure me, and he did! My heart and my intention is to GOD. The pattern here with the Jehovah's Witnesses is any time I bring GOD to what he has done in my life, they take GOD out of the picture.

One time in his house and in front of his wife, I told him that my loyalty is to Jehovah, not to any man when it comes to GOD, and I came to him as a child in the Word of GOD. And after one year and six months, I discovered that my false preacher and his group take advantage of people who are children in the Word of GOD; and manipulate them because they don't know their right hand from the left hand, like when GOD said to Jonah in 4:11, "But Nineveh has more than a hundred and twenty thousand people who cannot tell their right hand from their left, and many cattle as well. Should I not be concerned about that great city?"

So, I, Assaf Sawaya, declare that after I experienced the teaching of the Jehovah's Witnesses for one year and six months, I saw myself that I am the true witness to Jehovah, and I will face my former false preacher and teacher and/or all of them to a public debate by myself. Only the Holy Spirit will be with me, and that will make us the majority. GOD loves Job because Job testified to GOD at all times, and GOD said about Job in Job 1:8, "Then the LORD said to Satan, 'Have you considered my servant Job? There is no one on earth like him: he is blameless and upright a man who fears GOD and shuns evil.'"

GOD, our creator, is telling us that Job testified about him, unlike some brood of people who don't testify to GOD, but use GOD'S name in *vain*. One perfect example is the ones who call themselves Jehovah's Witnesses.

GOD said to Satan there was no one on earth like Job, and Job was born a sinner. He gives hope to all of us; wouldn't you, my brothers and sisters, like for GOD to say that about you? Unlike Adam and Eve when GOD gave them all things—dominion, authority, and forever-lasting life in paradise and no sickness or disease—but only one thing GOD asked of them: not to eat from the tree of life.

They disobeyed GOD, and we were condemned to death because of their actions; they blame Satan, and Satan gained their authority, and he is ruling the earth for a short time. But GOD is showing us and Satan when GOD defeated Satan in the story of Job. Satan knows that his days are short on earth, so are our days, unless we repent for our sins and be like Job—knowing, fearing, and obeying GOD. We have that option of redemption, unlike Satan, because our loving GOD, for his children, sent his Son to die for us, but not for Satan and his following angels. So when we believe in JESUS that he died for our sins and obey his Word, our lives will be restored, and we'll live forever unlike Adam and Eve. And GOD'S plan will be restored as he intended when GOD created Adam and Eve, and we'll live forever.

In Job 42:7–10,

> After the LORD had said these things to JOB, He said to Eliphaz the TEMANITE, "I am angry with you and your two friends because you have not spoken of me what is right as my servant JOB has. So now take seven bulls and seven rams and go to my servant JOB and sacrifice a burnt offering for yourselves. My servant JOB will pray for you, and I will accept his prayer and not deal with you according to your folly. You have not spoken of me what is right, as my servant JOB has."

So Eliphaz the TEMANITE, Bildad the SHUHITE and Zophar the NAAMATHITE did what the LORD told them: and the LORD accepted JOB'S prayer.

After JOB had prayed for his friends, the LORD made him prosperous again and gave him twice as much as he had before.

JOB 32:1–22—So these three men stopped answering JOB. But Elihu son of Barakel the BUZITE, of the family of Ram, became very angry with JOB for justifying himself rather than GOD. He was also angry with the three friends because they had found no way to refute JOB, and yet had condemned him. Now Elihu had waited before speaking to JOB because they were older than he. But when he saw that the three men had nothing more to say, his anger was aroused. So Elihu son of Barakel the BUZITE said: "I am young in years, and you are old; that is why I was fearful, not daring to tell you what I know. I thought age should speak; advanced years should teach wisdom. But it is the spirit in a man, the breath of the Almighty, that gives him understanding. It is not only the old who are wise, not only the age who understand what is right. Therefore, I say to you: Listen to me: I too will tell you what I know.

"I waited while you spoke. I listened to your reasoning: while you were searching for words, I gave you my full attention. But not one of you has proved JOB wrong: none of you has answered his arguments. Do not say 'We have found wisdom': let GOD refute him, not man. But JOB has not marshaled his words against me, and I will not answer him with your arguments.

"They are dismayed and have no more to say: words have failed them. Must I wait, now that they are silent? Now that they stand there with no reply? I too will have my say: I too will tell what I know. For I am full of words, and the spirit within me compels me: inside I am like bottled-up wine, like new wineskins ready to burst. I must speak and find relief: I must open my lips and reply. I will show partiality to no one, nor will I flatter any man: for I were skilled in flattery, my Maker would soon take me away."

In Job 32:1, A fourth counselor named Elihu, younger than the other three (32:4, 6–7, 9), has been standing on the sidelines, deference to age, and listening to the dialogue or dispute. But now he declared himself ready to show that both Job and the three other counselors were in the wrong. Elihu's four poetic speeches (32:5–33:33; ch.34; ch. 35; ch. 36–37) are preceded by a prose introduction written by the author of the book.

JOB 35:1–16—Then Elihu said: "Do you think this is just? You say, 'I will be cleared by GOD.' Yet you ask him, 'What profit is it to me?' and 'What do I gain by not sinning?' I would like to reply to you and to your friends with you.

"Look up at the heaven and see; gaze at the clouds so high above you. If you sin, how does that affect him? If you are righteous, what do you give to him, or what does he receive from your hand? Your wickedness affects only a man like yourself, and your righteousness only the sons of men.

"Men cry out under a load of oppression; they plead for relief from the arm of the powerful. But no one says, 'Where is GOD my Maker, who give in the night, who teaches more to us than to the beasts of the earth and makes us wiser than the birds of the air?' He does not answer when men cry out because of the arrogance of the wicked. Indeed, GOD does not listen to their empty plea; the Almighty pays no attention to it.

"How much less, then, will he listen when you say that you do not see him? That is your case before him and you must wait for him, and further, that his anger never punishes and he not take the least notice of wickedness." So JOB opens his mouth with empty talk: without knowledge he multiplies words.

Now I say to the Jehovah's Witnesses that GOD is angry with you because you have not spoken of GOD what is right as his servant Job. But you don't have to take any bulls or rams to sacrifice for your sins. GOD himself sent his only begotten Son as a sacrifice for our sins; but you have to go to GOD'S servant Job to pray for you, and GOD will accepts your sins. But in this lifetime, there are hundreds of millions of Jobs to pray for you sinners, and stop deceiving people with your own false teaching. The first lie you tell when you open the BIBLE is when you say that you teach what the Word of GOD says; and your last lie is when you say that you are the only group GOD will be saving to be with him in heaven or on earth when GOD accomplishes his kingdom. In 1 John 5:20, "We know also that the Son of GOD has come and has given us understanding, so that we may know him who is true. And we are in him who is true—even in his Son JESUS CHRIST. He is the true GOD and eternal life."

So I, Assaf Sawaya, say to you, false teachers: Stop deceiving people by saying that JESUS is the Son of GOD but not GOD himself! You false teachers. In Genesis 1:26, "Then GOD said, 'Let us make man in our image, in our likeness.'" In Genesis 11:7, "'Come, let us go down and confuse their language so they will not understand each other.'" What does *let us* mean? It is plural: GOD the Father, GOD the Son, and GOD the Holy Spirit; so is *let us go down*. And in Isaiah 6:8, "Then I heard the voice of the LORD saying, 'Whom shall I send? And who will go for us?'" *Us* is not a singular word. GOD'S intention is declaring again GOD the Father, GOD the Son, and GOD the Holy Spirit.

1 JOHN 1:1—The Word of Life

That which was from the beginning, which we have heard, which we have seen with our eyes, which we have looked at and our hands have touched—this we proclaim concerning the Word of Life. The life appeared; we have seen it and testify to it, and we proclaim to you the eternal life, which was with the Father and has appeared to us. We proclaim to you what we have seen and heard, so that you also may have fellowship with us. And our fellowship is with the Father and with his Son, JESUS CHRIST. We write this to make our joy complete.

This is the message we have heard from him and declare to you: GOD is light; in him there is no darkness at all. If we claim to have fellowship with him yet walk in the darkness, we lie and do not live by the truth. But if we walk in the light, as he is in the light, we have fellowship with one another, and the blood of JESUS, his Son, purifies us from all sin.

If we claim to be without sin, we deceive ourselves and the truth is not with us. If we confess our sins, he is faithful and just and will forgive us our sins and purify us from all unrighteousness. If we claim we have not sinned, we make him out to be a liar and his word has no place in our lives.

My friend Raja called me after the thirty years I have not seen him or heard from him; we got together for dinner with his brother and his family. They just moved to Las Vegas. It was a happy reunion. We talked about the old days when we met at the club where he played music, and we became friends ever since that time; but we lost track of each other by him moving back to Lebanon and me staying in the USA between San Diego and Las Vegas.

I invited Raja to visit me in my home, and when he came to visit me at home, he saw me occupied in my writing. When he asked me what I was doing, I said, "I am writing my life story and how GOD pulled me out from the deep pit." As in Psalm 40:2, "He lifted me out of the slimy pit, out of the mud and mire; he set my feet on a rock and gave me a firm place to stand."

Raja was impressed of what I am doing, and I showed him what I just finished writing about the prophet Jonah and the prophet Job. "You are writing about the prophet Job?" He was so excited about the news. He said, "Job, to us"—meaning the Druze faith—"he is the prophet that we build a shrine to worship at in Syria."

As you can see in the graph of the shrine the Druze, it's built on the highest point of a mountain and seems like it descended from heaven, comprised of twenty rooms. No one knows exactly when the shrine was built; but it was built in the memory of the prophet Job, who was born in the village of Aaddas in Syria in the Druze Mountain.

The elders of the Druze meet every Friday in the shrine; all the Druze visit the shrine, and others all year long. And in the summertime, they enjoy the yearly festival that is open to all. I relate to the minorities of the Druze because of the loving heart they are blessed with, as what GOD has blessed me also since my childhood and throughout my life. The Druze foreshadow the love of Job and his righteousness. As what you read in the Job story, GOD said to Satan (Job 1:8), "'Have you considered my servant Job? There is no one on earth like him; he is blameless and upright, a man who fears GOD and shuns evil.'"

The Druze are a minority. They live in Syria, Lebanon, and Israel. They also occupy seats in the parliament, and at all times, they have one or two seats as ministers in the government. They have no jealousy of who is in control in any of the countries they live in and always respect the law of the governing body. They are very successful people anywhere they live, and they live in most of the world.

GOD has defeated Satan by a man who inherited sin through the disobedience of Adam. GOD is showing us the contrast between

Adam and Job; Adam was created as a perfect man without any sin, and GOD gave Adam the authority and dominion on the animals of the earth, the birds of the air, and the fish of the sea.

Adam gave all the authority and the dominion to the deceiver Satan when he deceived Eve and Adam listened to his wife, Eve; and they were dead that same day as GOD had promised them: "'When you eat from the tree of life you will die." And they were dead spiritually that day.

الموحدون الدروز. والنبي أيوب عليه السلام

مدوّنة فيصل المصري

٢٠١٧

Satan tried to deceive Job through his wife (Job 2:9).

> His wife said to him, "Are you still holding on to your integrity? Curse GOD and die!"
> He replied, "You are talking like a foolish woman. Shall we accept good from GOD and not trouble?" In all this JOB did not sin in what he said.

Job did not sin against GOD, and he rebuked his wife, unlike Adam who listened to his wife and disobeyed GOD'S order when he told him not to eat from the forbidden tree. Satan the deceiver also deceived himself by thinking he could overthrow his creator, GOD.

The ultimate defeat to Satan came when JESUS shed his blood on the cross to redeem us, the sinners, of this world, and when JESUS rose from death, we were born again with him and whoever believes that JESUS died for our sins and rose from death. We Christians believe in JESUS, who was risen from death after three days, and there were more than five hundred who saw JESUS alive and stayed on earth for 40 days and then ascended to heaven and cast out Satan and his followers, the deceived angels.

The big question is, why did GOD allow Satan to deceive Adam but did not allow Satan to kill Job?

I asked GOD to reveal the big question for me; but what GOD revealed to me is not to explore on that question, and I obeyed GOD. GOD was with me when I was arrested and indicted under the criminal code CCE (continuing criminal enterprise), which carries a life sentence without the possibility of parole!

I cried out to the LORD, "Please help me, dear GOD. That is too big of a load to carry." I started to pray like I never did in my life. But GOD was there for me, and again GOD saved me by his grace when GOD sent his Son JESUS and took our sins by the stripes on his naked body and the shedding of his blood, for GOD so loved the world! But not for the sins of Satan and his angels and Adam and Eve's sins; because JESUS did not die for them, they were created as the perfect ones. They are doomed to spend their eternal life in the lake of fire with the coming Antichrist and all the false teachers and all false prophets and those who do not believe that we are saved by the blood of JESUS. Amen.

That is why Satan is so ferocious and doing all that GOD allows him to do until his coming time to be handed the CCE indictment.

My beloved, GOD'S message to us is to obey his commandments and all that GOD said to the world: "This is my Son, whom I love; with him I am well pleased." This is all written in the four books of the Gospel: Matthew 3:17, Mark 1:11, Luke 3:22, and John 1:34.

The Baptism of JESUS (Matthew 3:13–17)

> Then JESUS came from Galilee to the Jordan to be baptized by John. But John tried to deter him, saying, "I need to be baptized by you, and do you come to me?"
>
> JESUS replied, "Let it be so now; proper for us to do this to fulfill all righteousness." Then John consented.
>
> As soon as JESUS was baptized, he went up out of the water. At that moment heaven was opened, and he saw the Spirit of GOD descending like a dove and lighting on him. And a voice from heaven said, "This is my Son, whom I love; with him I am well pleased."

In 3:15, this occasion marked the beginning of CHRIST'S messianic ministry. There were several reasons for his baptism: the first mentioned here was "to fulfill all righteousness." The baptism indicated that he was consecrated to GOD and officially approved by him, as especially shown in the descent of the Holy Spirit (v. 16) and the words of the Father (v.17; cf. Ps 2:7 and Isa 42:1). All of GOD'S righteous requirements for the Messiah were fully met in JESUS. Second, at JESUS'S baptism, John publicly announced the arrival of the Messiah and the inception of his ministry (Jn 1:31–34). Third, by his baptism, JESUS completely identified himself with man's sin and failure, though he himself needed no repentance or cleansing from sin, becoming our substitute (2 Co 5:21). Fourth, his baptism was an example to his followers.

In Psalm 2:7, "'I will proclaim the decree of the LORD:' He said to me. 'You are my Son; today I have become your Father.'" In Isaiah 42:1, "'Here is my servant, whom I uphold, my chosen one in whom I delight; I will put my Spirit on him and he will bring justice to the nations.'" And in John 1:31–34,

> "I myself did not know him, but the reason I came baptizing with water was that he might be revealed to Israel."
>
> Then John gave this testimony: "I saw the Spirit come down from heaven as a dove and remain on him. I would not have known him, except that the one who sent me to baptize with water told me, 'The man on whom you see the Spirit come down and remain is he who will baptize with the Holy Spirit.' I have seen and I testify that this is the Son of GOD."

In 2 Corinthians 5:21, "GOD made him who had no sin to be sin for us, so that in him we might become the righteousness of GOD." In Mark 1:11, "And a voice came from heaven: 'You are my Son, whom I love; with you I am well pleased.'" In Luke 3:22, "And the Holy Spirit descended on him in bodily form like a dove. And a voice came from heaven: 'You are my Son. whom I love: with you I am well pleased.'"

LUKE 23:26—The Crucifixion of our LORD JESUS

> As they led him away, they seized Simon from Cyrene, who was on his way in from the country, and put the cross on him and made him carry it behind JESUS. A large number of people followed him, including women who mourned and wailed for him. JESUS turned and said to them, "Daughters of Jerusalem, do not weep for me: weep for yourselves and for your children. For the time will come when you will say, 'Blessed are the barren women, the wombs that never bore and the breast that never nursed!' Then they will say to the mountains, 'Fall on us!' and to the hills,

'Cover us!' For if men do these things when the tree is green, what will happen when it is dry?"

Two other men, both criminals, were also led out with him to be executed. When they came to the place called the Skull, there they crucified him, along with the criminals—one on his right, the other on his left. LUKE 23:34—JESUS said, "Father, forgive them, for they do not know what they are doing."

And they divided up his clothes by casting lots. The people stood watching, and the rulers even sneered at him. They said, "He saved others; let him save himself if he is the CHRIST of GOD, the chosen One."

The soldiers also came up and mocked him. They offered him wine vinegar and said, "If you are the king of the Jews, save yourself."

There was a written notice above him, which read: "THIS IS THE KING OF THE JEWS."

One of the criminals who hung there hurled insults at him: "Aren't you the CHRIST? Save yourself and us!"

But the other criminal rebuked him. "Don't you fear GOD?" He said, "Since you are under the same sentence? We are punished justly, for we are getting what our deeds deserve. But this man has done nothing wrong."

JESUS answered him, "I tell you the truth. Today you will be with me in paradise."

It was now about the sixth hour, and darkness came over the whole land until the ninth hour, for the sun stopped shining. And the curtain of the temple was torn in two. JESUS called out with a loud voice. "Father, into your hands I commit my spirit." When he had said this, he breathed his last.

> The centurion, seeing what had happened, praised GOD and said, "Surely this was a righteous man."
>
> When all the people who had gathered to witness this sight saw what took place, they beat their breast and went away. But all those who knew him, including the women who had followed him from Galilee, stood at a distance, watching these things.

Luke 23:26—*Simon*. His sons, Rufus and Alexander (Mk 15:21) must have been known in Christian circles at a later time and perhaps were associated with the church at Rome (Ro 16:13).

Cyrene. A leading city in Libya, west of Egypt. Put the cross on him. See note on Mark 15:21: "A certain man from Cyrene, Simon, the father of Alexander and Rufus, was passing by on his way in from the country, and they forced him to carry the cross."

In Luke 23:28, "'Weep for yourselves and for your children. Because of the terrible suffering to befall Jerusalem some 40 years later when the Roman would besiege the city and utterly destroy the temple.'"

23:29—*Blessed are the barren*. It would be better not to have children than to have them experience such suffering (cf. Jer. 16:1–4; 1 Co 7:25–35). In Jeremiah 16:1–4, "Then the word of the LORD came to me: 'You must not marry and have sons or daughters in this place. For this is what the LORD says about the sons and daughters born in this land and about the women who are their mothers and the men who are their fathers: They will die of deadly diseases. They will not be mourned or buried but will be like refuse lying on the ground. They will perish by sword and famine, and their dead bodies will become food for the birds of the air and the beasts of the earth.'" And in 1 Corinthians 7:25–35,

> Now about virgins: I have no command from the LORD, but I give a judgment as one who by the LORD's mercy is trustworthy.

Because of the present crisis I think that it is good for you to remain as you are. Are you married? Do not seek a divorce. Are you unmarried? Do not look for a wife. But if you do marry, you have not sinned: and if a virgin marries, she has not sinned. But those who marry will face many troubles in this life, and I want to spare you this.

What I mean, brothers, is that the time is short. From now on those who have wives should live as if they had none; those who mourn, as if they did not; those who are happy, as if they were, as if they were not; those who buy something, as if it were not theirs to keep; those who use the things or the world, as if not engrossed in them. For this world in its present form is passing away.

I would like you to be free from concern. An unmarried man is concerned about the LORD'S affairs—how he can please the LORD. But a married man is concerned about the affairs of this world—how he can please his wife—and his interests are divided. An unmarried woman or virgin is concerned about the LORD'S affairs: Her aim is to be devoted to the LORD in both body and spirit. But a married woman is concerned about the affairs of this world—how she can please her husband.

I am saying this for your own good, not to restrict you, but that you may live in a right way in undivided devotion to the lord.

1 Corinthians 7:25—*Now about virgins*. Paul answers another major question the Corinthians had asked (v. 1). *I give a judgement as one who…is trustworthy*. Paul is not giving a direct command from JESUS here (as in v. 10; cf. Ac 20:35). In this matter, which is not a question of right or wrong, Paul express his own judgment. Even though he put it this way, he is certainly not denying that he wrote under the influence

of divine inspiration (see v. 40). And since he writes under inspiration, what he recommends is clearly the better course of action.

In 1 Corinthians 7:1, "Now for the matters you wrote about: It is good for a man not to marry," and in 7:10, "To the married I give this command (not I, but the LORD): A wife must not separate from her husband." In Acts 20:35, "In everything I did, I showed you that by this kind of hard work we must help the weak, remembering the words the LORD JESUS himself said: 'It is more blessed to give than to receive.'" In 1 Corinthians 7:40, "In my judgment, she is happier if she stays as she is—and I think that I too have the Spirit of GOD."

7:26—*present crisis*. Probably a reference to the pressures of the Christian life in an immoral and particularly hostile environment (cf. vv. 2, 28; 5:1; 2 Ti 3:12). Paul's recommendation here does not apply to all times and all situations. In 1 Corinthians 7:2, "But since there is so much immorality, each man should have his own wife, and each woman her own husband," and in 5:1, "It is actually reported that there is sexual immorality among you, and of a kind that does not occur even among pagans: A man has his father's wife." In 2 Timothy 3:12, "In fact, everyone who wants to live a godly life in CHRIST JESUS will be persecuted."

7:28—*many troubles*. Times of suffering and persecution for CHRIST, when being married, would mean even greater hardship in taking care of one's mate. In 1 Corinthians 7:29, "Time is short. The time for doing the LORD'S work has become increasingly short. Life is fleeting, as times of persecution remind us. Do not be concerned with the affairs of this world [vv. 29–31] because material things are changing and disappearing [v. 31]." Some think the reference is to the LORD'S second coming.

7:34—*his interests are divided*. He cannot give undistracted service to CHRIST (v. 35). This is particularly true in times of persecution.

The Resurrection of Our LORD GOD JESUS CHRIST

Luke 24:1–11—On the first day of the week, very early in the morning the women took the spices they had prepared and went to the tomb. They found the stone rolled away from the tomb, but when they entered, they did not find the body of the LORD JESUS. While they were wondering about this, suddenly two men in clothes that gleamed like lightning stood beside them. In their fright the women bowed down with their faces to the ground, but the men said to them, "Why do you look for the living among the dead? He is not here: he has risen! Remember how he told you while he was still with you in Galilee: 'The Son of Man must be delivered into the hands of sinful men, be crucified and on the third day be raised again."

Then they remembered his words. When they came back from the tomb, they told all these things to the Eleven and to all the others. It was Mary Magdalene, Joanna, Mary the mother of James, and the others with them who told this to the apostles. But they did not believe the women, because their words seemed to them like nonsense. Peter, however, got up and ran to the tomb. Bending over, he saw the strips of linen lying by themselves, and he went away, wondering to himself what had happened.

24:1—*first day of the week*. Sunday began by Jewish time at sundown on Saturday. Spices could then be bought (Mk 16:1). And they were ready to set out early the next day. When the women started out, it was dark (Jn 20:1), and by the time they arrived at the tomb, it was still early dawn (see Mt 28:1; Mk 16: 2). In Mark 16:1–2, "When the Sabbath was over, Mary Magdalene, Mary the mother of James, and Salome bought spices so that they might go to anoint JESUS'S body. Very early on the first day of the week, just after sunrise, they were on their way to the tomb." In Matthew 28: 1, "After the Sabbath, at dawn on the first day of the week, Mary Magdalene and the other Mary went to look at the tomb."

24:2—*the stone rolled away.* A tomb's entrance was ordinarily closed to keep vandals and animals from disturbing the bodies. This stone, however, had been sealed by Roman authority for a different reason (see Mt 27:62–66):

> The next day, the one after Preparation Day, the chief priests and the Pharisees went to Pilate. "Sir," they said, "we remember that while he was still alive that deceiver said, 'After three days I will rise again.' So give the order for the tomb to be made secure until the third day. Otherwise, his disciples may come and steal the body and tell the people that he has been raised from the dead. This last deception will be worse than the first."
>
> "Take a guard," Pilate answered. "Go. Make the tomb as secure as you know how."
>
> So they went and made the tomb secure by putting a seal on the stone and posting the guard.

Luke 24:4—*two men.* They looked like men, but their clothes were remarkable (see 9:29; Ac 1:10; 10:30). Other reports referring to them call them angels (v. 23; see also Jn 20:12). Although Matthew speaks of one angel (not two, Mt 28:2 and Mk 16:5), this is not strange because frequently only the spokesman is noted and an accompanying figure is not mentioned. Words and posture (*sealed,* Jn 20:12; *standing,* Lk 24:4) often change in the course of events, so these variations are not necessarily contradictory. They are merely evidence of independent accounts.

In Luke 9:29, "As he was praying, the appearance of his face changed, and his clothes became as bright as a flash of lightning." In Acts 1:10, "They were looking intently up into the sky as he was going, when suddenly two men dressed in white stood beside them," and in 10:30, "Cornelius answered: 'Four days ago I was in my house praying at this hour, at three in the afternoon. Suddenly a man in shining clothes stood before me.'"

In Luke 23, "But didn't find his body. They came and told us that they had seen a vision of angels, who said he was alive." In John 20:12, "And saw two angels in white, seated where JESUS'S body had been, one at the head and the other at the foot." In Matthew 28:2, "There was a violent earthquake, for an angel of the LORD came down from heaven and going to the tomb, rolled back the stone and sat on it." And in Mark 16:5, "As they entered the tomb, they saw a young man dressed in a white robe sitting on the right side, and they were alarmed."

Luke 24:6—*While...in Galilee.* JESUS had predicted his death and resurrection on a number of occasions (9:22), but the disciples failed to comprehend or accept what he was saying. In Luke 9:22, "And JESUS said, 'The Son of Man must suffer many things and be rejected by the elders chief priests and teachers of the law, and he must be killed and on the third day be raised to life.'"

Luke 24:9—*to the Eleven and to all the others. Eleven* is sometimes used to refer to the group of apostles (Ac 1:26; 2:14) after the betrayal by Judas. Judas was dead at the time the apostles first met the risen CHRIST, but the group was still called the Twelve (Jn 20:24). The *others* included disciples who, for the most part, came from Galilee. In Acts 1:26, "Then they cast lots, and the lot fell to Matthias: so he was added to the eleven apostles." In John 20:24, "Now Thomas [called Didymus, one of the Twelve] was not with the disciples when JESUS came."

Luke 24:10—*Mary Magdalene.* See note on 8:2. She is named first in most of the lists of women (Mt 27:56; Mk 15:40; but cf. Jn 19:25) and was the first to see the risen CHRIST (Jn 20:13–18).

Joanna. See 8:3. She is named by only Luke at this point (Mark is the only one who adds Salome at this time; Mk 16:1).

Mary the mother of James. See Mk 16:1. She is the "other Mary" of Matthew 28:1. The absence of the mother of JESUS is significant. She was probably with John (cf. Jn 19:27).

In Luke 8:2, "And also some women who had been cured of evil spirit and diseases: Mary (called Magdalene) from whom seven demons had come out." In Matthew 27:56, "Among them were Mary Magdalene, Mary the mother of James and Joseph, and the mother of Zebedee's sons." In Mark 15:40, "Some women were watching from a distance. Among them were Mary Magdalene, Mary the mother of James the younger and Joseph, and Salome." And in John 19:25, "Near the cross of JESUS stood his mother, his mother's sister, Mary the wife of Clopas, and Mary Magdalene."

In John 20:13–18,

> They asked her. "Woman, why are you crying?"
>
> "They have taken my LORD away," she said, "and I don't know where they have put him."
>
> At this, she turned around and saw JESUS standing there, but she did not realize that it was JESUS. "Woman," he said, "why are you crying? Who is it you are looking for?"
>
> Thinking he was the gardener, she said, "Sir, if you have carried him away, tell me where you have put him, and I will get him."
>
> JESUS said to her, "Mary."
>
> She turned toward him and cried out in Aramaic, "RABBONI!" (which means "Teacher").
>
> JESUS said, "Do not hold on to me, for I have not yet returned to the Father. Go instead to my brothers and tell them, 'I am returning to my Father and your Father, to my GOD and your GOD.'"
>
> Mary Magdalene went to the disciples with the news: "I have seen the LORD!" and she told them that he said these things to her.

In Mark 16: 1, "When the Sabbath was over, Mary Magdalene, Mary the mother of James, and Salome bought spices so that they might go to JESUS' body." In Matthew 28:1, "After the Sabbath, at dawn on the first day of the week, Mary Magdalene and the other Mary went to look at the tomb." In John 19:27, "And to the disciples, 'Here is your mother.' From that time on, this disciple took her into his home."

Luke 24:12. *Peter…ran.* John's Gospel (20:3–9) includes another disciple: John himself. In John 20:3–9, "So Peter and the other disciple started for the tomb. BOTH were running, but the other disciple outran Peter and reached the tomb first. He bent over and looked in at the strips of linen lying there but did not go in. Then Simon Peter, who was behind him, arrived and went into the tomb. He saw the strips of linen lying there, as well as the burial cloth that had been around JESUS' head. The cloth was folded up by itself, separate from the linen. Finally the other disciple, who had reached the tomb first, also went inside. He saw and believed. (They still did not understand from Scripture that JESUS had to rise from the dead.)"

"Get behind me, Satan!" That is what JESUS said to his disciple Peter when he took JESUS aside and began to rebuke JESUS! "Never, Lord," he said. "This shall never happen to you."

After what JESUS was explaining to his disciples, that he must go to Jerusalem and suffer many things and he must be killed and on the third day, JESUS will be raised to life.

Peter was the first disciple JESUS had chosen. As he was fishing for a living, JESUS told Peter, "Follow me and I will make you a fisherman of men!" Peter obeyed JESUS, and for about three years, he was with JESUS and other disciples. JESUS had chosen as well; they all lived JESUS'S way of life, and they observed all the miracles JESUS had done to other people.

As he was teaching about the kingdom of GOD and how to get there, JESUS was feeding his followers spiritual food and bodily food. Let us read Matthew 16:5–28, "The Yeast of the Pharisees and Sadducees."

> When they went across the lake, the disciples forgot to take bread. "Be earful," JESUS said to them. "Be on your guard against the yeast of the Pharisees and Sadducees."
>
> They discussed this among themselves and said, "It is because we didn't bring any bread."
>
> Aware of their discussion, JESUS asked, "You of little faith. Why are you talking among yourselves about having no bread? Do you still not understand? Don't you remember the five loaves

for the five thousand, and how many basketfuls you gathered? Or the seven loaves for the four thousand, and how many basketfuls you gathered? How is it you don't understand that I was not talking to you about bread? But be on your guard against the yeast of the Pharisees and Sadducees."

Then they understood that he was not telling them to guard against the yeast used in bread but against the teaching of the Pharisees and Sadducees.

When JESUS came to the region of Caesarea Philippi, he asked his disciples, "Who do people say the Son of Man is?"

They replied, "Some say John the Baptist; others say Elijah; and still others, Jeremiah or one of the prophets."

"But what about you?" he asked. "Who do you say I am?"

Simon Peter answered, "You are the CHRIST, the Son of the living GOD."

JESUS replied, "Blessed are you, Simon son of Jonah. For this was not revealed to you by man, but by my Father in heaven. And I tell you that you are Peter, and on this rock I will build my church, and the gates of hades will not overcome it. I will give you the keys of the kingdom of heaven; whatever you bind on earth will be bound in heaven, and whatever you loose on earth will be loosed in heaven."

Then he warned his disciples not to tell anyone that he was the CHRIST.

From that time on JESUS began to explain to his disciples that he must go to Jerusalem and suffer many things at the hands of the elders, chief priests and teachers of the law, and that he must be killed and on the third day be raised to life.

Peter took him aside and began to rebuke him. "Never, LORD!" he said. "This shall never happen to you!"

JESUS turned and said to Peter, "Get behind me, Satan! You are a stumbling block to me; you do not have in mind the things of GOD, but the things of men."

Then JESUS said to his disciples, "If anyone would come after me, he must deny himself and take up his cross and follow me. For whoever wants to save his life will lose it, but whoever loses his life for me will find it. What good will it be for a man if he gains the whole world, yet forfeits his soul? Or what can a man give in exchange for his soul? For the Son of Man is going to come in his Father's glory with his angels, and then he will reward each person according to what he has done. I tell you the truth, some who are standing here will not taste death before they see the Son of Man coming in his kingdom."

In Matthew 16:12, Matthew often explains the meaning of JESUS'S words (cf. 17:13). Then the disciples understood that he was talking to them about John the Baptist.

16:13—*Caesarea Philippi.* To be distinguished from the magnificent city of Caesarea, which Herod the Great had built on the coast of the Mediterranean. Caesarea Philippi, rebuilt by Herod's son Philip (who named it after Tiberius Caesar and himself), was north of the sea of Galilee, near the slopes of Mount Hermon. Originally it was called Paneas (the ancient name survives today as Banias) in honor of the Greek god Pan, whose shrine was located there. The region was especially pagan.

16:18—*Peter...rock...church.* In Greek, *Peter* is "Petros" and *rock* is "petra." The rock on which the church is built may be Peter's inspired (v. 17) confession of faith in JESUS as the MESSIAH, "the Son of the living GOD," or it may be Peter himself since Ephesians

2:20 indicates that the church is "built on the foundation of the apostles and prophets."

Church. In the Gospels, this word is used only by Matthew (here and twice in 18:17). In the Septuagint, it is used for the congregation of Israel. In Greek circles of JESUS'S day, it indicated the assembly of free voting citizens in a city (cf. Ac 19:32, 38, 41).

Hades. The Greek name for the place of departed spirits, generally equivalent to the Hebrew *Sheol* (see note on Ge 37:35). The *gates of Hades* may mean the "powers of death," i.e., all forces opposed to CHRIST and his kingdom (but see note on Job 17:16).

In Ephesians 2:20, "Built on the foundation of the apostles and prophets with CHRIST JESUS himself as the chief cornerstone." In Acts 19:32, "The assembly was in confusion: Some were shouting one thing, some another. Most of the people did not even know why they were there."

16:19—*keys*. Perhaps Peter used these keys on the day of Pentecost (Ac 2) when he announced that the door of the kingdom was unlocked to Jews and proselytes and later when he acknowledged that it was also opened to Gentiles (Ac 10).

Bind loose. Not the authority to determine but to announce guilt or innocence (see 18:18 and the context there; cf. Ac 5:3, 9).

In Acts 2:1, "When the day of Pentecost came, they were all together in one place," and in 10:1, "At Caesarea there was a man named Cornelius, a centurion in what was known as the Italian Regiment." In Matthew 18:18, "'I tell you the truth. Whatever you bind on earth will be bound in heaven, and whatever you loose on earth will be loosed in heaven.'"

Matthew 16:20—*not to tell*. Because of the false concepts of the Jews who looked for an exclusively national and political Messiah, JESUS told his disciples not to publicize Peter's confession, lest it precipitate a revolution against Rome (see note on 8:4: "Then JESUS said to him, 'See that you don't tell anyone. But go, show yourself to the priest and offer the gift Moses commanded as a testimony to them.'"

16:21—*began*. The beginning of a new emphasis in JESUS'S ministry. Instead of teaching the crowds in parables, he concentrated on preparing the disciples for his coming suffering and death.

16:23—*Satan*. A loanword from Hebrew meaning "adversary" or "accuser." See NIV text note on Job 1:6; see also note on Revelation 2:9: "One day the angels came to present themselves before the LORD, and Satan also came with them," and "I know your afflictions and your poverty—yet you are rich! I know the slander of those who say they are Jews and are not, but are a synagogue of Satan," respectively. In Romans 2:28, "A man is not a Jew if he is only one outwardly, or is circumcision merely outward and Physical?"

16:24—*take up his cross*. See note on 10:38: "And anyone who does not take his cross and follow me is not worthy of me."

16:28—There are two main interpretations of this verse: (1) It is a prediction of the transfiguration, which happened a week later (17:1–2) and which demonstrated that JESUS will return in his Father's glory (16:27); and (2) It refers to the day of Pentecost and the rapid spread of the Gospel described in the book of Acts. The context seems to favor the first view. See note on 2 Pe 1:16.

In Matthew 17:1–2, "After six days JESUS took with him Peter, James and John the brother of James, and led them up a high mountain by themselves. There he was transfigured before them. His face shone like the sun, and his clothes became as white as the light." In 2 Peter 1:16–21,

> We did not follow cleverly invented stories when we told you about the power and coming of our LORD JESUS CHRIST, but we were eyewitnesses of his majesty. For he received honor and glory from GOD the Father when the voice came to him from the Majestic Glory, saying, "This is my Son. whom I love: with him I am well pleased." We ourselves heard this voice that came from heaven when we were with him on the sacred mountain.
>
> And we have the word of the prophets made more certain, and you will do well to pay attention to it, as to a light shining in a dark place, until the day dawns and the morning star rises

in your hearts. Above all you must understand that no prophecy of Scripture came about by the prophet's own interpretation. For prophecy never had its origin in the will of man, but men spoke from GOD as they were carried along by the Holy Spirit.

JESUS was telling his disciples in Matthew 16:9, "Do you still not understand? Don't you remember the five loaves for five thousand, and how many basketfuls you gathered?"

JESUS'S disciples, that day, gathered twelve basketfuls of bread and fish. After JESUS fed over five thousand people including women and children, they all were satisfied. But when JESUS said to his disciples about the spiritual food, they were not satisfied yet because they were still spiritually blind. And when JESUS asked them, "Who do people say the Son of man is?" only Simon Peter answered correctly by saying, "You are the CHRIST the Son of the living GOD." Then JESUS blessed Peter and promised to give him the keys of the kingdom of heaven.

But when JESUS was explaining to his disciples that he must be killed, they all were spiritually blind. But when Peter took JESUS aside to rebuke JESUS by saying to him, "No way! You are the Son of the living GOD. That could not happen to you, LORD!" then JESUS said to him, "Get behind me, Satan. You do not have in mind the things of GOD, but the things of men."

When I tell non-Christian people that JESUS came from heaven and shed his blood for all men, their response is, "That can't be true. Why does the Son of GOD have to die?" Because we cannot do it on our own and because GOD so loved the world he sent his only begotten Son to redeem us from what Satan brought on all men with his sinful nature. And whoever believes that JESUS died to save us from sin will inherit forever-lasting life with him in heaven.

Then JESUS said to them, "Whoever wants to save his life, will lose it, but whoever loses his life for JESUS will find it." In the book of Matthew chapter 16:19, JESUS told Peter, "I will give you the keys to the kingdom of heaven," and in the same chapter

(Matthew 16:23), JESUS said to Peter, "Get behind me, Satan." And in Matthew chapter 26:31–35,

> Then JESUS told them, "This very night you will all fall away on account of me, for it is written: 'I will strike the shepherd, and the sheep of the flock will be scattered.' But after I have risen, I will go ahead of you into Galilee."
>
> Peter replied, "Even if all fall away on account of you, I never will."
>
> "I tell you the truth," JESUS answered. "This very night, before the rooster crows, you will disown me three times."
>
> But Peter declared, "Even if I have to die with you, I will never disown you." And all the other disciples said the same.

Peter did not live to his promise. His heart was in the right, but his flesh was not. Even though he lived with JESUS, in contrast with the prophet Job when his wife came to him and said to Job, "Why don't you curse GOD and die?" Job rebuked his wife and said to her, "You are talking like a foolish woman; should we accept good from GOD and not trouble?" And Job defeated Satan for what he went through in his life and never cursed GOD! And GOD said, "There is no one on earth like Job!" My beloved, we all could be Job when we believe and obey all that GOD said to us. Glory to GOD and the love he has for us. Amen.

After JESUS was arrested, and in the same chapter in Matthew (26:69–75), Peter disowned JESUS:

Peter Disowns JESUS

> Now Peter was sitting out in the courtyard, and a servant girl came to him. "You also were with JESUS of Galilee," she said.

But he denied it before them all. "I don't know what you're talking about," he said.

Then he went out to the gateway, where another girl saw him and said to the people there, "This fellow was with JESUS of Nazareth."

He denied it again with an oath: "I don't know the man!"

After a little while, those standing there went up to Peter and said, "Surely you are one of them, for your accent gives you away."

Then he began to call down curses on himself and he swore to them, "I don't know the man!"

Immediately a rooster crowed. Then Peter remembered the word JESUS had spoken: "Before the rooster crows, you will disown me three times." And he went outside and wept bitterly.

26:73—*your accent gives you away*. Peter had a decidedly Galilean accent that was conspicuous in Jerusalem.

After Peter experienced all that JESUS said to him and predicted his behavior, Peter wept bitterly. JESUS already knew Peter's loving heart, and that is why he had chosen him and then said to him, "I will give you the keys to the kingdom of heaven." Peter loved JESUS, but he behaved like the ordinary man at that situation. But then he remembered that JESUS also said, "Whoever loses his life for me will find it." Peter found his life when he was condemned, to be crucified, but he asked the persecutor, "I am not worthy to be crucified like JESUS. I wish you crucify me upside down." And that was how Peter saved his life by losing it, serving JESUS.

GOD is with the ones who have a loving heart, and GOD will not abandon you even in your worst trials. I am the perfect example; GOD has lifted me up from the slimy pit not only once but more than one time! That is why I am testifying to the loving GOD and his mercy on his children, and when I knew that was GOD'S will for me; now I am devoting my life to serve GOD all the way.

When JESUS told his disciples that he must be killed, they all rejected the thought that the Son of GOD will go through that painful death, even if they were with JESUS for about three years. But when they saw JESUS suffering on the cross, they could not escape the fact that JESUS came to earth for that purpose to save us, the sinners, and rise from death to rise up with him. Whoever believes in his sacrifice will be with JESUS in heaven in forever-lasting life.

It is that simple. We all were condemned to death for the sin of one man, Adam, and we will live forever because of the sacrifice of one man, JESUS.

I believe in all that JESUS had said and done for us, and I am devoting my life for him to be with him. Glory to GOD and our Savior, the LORD JESUS. And when I fail him, JESUS will forgive me as long as I don't make a continuous habit of my sin.

Not because we are good; that is not enough. We have to believe that JESUS died for us. To know more about JESUS, you have to study the BIBLE, GOD'S Word, every day. And don't leave the BIBLE on the shelf, collecting dust, but take it in your hands and let the pages of the BIBLE collect your fingerprints every day because if you leave it on the shelf, GOD also will leave you on the shelf and you will not collect GOD'S fingerprint on your life to live forever with him!

I wish I came to the LORD when I was introduced to him in my forties, after I was baptized. One good Christian came to me and said, "Now that you are baptized, you should devote your life to serve our LORD JESUS!" His words came like a ton of bricks on my shoulder, and I said to myself, *Oh no, I want to enjoy my life before I commit myself to the LORD.* It took me about thirty years to come to the LORD, and the joy I was looking for was with GOD! The GOD that I am serving now and returning his love after what GOD has done in my life and the love GOD has showed me. Now I live the real joy by serving GOD and studying his Word, which lifts you up; and when I get that feeling, I jump up in the air and shout, "How delicious you are, my beloved GOD!"

My message to the young people is, the joy that you are looking for in your life is to study the Word of GOD, the BIBLE, and don't put it on the shelf. By the time you read my testimony, I will be seventy-two years old. GOD will welcome you any time you come to him and will give you the same wages as if you started to serve him since your teenage years; but please don't wait as long as I did at a late age because you will miss what I missed in my youth. The ultimate joy is to love GOD back! And you will know it when you do the exact way I did at the autumn of my life.

Please read the "Parable of the Workers in the Vineyard," Matthew 20:1–16:

> "For the kingdom of heaven is like a landowner who went out early in the morning to hire men to work in his vineyard. He agreed to pay them a denarius for the day and sent them into his vineyard. About the third hour he went out and saw others standing in the marketplace doing nothing. He told them, 'You also go and work in my vineyard, and I will pay you whatever is right.' 5 So they went. He went out again about the sixth hour and the ninth hour and did the same thing. About the eleventh hour, he went out and found still others standing around. He asked them, 'Why have you been standing here all day long doing nothing?'
>
> "'Because no one has hired us,' they answered.
>
> "He said to them, 'You also go and work in my vineyard.'
>
> "When evening came, the owner of the vineyard said to his foreman, 'Call the workers and pay them their wages, beginning with the last ones hired and going on to the first.'
>
> "The workers who were hired about the eleventh hour came and each received a denarius. So when those came who were hired first, they expected to receive more. But each one of them also received denarius. When they received it they began to grumble against the landowner.

'These men who were hired last worked only one hour,' they said, 'and you have made them equal to us who have borne the burden of the work and the heat of the day.'

"But he answered one of them, 'Friend, I am not being unfair to you. Didn't you agree to work for a denarius? Take your pay and go. I want to give the man who hired last the same as I gave you. Don't I have the right to do what I want with my money? Or are you envious because I am generous?'

"So the last will be first, and the first will be last."

1 JOHN 2:28–29—And now, dear children, continue in him, so that when he appears we may be confident and unashamed before him at his coming. If you know that he is righteous, you know that everyone who does what is right has been born of him.

3:1–24—How great is the love the Father has lavished on us, that we should be called children of GOD! And that is what we are! The reason the world does not know us is that it did not know him. Dear friends, now we are children of GOD, and what we will be has not yet been made known. But we know that when he appears, we shall be like him, for we shall see him as he is. Everyone who has this hope in him purifies himself, just as he is pure.

Everyone who sins breaks the law; in fact, sin is lawlessness. But in him is no sin. No one who lives in him keeps on sinning. NO one who continues to sin has either seen him or known him.

Dear children, do not let anyone lead you astray. He who does what is right is righteous, just as he is righteous. He who does what is sinful is of the evil, because the devil has been sinning from the beginning. The reason the son of GOD appeared was to destroy the devil's work.

No one who is born of GOD will continue to sin, because GOD'S seed remains in him; he cannot go on sinning, because he has been born of GOD. This is who we know who the children of GOD are and who the children of the devil are: Anyone who does not do what is right is not a child of GOD; nor is anyone who does not love his brother.

This is the message you heard from the beginning: We should love one another. Do not be like Cain, who belonged to the evil one and murdered his brother. And why did he murder him? Because his own actions were evil and his brother's were righteous.

Do not be surprised, my brothers, if the world hates you. We know that we have passed from death to life, because we love our brothers. Anyone who does not love remains in death. Anyone who hates his brother is a murderer, and you know that no murderer has eternal life in him. This is how we know what love is: JESUS CHRIST laid down his life for us. And we ought to lay down our lives for our brothers. If anyone has material possessions and sees his brother in need but has no pity on him, how can the love of GOD be in him? Dear children, let us not love with words or tongue but with actions and in truth.

This then is how we know that we belong to the truth, and how we set our hearts at rest in his presence whenever our hearts condemn us, for GOD is greater than our hearts. He knows everything. Dear friends, if our hearts, do not condemn us, we have confidence before GOD and receive from him anything we ask, because we obey his commands and do what pleases him. And this is his command: to believe in the name of his Son, JESUS CHRIST, and to love one another as he commanded us. Those who obey his commands live in him, and he in them, and this is how we know that he lives in us. We know it by the Spirit he gave us.

4:1–21—Dear friends, do not believe every spirit, but test the spirits to see whether they are from GOD, because many false prophets have gone out into the world. This is how you can recognize the spirit of GOD: Every spirit that acknowledges that JESUS CHRIST has come in the flesh is from GOD, but every spirit that does not acknowledge JESUS is not from GOD. This is the spirit of the antichrist, which you have heard is coming and even now is already in the world.

You, dear children, are from GOD and have overcome them, because the one who is in you is greater than the one who is in the world. They are from the world and speak from the viewpoint of the world, and the world listens to them. We are from GOD, and whoever knows GOD listens to us: but whoever is not from GOD does not listen to us. This is how we recognize the Spirit of truth and the spirit of falsehood.

Dear friends, let us love one another, for love comes from GOD. Everybody who loves has been born of GOD and knows GOD. Whoever does not love does not know GOD, because GOD is love. This is how GOD showed his love among us: He sent his one and only Son into the world that we might live through him. This is love: not that we loved GOD, but that he loved us and sent his Son as an atoning sacrifice for our sins.

Dear friends, since GOD so loved us, we also ought to love one another. No one has ever seen GOD; but if we love one another, GOD lives in us and his love made complete in us.

We know that we live in him and he in us, because he has given us of his Spirit. And we have seen and testify that the Father has sent his Son to be the Savior of the world. If anyone acknowledges that JESUS is the Son of GOD, GOD lives in him and he in GOD. And so we know and rely on the love of GOD has for us.

GOD is love. Whoever lives in love lives in GOD, and GOD in him. In this way, love is made complete among us so that we will have confidence on the day of judgment, because in this world we are like him. There is no fear in love. But perfect love drives out fear, because fear has to do with punishment. The one who fears is not made perfect in love.

We love because he first loved us. If anyone says, "I love GOD," yet hates his brother, he is liar. For anyone who does not love his brother, whom he has seen, cannot love GOD, whom he has not seen. And he has given us his command: Whoever loves GOD must also love his brother.

5:1–21—Everyone who believes that JESUS is the CHRIST is born of GOD, and everyone who loves the father loves his child as well. This is how we know that we love the children of GOD: by loving GOD and carrying out his commands. This is love for GOD: to obey his commands. And his commands are not burdensome. For everyone born of GOD overcomes the world, even our faith. Who is it that overcomes the world? Only he who believes that JESUS is the Son of GOD.

This is the one who came by water and blood—JESUS. He did not come by water only, but by water and blood. And it is the Spirit who testifies, because the Spirit of the truth. For there are three that testify: the Spirit, the water and blood; and the three are in agreement. We accept man's testimony, but GOD'S testimony is greater because it is the testimony of GOD, which he has given about his Son. Anyone who believes in the Son of GOD has this testimony in his heart. Anyone who does not believe GOD has made him out to be a liar, because he has not believed the testimony GOD has given about his Son. And this is the testimony: GOD has given us eternal life, and this life is in his Son. He who has the Son has life; he who does not have the Son of GOD does not have life.

I write these things to you who believe in the name of the Son of GOD so that you know that you have eternal life. This is the confidence we have in approaching GOD: that if we ask anything according to his will, he hears us. And if we know that he hears us—whatever we ask—we know that we have what we asked him.

If anyone sees his brother commit a sin that does not lead to death, he should pray and GOD will give him life. I refer to those whose sin does not lead to death. I am not saying that he should pray about that. All wrongdoing is sin, and there is sin that does not lead to death.

We know that anyone born of GOD does not continue to sin; the one who has born of GOD keeps him safe, and the evil one cannot harm him. We know that we are children of GOD, and that the whole world is under the control of the evil one. We know also that the

Son of GOD has come and has given us understanding, so that we may know him who is true.
And we are in him who is true—even in his Son
JESUS CHRIST. He is the true GOD and eternal life.

Dear children, keep yourselves from idols.

The introduction to this letter deals with the same subject and
uses several of the same words as the introduction to John's Gospel
(1:1–4): *beginning, word, life,* and *with.*

*Was from the beginning. Has always existed. We. John and the other
apostles. Heard...seen...looked at...touched.* The apostles had made a
careful examination of the Word of life. He testifies the one who has
existed from eternity.

Because flesh (John 1:14). A flesh-and-blood man. He was true
GOD and true man. At the outset, John contradicts the heresy of the
Gnostics. Gnosticism—One of the most dangerous heresies of the
first two centuries of the church was Gnosticism. Its central teaching
was that the spirit is entirely good and matter is entirely evil. From
this unbiblical dualism flowed five important errors:

1. Man's body, which is matter, is therefore evil. It is to be in
    contrast with GOD, who is worthy in spirit and therefore
    good.
2. Salvation is the escape from the body, achieved not by faith
    in CHRIST but by special knowledge (the Greek word for
    knowledge is *gnosis,* hence Gnosticism).
3. CHRIST's true humanity was denied in two ways: (a)
    Some said that CHRIST only seemed to have a body, a
    view called Docetism, from the Greek *dokeo* ("to seem");
    and (b) others said that the divine CHRIST joined the
    man JESUS at baptism and left him before he died, a view
    called Cerinthianism, after its most prominent spokesman,
    Cerinthus. This view is the background of much of 1 John
    (see 1:1; 2:22; 4:2–3).

4. Since the body was considered evil, it was to be treated harshly. This ascetic form of Gnosticism is the background of part of the letter to the Colossians (2:21–23).
5. Paradoxically, this dualism also led to licentiousness. The reasoning was that since matter—and not the breaking of GOD'S law (1 John 3:4)—was considered evil, breaking his law was of no moral consequence.

The Gnosticism addressed in the NT was an early form of heresy, not the intricately developed system of the second and third centuries. In addition to that seen in Colossians and in John's letters, acquaintance with early Gnosticism is reflected in 1 and 2 Timothy, Titus, 2 Peter, and perhaps 1 Corinthians.

Occasion and purpose. John's readers were confronted with an early form of Gnostic teaching of the Cerinthian variety (see Gnosticism). This heresy was also libertine, throwing off all moral restraints. Consequently, John wrote this letter with two basic purposes in mind: (1) to expose false teachers (1 John 2:26) and (2) to give believers assurance of salvation (5:13). In keeping with his intention to combat Gnostic teachers, John specifically struck at their total lack of morality (3:8–10); and by giving eyewitness testimony to the incarnation, he sought to confirm his readers, belief in the incarnate CHRIST (1:3). Success in this would give the writer joy (1:4).

The life...the eternal life. CHRIST. He is called "the life" because he is the living one who has life in himself (see John 11:25; 14:6). "JESUS said to her, 'I am the resurrection and the life. He who believes in me will live, even though he dies; and whoever lives and believes in me will never die. Do you believe this?'" JESUS was talking to Martha, Lazarus's sister, to comfort her for Lazarus death. But in John 11:21–24 and 32–44,

> "LORD," Martha said to JESUS, "if you had been here, my brother would not have died. But I know that even now GOD will give you whatever you ask."

JESUS said to her, "Your brother will rise again."

Martha answered, "I know he will rise again in the resurrection at the last day." Martha was weeping and her sister Mary.

When Mary reached the place where JESUS was and saw him, she fell at his feet and said, "LORD if you had been here, my brother would not have died."

JESUS was deeply moved in spirit and troubled, because He loved Lazarus. "Where have you laid him?" he asked.

"Come and see LORD," they replied.

JESUS wept. Then the Jews said, "See how he loved him!" But some of them said, "Could not he who opened the eyes of the blind man have kept this man from dying?"

JESUS, once more deeply moved, came to the tomb. It was a cave with a stone laid across the entrance. "Take away the stone," he said.

"But, LORD," said Martha, the sister of the dead man, "by this time there is a bad odor, for he has been there four days."

Then JESUS said, "Did I not tell you that if you believe, you would see the glory of GOD?" So they took away the stone. Then JESUS looked up and said, "Father, I thank you that you have heard me. I knew that you always hear me, but I said this for the benefit of the people standing here, that they may believe that you sent me." When he had said this, JESUS called in a loud voice, "Lazarus, come out!" The dead man came out, his hands and feet wrapped with strips of linen, and a cloth around his face. JESUS said to them, "Take off the grave clothes and let him go."

In John 14:6, after the prophet Thomas asked JESUS, "LORD, we don't know where you are going, so how can we know the way?" JESUS answered, "I am the way and the truth and the life. No one comes to the Father except through me. If you really knew me, you would know my Father as well. From now on, you do know him and have seen him." He is also the source of life and sovereign over life (5:11). The letter begins and ends (5:20) with the theme of eternal life.

Fellowship with us. Participation with us (vicariously) in our experience of hearing, seeing, and touching the incarnate CHRIST (1 John 1:1). Fellowship (Greek *koinonia*) is the spiritual union of the believer with CHRIST. As described in the figures of the vine and branches (John 15:1–5), "I am the true vine, and my Father is the gardener. He cuts off every branch in me that bears no fruit, while every branch that does bear fruit he prunes so that it will be even more fruitful. You are already clean because of the word I have spoken to you. Remain in me, and I will remain in you. No branch can bear fruit by itself: it must remain in the vine. Neither can you bear fruit unless you remain in me. I am the vine: you are the branches. If a man remains in me and I in him, he will bear much fruit; apart from me you can do nothing."

In 1 Corinthians 12:12, "One Body, Many Parts," "The body is a unit, though it is made up of many parts; and though all its parts are many, they form one body. So it is with CHRIST." And in Colossians 1:18, "And he is the head of the body, the church: he is the beginning and the firstborn from among the dead. So that in everything he might have the supremacy—as well as communion with the Father and with fellow believers."

Our joy complete. John's joy in the LORD could not be complete unless his readers shared the true knowledge of the CHRIST (2 John 1:12): "I have much to write to you, but I do not want to use paper and ink. Instead, I hope to visit you and talk with you face to face, so that our joy may be complete."

From him. From CHRIST. Light and darkness. Light represents what is good, true, and holy; while darkness represents what is evil and false. In John 3:19, "This is the verdict: Light has come into the world, but men loved darkness instead of light because their deeds were evil." Walk in the darkness…in the light. Two lifestyles—one characterized by wickedness and error, the other by holiness and truth.

We. John and his readers. To have fellowship with him. To be in living, spiritual union with GOD. Walk. A metaphor with living truth (John 1:14). In the temple courts, he found men selling cattle, sheep, and doves and others sitting at tables exchanging money.

Faithful and just. Here, the phrase is virtually a single concept. It indicates that GOD'S response toward those who confess their sins will be in accordance with his nature and his gracious commitment to his people. In Psalm 143:1, "O LORD, hear my prayer, listen to my cry for mercy; in your faithfulness and righteousness come to my relief." In ZECHARIAH 8:8, "'I will bring them back to live in Jerusalem; they will be my people, and I will be faithful and righteous to them as their GOD.'" Faithful—to his promise to forgive.

In Jeremiah 31:34, "'No longer will a man teach his neighbor, or a man his brother, saying, "Know the LORD," because they will all know me from the least of them to the greatest,' declares the LORD." In Micah 7:18–20, "Who is a GOD like you, who pardons sin and forgives the transgression of the remnant of his inheritance? You do not stay angry forever but delight to show mercy. You will again have compassion on us; you will tread our sins underfoot and hurl our iniquities into the depths of the sea. You will be true to Jacob, and show mercy to Abraham, as you pledge on oath to our fathers in days long ago."

Will forgive us. Will provide the forgiveness that restores the communion with GOD that had been interrupted by sin (as requested in the LORD'S prayer, Matthew 6:12): "Forgive us our debts, as we also have forgiven our debtors."

We have not sinned. Gnostics denied that their immoral actions were sinful.

2:1—*dear children.* John, the aged apostle, often used this expression of endearment.

2:8—*true light.* Used in the NT only here and in John 1:9: "The true light that gives light to every man was coming into the world." This phrase refers to the gospel of JESUS CHRIST, who is the light of the world, and to its saving effects in the lives of believers. Read John 8:12: "When JESUS spoke again to the people, he said, 'I am the light of the world. Whoever follows me will never walk in darkness but will have the light of life.'"

2:18—*last hour*. With other NT writers, John viewed the whole period beginning with CHRIST'S first coming as the last days. They understood this to be the "last" of the days because neither former prophecy nor new revelation concerning the history of salvation indicated the coming of another era before the return of CHRIST. The word *last* in *last days*, *last times*, and *last hour* also expresses a sense of urgency and imminence. The Christian is to be alert, waiting for the return of CHRIST (see Acts 2:17; 2 Timothy 3:1; Hebrews 1:2; 1 Peter 1:20).

In Acts 2:17, "In the last days, GOD says, 'I will pour out my Spirit on all people. Your sons and daughters will prophesy, your young men will see visions, your old men will dream dreams." In 2 Timothy 3:1–3, "But mark this: There will be terrible times in the last days. People will be lovers of themselves, lovers of money, boastful, proud, abusive, disobedient to their parents, ungrateful, unholy, without love, unforgiving, slanderous, without self-control, brutal, not lovers of the good, treacherous, rash, conceited, lovers of pleasure rather than lovers of GOD—having a form of godliness but denying its power. Have nothing to do with them." In Hebrews 1:2, "But in these last days he has spoken to us by his Son, whom he appointed heir of all things, and through whom he made the universe." And in 1 Peter 1:20, "He was chosen before the creation of the world, but was revealed in these last times for your sake."

The Antichrist. Many Antichrists. John assumed his readers knew that a great enemy of GOD and his people will arise before CHRIST'S return. That person is called Antichrist. In 1 John 2:18, "Dear children, this is the last hour; and as you have heard that the antichrist is coming. Even now many antichrists have come. This is how we know it is the last hour." In "The Man of Lawlessness" in 2 Thessalonians 2:3, "Don't let anyone deceive you in any way, for that day will come until the rebellion occurs and the man of lawlessness is revealed, the man doomed to destruction. And 'the beast.'" And in Revelation 13:1–10,

> And I saw a beast coming out of the sea. He had ten horns and seven heads, with ten crowns on his horns, and on each head a blasphemous name. The beast I saw resembled a leopard, but had feet like those of a bear and a mouth like that of a lion. The dragon gave the beast his power and his throne and great authority. One of the heads of the beast seemed to have had fatal wound, but the fatal wound had been healed. The whole world was astonished and followed the beast. Men worshiped the dragon because he had given authority to the beast and they also worshiped the beast and asked, "Who is like the beast? Who can make war against him?"
>
> The beast was given a mouth to utter proud words and blasphemies and to exercise his authority for forty-two months. He opened his mouth to blaspheme GOD, and to slander his name and his dwelling place and those who live in heaven. He was given power to make war against the saints and to conquer them. And he was given authority over every tribe, people, language and nation. All inhabitants of the earth will worship the beast—all whose names have not been written in the book of life belonging to the lamb that was slain from the creation of the world.
>
> He who has ear, let him hear. If anyone is to go into captivity, into captivity he will go. If anyone is to be killed with the sword, with the sword he will be killed. This calls for patient endurance and faithfulness on the part of the saints.

But prior to him, there will be many Antichrists. These are characterized by the following: (1) They deny the incarnation and that JESUS is the divine CHRIST; (2) They deny the Father; (3) They do not have the Father; (4) They are liars and deceivers; (5) They are many; and (6) in John's day, they left the church because they had nothing in common with believers. The Antichrists referred to in John's letter were the early Gnostics. The *anti* in Antichrist means "against." In 2 Thessalonians 2:4, "He will oppose and will exalt himself over everything that is called GOD or is worshiped, so that he sets himself up in GOD'S temple, proclaiming himself to be GOD."

Anointing. The Holy Spirit. Holy One. Either JESUS CHRIST or the Father.

Do not need anyone to teach you. Since the BIBLE constantly advocates teaching Matthew 28:20: "'And teaching them to obey everything I have commanded you. And surely I am with you always, to the very end of the age.'"

In 1 Corinthians 12:28, "And in the church GOD has appointed first of all apostles, second prophets, third teachers; then workers of miracles, also those having gifts of healing, those able to help others, those with gifts of administration, and those speaking in different kinds of tongues." In Ephesians 4:11, "It was he who gave some to be apostles, some to be prophets, some to be evangelists and some to be pastors and teachers." In Colossians 3:16, "Let the word of CHRIST dwell in you richly as you teach and admonish one another with all wisdom, and as you sing psalms, hymns and spiritual songs with gratitude in your hearts to GOD." And in 2 Timothy 2:2, 24: "And the things you have heard me say in the presence of many witnesses entrust to reliable men who will also be qualified to teach others. And the LORD'S servants must not quarrel; instead, he must be kind to everyone, able to teach, not resentful."

John is not ruling out human teachers. At the time when he wrote this, however, Gnostic teachers were insisting that the teaching of the apostles was to be supplemented with the "higher knowledge" that they (the Gnostics) claimed to possess. John's response was that what the readers were taught under the Spirit's ministry through the apostles not only was adequate but was the only reliable truth.

Teaches you. The teaching ministry of the Holy Spirit (what is commonly called illumination) does not involve revelation of new truth or the explanation of all difficult passages of Scripture to our satisfaction. Rather, it is the development of the capacity to appreciate and appropriate GOD'S truth already revealed—making the BIBLE meaningful in thought and daily living.

All things. All things necessary to know for salvation and Christian living. Continue in him.

Remains in—2:24–27. "See that what you have heard from the beginning remains in you. If it does you also will remain in the Son and in the Father. As for you the anointing you received from him remains in you, and you do not need anyone to teach you. But as his anointing teaches you about all things and as that anointing is real, not counterfeit—just as it has taught you, remain in him."

Confident. In 3:21, "Dear friends, if our hearts do not condemn us, we have confidence before GOD," and in 4:17, "In this way, love is made complete among us so that we will have confidence on the day of judgement, because in this world we are like him. GOD the Father does what is right. Members of GOD'S family are marked by Holy living children of GOD." And in John 1:12, "Yet lo all who received him, to those who believe in his name, he gave the right to become children of GOD."

Hope. Not a mere wish, but unshakable confidence concerning the future. In Romans 5:2, "Through whom we have gained access by faith into this grace in which we now stand. And we rejoice in the hope of the glory of GOD."

Him. CHRIST. Purifies himself. By turning from sin. Keeps on sinning. John is not sinless perfection, but explains that the believer's life is characterized not by sin but by doing what is right. In 1 John 1:8–10, "If we claim to be without sin, we deceive ourselves and the truth is not in us. If we confess our sins, he is faithful and just and will forgive us our sins and purify us from all unrighteousness. If we claim we have not sinned, we make him out to be a liar and his word has no place in our lives." In 2:1, "My dear children, I write this to you so that you will not sin. But if anybody does sin, we have one who speaks to the Father in our defense—JESUS CHRIST, the righteous One."

Devil. In this short letter, John says much about the devil:

1. He is called "the devil" and "the evil one." In 1 John 3:12, "Do not be like Cain, who belonged to the evil one and murdered his brother. And why did he murder him? Because his own actions were evil and his brother's were righteous." In 1 John 2:13–14, "I write to you, fathers, because you have known him who is from the beginning. I write to you, young men, because you have overcome the evil one. I write to you, dear children, because you have known the Father. I write to you, fathers, because you have known him who is from the beginning. I write to you, young men, because you are strong, and the word of GOD lives in you, and you have overcome the evil one." In 1 John 5:18–19, "We know that anyone born of GOD does not continue to sin; the one who has born of GOD keeps him safe, and the evil one cannot harm him. We know that we are children of GOD, and that the whole world is under the control of the evil one."

2. He "has been sinning from the beginning," from the time he first rebelled against GOD, before the fall of Adam and Eve. In John 8:44, "You belong to your father, the devil, and you want to carry out your father's desire. He was a murderer from the beginning, not holding to the truth, for there is nontruth in him. When he lies, he speaks his native language, for he is a liar and the father of lies."

3. He is the instigator of human sin, and those who continue to sin belong to him and are his children.

4. He is in the world and has "the whole world" of unbelievers under his control.

5. But he cannot lay hold of the believer to harm him.

6. On the contrary, the Christian will overcome him, and CHRIST will destroy his work.

God's seed. The picture is of human reproduction, in which the sperm (the Greek for *seed* is *sperma*) bears the life principle and transfers the paternal characteristics, cannot go on sinning. Not a complete cessation of sin, but a life that is not characterized by sin.

Cain. In Hebrews 11:4, "By faith ABEL offered GOD a better sacrifice than Cain did. By faith he was commended as a righteous man, when GOD spoke well of his offerings. And by faith he still speaks, even though he is dead."

Hates. 1 John 2:9–10, "Anyone who claims to be in the light but hates his brother is still in the darkness. Whoever loves his brother lives in the light, and there is nothing in him to make him stumble." In James 2:14–17, "What good is it, my brothers, if a man claims to have faith but has no deeds? Can such faith save him? Suppose a brother or sister is without clothes and daily food. If one of you says to him, "Go. I wish you well: keep warm and well fed," but does nothing about his physical needs, what good is it? In the same way, faith by itself, if it is not accompanied by action, is dead."

Love of God. GOD'S kind of love, which he pours out in the believer's heart. And which in Christians to each other. Or it may speak of the believer's love for GOD. In Romans 5:5, "And hope does not disappoint us, because GOD has poured out his love into our hearts by the Holy Spirit, whom he has given us."

God is greater than out hearts. An oversensitive conscience can be quieted by the knowledge that GOD himself has declared active love to be an evidence of salvation. He knows the hearts of all—in spite of shortcomings—have been born of him. In 1 John 3:23, this command has two parts: (1) believe in CHRIST (Jn 6:29) and (2) love each other (Jn 13:34–35). The first part is developed in 4:1–6 and the second part in 4:7–12.

In John 6:29, "JESUS answered. 'The work of GOD is this: to believe in the one he has sent.'" In John 13:34–35, "'A new command I give you: Love one another. As I have loved you. So you must love one another. By this all men will know that you are my disciples, if you love one another.'"

1 John 4:1—*spirit.* A person moved by a Spirit, whether by the Holy Spirit or an evil one. Test the spirits (1 Th 5:21). Matthew 7:1

does not refer to such testing or judgment; it speaks of self-righteous moral judgment of others.

False prophets. A true prophet speaks from GOD, being "carried along" by the Holy Spirit (2 Pe 1:21). False prophets, such as the Gnostics of John's day, speak under the influence of spirits alienated from GOD. CHRIST warned against false prophets (Mt 7:15; 24:11), as did Paul (1 Ti 4:1) and Peter (2 Pe 2:1).

In 1 Thessalonians 5:21, "Test everything. Hold on the good." In Matthew 7:1, "Do not judge, or you too will be judged." In 2 Peter 1:21, "For prophecy never had its origin in the will of man, but men spoke from GOD as they were carried along by the Holy Spirit."

In Matthew 7:15 and 24:11, "Watch out for false prophets. They come to you in sheep's clothing, but inwardly they are ferocious wolves...and many false prophets will appear and deceive many people." In 1 Timothy 4:1, "The Spirit clearly say that later times some will abandon the faith and follow deceiving spirits and things taught by demons." In 2 Peter 2: 1, "But there were also false prophets among the people, just as there will be false teachers among you. They will Secretly introduce destructive heresies, even denying the sovereign LORD who bought them, bringing swift destruction on themselves."

Acknowledges. Not only knows intellectually—for demons know and shudder (Jas 2:19; Mk 1:24)—but also confesses publicly. JESUS CHRIST has come in the flesh. Read 1 John 1:1. Thus, John excludes the Gnostics, especially the Cerinthians, who taught that the divine CHRIST came upon the human JESUS at his baptism and then left him at the cross so that it was only the man JESUS who died. In James 2:19, "You believe that there is one GOD. Good! Even the demons believe that—and shudder." In Mark 1:24, "'What do you want with us, JESUS of Nazareth? Have you come to destroy us? I know who you are the Holy One of GOD!'"

1 John 4:4—*from GOD.* An abbreviated form of the expression "born of GOD" (2:29; 3:9–10).

Them. The false prophets (4:1) who were inspired by the spirit of the Antichrist (4:3).

The one who is in the world. The devil (Jn 12:31; 16:11). *World* (4:3) means the inhabited earth; but in 4:4–5, it means the community or system of those born of GOD—including the Antichrist (John1:10). In John 12:31 and 16:11, "Now is the time for judgment on this world; now the prince of this world will be driven out… And in regard to judgment, because the prince of this world now stands condemned." In John 1:10, "He was in the world, and though the world was made through him, the world did not recognize him."

Spirit of truth (1 John 5:6). Also read John 14:17 about the Spirit of truth: "'The world cannot accept him, because it neither sees him nor knows him. But you know him, for he lives with you and will be in you.'"

The word *love* in its various forms is used forty-three times in the letter and thirty-two times in this short section.

1 John 4:8—*does not know GOD.* Only those who are to some degree like him truly know him. GOD is love. In his essential nature and in all his actions, GOD is loving. John similarly affirms that GOD is spirit (Jn 4:24) and light. In 1 John 1:5, "As well as Holy, powerful, faithful, true and just." In John 4:24, "GOD is spirit, and his worshipers must worship in spirit and truth."

1 John 4:9—*one and only Son.* Read John 1:18: "No one has ever seen GOD, but GOD the One and Only, who is at the Father's side, has made him known." No one has ever seen GOD. Since our love has its source in GOD'S love, his love reaches full expression (is made complete) when we love fellow Christians. Thus, the GOD whom "no one has ever seen" is seen in those who love because GOD lives in them.

God is love (1 John 4:8). "Whoever does not love does not know GOD, because GOD is love."

Like him. Like CHRIST. The fact that we are like CHRIST in love is a sign that GOD, who is love, lives in us; therefore, we may have confidence on the day of judgment that we are saved.

No fear in love. There is no fear of GOD'S judgment because genuine love confirms salvation. In 1 John 4:19, "All love comes ultimately from GOD; genuine love is never self-generated by his creatures." 1 John 4:21, "And he has given us this command: Whoever loves GOD must also love his brother." In John 13:34, "'A new command I give you: Love one another. As I have loved you, so you must love one another.'" In 1 John 5:1. Everyone who believes that JESUS is the CHRIST is born of GOD." Faith in JESUS as the CHRIST is a sign of being born again, just as love is (4:7).

The CHRIST. John wrote at a time when members of a family were closely associated as a unit under the headship of the father. He could therefore use the family as an illustration to show that anyone who loves GOD the Father will naturally love GOD'S children.

5:3—*his commands are not burdensome.* Not because the commands themselves are light or easy to obey but, as John explains in verse 4, because of the new birth. The one born of GOD by faith is enabled by the Holy Spirit to obey.

5:4—*overcomes...has overcome.* To overcome the world is to gain victory over its sinful pattern of life, which is another way of describing obedience to GOD (v 3). Such obedience is not impossible for the believer because he has been born again and the Holy Spirit dwells within him and gives him strength. John speaks of two aspects of victory: (1)]the initial victory of turning in faith from the world to GOD ("has overcome"); and (2) the continuing day-by-day victory of Christian living ("overcomes" the world). Read 1 John 2:15.

5:6—Water symbolizes JESUS'S baptism, and blood symbolizes his death. These are mentioned because JESUS'S ministry began at his baptism and ended at his death. John is reaching to the heretics of his day (read Gnosticism, page 5). Who said that JESUS was born only a man and remained so until his baptism? At that time, they maintained the CHRIST (the Son of GOD) descended on the human JESUS, but left him before his suffering on the cross so that it was only the man JESUS who died. Throughout this letter, John has been insisting that JESUS CHRIST is GOD as well as man. Please read 1 JOHN 1:1–4; 4:2; and 5:5. He now asserts that it was this GOD—man JESUS CHRIST who came into our world—who was baptized and died. JESUS was the son of GOD not only at his baptism but also at his death. Read 1 John 2:2. "He is atoning sacrifice for our sins, and not only for ours but also for the sins of the whole world." He has to be God to be the sacrifice, because he is love. Please read 1 John 4:10. "This is love: not that we loved God, but that he loved us and sent his Son as an atoning sacrifice for our sins."

The Spirit who testifies. The Holy Spirit testifies that JESUS is the Son of GOD in two ways:

1. The Spirit descended on JESUS at his baptism. In John 1:32–34, "Then JOHN gave this testimony: 'I saw the SPIRIT come down from heaven as a dove and remain on him. I would not have known him, except that the one who sent me to baptize with water told me, "The man on whom you see the Spirit come down and remain is he who will baptize with the Holy Spirit." I have seen and I testify that this is the Son of GOD.'"

2. He continues to confirm in the hearts of believers the apostolic testimony that JESUS'S baptism and death verifies that he is CHRIST, the Son of GOD (1 John 2:27). In 1 Corinthians 12:3, "Therefore I tell you that no one who is speaking by the Spirit of GOD says, 'JESUS be cursed,' and no one can say, 'JESUS is LORD,' except by the Holy Spirit."

1 John 5:7—*three.* The OT law required "two or three witnesses" (Dt 17:6; 19:15; see 1 Ti 5:19). At the end of this verse, some older English versions added the words found in the NIV text note. But the addition is not found in any Greek manuscript or NT translation prior to the sixteenth century. In Deuteronomy 17:6 and 19:15, "On the testimony of two or three witnesses a man shall be put to death, but no one shall be put to death on the testimony of only on witness… One witness is not enough to convict a man accused of any crime or offense he may have committed. A matter must be established by the testimony of two or three witnesses." In 1 Timothy 5:19, "Do not entertain an accusation against an elder unless it is brought by two or three witnesses."

God's testimony. The Holy Spirit's testimony, mentioned in 1 John 5:6–8 and 1 John 5:11, has given us eternal life. As a present possession, read notes on John 3:15, 36: "That everyone who believes in him may have eternal life… Whoever believes in the Son has eternal life, but whoever rejects the Son will not see life, for GOD'S wrath remains on him."

1 John 5:14—*If we ask anything according to his will.* For another condition for prayer. Read 1 John 3:21–22.

In 1 John 5:16, verses 16–17 illustrate the kind of petition we can be sure GOD will answer. Read 1 John 5:14–15. *Sin that leads to death.* In the context of this letter directed against Gnostic teaching, which denied the incarnation and threw off all moral restraints, it is probable that the *sin that leads to death* refers to the Gnostics' adamant and persistent denial of the truth and to their shameless immorality. This kind of unrepentant sin leads to spiritual death. Another view is that this is sin that results in physical death. It is held that because a believer continues to sin, GOD in judgment takes his life (1 Co 11:30). In either case, "sin that does not lead to death" is of a less serious nature.

In 1 Corinthians 11:30, "That is why many among you are weak and sick, and a number of you have fallen asleep." *Have fallen asleep.* A common first-century figure of speech for death.

We know. The letter ends with three striking statements, affirming the truths that *we know* and summarizing some of the letter's major themes.

1 John 5:18—*the one who was born of GOD.* JESUS, the Son of GOD.

5:20—*him who is* true. GOD the Father. He is the true GOD. Could refer to either GOD the Father or GOD the Son.

Eternal life. The letter began with this theme (1:1–2) and now ends with it. In 1 JOHN 1:1–2, "That which was from the beginning which we have heard, which we have seen with our eyes, which we have looked at and our hands have touched—this we proclaim concerning the word of life. The life appeared: we have seen it and testify to it, and we proclaim to you the eternal life, which was with the Father and has appeared to us."

1 John 5:21—*Idols.* False gods, as opposed to the one true GOD. Read 1 John 5:20: "We know also that the Son of GOD has come and has given us understanding, so that we may know him who is true. And we are in him who is true—even in his Son JESUS CHRIST. He is the true GOD and eternal life."

April 9, 2018. The time was 9:00 a.m. Getting ready to go to work, the TV was on at the same channel, Daystar. I do not change channels. I always watch TBN, Hillsong, and Daystar at all times because I am trying to learn as much as I can about the Word of GOD to finish writing my book. After I left the false teaching of the Jehovah's Witnesses, the graceful host Joni Lamb was on, and her lovely daughter Rebeca was counting down the thirty-ninth day to her wedding. They got my attention about the name of their guest, Salam, that I watched a few nights before, but I did not get the whole story that evening. And I was praying to GOD to see that meeting they had, so I called work to let them know that I will be late; to me, GOD comes first.

I wanted to hear their guest's full story to add it to my book. Ms. Salam—Cheryl Prewitt—was telling her story. As a little girl, the milkman told her, "You pretty girl. One day, you are going to be Miss America," as what he told all the angel girls. But Cheryl took the milkman's word to heart, believing that comment was a message from GOD.

Cheryl, at the age of eleven, was in a severe car accident; her doctor prepared her to accept the fact that her severe injury will not allow her to be able to walk again. Cheryl, for six years, was going through many operations to restore her feet, her face, and other parts of her body. But she kept remembering the milkman's word that she was going to be Miss America, and she took the word of the milkman as a word of GOD.

Cheryl kept telling herself and others, "If I am going to be Miss America, that means I have to be able to walk." By faith and by trusting GOD, Cheryl walked on the runway and became Miss Mississippi, and then Miss America in 1980! Cheryl Prewitt met Harry Salam and were married in 1985; they both are Pastors, and they have their own ministry.

When we study the BIBLE and know the Word of GOD and what GOD could do with the people who has faith in him, you could walk through a burning furnace, and not even one hair from your head will burn, like what happened with the three Jews who believed in GOD and obeyed him and refused to obey the order of King Nebuchadnezzar and bow to his golden idol.

> DANIEL 3:1–30—King Nebuchadnezzar made an image of gold, ninety feet high and nine feet wide, and set it up on the plain of Dura in the province of Babylon. He then summoned the satraps, prefects, governors, advisers, treasurers, judges, magistrates and all the other provincial officials to come to the dedication of the image he had set up. So the satraps, prefects, governors, advisors, treasurers, judges, magistrates and all the other provincial officials assembled for the dedication of the image that King Nebuchadnezzar had set up, and they stood before it.
>
> Then the herald loudly proclaimed, "This is what you are commanded to do, O people, nations and men of every language: As soon as you hear the sound of the horn, flute, zither, lyre, harp pipes and all kinds of music, you must fall down and worship the image of gold that King Nebuchadnezzar has set up. Whoever does not fall down and worship will immediately be thrown into a blazing furnace." Therefore, as soon as they heard the sound of the horn, flute, zither, lyre, harp and all kinds of music, all the peoples, nations and men of every language fell down and worshiped the image of gold that King Nebuchadnezzar had set up.
>
> At this time some astrologers came forward and denounced the Jews. They said to King Nebuchadnezzar, "O King, live forever! You have issued a decree. O King, that everyone who hears the sound of the horn, flute, zither, lyre, harp, pipes and all kinds of music must fall down and worship the image of gold, and that whoever does

not fall down and worship will be thrown into a blazing furnace. But there are some Jews whom you have set over the affairs of the province of Babylon—Shadrach, Meshach and Abednego—who pay no attention to you, O King. They neither serve your gods nor worship the image of gold you have set up."

Furious with rage, Nebuchadnezzar summoned Shadrach, Meshach and Abednego. So these men were brought before the King, and Nebuchadnezzar said to them, "Is it true, Shadrach, Meshach and Abednego, that you do not serve my gods or worship the image of gold I have set up? Now when you hear the sound of the horn, flute, zither, lyre, harp, pipes and all kinds of music, if you are ready to fall down and worship the image I made, very good. But if you do not worship it, you will be thrown immediately into a blazing furnace. Then what god will be able to rescue you from my hand?"

Shadrach, Meshach and Abednego replied to the King, "O Nebuchadnezzar, we do not need to defend ourselves before you in this matter. If we are thrown into the blazing furnace, the GOD we serve is able to save us from it, and he will rescue us from your hand, O King. But even if he does not, we want you to know, O King, that we will not serve your gods or worship the image of gold you have set up."

Then Nebuchadnezzar was furious with Shadrach, Meshach and Abednego, and his attitude toward them changed. He ordered the furnace heated seven times hotter than usual and commanded some of the strongest soldiers in his army to tie up Shadrach, Meshach and Abednego and throw them into the blazing furnace. So these men, wearing their robes, trousers, turbans and other clothes, were bound and thrown into the blazing furnace. The King's command was so urgent and the furnace so hot that the flames of the fire killed the soldiers who took up Shadrach, Meshach and Abednego, and these three men, firmly tied, fell into the blazing furnace.

Then King Nebuchadnezzar leaped to his feet in amazement and asked his advisors, "Weren't there three men that we tied up and threw into the fire?"

They replied, "Certainly, O King."

He said, "Look! I see four men walking around in the fire, unbound and unharmed, and the fourth looks like a Son of the gods." Nebuchadnezzar then approached the opening of the blazing furnace and shouted, "Shadrach. Meshach and Abednego, servants of the most high GOD, come out! Come here!"

So Shadrach, Meshach and Abednego came out of the fire, and the satraps, prefects, governors, and royal advisers crowded around them. They saw that the fire had not harmed their bodies, nor was a hair of their heads singed; their robes were not scorched, and there was no smell of fire on them.

Then Nebuchadnezzar said, "Praise be to the GOD of Shadrach, Meshach and Abednego, who has sent his angel and rescued his servants! They trusted in him and defied the King's command and were willing to give up their lives rather than serve or worship any god except their own GOD. Therefore, I decree that the people of any nation or language who say anything against the GOD of Shadrach, Meshach and Abednego be cut into pieces and their houses be turned in to piles of rubble, for no other god can save in this way."

Then the king promoted Shadrach, Meshach and Abednego in the province of Babylon.

The seven classifications of government officials were to pledge full allegiance to the newly established empire as they stood before the image. The image probably represented the god Nabu, whose name is the first element in Nebuchadnezzar's name, meaning "Nabu, protect my son!" or "Nabu, protect my boundary!" *They neither serve your god nor worship the image.* They obeyed the Word of GOD above the word of the King.

In Exodus 20:3–5, "'You shall have no gods before me. You shall not make for yourself an idol in the form of anything in heaven above or on the earth beneath or in the waters below. You shall not bow down to them or worship them; for I, the LORD your GOD, am a jealous GOD, punishing the children for the sin of the fathers to the third and fourth generation of those who hate me." In Hebrews 11:34, "Quenched the fury of the flames, and escaped the edge of the sword: whose weakness was turned to strength; and who became powerful in battle and routed foreign armies." If he does not, whether GOD decided to rescue them or not, their faith is resigned to his will. In Psalm 91:9. "If you make the Most High your dwelling even the LORD, who is my refuge then no harm will befall you, no disaster will come near your tent. For he will command his angels concerning you to guard you in all your ways: they will lift you up in their hands, so that you will not strike your foot against a stone."

Son of the gods. Nebuchadnezzar was speaking as a pagan polytheist and was content to conceive of the fourth figure as a lesser heavenly being sent by all—powerful GOD of the Israelites.

The reason I am sharing Cheryl's testimony is to show what happened to me when GOD directed me to learn his Word from the Jehovah's Witnesses, and then I was redirected by GOD to leave them and expose them because of their false teaching and finish writing my book, regardless of my preacher's discouragement and intention not to ever come to that point on my own. I believe that is that group's policy. But who cares? The ALLMIGHTY is with me; GOD knew me, before I was in my mother's womb.

As you read before, Jehovah was with me throughout my life since my childhood! I also believe that GOD'S purpose was for me to expose those false Christians with their false ideology that our LORD JESUS warned us about them toward the end of age.

What Cheryl shared with the world was, she kept telling herself that GOD says she was going to be Miss America, and she believed that GOD was talking to her through the milkman; and her faith in GOD came true, and she became Miss America. She also became a pastor with her husband. If Cheryl was born into the Jehovah's Witnesses family, they would not believe that GOD was talking to her because they will take that hope from her by manipulating her that GOD will not talk to the individual—like my false preacher who, one time, told me, "Do you think that GOD has time for you?"

So we noticed that their interpretation to the Word of GOD is manipulative and false. They use the Word of GOD in vain, and that is blasphemy. But they make sure they give hope to the sinners and the wicked by telling another false Word of GOD. My false preacher told me that at the end of the world when JESUS comes to establish his kingdom, JESUS our LORD will raise the dead who believe in Him, and the wicked will stay as dust as we were created from dust. The Jehovah's Witnesses believe there is no hell and suffering forever; that way, they give comfort to the sinners and the wicked. That means they comfort themselves by just living in Satan's world and serving him. JESUS preached more about hell than he did heaven and was the greatest hellfire preacher ever.

The Jehovah's Witnesses manipulate us for their wicked agenda. In Matthew 13:49–50, "'This is how it will be at the end of age. The angels will come and separate the wicked from the righteous; and throw them into the fiery furnace, where there will be weeping and gnashing of teeth.'" In Matthew 25:41, "Then he will say to those on his left, 'Depart from me, you who are cursed into the eternal fire prepared for the evil and his angels.'" In 2 Thessalonians 2:8–9, "He will punish those who do not know GOD and do not obey the gospel of our LORD JESUS. They will be punished with everlasting destruction and shut out from the presence of the LORD and from the majesty of his power." In Revelation 20:10, "And the devil, who deceived them, was thrown into the lake of burning sulfur, where the beast and the false prophet had been thrown. They will be tormented day and night for ever and ever." And in Revelation 21:8, "But the cowardly, the unbelieving, the vile, the murderers, the sexually immoral, those who practice magic arts, the idolaters and all liars—their place will be in the fiery lake of burning sulfur. This is the second death."

My purpose in life is to serve our LORD GOD, the GOD of Abraham, Isaac, and Jacob, the loving and compassionate GOD who loves us all even when we are sinners. And when we come to him as a sinners to forgive us, GOD will not say to us, "Let me see how you will do the next six months or the next year"; GOD forgives us at that moment, and he does not remember our sins or reminds us of them, like what the false Jehovah's Witnesses do. They punish their own sons and daughters for six months or one year—and in some cases, more time—and they claim that they teach the truth about Jehovah. They are liars, and I caught them in many lies.

I, Assaf Sawaya, stand behind every testimony to Jehovah, our GOD and Savior.

At the age of forty-two, I was baptized as a born-again Christian, and after the ceremony, one of the musicians came to me shook my hand and wished me good life with JESUS and said, "Now you have to serve him and dedicate your life for JESUS"; and that hit me like a ton of brick that fell on my shoulders. I said to myself, *I am in my prime of my life. Before I commit myself to serve GOD, I should enjoy myself;* and that was the biggest mistake I made in my life. By ignoring GOD'S call for me to serve him, I paid a big price for my ignorance.

I did not come to GOD until my late sixties, and now I am a seventy-one year-old about to finish writing a book about my life story and what GOD has done in my life; and I am the happiest man I've ever been. I dance and sing every day from the pleasure I feel by studying the BIBLE and knowing what GOD has for me. It is a pleasure beyond any word I could describe that ecstasy. I could give an example; every day I can't wait to get home to study and write about the Word of GOD. The feeling I have is like when I first got married; I couldn't wait to get home to see and hug my wife. And another example is when you have a baby, and you can't wait to get home to see hug and cuddle that baby angel. It is that kind of feeling when I read, study, and write about the Word of GOD.

So if you are in the autumn of your life, don't feel it is too late to come to GOD. He will welcome you any time of your life, and you will receive the same wages as a teenager serving GOD all his life; that is how loving GOD is. Let us read what GOD says in Matthew 20:1–19:

> "For the kingdom of heaven is like a landowner
> who went out early in the morning to hire men

to work in his vineyard. He agreed to pay them a denarius for the day and sent them into his vineyard. About the third hour he went out and saw others standing in the marketplace doing nothing. He told them, 'You also go and work in my vineyard, and I will pay you whatever is right.' So they went. He went out again about the sixth hour and the ninth hour and did the same thing. About the eleventh hour he went out and found still others standing around. He asked them, 'Why have you been standing here all day long doing nothing?'

"'Because no one has hired us,' they answered

"He said to them, 'You also go and work in my vineyard.'

"When evening came, the owner of the vineyard said to his foreman, 'Call the workers and pay them their wages, beginning with the last ones hired and going on to the first.'

"The workers who were hired about the eleventh hour came and each received a denarius. So when those came who were hired first, they expected to receive more. But each one of them also received a denarius. When they received it, they began to grumble against the landowner, 'These men who were hired last worked only one hour,' they said, 'and you have made them equal to us who have borne the burden of the work and the heat of the day.'

"But he answered one of them, 'Friend, I am not being unfair to you. Take your pay and go. I want to give the man who was hired last the same as I gave you. Don't I have the right to do what I want with my own money? Or are you envious because I am generous?'

"So the last will be first, and the first will be last."

The O'Reilly Factor

I was waiting for Bill to ask the intelligent question, and he did to his guest, the nun. She was in her autumn years like myself, but when she was eighteen years old, she was the leading lady in a film with the King of Rock and Roll, Elvis. I remember when I saw that film in Lebanon; I also was eighteen years old.

She told Mr. O'Reilly she left Hollywood to answer the divine call from GOD to become a nun, and she pursued her call by going to a convent, asking the mother superior about devoting her life to serve our LORD JESUS and becoming a nun. The mother superior's advice was "You are so young, my child, and famous. Enjoy your life in Hollywood."

Six years passed, and the famous star went back to the same convent, asking the mother superior again to join them because she has been called again by GOD to serve him. This time, the mother superior knew and obeyed GOD's call for that angel who has the desire to become a star by serving GOD; some of us know when to obey GOD. Yes. GOD has time for the individual; here I am answering my former false preacher.

That lovely young famous star left the glamor of this world by the faith of GOD'S Word about his promise to us: forever lasting life with him in heaven and a million times more a glamorous life than this world. Our famous star is still in that convent, obeying GOD and serving him, and I was so lucky to watch that episode with *The O'Reilly Factor* show.

Mr. O'Reilly asked his guest the intelligent question I was waiting for: "What is evil? Is there an evil?" "Yes, there is," the guest answered. "Anybody who doesn't have a loving heart is evil!" To me, that was the magic answer from that angel who devoted her life to obey and serve our LORD GOD while she was in her prime and famous life!

I could relate to her story myself, but I did not know that time, it was my time to obey GOD until what happened to my life—when GOD showed me that he was with me all the time to be a lesson for others to learn from my mistakes and obey GOD when he calls on you and enjoy your life doing GOD'S will; and then forever lasting life in heaven or in paradise on earth when GOD establishes his kingdom forever. Amen.

A denarius. The usual daily wage. A Roman soldier also received one denarius a day.

Third hour. 9:00 a.m.

Sixth hour, ninth hour. Noon and 3:00 p.m. respectively.

Eleventh hour. 5:00 p.m.

In the "Parable of the Workers in the Vineyard," Jesus illustrated to his children the love he has for them and, no matter how long it take us, to know him and come to our LORD. He welcomes us and doesn't say to us, "What took you so long?" For the kingdom of heaven is like a landowner. The landowner in this parable represents GOD. We understand from this parable that all the workers who came to work at the vineyard were brought by the landowner at a different time, and at the end of the day, he paid them the same wages. But the ones who came early were complaining because they worked longer hours, but GOD is showing us that any time we come to him, GOD welcomes us. As I showed in my testimony, I was baptized when I was forty-two years old, but I did not serve GOD then. I waited until I was in my late sixties. I did that because of my ignorance, not by planning. How if we do that by planning? We wait until we get old and then will come to GOD because we know he is a loving GOD and will welcome us; so we could have it both ways?

Yes, GOD may do that because of his love for us, but look at what happened to me; I was baptized in my late forties, but I did not serve GOD then. I was thinking of getting the fleshly pleasure, where the pleasure is not knowing and serving GOD. As long as we think like a human and we believe that we are so smart, the smartest people on earth and their intelligence is ignorant with GOD.

So if our goal is for fleshly desire, that is temporary and short pleasure; but if we serve GOD and obey his Word, we will have all our desires satisfied and at all times, and that pleases GOD because he is our Father and GOD loves us more than we know and beyond our comprehension. Let me share my experience with you since I have been studying the Word of GOD, the BIBLE. I overcame all my sins, and that is the ultimate ecstasy; I do know now that GOD is with me, and he provides all my needs. I am in a state of pleasure at all times; I sing and dance from the time I wake up throughout the day. Even at work, my coworkers sometimes make the comment, "What are you happy about? Tell us the secret."

Yes, I'd love to share that with you and the whole world as well, and I am writing a book to share and show the globe how all of us could reach that ecstasy. I have a loving heart, and I recognize GOD'S love for me; and I obey his will, and GOD does the rest. I always had a loving heart since my childhood, but also I always saw myself in the valley; and I used to question myself, *Why? I can't reach the mountaintop?* GOD manifested himself into my heart, and I was flowing with love, my heart about to burst out of my chest. And GOD told me what to do; I obeyed, and GOD showed me the result of my obedience, and I am sharing all this with you. GOD loves you, and he wants you to know him; and when you do that, GOD has promised for you to own the world with him. GOD loves you and loves to have your love!

In 1 John 3:1, "How great is the love the Father has lavished on us that we should be called children of GOD! And that is what we are! The reason the world does not know us is that it did not know him." In John 3:16, "For GOD so loved the world that he gave his one and only Son, that whoever believes in him shall not perish but have eternal life."

I was eleven years old at the basic education class when our French teacher emphasized to the class about a French author; the trace still there. It's the story of a father disciplining his son how to behave, telling him, "From now on, with every mistake you make, you have to hammer a nail at the door, and when you do good, you will take one nail off the door."

After that disciplinary agreement, a few months passed, and the door was covered with nails. Then the father brought his son to show him the door already covered with nails and told his son, "There is no more room at the door to nail. The time has come to redeem yourself, my son, and start doing good. There is no more room to make another mistake. Now is the time to start to take the nails out one at a time." He agreed to his father's instruction.

A long period passed, and the son was making an effort to please his father; and he did by taking all the nails off the door. The father was extremely pleased with his son's effort and to show him his love, bought him gifts and brought him to the door to express his satisfaction by taking all the nails off the door completely. The father hugged his son, showing him his love and how proud and happy he was with him. "You see, my beloved son, all the nails you hammered on the door. You've also undone yourself. You have learned how to discipline yourself. You have done good, my son."

The son was sad and told his father, "Look, my father, but the trace of the nails are still showing on the door."

As a kid, I did not know the depth of that message, and probably the author did not have the message that I am interpreting now after I studied the BIBLE. Our LORD GOD does not see the trace of the nails on the door when we make mistakes and sin, but GOD tells us, "Any time you repent and come to me for forgiveness, all your sins will be forgotten, and I will not see the trace of your sins anymore." Only Satan reminds us of our sins because he is hateful and a deceiver; he comes to destroy, steal, and kill.

Our GOD is love and shows his love to us by sending his only Son, JESUS, and became a carpenter and replaced the door with a new one and took all the nails of the world into his hands and feet for JESUS our GOD loves us so much not for our merit but for who he is; and GOD is love.

The Parable of the Lost Son (Luke 15:11)

JESUS continued: "There was a man who had two sons. The younger one said to his father, 'Father, give me my share of the estate.' So he divided his property between them. Not long after that, the younger son got together all he had, set off for a distant country and there squandered his wealth in wild living. After he had spent everything, there was a severe famine in that whole country, and he began to be in need. So he went and hired himself out to a citizen of that country, who sent him to his fields to feed pigs. He longed to fill his stomach with the pods that the pigs were eating, but no one gave him anything. When he came to his senses, he said, 'How many of my father's hired men have food to spare? And here I am starving to death! I will set out and go back to my father and say to him: "Father. I have sinned against heaven and against you. I am no longer worthy to be called your son: make me like one of your hired men."' So he got up and went to his father.

"But while he was still a long way off, his father saw him and was filled with compassion for him; he ran to his son, threw his arms around him and kissed him. The son said to him, 'Father. I have sinned against heaven and against you. I am no longer worthy to be called your son.'

"But the father said to his servants, 'Quick! Bring the best robe and put it on him. Put a ring on his finger and sandals on his feet. Bring the fattened calf and kill it. Let's have a feast and celebrate. For this son of mine was dead and is alive again: he was lost and is found.' So they began to celebrate.

"Meanwhile, the older son was in the field. When he came near the house, he heard music and dancing. So he called one of the servants and asked him what was going on. 'Your brother has come,' he replied, 'and your father has killed the fattened calf because he has him back safe and sound.'

"The older brother became angry and refused to go in. So his father went out and pleaded with him. But he answered his father, 'Look! All these years I've been slaving for you and never disobeyed your orders. Yet you never gave me even a young goat so I could celebrate with my friends. But when this son of yours who has squandered your property with prostitutes comes home, you kill the fattened calf for him!'

"'My son,' the father said, 'you are always with me, and everything I have is yours. But we had to celebrate and be glad, because this brother of yours was dead and is alive again; he was lost and is found.'"

Share of the estate. The father might divide the inheritance (double to the older son; and note on Luke 12:13: "'Teacher, tell my brother to divide the inheritance with me'"). In Deuteronomy 21:17, "He must acknowledge the son of his unloved wife as the firstborn by giving him a double share of all he has." That son is the first sign of his father's strength. The right of the firstborn belongs to him. But retain the income from it until his death. But to give a younger son his portion of the inheritance upon request was highly unusual.

Got together all he had. The son's motive becomes apparent when he departs, taking with him all his possessions and leaving nothing behind to come back to. He wants to be free of parental restraint and to spend his share of the family wealth as he pleases.

Wild living. More specific in v. 30, though the older brother may have exaggerated because of his bitter attitude.

15:15—*to feed pigs.* The ultimate indignity for a Jew; not only was the work distasteful but pigs were "unclean" animals (Lev 11:7). And the pig, though it has a split hoof completely divided, does not chew the cud: it is unclean for you.

Pods. Seeds of the carob tree.

Best robe...ring...sandals...feast. Each was a sign of position and acceptance (Ge 41:42; Zec 3:4): a long robe of distinction, a signet ring of authority, sandals like a son (slave went barefoot), and the fattened calf for a special occasion.

The older brother. The forgiving love of the father symbolizes the divine mercy of GOD, and the older brother's resentment is like the attitude of the Pharisees and teachers of the law who opposed JESUS.

Even a young goat. Cheaper food than a fattened calf.

This son of yours. The older brother would not even recognize him as his brother; so bitter was his hatred.

Everything I have is yours. The father's love included both brothers. The parable might better be called the Parable of the Father's Love" rather than "The Prodigal Son." It shows a contrast between the self-centered exclusiveness of the Pharisees, who failed to understand GOD's love and the concern and joy of GOD at the repentance of sinners.

Dead and is alive. A beautiful picture of the return of the younger son, which also pictures Christian conversion (see Ro 6:13; Eph 2:1, 5). The words *lost and is found* are often used to mean "perished and saved" (19:10; Mt 10:6; 18:10–14). In Romans 6:13, "Do not offer the parts of your body to sin, as instruments of wickedness, but rather offer yourselves to GOD, as those who have been brought from death to life: and offer the parts of your body to him as instruments of righteousness." In Ephesians 2:1–5, "As for you, you were dead in your transgressions and sins, in which you used to live when you followed the ways of this world and of the ruler of the kingdom of the air, the spirit who is now at work in those who are disobedient. All of us also lived among them at one time, gratifying the craving of our sinful nature and following its desires and thoughts. Like the rest, we were by nature objects of wrath. But because of his great love for us, GOD, who is rich in mercy, made us alive with CHRIST even when we were dead in transgressions—it is by grace you have been saved." In Matthew 10:6, "Go rather to the lost sheep of Israel." And in Luke 18:10–14,

> "Two men went up to the temple to pray, one a Pharisee and the other a tax collector. The Pharisee stood up and prayed about himself: 'GOD, I thank you that I am not like other

men—robbers, evildoers, adulterers—or even like this tax collector. I fast twice a week and give a tenth of all I get.'

"But the tax collector stood at a distance. He would not even look up to heaven, but beat his breast and said, 'GOD, have mercy on me, a sinner.'

"I tell you that this man, rather than the other, went home justified before GOD. For everyone who humbles himself will be exalted."

JESUS often talks in parables to the tax collectors, the sinners, the Pharisees, and the teachers of the law. JESUS was telling them this parable: there was a man who had two sons. The younger one asked his father to give him his share of the estate! So the father divided his property between his two sons. The younger son collected all that he had and set off for a distant country; there he squandered all his inheritance in wild living. After he spent all that he had, he was longing for food. He found a job feeding pigs in a remote field. He even longed to fill his stomach with the pods that the pigs were eating, but no one gave him anything.

When he came to his senses, he said to himself, "My father's hired men have food to spare, and here I am starving to death! Let me go back to my father and tell him, 'I have sinned against heaven and against you. I am no longer worthy to be called your son. Make me like one of your hired men.' So he got up and went back to his father.

But while he was still a long way off, his father saw him and was filled with compassion for him; the father ran to his son, threw his arms around him, and kissed him. The son said to his father, "I have sinned against heaven and against you. I am no longer worthy to be called your son." That was the feeling of the son because of the wrong he did to his father.

But the son did not know how much his father loved him despite of the wrong and the heartbreak caused to his father; the father dismissed his son's wrong feeling and ignorance. The father called his servants, "Quick, bring the best robe and put it on him and put a ring on his finger and sandals on his feet. Bring the fattened calf and kill it." All of these were a sign of position and acceptance. Long robe as a sign of distinction; a ring, a sign of authority; and the fattened calf, for a special occasion. "For my son was dead and is alive again; he was lost and is found," so they began to celebrate. The father symbolizes the divine mercy of GOD, our heavenly father. He loves us regardless of our mistakes and sins, and when we come to him, GOD welcomes us with open arms and does not remember our sins.

When the older son came near the house and heard music and dancing, he called one of the servants and asked him what was going on. "Your brother has come home, and your father has killed the fattened calf because he is back safe and sound." The older brother became angry and prodigal like his young brother and refused to go inside, so the father came out and pleaded with him; but he said to his father, "Look! All these years, I've been slaving for you and never disobeyed your orders. Yet you never gave me even a young goat so I could celebrate with my friends."

The older brother resented his father's love for his younger prodigal brother; yet he is sinning toward his heavenly father by judging his brother's mistakes and not leaving the judgment to our only judge, our loving GOD. Our LORD GOD, JESUS, said in Luke 6:37, "'Do not judge, and you will not be judged. Do not condemn, and you will not be condemned. Forgive, and you will be forgiven.'"

The older son kept on reminding his father about his brother by calling him "that son of yours who has squandered your wealth on prostitutes, and you killed the fattened calf for him." The older brother is showing envy and hate for his younger brother because of his father's loving heart, in contrast with his hateful heart. The older son's resentment toward his brother is like the attitude of the Pharisees and the tax collector. JESUS gave them this parable:

> Luke 18:9—To some who were confident of their own righteousness and looked down on everybody else, JESUS told this parable: "Two men went up to pray, one a Pharisee and the other a

tax collector. The Pharisee stood up and prayed about himself: 'GOD, I thank you that I am not like other men—robbers, evildoers, adulterers—or even like this tax collector. I fast twice a week and give a tenth of all I get.'

"But the tax collector stood at a distance. He would not even look up to heaven, but beat his breast and said, 'GOD, have mercy on me, a sinner.'

"I tell you that this man, rather than the other, went home justified before GOD. For everyone who exalts himself will be humbled, and he who humbles himself will be exalted."

The older son kept on reminding his father about his brother's sin, not realizing that he is a sinner as well. JESUS is reminding all of us not to judge our brothers, or we will be judged. Also JESUS reminds us in Matthew 7:1–5: "'Do not judge, or you too will be judged. For in the same way you judge others, you will be judged, and with the measure you use, it will be measured to you. Why do you look at the speck of sawdust in your brother's eye and pay attention to the plank in your own eye? How can you say to your brother, 'Let me take the speck out of your eye,' when all the time there is a plank in your own eye? You hypocrite, first take the plank out of your own eye, and then you will see clearly to remove the speck from your brother's eye."

Now that I am saved and trying to overcome all my fleshly desires by studying the Word of GOD and listening to other different preachers to learn more about the BIBLE, I do urge you, my brothers and sisters, to study the BIBLE, the Word of GOD, because it is your responsibility toward your eternal life. And there is an eternal life after we die, and if we don't believe in that, we will be missing GOD'S divine gift for us because of our ignorance or stubbornness. I am testifying to all the world about my experience with our creator, the Almighty GOD. When I cried out my heart to him to cure my stomach ulcer, GOD cured me in that second.

Now I know GOD'S presence in my life, and I enjoy studying his Word, the BIBLE every day, by returning his love for me and sharing his Word with every person I associate with anywhere; and that is the happiest time forever. GOD want us to be his apostles and tell the world about him so we could be saved when our LORD JESUS comes back again to establish his kingdom on earth

I have to go now. I don't want to miss the CBS News at 5:30 p.m. with Walter Cronkite.

That evening, the dominant news was about the death of the greatest singer, the beloved Oum Kalthoum of EGYPT, also spelled Umm Kulthum. Walter Cronkite talked about her for over five minutes, and in closing, he said: "In the Middle East, the Jews, the Muslims, and the Christians don't agree on anything, and they have been fighting among each other for centuries. But they all agree and enjoy the voice and the music of Oum Kalthoum!"

"Indisputably the greatest Arab singer," over four million Egyptians lined the street for her funeral cortege in February 3, 1975. How true Mr. Cronkite was by his statement about the Middle East; they all fight among themselves, but they all agree on the beautiful voice and the music of one of GOD'S creation, a person called Oum Kalthoum. But they don't agree on our GOD the Creator of that talented person called Oum Kalthoum, who brings joy among enemies and ignores the joy of GOD when he sees them loving one another.

JESUS was asked in Matthew 22:36, "Teacher, which is the greatest commandment in the Law?" JESUS replied: "Love the LORD your GOD with all your heart and with all your soul and with all your mind. This is the first and greatest commandment. And the second is like it: Love your neighbor as yourself. All the Law and the Prophets hang on these two commandments."

22:37—*with all your heart...soul...mind.* With your whole being. The Hebrew of Deuteronomy 6:5 has "heart...soul... strength," but some manuscripts of the Septuagint (the Greek translation of the OT) add *mind.* JESUS combined all four terms in Mark 12:30.

In Deuteronomy 6:5–25,

> "Love the LORD your GOD with all your heart
> and with all your soul and with all your strength.
> These commandments that I give you today are
> to be upon your hearts. Impress them on your
> children. Talk about them when you sit at home
> and when you walk along the road, when you lie
> down and when you get up. Tie them as symbols
> on your hands and bind them on your foreheads.
> Write them on the doorframes of your houses
> and on your gates.
>
> "When the LORD your GOD brings
> you into the land he swore to your fathers, to
> Abraham, Isaac and Jacob, to give you—a land
> with large, flourishing cities you did not build,
> houses filled with all kinds of good things you
> did not provide, wells you did not dig, and vine-
> yards and olive groves you did not plant—then
> when you eat and are satisfied, be earful that
> you do not forget the LORD, who brought you
> out of Egypt, out of the land of slavery. Fear the
> LORD your GOD, serve him only and take your
> oaths in his name. Do not follow other gods, the
> gods of the peoples around you; for the LORD
> your GOD, who is among you, is a jealous GOD
> and his anger will burn against you, and he will
> destroy you from the face of the earth.
>
> "Do not test the LORD your GOD as you
> did at MASSAH. Be sure to keep the commands
> of the LORD your GOD and the stipulations
> and decrees he has given you. Do what is right
> and good in the LORD'S sight, so that it may go
> well with you and may go in and take over the
> good land that the LORD promised on oath to

your forefathers, thrusting out all your enemies before you, as the LORD said.

"In the future, when your son asks you, 'What is the meaning of the stipulations, decrees and laws the LORD our GOD has commanded you?' tell him: 'we were slaves of Pharaoh in Egypt, but the LORD brought us out of Egypt with a mighty hand. Before our eyes the LORD sent miraculous signs and wonders—great and terrible—upon Egypt and Pharaoh and his whole household. But he brought us out from there to bring us in and give us the land that he promised on oath to our forefathers. The LORD commanded us to obey all these decrees and to fear the LORD our GOD, so that we might always prosper and be kept alive, as is the case today. And if we are careful to obey all this law before the LORD our GOD, as he has commanded us, that will be our righteousness.'

In Mark 12:30, "'Love the LORD your GOD with all your heart and with all your soul and with all your mind and with all your strength. The second is this: Love your neighbor as yourself. There is no commandment greater than these.'"

Deuteronomy 6:5—*Love the LORD*. Love for GOD and neighbor (see Lev 19:18) is built on the love that the LORD has for his people (1 Jn 4:19–21) and on his identification with them. Such love is to be total, involving one's whole being (see notes on 4:29; Jos 22:5).

In Leviticus 19:18, "'Do not seek revenge or bear a grudge against one of your people, but love your neighbor as yourself. I am the LORD.'" In 1 John 4:19–21, "We love because he first loved us. If anyone says, 'I love GOD,' yet hates his brother, he is a liar. For anyone who does not love his brother, whom he has seen, cannot love GOD, whom he has not seen. And he has given us this command: Whoever loves GOD must also love his brother." In Deuteronomy 4:29, "But if from there you seek the LORD your GOD, you will find him if you look for him with all your heart and with all your soul." In Joshua 22:5, "But be very careful to keep the commandment and the law that Moses the servant of the LORD gave you: to love the LORD your GOD, to walk in all his ways, to obey his commands, to hold fast to him and to serve him with all your heart and all your soul."

6:6—*commandments…upon your heart.* A feature that would especially characterize the "new covenant" (see Jer 31:33: "'This is the covenant I will make with the house of Israel after that time,' declares the LORD. 'I will put my law in their minds and write it on their hearts. I will be their GOD, and they will be my people.'")

6:8–9—Many Jews take these verses literally and the phylacteries (see note on Mt 23:5) to their foreheads and left arms. They also attach mezuzot (small wooden or metal containers in which passages of Scripture are placed) to the doorframes of their houses. But a figurative interpretation is supported by 11:18–20; Exodus 13:9, 16. See note on Exodus 13:9. In Matthew 23:5, "Everything they do is done for men to see: They make their phylacteries wide and the tassels on their garments long."

11:18–20—*Fix these words of mine in your hearts and minds; tie them as symbols on your hands and bind them on your foreheads.* In Exodus 13:9, 16, "This observance will be for you like a sign on your hand and a reminder on your forehead that the law of the LORD is to be on your lips. For the LORD brought you out of Egypt with his mighty hand… And it will be like a sign on your hand and a symbol on your forehead that the LORD brought us out of Egypt with his mighty hand."

6:10–12—Because the emphasis in the Scripture is always on what GOD does and not on what his people achieves. They are never to forget what he has done for them.

6:13—Quoted in part by JESUS in response to Satan's temptation (Mt 4:10; Lk 4:8). JESUS quoted from Deuteronomy in response to the devil's other two temptations as well (see notes on v. 16; 8:3). In Matthew 4:10, "JESUS said to him, 'Away from me, Satan! For it is written: Worship the LORD your GOD, and serve him only.'" In Luke 4:8, "JESUS answered, 'It is written: "Worship the LORD your GOD and serve him only."'"

Deuteronomy 6:16—*Do not test the LORD your GOD as you did at Massah*. In 8:3, "He humbled you, causing you to hunger and then feeding you with manna, which neither you nor your fathers had known, to teach you that man does not live on bread alone but on every word that comes from the mouth of the LORD."

6:15—*jealous GOD*. See note on Exodus 20:5: "'You shall not bow down to them or worship them: for I, the LORD your GOD, am a jealous GOD, punishing the children for the sin of the fathers to the third and fourth generation of those who hate me.'"

Deuteronomy 6:16—Quoted in part by JESUS in Matthew 4:7 and Luke 4:12 (see also note on v. 13). *As you did at Massah* (9:22; 33:8; see also note on Ex 17:7). In Matthew 4:7, "JESUS answered him, 'It is also written: "Do not put the LORD your GOD to the test."'" In Luke 4:12, "JESUS answered, 'It says: "Do not put the LORD your GOD to the test."'"

Deuteronomy 6:13—*Fear the LORD your GOD, serve him only and take your oaths in his name*. In Deuteronomy 9:22, "You also made the LORD angry at Taberah, at Massah and at Kibroth Hattaavah,'" and in 33:8, "About Levi he said: 'Your Thummim and Urim belong to the man you favored. You tested him at Massah: you contended with him at the waters of Meribah.'" In Exodus 17:7, "And he called the place Massah and Meribah because the Israelites quarreled and because they tested the LORD saying, 'Is the LORD among us or not?'"

6:23—*brought us out…to bring us in*. See note on Exodus 6:7– 8: "'I will take you as my people, and I will be your GOD. Then you will know that I am the LORD your GOD, who brought you out from under the yoke of the Egyptians. And I will bring you to the land I swore with uplifted hand to give to Abraham, to Isaac and to Jacob. I will give it to you as a possession. I am the LORD.'"

6:25—*righteousness*. Probably here refers to a true, personal relationship with the covenant of the LORD that manifests itself in the daily lives of GOD's people. See Deuteronomy 24:13: "'Return his cloak to him by sunset so that he may sleep in it. Then he will thank you, and it will be regarded as a righteous act in the sight of the LORD your GOD.'"

JESUS was asked in Matthew, "What is the greatest commandment in the Law, teacher?" JESUS said: "Love your GOD with all your heart, your soul and your mind. This is the first, and the second is like it: Love your neighbor as yourself." So when you love your neighbor, you will not do anything to harm him, rob him, hate him, and hurt him in any way.

During Moses's time, it also was said in Deuteronomy to "love the LORD your GOD with all your heart, soul, and strength." GOD also said to impress these commandments on your children to have them in your heart, to tell your coworkers about them, and anyone you engage with at all times. "Write them on the doorframe of your house or on your gate."

Fear the LORD your GOD and serve him only; do not follow other gods, the gods of people, made out of their own hands, or the love of money, power, and what this world offers. Do not follow your selfish fleshly desires. Be sure to keep GOD's commands and the stipulations and decrees GOD has given you. Always do what is right and good in the eyes of GOD so that it may go well with you, and go and take the land that GOD promised on oath to your forefathers: Abraham, Isaac, and Jacob. And when your son asks you, "What is the meaning of the stipulations and decrees and the laws the LORD our GOD has commanded you?" tell him, "We were slaves in Egypt, but GOD brought us out of Egypt with a mighty hand. Our LORD GOD commanded us to obey all his decrees and fear him so that we might always be prosper and kept alive. That will be our righteousness."

But the devil has a wicked heart, and he transfers his wickedness into the heart of the first man who was born on this earth, Cain, who killed his own brother, Abel, because of jealousy. Read Genesis 4:1–12, "Cain and Abel":

> Adam lay with his wife Eve, and she became pregnant and gave birth to Cain. She said, "With the help of the LORD I have brought forth a man." Later she gave birth to his brother Abel.
>
> Now Abel kept flocks, and Cain worked the soil. In the course of time Cain brought some of

the fruits of the soil as an offering to the LORD. But Abel brought fat portions from some of the firstborn of his flock. The LORD looked with favor on Abel and his offering, but on Cain and his offering he did not look with favor. So Cain was very angry, and his face was downcast. Then the LORD said to Cain, "Why are you angry? Why is your face downcast? If you do what is right, will you not be accepted? But if you do not what is right, sin is crouching at your door: it desires to have you, but you must maser it."

Now Cain said to his brother Abel, "Let's go out to the field." And while they were in the field, Cain attacked his brother Abel and killed him.

Then the LORD said to Cain, "Where is your brother Abel?"

"I don't know," he replied. "Am I my brother's keeper?"

The LORD said, "What have you done? Listen! Your brother's blood cries out to me from the ground. Now you are under a curse and driven from the ground, which opened its mouth to receive your brother's blood from your hand. When you work the ground, it will no longer yield its crops for you. You will be a restless wanderer on the earth."

Genesis 4:1—*With the help of the LORD*. Eve acknowledged that GOD is the ultimate source of life (see Acts 17:25: "And he is not served by human hands, as if he needed anything, because he himself gives all men life and breath and everything else."

Abel. The name means "breath" or "temporary" or "meaningless" (the translation of the same Hebrew word that is in Ecc 1:2; 12:8) and hints at the shortness of Abel' s life. In Ecclesiastes 1:2 and 12:8, "'Meaningless! Meaningless!' says the Teacher. 'Utterly meaningless! Everything is meaningless… Meaningless! Meaningless!' says the Teacher. 'Everything is meaningless!'"

4:3–4. *Cain brought some of the fruits… But Abel brought fat portions from some of the firstborn of his flock.* The contrast is not between an offering of plant life and an offering of animal life but between a careless, thoughtless offering and a choice, generous offering (cf. Le 3:16). Motivation and heart attitude are all important, and GOD looked with favor on Abel and his offering because of Abel's faith (Heb 11:4). *Firstborn*—indicative of the recognition that all the productivity of the flock is from the LORD and all of it belongs to him. In Leviticus 3:16, "The priest shall burn them on the alter as food, an offering made by fire, a pleasing aroma. All the fat is the LORD's." In Hebrews 11:4, "By faith Abel offered GOD a better sacrifice than Cain did. By faith he was commanded as a righteous man, when GOD spoke well of his offerings. And by faith he still speaks, even though he is dead."

4:5—*angry.* GOD did not look with favor on Cain and his offering, and Cain (whose motivation and attitude were bad from the outset) reacted predictably.

4:7—*sin is crouching at your door.* The Hebrew word for *crouching* is the same as an ancient Babylonian word referring to an evil demon crouching at the door of a building to threaten the people inside. Sin may thus be pictured here as just such a demon, waiting to pounce on Cain; it desires to have him. He may already have been plotting his brother' s murder. It desires to have you. In Hebrew, the same expression as that for "your desire will be for [your husband]" in Genesis 3:16: "To the woman he said, 'I will greatly increase your pain in childbearing; with pain you will give birth to children. Your desire will be for your husband, and he will rule over you.'"

4:8—*attacked his brother…and killed him.* The first murder was especially monstrous because it was committed with deliberate deceit ("Let' s go out to the field") against a brother (see vv. 9–11; 1 Jn 3:12) and against a good man (Mt 23:35; Heb 11:4), a striking illustration of the awful consequences of the fall. In 1 John 3:12, "Do not be like Cain, who belonged to the evil one and murdered his brother. And why did he murder him? Because his own actions were evil and his brother's were righteous." In Matthew 23:35, "'And so upon you will come all the righteous blood that has been shed on earth, from the blood of righteous Abel to the blood of Zechariah son of BEREKIAH, whom you murdered between the temple and the altar."

Genesis 4:9—*Where...?* A rhetorical question (see 3:9). *I don't know.* An outright lie. *Am I my brother's keeper?* A statement of callous indifference—all too common through the whole course of human history. In Genesis 3:9, "But the LORD GOD called to the man, 'Where are you?'"

4:10—*Your brother's blood cries out.* Abel—in one sense, a prophet (Lk 11:50–51)—"still speaks, even though he is dead" (Heb 11:4) for his spilled blood continues to cry out to GOD against all those who do violence to their human brothers. But the blood of CHRIST "speaks a better word" (Heb 12). In Luke 11:50–51, "'Therefore this generation will be held responsible for the blood of all the prophets that has been shed since the beginning of the world, from the blood of Abel to the blood of Zechariah, who was killed between the altar and the sanctuary. Yes I tell you, this generation will be held responsible for it all." In Hebrews 12:24, "To JESUS the mediator of a new covenant, and to the sprinkled blood that speaks a better word than the blood of Abel."

4:11—*curse.* The ground had been cursed because of human sin (3:17), and now Cain himself is cursed. Formerly he had worked the ground, and it had produced life for him (vv. 2–3). Now the ground, soaked with his brother's blood, would symbolize death and would no longer yield for him its produce (v. 12]). In Genesis 3: 17, "To Adam he said, 'Because you listened to your wife and ate from the tree about which I commanded you, "You must not eat of it": Cursed is the ground because of you; through painful toil you will eat of it all the days of your life.'"

4:12—*wanderer.* Estranged from his fellowmen and finding even the ground inhospitable, he became a wanderer in the land of wandering (see NIV text note on v. 16).

I have been studying the Word of GOD, the BIBLE, to learn about him and return his love for me, and when I say *me,* I also mean *us.* GOD has shown me his love by the mistakes I have had made against him; but GOD always pulled me up from the deepest of the deep because of my loving heart, and now I am committing my life to serve him all the way until I breathe my last.

Let us read Ephesians 2:1–10:

> As for you, you were dead in your transgressions and sins, in which you used to live when you followed the ways of this world and of the ruler of the kingdom of the air, the spirit who is now at work in those who are disobedient. All of us also lived among them at one time, gratifying the cravings of our sinful nature and following its desires and thoughts. Like the rest, we were by nature objects of wrath.
>
> But because of his great love for us, GOD, who is rich in mercy, made us alive with CHRIST even when we were dead in transgressions—it is by grace you have been saved. And GOD raised us up with CHRIST and seated us with him in the heavenly realms in CHRIST JESUS, in order that in the coming ages he might show the incomparable riches of his grace, expressed in his kindness to us in CHRIST JESUS. For it is by grace you have been saved, through faith—and this not from yourselves. It is the gift of GOD—not by works, so that no one can boast. For we are GOD' S workmanship, created in CHRIST JESUS to do good works, which GOD prepared in advance for us to do.

In Ephesians 2:1–10, in chapter 1, Paul wrote of the great purposes and plans of GOD, culminating in the universal headship of CHRIST (1:10), all of which is to be for "the praise of his glory" (1:14). He now proceeds to explain the steps by which GOD will accomplish his purposes, beginning with the salvation of individuals.

2:1—A description of their past moral and spiritual condition, separated from the life of GOD.

2:2—*ruler*. Satan (cf. Jn 14:30, "prince"). *Air*. Satan is no mere earthbound enemy (cf. 6:12). *Spirit*. Satan is a created, but not a human being (cf. Job 1:6; Eze 28:15; see note on Isa 14:12–15). In John 14:30, "I will not speak with you much longer, for the prince of this world is coming. He has no hold on me." In 6:12, "For our struggle is not against flesh and blood, but against the rulers, against the authorities, against the powers of this dark world and against the spiritual forces of evil in the heavenly realms." In Job 1:6, "One day the angels came to present themselves before the LORD, and Satan also came with them." In Ezekiel 28:15, "You were blameless in your ways from the day you were created till wickedness was found in you." And in Isaiah 14:12–15, "How you have fallen from heaven, O morning star, son of the dawn! You have been cast down to the earth, you who once laid low the nations! You said in your heart, 'I will ascend to heaven; I will raise my throne above the stars of GOD; I will sit enthroned on the mount of assembly, on the utmost heights of the sacred mountain. I will ascend above the tops of the clouds; f will make myself like the Most High.' But you are brought down to the grave, to the depths of the pit."

Ephesians 2:3—*All of us*. Jews and Gentiles. *Objects of wrath* (see Ro 1:18; 2:5; 9:22). In Romans 1:18, "The wrath of GOD is being revealed from heaven against all the godlessness and wickedness of men who suppress the truth by their wickedness." In 2:5, "But because of your stubbornness and your unrepentant heart you are storing up wrath against yourselves for the day of GOD'S wrath, when his righteous judgment will be revealed." In 9:22, "What if GOD, choosing to show his wrath and make his power known, bore with great patience the objects of his wrath—prepared for destruction?"

2:5—*made us alive with CHRIST*. This truth is expanded in Romans 6:1–10:

> What shall we say, then? Shall we go on sinning
> so that grace may increase? By no means! We died

to sin; how can we live in it any longer? Or don't you know that all of us who were baptized into CHRIST JESUS were baptized into his death? We were therefore buried with him through baptism into death in order that just as CHRIST was raised from the dead through the glory of the Father, we too may live a new life.

If we have been united with him like this in his death, we will certainly also be united with him in his resurrection. For we know that our old self was crucified with him so that the body of sin might be done away with, that we should no longer be slaves to sin—7because anyone who has died has been freed from sin. Now if we died with CHRIST, we believe that we will also live with him. For we know that since CHRIST was raised from the dead, he cannot die again; death no longer has mastery over him. The death he died, he died to sin once for all; but the life he lives, he lives to GOD.

2:6—*heavenly realms.* See note on 1:3. *In CHRIST JESUS.* Through our union with CHRIST. In 1:3, "Praise be to the GOD and Father of our LORD JESUS CHRIST, who has blessed us in the heavenly realms with every spiritual blessing in CHRIST."

2:7—*coming ages.* Cf. 1:21; probably refers to the future of eternal blessing with CHRIST. *Show.* Or *exhibit* or *prove.* Far above all rule and authority and power and dominion and every title that can be given, not only in present age but also in the one to come.

2:8—A major passage for understanding GOD'S grace, i.e., his kindness, unmerited favor, and forgiving love. *You have been saved. Saved* has a wide range of meanings. It includes salvation from GOD'S wrath, which we all had incurred by our sinfulness. The tense of the verb (also in v. 5) suggests a complete action with emphasis on its present effect. *Through faith.* See Romans 3:21–31 (and notes on that passage), which establishes the necessity of faith in CHRIST as the only means of being made right with GOD. *Not from yourselves.* No human effort can contribute to our salvation; it is the gift of GOD. Verse 5 made us alive with CHRIST even when we were dead in transgressions. *It is by grace you have been saved.* In Romans 3:21–31,

> But now a righteousness from GOD, apart from law, has been made known, to which the Law and the Prophets testify. This righteousness from GOD comes through faith in JESUS CHRIST to all who believe. There is no difference, for all have sinned and fall short of the glory of GOD, and are justified freely by his grace through the redemption that came by CHRIST JESUS. GOD presented him as a sacrifice of atonement, through faith in his blood. He did this to demonstrate his justice, because in his forbearance he had left the sins committed beforehand unpunished. He did it to demonstrate his justice, at the present time, so as to be just and the one who justifies those who have faith in JESUS.
>
> Where, then, is boasting? It is excluded. On what principle? On that of observing the law? No, but on that of faith. For we maintain that a man is justified by faith apart from observing the law. Is GOD the GOD of Jews only? Is he not the GOD of Gentiles too? Yes, of Gentiles too, since there is only one GOD, who will justify the circumcised by faith and the uncircumcised through that same faith. Do we, then, nullify the law by this faith? Not at all! Rather, we uphold the law.

2:9—*not by work.* One cannot earn salvation by "observing the law" (Ro 3:20, 28). Such a legalistic approach to salvation (or sanctification) is consistently condemned in Scripture. No one can boast.

No one can take credit for his or her salvation. In Romans 3:20, 28, "Therefore no one will be declared righteous in his sight by observing the law; rather, through the law we become conscious of sin... For we maintain that a man is justified by faith apart from observing the law."

2:10—*workmanship*. The Greek for this word sometimes has the connotation of a "work of art." *Prepared in advance*. Carries forward the theme of GOD'S sovereign purpose and planning, seen in chapter 1.

We have seen that Satan's wickedness manifested in the heart of the first man was born on earth, Cain, who killed his brother, Abel. Cain killed his own brother because of jealousy. GOD looked with favor on Abel's offering; Abel has loved and had faith in GOD; but Cain also gave an offering for GOD, but he did not have the faith and love for GOD like his brother, Abel.

All offerings presented to the LORD shall be burned by the priest on the altar as food. Abel's offering was the firstborn of the animal without any blemish, and when the animal was burned by fire on the altar, its aroma was pleasing to GOD. And when the angels in heaven praise GOD and give him glory, that also is pleasing to GOD.

As I am writing about the subject, I asked GOD why Satan rebelled against GOD. GOD revealed to me Satan was jealous of GOD being praised and glorified. Satan wanted to be praised himself, and his wickedness manifested in one third of the angels in heaven; and he deceived them. The LORD says Satan rebelled against GOD because he was not satisfied in his position as the most beautiful angel that the LORD created. Evidently, because of his beauty and splendor, he chose to rebel against GOD. His sin was a self-caused action that led to his losing his position, his place, and his possession.

The word *rebel* or a form of it is used in the BIBLE ninety-eight times. When a person *rebels*, it simply means that they refuse to come under the authority of someone who is above them. So Satan rebelled. GOD does not put up with things like that, so GOD kicked Satan and his deceiving angels out of heaven. Satan hates GOD, and so he still tries to keep people from coming to his enemy, GOD.

The war was going on between Satan and GOD before Satan deceived Adam and Eve. When Satan deceived, Adam was to interrupt GOD'S plan for having a human to GOD'S image and to fill the earth with his children. Satan succeeded by deceiving Adam and Eve. The story of Adam and Eve is the story about how GOD gave us the free will to choose and discern between good and evil. GOD forbade Adam from eating the forbidden fruit, but GOD allowed Adam to make the choice to obey or to disobey GOD.

Another good example is the first son born to Adam and Eve, Cain, who killed his brother, Abel, because of his carelessness about what pleases GOD. Then the LORD said to Cain, "Why are you angry? Why is your face downcast? If you do what is right, will you not be accepted? But if you do not what is right, sin is crouching at your door." And it did. Cain said to his brother, "Let us go to the field," and there he attacked his brother, Abel, and killed him.

Cain did the same mistake his father and mother did when they allowed Satan to get into their hearts and deceived them by telling them part of the truth. That is why I pray to GOD every day to bless me with wisdom to be able to discern between what is truth and false. As you read earlier when I was studying the BIBLE with a false and deceiving teacher, my prayer saved me and stopped me from being deceived. Glory to GOD.

The message is, Don't let any man program you for their purpose, but let GOD program you to his purpose. Satan is still deceiving GOD'S children since the beginning of time, and he rules this corrupt world. But the end of time is near. As GOD'S children, we should realize by the mistakes of generations of mankind through history that when we don't listen to GOD and his commandments, we will be judged according to our sins; and when we don't wait for his instruction and obey him and decide on our own intelligence, as humans, we fail. But GOD loves us and he takes good care of us at all times; GOD is love, and GOD loves life.

This is the story of Terah's son, Abram, born in Ur in the Chaldeans. Abram married Sarai, who was barren (has no children). TERAH took his son Abram and his wife Sarai, his grandson Lot, to go to Canaan, but they settled in Haran. In Genesis 12:1–3, "The

LORD had said to Abram, 'Leave your country, your people and your father's household and go to the land I will show you. I will make you into a great nation and I will bless you; I will make your name great and you will be a blessing. I will bless those who bless you, and whoever curse you I will curse; and all peoples on earth will be blessed through you.'"

12:1—*had said*. GOD had spoken to Abram "while he was still in Mesopotamia, before he lived in Haran" (Ac 7:2). *Leave...show you*. Abram must leave the settled world of the post-Babel nations and begin a pilgrimage with GOD to a better world of GOD'S making (see 24:7). In Acts 7:2, "To this he replied: 'Brothers and fathers, listen to me! The GOD of glory appeared to our father Abraham while he was still in Mesopotamia, before he lived in Haran. "Leave your country and your people," GOD said, "and go to the land I will show you."'" In Genesis 24:7, "'The LORD, GOD of heaven, who brought me out of my father's household and my native land and who spoke to me and promised me on oath, "To your offspring I will give this land"—he will send his angel before you so that you can get a wife for my son from there.'"

My brothers and sisters, the apostle Paul said in Acts 7:2, "'The GOD of glory appeared to our father Abraham while he was still in Mesopotamia, before he lived in Haran. "Leave your country and your people," GOD said, "and go to the land I will show you."'" Our father Abraham was seventy-five years old when GOD spoke to him and said, "I will make you into a great nation and I will bless you." GOD was saying to Abram, "Your wife Sarai, the barren, I will bless her with a son through her womb and call him Isaac."

Genesis 12:2–3—GOD'S promise to Abram has a sevenfold structure: (1) "I will make you into a great nation"; (2) "I will bless you"; (3) "I will make your name great"; (4) "You will be a blessing"; (5) "I will bless those who bless you"; (6) "Whoever curses you I will curse"; and (7) "All peoples on earth will be blessed through you." GOD'S original blessing on all mankind (1:28) would be restored and fulfilled through Abram and his offspring. In various ways and degrees, these promises were reaffirmed to Abram (v. 7; 15; 5–21; 17:4–8; 18:18–19; 22:17–18), to Isaac (26:2–4), to Jacob

(28:13–15; 35:11–12; 46:3), and to Moses (Ex 3:6–8; 6:2–8). The seventh promise is quoted in Acts 3:25 with reference to Peter's Jewish listeners (see Ac 3:12)—Abram's physical descendants—and in Galatians 3:8 with reference to Paul's Gentile listeners, Abram's spiritual descendants.

Genesis 12:2–3—In Genesis 1:28, "GOD blessed them and said to them, 'Be fruitful and increase in number; fill the earth and subdue it. Rule over the fish of the sea and the birds of the air and over every living creature that moves on the ground.'" In Genesis 12:7, "The LORD appeared to Abram and said, 'To your offspring I will give this land.' So he built an altar there to the LORD, who had appeared to him."

In Genesis 1:28, GOD blessed Adam and Eve. But the enemy of GOD, Satan, deceived them; they lost their everlasting life, and we, the rest of humanity, inherited their sentence. And in Genesis 6:5, "The LORD saw how great man's wickedness on the earth had become, and that every inclination of the thoughts of his heart was only evil all the time. The LORD was grieved that he had made man on the earth, and his heart was filled with pain. So the LORD said, 'I will wipe mankind, whom I have created from the face of the earth—men and animals, and creatures that move along the ground, and birds of the air—for I am grieved that I have made them.' But Noah found favor in the eyes of the LORD."

Noah was a righteous man, blameless among the people of his time, and he walked with GOD. GOD was grieved because of the wickedness of man that he created; but GOD saw the righteousness in one man, Noah, and his family and showed him favor and told him to build an ark to save him and his family and the animals and the birds of the air because GOD was going to bring a flood on earth and perish it! Every living thing on earth perished; and a new generation came to life through Noah and his children.

The new generations were wicked as well as the first man; GOD'S enemy, Satan, got into their hearts. But a man called Abram found favor in the eyes of GOD. GOD appeared to Abram and said to him, "This land I will give to your offspring."

GENESIS 15:5—GOD took Abram outside and said, "Look up at the heavens and count the stars—if indeed you can count them." Then he said to him, "So shall your offspring be." Abram believed the LORD, and he credited it to him as righteousness. He also said to him, "I am the LORD, who brought you out of Ur of the Chaldeans to give you this land to take possession of it."

But Abram said, "O Sovereign LORD, how can I know that I will gain possession of it?"

So the LORD said to him, "Bring me a heifer, a goat and a ram, each three years old, along with a dove and a young pigeon." Abram brought all these to him, cut them in two and arranged the halves opposite each other. Then birds of prey came down on the carcasses, but Abram drove them away.

As the sun was setting, Abram fell into a deep sleep, and a thick and dreadful darkness came over him. Then the LORD said to him, "Know for certain that your descendants will be strangers in a country not their own, and they will be enslaved and mistreated four hundred years. But I will punish the nation they serve as slaves, and afterward they will come out with great possessions. You, however, will go to your fathers in peace and be buried at a good age. In the fourth generation your descendants will come back here, for the sin of the Amorites has not yet reached its full measure."

When the sun had set and darkness had fallen, a smoking firepot with a blazing torch appeared and passed between the pieces. On that day the LORD made a covenant with Abram and said, "To your descendants I give this land, from the river of Egypt to great river, the Euphrates— the land of the Kenites, Kenizzites, Kadmonites, Hittites, Perizzites, Rephaites, Amorites, Canaanites, Girgashites and Jebusites."

GENESIS 17:4–8—"As for me, this is my covenant with you: You will be the father of many nations. No longer will you be called Abram; your name will be Abraham, for I have made you a father of many nations. I will make you very fruitful: I will make nations of you, and kings will come from you. I will establish my covenant as an everlasting covenant between me and you and your descendants after you for the generations to come, to be your GOD and the GOD of your descendants after you. The whole land of Canaan, where you are now an alien. I will give as an everlasting possession to you and your descendants after you; and I will be their GOD."

18:18–19—"Abraham will surely become a great and powerful nation, and all nations on earth will be blessed through him. For I have chosen him, so that he will direct his children and his household after him to keep the way of the LORD by doing what is right and just, so that the LORD will bring about for Abraham what he has promised him."

GENESIS 17:15—GOD also said to Abraham, "As for Sarai your wife, you are no longer to call her Sarai; her name will be Sarah. I will bless her and will surely give you a son by her. I will bless her so that she will be the mother of nations; kings of people will come from her."

Abraham fell facedown; he laughed and said to himself, "Will a son be born to a man a hundred years old? Will Sarah bear a child at the age of ninety?" and Abraham said to GOD, "If only Ishmael might live under your blessing!"

Then GOD said, "Yes, but your wife Sarah will bear you a son, and you will call him Isaac. I will establish my covenant with him as an everlasting covenant for his descendants after him. And as for Ishmael, I have heard you: I will surely bless him; I will make him fruitful and will greatly increase his numbers. He will be the father of twelve rulers, and I will make him into a great nation. But my covenant I will establish with Isaac, whom Sarah will bear to you by this time next year."

GENESIS 22:17–18—"I will surely bless you and make your descendants as numerous as the stars in the sky and as the sand on the seashore. Your descendants will take possession of the cities of their enemies, and through your offspring all nations on earth will be blessed, because you have obeyed me."

GENESIS 26:2–4—The LORD appeared to Isaac and said, "Do not go down to Egypt: live in the land where I tell you to live. Stay in this land for a while, and I will be with you and will bless you. For to you and your descendants I will give all these lands and will confirm the oath I swore to your father Abraham. I will make your descendants as numerous as the stars in the sky and will give them all these lands, and through your offspring all nations on earth will be blessed,

28:13–15—[To Jacob:] There above it stood the LORD, and said: "I am the LORD, the GOD of your father Abraham and the GOD of Isaac. I will give you and your descendants the land on which you are lying. Your descendants will be like the dust of the earth, and you will spread out to the west and to the east, to the north and to the south. All peoples on earth will be blessed through you and your offspring. I am with you and will watch over you wherever you go, and I will bring you back to this land. I will not leave you until I have done what I have promised you."

GENESIS 35:11–12—[To Jacob:] And GOD said to him. "I am GOD Almighty: be fruitful and increase in number. A nation and a community of nations will come from you, and kings will come from our body. The land I gave to Abraham and Isaac I also give to you, and I will give this land to your descendants after you."

46:3—"I am GOD, the GOD of your father," he said. "Do not be afraid to go down to Egypt, for I will make you into a great nation there."

[To Moses said in] EXODUS 3:6–8—Then he said, "I am the GOD of your father, the GOD of Abraham, the GOD of Isaac and the GOD of Jacob." At this, Moses hid his face, because he was afraid to look at GOD.

The LORD said, "I have indeed seen the misery of my people in Egypt. I have heard them crying out because of their slave drivers, and I am concerned about their suffering. So I have come down to rescue them from the hand of the Egyptians and to bring them up out of that land into a good and spacious land, a land flowing with milk and honey—the home of the Canaanites, Hittites, Amorites, Perizzites, Hivites and Jebusites."

6:2–8—GOD also said to Moses, "I am the lord. I appeared to Abraham, to Isaac and to Jacob as GOD Almighty, but by my name the LORD I did not make myself known to them. I also established my covenant with them to give them the land of Canaan, where they lived as aliens. Moreover, I have heard the groaning of the Israelites, whom the Egyptians are enslaving, and I have remembered my covenant. Therefore, say to the Israelites: I am the lord, and I will bring you out from under the yoke of the Egyptians. I will free you from being slaves to them, and I will redeem you with an outstretched arm and with mighty acts of judgment. I will take you as my own people, and I will be your GOD. Then you will know that I am the LORD your GOD, who brought you out from under the yoke of the Egyptians. And I will bring you to the land I swore with uplifted hand to give to Abraham, to Isaac and to Jacob. I will give it to you as a possession. I am the LORD."

In Acts 3:25, "And you are heirs of the prophets and of the covenant GOD made with your fathers. He said to Abraham. 'Through your offspring all peoples on earth will be blessed.'" In Acts 3:12, "When Peter saw this, he said to them: 'Men of Israel, why does this surprise you? Why do you stare at us as if by our own power or godliness we had made this man walk?'" In Galatians 3:8, "The Scripture foresaw that GOD would justify the Gentiles by faith, and announced the gospel in advance to Abraham: 'All nations will be blessed through you.'"

Abraham left as GOD said to him, with his wife Sarai and nephew Lot, leaving behind his people and his father's household. Abraham was seventy-five years old when he left Haran to settle in the land of Canaan; at that time, they lived there. The LORD appeared to Abram and said, "To your offspring I will give this land." So Abram built an altar there to the LORD, who had appeared to him.

We are on this earth to love GOD, our creator, and serve him only and not to follow other gods because our GOD is a jealous GOD, and we should not do anything to arouse his anger against us. GOD will destroy us from the face of the earth. GOD is love, and he wants us to love him and to love one another, and that act of love is pleasing to GOD when GOD sees his children love and care for one another and overcome hatred, jealousy, envy, and coveting our brother's belongings of any kind and follow all of GOD'S commandments.

My brothers and sisters, let us please GOD so he will give us all our hearts' desires, unlike Adam and Eve and their first son, Cain. GOD does not need to be served by human hands because GOD gave man life, breath, and everything else. GOD loves to be praised for all that he has done for all of us, and when we praise him, we are showing our love for him; and that is the state of mind GOD wants us to be in. It pleases GOD to see us pleased.

When Cain killed his brother, Abel, GOD said to him, "Your brother's blood cries out to me from the ground." Any bloodshed by any man to any man will be held responsible against who shed the blood, and the wages for that act is GOD'S curse on him in this lifetime and the other life tormented in hell where there is burning fire forever. It is our choice; obey GOD and live forever in heaven, or disobey GOD and live forever in hell in a burning fire.

From the fall of Adam and Eve to the first murder committed by the first man born on earth, Cain, who killed his brother, Abel, to the days of Noah; man's wickedness grieves GOD. The Flood is in Genesis 6:1–21:

> When men began to increase in number on the
> earth and daughters were born to them, the sons
> of GOD saw that the daughters of men were

beautiful, and they married any of them they chose. Then the LORD said, "My Spirit will not contend with man forever, for he is mortal: his days will be a hundred and twenty years." The Nephilim were on the earth in those days—and also afterward—when the sons of GOD went to the daughters of men and had children by them. They were the heroes of old, men renown.

The LORD saw how great man's wickedness on the earth had become, and that every inclination of the thoughts or his heart was only evil all the time. The LORD was grieved that he had made man on the earth, and his heart was filled with pain. So the LORD said, "I will wipe mankind, whom I have created from the face of the earth—men and animals, and creatures that move along the ground, and birds of the air—for I am grieved that I have made them." But Noah found favor in the eyes of the LORD.

This is the account of Noah. Noah was a righteous man, blameless among the people of his time, and he walked with GOD. Noah had three sons: Shem, Ham and Japhet. Now the earth was corrupt in GOD'S sight and was full of violence. GOD saw how corrupt the earth had become, for all the people on earth had corrupted their ways.

So GOD said to Noah, "I am going to put an end to all people, for the earth is filled with violence because of them. I am surely going to destroy both them and the earth. So make yourself an ark of cypress wood: make rooms in it and coat it with pitch inside and out. This is how you are to build it: The ark is to be 450 feet long, 75 feet wide and 45 feet high. Make a roof for it and finish the ark to within 18 inches of the top.

Put a door in the side of the ark and make lower, middle and upper decks. I am going to bring floodwaters on the earth to destroy all life under the heavens, every creature that has the breath or life in it. Everything on earth will perish. But I will establish my covenant with you, and you will enter the ark—you and your sons and your wife and your sons' wives with you. You are to bring into the ark two of all living creatures, male and female, to keep them alive with you. Two of every kind of bird, of every kind of animal and every kind of creature that moves along the ground will come to you to be kept alive. You are to take every kind of food that is to be eaten and store it away as food for you and for them."

Noah did everything just as GOD commanded him.

GENESIS 7:1—The LORD then said to Noah, "Go into the ark you and your whole family, because I have found you righteous in this generation. Seven days from now I will send rain on the earth for forty days and forty nights, and I will wipe from the face of the earth every living creature I have made.' And Noah did all that the LORD commanded him.

And after the seven days the floodwaters came on the earth.

For forty days the flood kept coming on the earth, and as the waters increased they lifted the ark high above the earth. The waters rose and increased greatly on the earth, and the ark floated on the surface of the water. They rose greatly on the earth, and all the high mountains under the entire heavens were covered. The waters rose and covered the mountains to a depth of more than twenty feet. Every living thing that moved on the earth perished—birds, livestock, wild animals, all the creatures that swarm over the earth, and all mankind. Everything on dry land that had breath of life in its nostrils died. Every living thing on the face of the earth was wiped out; men and animals and the creatures that moved along the ground and the birds of the air were wiped from the earth. Only Noah was left, and those with him in the ark. The waters flooded the earth for a hundred and fifty days.

GENESIS 8:18—So Noah came out, together with his sons and his wife and his sons' wives. All the animals and all the creatures that move along the ground and all the birds—everything that moves on the earth came out of the ark, one kind after another.

Then Noah built an altar to the LORD and, taking some of all the clean animals and clean birds, he sacrificed burnt offerings on it. The LORD smelled the pleasing aroma and said in his heart: "Never again will I curse the ground because of man, even though every inclination of his heart is evil from childhood. And never again will I destroy all living creatures, as I have done. As long as the earth endures, seedtime and harvest, cold and heat, summer and winter, day and night will never cease."

GENESIS 9:6—"Whoever sheds the blood of man, by man shall his blood be shed: for in the image of GOD has GOD made man."

Sons of GOD has been interpreted to refer either to angels or to human beings. Nephilim are a people of great size and strength.

The Hebrew word means "fallen ones." In men's eyes, they were "the heroes of old men of renown"; but in GOD'S eyes, they were sinners, "fallen ones" ripe for judgment, one of the BIBLE'S most vivid descriptions of total depravity. And because man's nature remained unchanged, things were no better after the flood. You could read Genesis 8:21.

The LORD was grieved...his heart was filled with pain. Man's sin is GOD'S sorrow.

I will wipe mankind...from the face of the earth. The period of grace was coming to an end. *Animals...creatures...birds.* Though morally innocent, the animal world, as creatures under man's corrupted rule, shared in his judgment.

Noah's godly life was a powerful contrast to the wicked lives of his contemporaries. This description of Noah does not imply sinless perfection. Read Genesis 8:22.

We read the story of Noah, the only righteous man, and his family survived the flood, where GOD said, "I will wipe mankind, whom I have created, from the face of the earth." From Adam to Noah, there is about a 1,100-year span. But only Noah and his family were saved. All sinned against GOD. On all the earth, there was not another person GOD could save; all sinned. Satan was winning, but not forever. Only GOD and his servants and his obedient children will live forever, from Abel to Noah and to Abraham.

Abel was the first man that GOD looked with favor on and, by his faith, was commanded as a righteous man. Noah was the second man. GOD looked with favor on him when he was warned about things not yet seen; through faith and obedience, Noah built an ark, and GOD credited it to him as righteousness. Abraham was the third man GOD looked with favor on. Abram obeyed GOD when he said to him to leave his country, his people, and his father's household. By faith, Abram made his home in the promised land. By faith, even when he was past age and Sarah, his wife, was barren; both of them were able to become father and mother. But GOD consider him faithful and kept his promise for Abraham to have a son and his descendants to become as numerous as the stars in the sky and as countless as the sands on the seashore.

In Hebrews 11:17–20, "By faith Abraham, when GOD tested him, offered Isaac as a sacrifice. He who had received the promises was about to sacrifice his one and only son, even though GOD had said to him, 'It is through Isaac that your offspring will be reckoned.' Abraham reasoned that GOD could raise the dead, and figuratively speaking, he did receive Isaac back from death. By faith Isaac blessed Jacob and Esau in regard to their future."

When Abram was seventy-five years old, GOD said to him, "Leave your country and go to the land I will show you." Let us read how many times GOD said to Abram, "I will… I will… I will!"

- "I will make you into a great nation and I will bless you."
- "I will make your name great and you will be a blessing."
- "I will bless those who bless you, and whoever curse you I will curse."
- "I will give this land to your offspring."
- "I will give to you and your offspring forever."
- "I will make your offspring like the dust of the earth."

GENESIS 16:1–16—Now Sarai, Abram's wife, had born him no children. But she had an Egyptian maidservant named Hagar; so she said to Abram. "The LORD has kept me from having children. Go, sleep with my maidservant; perhaps I can build a family through her." Abram agreed to what Sarai said. So after Abram had been living in Canaan ten years, Sarai his wife took her Egyptian maidservant Hagar and gave her to her husband to be his wife. He slept with Hagar, and she conceived. When she knew she was pregnant, she began to despise her mistress.

Then Sarai said to Abram, "You are responsible for the wrong I am suffering. I put my servant in your arms, and now that she knows she is pregnant, she despises me. May the LORD judge between you and me."

"Your servant is in your hand," Abram said. "Do with her whatever you think best." Then Sarai mistreated Hagar; so she fled from her.

The angel of the LORD found Hagar near a spring in the desert; it was the spring that is beside the road to SHUR. And he said, "Hagar, servant of Sarai, where have you come from, and where are you going?"

"I'm running away from my mistress Sarai," she answered.

Then the angel of the LORD told her, "Go back to your mistress and submit to her." The angel added, "I will so increase your descendants that they will be too numerous to count." The angel of the LORD also said to her: "You are now with child and you will have a son. You shall name him Ishmael, for the LORD has heard of your misery. He will be a wild donkey of a man; his hand will be against everyone and everyone's hand against him, and he will live in hostility toward all his brothers."

She gave this name to the LORD who spoke to her: "You are the GOD who sees me." For she said, "I have now seen the One who sees me." That is why the well was called Beer LAHAI Roi; it is still there, between Kadesh and BERED.

So Hagar bore Abram a son, and Abram gave the name Ishmael to the son she had borne. Abram was eighty-six years old when Hagar bore him Ishmael.

16:1—*no children.* See note on 11:30. *Egyptian.* Perhaps Hagar was acquired while Abram and Sarai were in Egypt (see 12:10–20).

16:2—*The LORD has kept me from having children.* Some time had passed since the revelation of 15:4 (see 16:3), and Sarai impatiently implied that GOD was not keeping his promise. *Go, sleep with my maidservant.* An ancient custom illustrated in Old Assyrian marriage contracts, the code of Hammurapi and the Nuzi tablets (see note on 15:3–4) to ensure the birth of a male heir. Sarai would herself solve the problem of her barrenness. In Genesis 15:4, "Then the word of the LORD came to him: 'This man will not be your heir, but a son coming from your own body will be your heir,'" and in 15:3, "And Abram said, 'You have given me no children; so a servant in my household will be my heir.'"

16:3—*ten years.* Abram was eighty-five years old (see 12:4; 16:16).

16:4—*despise her mistress.* Peninnah acted similarly toward Hannah (see 1 Sa 1:6). In 1 Samuel 1:6, "And because the LORD had closed her womb, her rival kept provoking her in order to irritate her."

16:5—*May the LORD judge between you and me.* An expression of hostility or suspicion (see 31:53; see also 31:49). In Genesis 31:53, "May the GOD of Abraham and the GOD of Nahor, the GOD of their father, judge between us," and in 31:49, "It was also called Mizpah, because he said, 'May the LORD keep watch between you and me when we are away from each other.'"

16:7—*The angel of the LORD.* Since the angel of the LORD speaks for GOD in the first person (v. 10) and Hagar is said to name "the LORD who spoke to her: 'You are the GOD who sees me'" (v. 13), the angel appears to be both distinguished from the LORD (in that he is called "messenger"—the Hebrew for *angel* means "messenger") and identified with him. Similar distinction and identification can be found in 19:1, 21; 31:11, 13; Ex 3:2, 4; Jdg 2:1–5; 6:11–12, 14; 13:3, 6, 8–23; Zec 3:1–6; 12:8. Traditional Christian interpretation has held that this "angel" was a pre-incarnate manifestation of CHRIST as GOD'S messenger-servant. It may be that whoever, as the LORD'S personal messenger, represented him and bore his credentials, the angel could speak on behalf of (and so be identified with) the One who sent him (see especially 19:21; cf. 18:2, 22; 19:2). Whether this "angel" was the second person of the Trinity remains therefore uncertain. *Shur.* Located east of Egypt (see 25:18; 1 Sa 15:7).

In Genesis 19:1, 21, "The two angels arrived at Sodom in the evening, and Lot was sitting in the gateway of the city. When he saw them, he got up to meet them and bowed down with his face to the ground... He said to him, 'Very well, I will grant this request too; I will not overthrow the town you speak of.'" In 31:11, 13,

> "The angel of GOD said to me in the dream, 'Jacob.'
> I answered, 'Here I am...'
> 'I am the GOD of Bethel, where you made a vow to me. Now leave this land at once and go back to your native land.'"

In Exodus 3:2, 4, "There the angel of the LORD appeared to him in flames of fire though the bush was on fire it did not burn up... When the LORD saw that he had gone over to look, GOD called to him from within the bush, "Moses! Moses!" And Moses said, "Here I am."

In Judges 2:1–5: 6:11–12. 14; 13:3, 6, 8–23,

> The angel of the LORD went up from Gilgal to Bokim and said, "I brought you up out of Egypt and led you into the land that I swore to give to your forefathers. I said, 'I will never break my covenant with you, and you shall not make a covenant with the people of this land, but you shall break down their altars.' Yet you have disobeyed me. Why have you done this? Now therefore I tell you that I will not drive them out before you: they will be thorns in your sides and their gods will be a snare to you." When the angel of the LORD had spoken these things to all the Israelites, the people wept aloud, and they called that place BOKIM. There they offered sacrifices to the LORD.

The angel of the LORD came and sat down under the oak in OPHRAH that belonged to JOASH the ABIEZRITE, where his son GIDEON was threshing wheat in a winepress to keep it from the MIDIANITES. When the angel of the LORD appeared to GIDEON, he said, "The LORD is with you, mighty warrior."

The LORD turned to him and said, "Go in the strength you have and save Israel out of MIDIAN'S hand. Am I not sending you?"

The angel of the LORD appeared to her and said, "You are sterile and childless, but you are going to conceive and have a son.

Then the woman went to her husband and told him, "A man of GOD came to me. He looked like an angel of GOD, very awesome. I didn't ask him where he came from, and he didn't tell me his name."

Then MANOAH prayed to the LORD: "O LORD, I beg you, let the man of GOD you sent to us come again to teach us how to bring up the boy who is to be born."

GOD heard MONOAH, and the angel of GOD came again to the woman while she was out in the field: but her husband MANOAH was not with her. The woman hurried to tell her husband, "He's here! The man who appeared to me the other day!"

Manoah got up and followed his wife. When he came to the man, he said. "Are you the one who talked to my wife?"

"I am," he said.

So Manoah asked him, "When your words are fulfilled, what is to be the rule for the boy's life and work?"

The angel of the LORD answered, "Your wife must do all that I have told her. She must not eat anything that comes from the grapevine, nor drink any wine or other fermented drink nor eat anything unclean. She must do everything I have commanded her."

Manoah said to the angel of the LORD, "We would like you to stay until we prepare a young goat for you."

The angel of the LORD replied, "Even though you detain me, I will not eat any of your food. But if you prepare a burnt offering, offer it to the LORD." [Manoah did not realize that it was the angel of the LORD.]

Then Manoah inquired of the angel of the LORD, "What is your name, so that we may honor you when your word comes true?"

He replied, "Why do you ask my name? It is beyond understanding."

Then Manoah took a young goat, together with the grain offering, and sacrificed it on a rock to the LORD. And the LORD did an amazing thing while Manoah and his wife watched: As the flame blazed up from the altar toward heaven, the angel of the LORD ascended in the flame. Seeing this, Manoah and his wife fell with their faces to the ground. When the angel of the LORD did not show himself again to Manoah and his wife, Manoah realized that it was the angel of the LORD.

"We are doomed to die!" he said to his wife. "We have seen GOD!"

But his wife answered, "If the LORD had meant to kill us, he would not have accepted a burnt offering and grain offering from our hands, nor shown us all these things or now told us this."

In Zechariah 3:1–6; 12:8,

Then he showed me Joshua the high priest standing before the angel of the LORD, and Satan standing at his right side to accuse him. The LORD said to Satan, "The LORD rebuke you, Satan! The LORD, who has chosen Jerusalem, rebuke you! Is not this man a burning stick snatched from the fire?"

Now Joshua was dressed in filthy clothes as he stood before them. The angel said to those who were standing before him, "Take off his filthy clothes." Then he said to Joshua, "See, I have taken away your sin, and I will put rich garments on you." Then he said, "Put a clean turban on his head." So they put a clean turban on his head and clothed him, while the angel of the LORD stood by.

The angel of the LORD gave this charge to Joshua.

"On that day the LORD will shield those who live in Jerusalem, so that the feeblest among them will be like David, and the house of David will be like GOD, like the angel of the LORD going before them. On that day I will set out to destroy all the nations that attack Jerusalem."

In Genesis 19:21, "He said to him, 'Very well, I will grant this request too: I will not overthrow the town you speak of.'" In 18:2, 22, "Abraham looked up and saw three men standing nearby. When he saw them, he hurried from the entrance of his tent to meet them and bowed low to the ground... The men turned away and went toward Sodom, but Abraham remained standing before the LORD." And in 19:2, "'My Lords,' he said, 'please turn aside to your servant's house. You can wash your feet and spend the night and then go on your way early in the morning.'"

In 25:18, "His descendants settled in the area from Havilah to Shur, near the border of Egypt, as you go toward Asshur. And they lived in hostility toward all their brothers." In 1 Samuel 15:7, "Then Saul attacked the Amalekites all the way from Havilah to Shur, to the east of Egypt."

16:8—*I'm running away from my mistress.* Not yet knowing exactly where she was going, Hagar answered only the first of the angel' s question.

16:10—A promise reaffirmed in 17:20 and fulfilled in 25:13–16. In Genesis 17:20, "And as for Ishmael, I have heard you: I will surely bless him; I will make him fruitful and will greatly increase his numbers. He will be the father of twelve rulers, and I will make him in to a great nation." In 25:13–16, "These are the names of the sons of Ishmael, listed in the order of their birth: NEBAIOTII the firstborn of Ishmael, KEDAR, ADBEEL, MIBSAM, MISHMA, DUMAH, MASSA, HADAD, TEMA, JETUR, NAPHISH and KEDEMAH. These were the sons of Ishmael, and these are the names of the twelve rulers according to their settlements and camps."

16:11—*Ishmael.* See NIV text note and 17:20.

16:12—*wild donkey.* Away from human settlements, Ishmael would roam the desert like a wild donkey (see Job 24:5; Hos 8:9). *Hostility.* The hostility between Sarai and Hagar (see vv. 4–6) was passed on to their descendants (see 25:18).

In Job 24:5, "Like wild donkeys in the desert, the poor go about their labor of foraging food; the wasteland provides food for their children." In Hosea 8:9, "For they have gone up to Assyria like a wild donkey wandering alone. Ephraim has sold herself to lovers." In Genesis 16:46,

> He slept with Hagar and she conceived. When she knew she was pregnant, she began to despise her mistress.
>
> Then Sarai said to Abram, "You are responsible for the wrong I am suffering. I put my servant in your arms, and now that she knows she is

pregnant, she despises me. May the LORD judge between you and me."

"Your servant is in your hands," Abram said. "Do with her whatever you think best." Then Sarai mistreated Hagar; so she fled from her.

16:13—*I have now seen the One who sees me.* See NIV text note and cf. Ex 33:23. To see GOD'S face was believed to bring death (see 32:30; Ex 33:20).

16:14—*Beer LAHAI Roi.* See NIV text note. Another possible translation that fits the context equally well is "Well of the one who sees me and who lives." *Kadesh.* See note on 14:7.

In Exodus 33:23, "'Then I will remove my hand and you will see my back; but my face must not be seen.'" In Genesis 32:30, "So Jacob called the place Peniel, saying, 'It is because I saw GOD face to face, and yet my life was spared.'" In Exodus 33:20, "'But,' he said, 'you cannot see my face, for no one may see me and live.'"

In Genesis 14:7, "Then they turned back and went to ENMISHPAT [that is, Kadesh], and they conquered the whole territory of the Amalekites, as well as the Amorites who were living in IIAZAZON TAMAR."

When JESUS was asked, "Which is the greatest commandment?" JESUS said to them, "Love the LORD your GOD with all your heart and with all your soul and with all your mind. And the second is like it: love your neighbor as yourself." These two are the most important commandments. GOD has to be first in our lives, then ourselves and our families because GOD loved us first; and when GOD acknowledges our delight in him by knowing our loving heart for him, GOD will uphold us in his hand.

In Psalm 37:23–24, "If the LORD delights in a man's way, he makes his steps firm; though he stumble, he will not fall for the LORD upholds him with his hand." In Proverbs 24:16, "For though a righteous man falls seven times, he rises again, but the wicked are brought down by calamity." In Proverbs 8:17–18, "'I love those who love me, and those who seek me find me. With me are riches and honor, enduring wealth and prosperity.'"

From the first man GOD put on earth, Adam and Eve, there were three men who believed in GOD and obeyed him and kept his will: Abel, who was killed by his own brother Cain; Enoch, the son of Jared, not to be confused with Cain's son Enoch; to Noah and his family. Only those few people loved and obeyed GOD. In Genesis 6:5–8, "The LORD saw how great man's wickedness on the earth had become, and that every inclination of the thoughts of his heart was only evil ail the time. The LORD was grieved that he had made man on the earth and his heart was filled with pain. So the LORD said, 'I will wipe mankind, whom I have created, from the face of the earth—men and animals, and creatures that move along the ground, and birds of the air—for I am grieved that I have made them.' But Noah found favor in the eyes of the LORD."

GOD said to Noah to build an ark to save his family and the creatures of the earth because GOD was going to bring flood on earth to destroy every living thing on earth. It took Noah 120 years to build the ark! The BIBLE says all the people laughed at him, saying, "You are building an ark in dry land. How stupid that is, Noah." Then they realized how stupid they were when the flood came, but then it was too late to have faith in the LORD who created them. That is the message here, my beloved: to listen and obey GOD'S Word, the BIBLE, before it is too late. We must be ready by studying and preaching GOD'S Word, only the BIBLE, because GOD says so; and we saw what happened to the generation from Adam to Noah's time.

And from Noah to Abraham's time, man did not learn. GOD also destroyed Sodom and Gomorrah because of their wickedness. Again only a few men were saved, like Abraham, his wife Sarah, and his nephew Lot; you already read that story in the BIBLE and how righteous Abraham was and how obedient to GOD even when GOD told him to sacrifice his only son, Isaac.

Of course, we already read that Abraham has another son, Ishmael, who was born to him after his wife Sarah told him to sleep with her servant, Hagar, because Sarah was barren and she did not wait for GOD'S promise when GOD said to Abraham, "You will have a son by your wife Sarah." After ten years of waiting, Sarah gave up then said to her husband, Abraham, to sleep with Hagar. We, as people, do not have the passion GOD has, and we forget his promise to us. But fifteen years after Ishmael was born, Sarah got pregnant and had her only son, Isaac, at the age of ninety years, and Abraham was at the age of one hundred years!

My question here is, why did GOD not interrupt Abraham and remind him of his promise to him when GOD said to Abraham that through Sarah, "You will have a child and call him Isaac, and he will be into a great nation"? Oh no. Please forgive me, dear LORD. Who am I to judge your Word? Or any human has no right to do so. You are the only judge on earth and in heaven. Praise be to GOD.

For sure, men do not listen to GOD no matter what the penalty is. From Adam, by disobeying GOD when he made it clear to Adam not to eat from the forbidden tree, he did pay the price for his disobedience. So does the rest of humanity. Again after Noah as well, man did not learn how to listen or obey GOD'S commandments; except a few righteous men like Abraham, Isaac, Jacob, Moses, and the prophets who, through faith, conquered kingdoms, administered justice, and gained what was promised to them by GOD.

From the three young Jews—Shadrach, Meshach, and Abednego—when GOD sent his angel and rescued them from the fire because they defied the king's command and they were willing to give up their lives rather than serve or worship any god except their own GOD. GOD also sent his angel and rescued Daniel from the lion's den. And the king himself said to Daniel, "May your GOD, whom you serve continually, rescue you!" GOD rescued Daniel by sending his angel and shut the mouths of the lions. Glory be to GOD.

The greatest story of all was when GOD said to Satan, "There is no man on earth like Job!" And Job came through and defeated Satan as a man—until the coming of our LORD and Savior JESUS CHRIST, who did the ultimate sacrifice by shedding his blood to save us from death! Glory be to our LORD and Savior JESUS CHRIST.

Did we learn from the history that man experienced since Adam until now? When we don't obey GOD, there is a penalty for our sins. No, we did not learn regardless of the lesson "man has an evil heart," and we still hate each other and are becoming creative in hate by killing one another as a group or as a nation! We invent weapons and train our children to hate and kill who does not agree with our thinking, and when we are at war with one another, sometimes we call for a cease fire either to talk or to reload our weapons.

I was born in Lebanon in 1947, just few months before the birth of the state of Israel. My birthplace, Douma, is a small village in the northern part of Lebanon, not too far from where the cedar grows, the famous tree in the BIBLE. I quit school at an early age and moved down to the city where my older brothers live in Antelias, a suburb of Beirut, to learn a trade. I helped my brother in his shop for a few months and said to my brother, "I would like to learn to be a tailor," He helped me and got me a job with his own tailor and said to him, "You don't have to pay him, but my youngest brother would like to learn the trade fast"; and I became a tailor in two years. My big brother opened a tailor shop for me next to his shop. I was an instant success; in three months' time, I had ten people working for me, and I was the youngest of them all. The people who worked for me were of different religious backgrounds: Muslim Sunnah, Muslim Sheaat, Catholics, and born-again Christians.

During the war between Israel and the Arab nations in 1967, which is known as the Six-Days War, Israel won the war. The hate escalated to its peek among all of us in the Middle East; I had to step in between my staff and calm them down because of the high tension among themselves and made it clear to them that there will be no talk about politics in my place of business. And I said to them, "Look at me. I love everyone. My mother taught me to love all people because GOD created us to love one another the way GOD loves us."

After the cease fire between Israel and the Arab nations, I felt the hate everywhere. There was no room for love among people, and several different parties started to train their followers how to kill and hate their enemies and to worship their leaders instead of their GOD! The theme was to hate and kill. I saw and lived that part of time.

I decided to leave everything behind when I got my immigration visa to come to the USA. I arrived at the New York airport on February 14, 1970. The officer handed me the green card at the entryway and said to me, "Welcome to the USA." What a great feeling that was! In the same day, I arrived at my sister's house in San Diego; and I was told it was Valentine's Day, and they explained it to me, what it means. I said to them, "What a country! Here in the USA, you celebrate love, and in the Middle East, they celebrate hate."

How about this idea, my beloved? *When we cease the hate, we cease the fire.* That is the name of my ministry when I will announce it!

Let us go back and read what Mr. Walter Cronkite said about the Middle East when the greatest singer Oum Kalthoum died. "In the Middle East, the Jews, the Muslim, and the Christians don't agree on anything, and they have been fighting among each other for centuries. But they all agree and enjoy the voice and the music of Oum Kalthoum!" That comment by Mr. Cronkite on the CBS evening news was on February 1975, and nothing has changed since that time. We all still harbor hate in our heart toward one another. And we are not able to discern and recognize GOD'S love for us unless we come, all of us, and show our loving GOD that we are loving one another the way GOD want us to by respecting his promise to all his children and obeying the continued promise GOD said to his servant Abraham: "I will make Isaac into a great nation." And when Abraham asked GOD, "What about Ishmael?" GOD also said to him, "I will make Ishmael into a great nation."

Oum Kalthoum's era should be a time-changer in the life of the people in the Middle East; she was godsend, a symbol of love to all the people in the Middle East. They all loved her, but they did not recognize GOD'S hand in that blessing. They were busy hating one another. If you claim that you love GOD and serve him, you will hear GOD and do what GOD says!

Let us read John 8:47: "He who belongs to GOD hears what GOD says. The reason you do not hear is that you do not belong to GOD." So let us hear what GOD says in Deuteronomy 6:5 and Matthew 22:39. Now that we know what GOD says, love the LORD your GOD with all your heart, and love your neighbor as yourself. And when we do what GOD says, GOD will give us our heart's desires. Let us do that: love GOD and love our neighbor.

I would hope for a Muslim person to take the latest song of Oum Kalthoum with some homemade hummus and shish kebab to visit his Jewish neighbor and tell him, "Let us celebrate and enjoy Oum Kalthoum's voice and music and our foods by having one glass of wine, raising it up to our health and saying, '*Lakaiem and Sahah*,' and dancing to the Oum Kalthoum music and to the "Hava Nagila" and stop the hate. After all, we are brothers. Give a hug." They both hug each other and keep on dancing. Suddenly, the music stops. They sit with their heads down, silent in the room; and when they lift their heads up, looking at their tears dropping from their cheeks, simultaneously with a choking voice, they say, "We should have done this before our sons were killed, but now that we have found GOD'S love in our hearts, for the next generations, we hope that they will cease the hate, to cease the fire, so our sons could live." When our Loving GOD will see his children living in harmony and loving one another, he will pour his blessings on all of us. Praise be to our loving GOD.

And the same thing with a Jewish person: take the latest song of Oum Kalthoum with some homemade baba ghanouj, falafel, and kofta and go visit his Muslim neighbor and celebrate the music and the food together.

The same thing with a Christian person: go to the home of the Muslim and to the home of the Jewish and invite them over his house to enjoy the music of Oum Kalthoum and the food his wife prepared all week for that occasion. On the menu is hummus, tabbouleh, kibbeh, shish kebab, shawarma and other delicious food they all enjoy. And the center of their conversation is all about the love of GOD to everybody. When GOD sees us all loving one another, he will be with us and bless us with all that pleases us because GOD is pleased with the love we have for one another.

That act of love of these loving people will catch on throughout the Middle East and then throughout the universe. Is this wishful thinking? Yes, it is, and it could take place when man starts to think about why he is on this earth and what GOD has for man. When we take the time and study the Word of GOD, the BIBLE, we will know GOD'S plan for man from the beginning of time before Satan interrupted GOD'S plan by deceiving Adam and Eve. But GOD'S plan will take place soon. We now are at the end of an age; all the signs show that. My beloved, be ready and don' t let anybody deceive you. You are responsible for you own destiny, and there is an eternal life! If you believe that or not, the choice is yours; make the right choice!

Invite JESUS into your heart, and JESUS will show you the way; JESUS said that himself. Read John 14:6: "JESUS answered, 'I am the way and the truth and the life. No one comes to the Father except through me." *I am* (see note on 6:35). *The way*. To GOD. JESUS is not one way among many, but the way. In John 6:35, "Then JESUS declared, 'I am the bread of life. He who comes to me will never go hungry, and he who believes in me will never be thirsty.'"

Daniel

Author, Date, and Authenticity

The book mentions Daniel as its author in several passages, such as 9:2 and 10:2. That JESUS concurred is clear from his reference to "the abomination that causes desolation, spoken of through the prophet Daniel" (Mt 24:15), quoting 9:27; 12:11. The book was probably completed c. 530 BC, shortly after the capture of Babylon by Cyrus in 539.

The widely held view that the book of Daniel is largely fictional rests mainly on the modern philosophical assumption that long-range predictive prophecy is impossible. Therefore, all fulfilled predictions in Daniel, as it is claimed, had to have been composed no earlier than the Maccabean period (second-century BC] after the fulfillments had taken place. But objective evidence excludes this hypothesis on several counts.

1. To avoid fulfillment of long-range predictive prophecy in the book, the adherent of the late-date view usually maintains that the four empires of chs. 2 and 7 are Babylon, Media, Persia, and Greece. But in the mind of the author, "the Medes and Persians" (5:28) together constituted the second in the series of four kingdoms (2:36–43). Thus, it becomes clear that the four empires are the Babylonian, Medo-Persian, Greek, and Roman. See chart on "Identification of the Four Kingdoms," p. 1311.

2. The language itself argues for a date earlier than the second century. Linguistic evidence from the Dead Sea Scrolls (which furnish authentic samples of Hebrew and Aramaic writing from the second-century BC; see "The Time between the Testaments," p.1431) demonstrates that the Hebrew and Aramaic chapters of

Daniel must have been composed centuries earlier. Furthermore, as recently demonstrated, the Persian and Greek words in Daniel do not require a late date. Some of the technical terms appearing in ch. 3 were already so obsolete by the second-century BC that translators of the Septuagint (the Greek translation of the OT) translated them incorrectly.

3. Several of the fulfillments of prophecies in Daniel could not have taken place by the second century anyway, so the prophetic element cannot be dismissed. The symbolism connected with the fourth kingdom makes it unmistakably predictive of the Roman Empire (see 2:33; 7:7, 19), which did not take control of Syro-Palestine until 163 BC. Also, the prophecy concerning the coming of "the Anointed One, the ruler" 483 years after "the issuing of the decree to restore and rebuild Jerusalem" (9:25) works out to the time of JESUS's ministry.

Objective evidence, therefore, appears to exclude the late-date hypothesis and indicates that there is insufficient reason to deny Daniel's authorship.

Theme

The theological theme of the book is GOD'S sovereignty: "The Most High GOD is sovereign over the kingdoms of men" (5:21). Daniel's visions always show GOD as triumphant (7:11; 8:25; 9:27; 11:45; 12:13). The climax of his sovereignty is described in Revelation: "The kingdom of the world has become the kingdom of our LORD and of his CHRIST, and he will reign for ever" (Rev 11:15; cf. Da 2:44; 7:27).

Literary Form

The book is made up primarily of historical narrative (found mainly in chs. 1–6) and apocalyptic (revelatory) material (found mainly in chs. 7–12). The latter may be defined as symbolic, vision-ary, prophetic literature, usually composed during oppressive conditions and being chiefly eschatological in theological content.

Daniel, Chapter 1 and Chapter 2

DANIEL 1:1—In the third year of the reign of JEHOIAKIM king of Judah, Nebuchadnezzar, king of Babylon came to Jerusalem and besieged it. And the LORD delivered JEHOIAKIM king of Judah into his hand, along with some of the articles from the temple of GOD. These he carried off to put in the treasure house of his god.

Then the king ordered Ashpenaz, chief of his court officials, to bring in some of the Israelites from the royal family and the nobility—young men without any physical defect, handsome, showing aptitude for every kind of learning, well informed, quick to understand, and qualified to serve in the king's palace. He was to teach them the language and literature of the Babylonians. The king assigned them a daily amount of food and wine from the king's table. They were to be trained for three years, and after that they were to enter the king's service. Among these were some from Judah: Daniel, Hananiah, MISHAEL and Azariah. The chief official gave them new names: to Daniel, the name Belteshazzar; to Hananiah, Shadrach; to MISHAEL, Meshach; and to Azariah, Abednego.

But Daniel resolved not to defile himself with the royal food and wine, and he asked the chief official for permission not to defile himself this way. Now GOD had caused the official to show favor and sympathy to Daniel, but the official told Daniel, "I am afraid of my lord the king, who has assigned your food and drink. Why should he see you looking worse than the other young men your age? The king would then have my head because of you."

Daniel then said to the guard whom the chief official had appointed over Daniel, Hananiah, MISHAEL and Azariah, "Please test your servant for ten days: Give us nothing but vegetables to eat and water to drink. Then compare our appearance with that of the young men who eat the royal food, and treat your servants in accordance with what you see."

So he agreed to this and tested them for ten days. At the end of the ten days they looked healthier and better nourished than any of the young men who ate the royal food. So the guard took away their choice food and the wine they were to drink and gave them vegetables instead.

To these four young men GOD gave knowledge and understanding of all kinds of literature and learning. And Daniel could understand visions and dreams of all kinds.

At the end of the time set by the king to bring them in, the chief official presented them to Nebuchadnezzar. The king talked with them, and he found none equal to Daniel, Hananiah, MISHAEL and Azariah; so they entered the king's service. In every matter of wisdom and understanding about which the king questioned them, he found them ten times better than all the magicians and enchanters in his whole kingdom. And Daniel remained there until the first year of king Cyrus.

*T*hird year. According to the Babylonian system of computing the years of a king's reign, the third year of Jehoiakim would have been 605 BC since his first full year of kingship began on New Year's Day after his in 608. But according to the Judahite system, which counted the year of accession as the first year of reign, this was the fourth year of Jehoiakim (Jer 25:1; 46:2). In Jeremiah 25:1; 46:2, "The word came to Jeremiah concerning all the people of Judah in the fourth year of Jehoiakim son of Josiah king of Judah, which was the first year of Nebuchadnezzar king of Babylon... Concerning Egypt: This is the message against the army of Pharaoh NECO king of Egypt, which was defeated at Carchemish on the Euphrates river by Nebuchadnezzar king of Babylon in the fourth year of Jehoiakim son of Josiah king of Judah."

Carried off. Judah was exiled to Babylonia because she disobeyed GOD'S Word regarding covenant-keeping, the Sabbath years, and idolatry (see Lev 25:1–7; 26:27–35; 2 Ch 36:14–21). The first deportation (605 BC) included Daniel, and the second (597) included Ezekiel. A third deportation took place in 586, when the Babylonians destroyed Jerusalem and the temple.

In Leviticus 25:1–7,

> The LORD said to Moses on Mount Sinai, "Speak to the Israelites and say to them: When you enter the land I am going to give you, the land itself must observe a sabbath to the LORD. For six years sow your fields and for six years prune your vineyards and gather their crops. But in the seventh year the land is to have a sabbath of rest, a sabbath to the LORD. Do not sow your fields or prune your vineyards. Do not reap what grows of itself for harvest the grapes of your untended vines. The land is to have a year of rest.

Whatever the land yields during the sabbath year will be food for you—for yourself, your manservant and maidservant, and the hired worker and temporary resident who live among you, as well as for your livestock and the wild animals in your land. Whatever the land produces may be eaten."

In Leviticus 26:27–35,

"If in spite of this you still do not listen to me but continue to be hostile toward me then in my anger I will be hostile toward you, and I myself will punish you for your sins seven times over. You will eat the flesh of your daughters. I will destroy your high places, cut down your incense altars and pile your dead bodies on the life less forms of your idols, and I will abhor you. I will turn your cities into ruins and lay waste your sanctuaries, and I will take no delight in the pleasing aroma of your offerings. I will waste the land so that your enemies who live there will be appalled. I will scatter you among the nations and will draw out my sword and pursue you. Your land will be laid waste, and your cities will lie in ruins. Then the land will enjoy its sabbath years all the time that it lies desolate and you are in the country of your enemies; then the land will rest and enjoy its sabbaths. All the time that it lies desolate, the land will have the rest it did not have during the sabbaths you lived in it."

And in 2 Chronicles 36:14–21,

Furthermore, all the leaders of the priests and the people became more and more unfaithful, following all the detestable practices of the nations and defiling the temple of the LORD, which he had consecrated in Jerusalem. The LORD, the GOD of their fathers, sent word to them through his messengers again and again, because he had pity on his people and on his dwelling place. But they mocked GOD'S messengers, despised his words and scoffed at his prophets until the wrath of the LORD was aroused against his people and there was no remedy.

He brought up against them the king of the Babylonians who killed their young men with the sword in the sanctuary, and spared neither young man nor young woman, old man or aged. GOD handed all of them over to Nebuchadnezzar. He carried to Babylon all the articles from the temple of GOD, both large and small, and the treasures of the LORD'S temple and the treasures of the king and his officials. They set fire to GOD'S temple and broke down the wall of Jerusalem; they burned all the palaces and destroyed everything of value there. He carried into exile to Babylon the remnant, who escaped from the sword and they became servants to him and his sons until the kingdom of Persia came to power. The land enjoyed its sabbath rests: all the time of its desolation it rested, until the seventy years were completed in fulfillment of the word of the LORD spoken by Jeremiah and he did not eat or drink anything.

1:4—*language and literature of the Babylonians.* Including the classical literature in Sumerian and Akkadian cuneiform, a complicated syllabic writing system. But the language of normal communication in multiracial Babylon was Aramaic, written in an easily learned alphabetic script.

Daniel means "GOD is my judge." *Hananiah* means "The LORD shows grace." *Mishael* means "Who is what GOD is?" *Azariah* means "The LORD helps."

1:7—*Belteshazzar.* Probably means, in Babylonian, "Bel [i.e., Marduk], protect his life!" *Shadrach.* Probably means "command of Aku [Sumerian moon god]." *Meshach.* Probably means "Who is what Aku is?" *Abednego.* Means "servant of Nego or Nebo [i.e., Nabu]."

1:8—*royal food and wine.* Israelites considered food from Nebuchadnezzar's table to be contaminated because the first portion of it was offered to idols. Likewise, a portion of the wine was poured out on a pagan altar. Ceremonially unclean animals were used neither slaughtered nor prepared according to the regulations of the law.

He asked…not to defile himself. He demonstrated the courage of his convictions.

1:9—*GOD had caused the official to show favor…to Daniel.* The careers of Joseph and Daniel were similar in many respects (see Ge 39 and 41). In Genesis 39, "Now Joseph had been taken down to Egypt. Potiphar, an Egyptian who was one of Pharaoh's officials, the captain of the guard, bought him from the Ishmaelites who had taken him there." In 41, "When two full years had passed, Pharaoh had a dream by the Nile."

1:12—*test your servants.* Daniel used good judgment by offering an alternative instead of rebelling. *Ten.* Often had the symbolic significance of completeness.

1:17—With GOD' s help, Daniel and his friends mastered the Babylonian literature on astrology and divination by dreams. But in the crucial tests of interpretation and prediction (see 2:3–11; 4:7), all the pagan literature proved worthless. Only by GOD'S special revelation (2:17–28) was Daniel able to interpret correctly.

1:21—*first year of king Cyrus.* Over Babylon (539 BC). Daniel was still living in the year 537 (10:1), so he saw the exiles return to Judah from Babylonian captivity. In Daniel 10:1, "In the third year of Cyrus king of Persia, a revelation was given to Daniel (who was called Belteshazzar). Its message was true and it concerned a great war. The understanding of the message came to him in a vision."

DANIEL chapter 2:1—In the second year of his reign, Nebuchadnezzar had dreams: his mind was troubled and he could not sleep. So the king summoned the magicians, enchanters, sorcerers and the astrologers to tell him what he had dreamed. When they came in and stood before the king, he said to them. "I have had a dream that troubles me and I want to know what it means."

Then the astrologers answered the king in Aramaic, "O king, live forever! Tell your servants the dream, and we will interpret it."

The king replied to the astrologers, "This is what I have firmly decided: If you do not tell me what my dream was and interpret it, I will have you cut into pieces and your houses turned into piles of rubble. But if you tell me the dream and explain it, you will receive from me gifts and rewards and great honor. So tell me the dream and interpret it for me."

Once more they replied, "Let the king tell his servants the dream, and we will interpret it."

Then the king answered, "I am certain that you are trying to gain time, because you realize that this is what I have firmly decided: If you do not tell me the dream, there is just one penalty for you. You have conspired to tell me misleading and wicked things, hoping the situation will change. So then, tell me the dream, and I will know that you can interpret it for me."

The astrologers answered the king, "There is not a man on earth who can do what the king asks! No king, whoever great and mighty, has ever asked such a thing of any magician or enchanter or astrologers. What the king asks is too difficult. No one can reveal it to the king except the gods, and they do not live among us."

This made the king so angry and furious that he ordered the execution of all the wise men in Babylon. So the decree was issued to put the wise men to death, and men were sent to look for DANIEL and his friends to put them to death.

When Arioch, the commander of the king's guard, had gone out to put to death the wise men of Babylon, Daniel spoke to him with wisdom and tact. He asked the king's officer, "Why did the king issue such a harsh decree?" Arioch then explained the matter to Daniel. At this, Daniel went in to the king and asked for time, so that he might interpret the dream for him.

Then Daniel returned to his house and explained the matter to his friends Hananiah, MISHAEL and Azariah. He urged them to plead for mercy from the GOD of heaven concerning this mystery, so that he and his friends might not be executed with the rest of the wise men of Babylon. During the night the mystery was revealed to Daniel in a vision. Then Daniel praised the GOD of heaven and said: "Praise be to the name of GOD for ever and ever; wisdom and power are his. He changes times and seasons; he sets up kings and deposes them. He gives wisdom to the wise and knowledge to the discerning. He reveals deep and hidden things; he knows what lies in darkness, and light dwells with him. I thank and praise you, O GOD of my fathers: You have given me wisdom and power, you have made known to me what we asked of you. You have made known to us the dream of the king.

Daniel Interprets the Dream

Then Daniel went to Arioch, whom the king had appointed to execute the wise men of Babylon, and said to him, "Do not execute the wise men of Babylon. Take me to the king and I will interpret his dream for him.

Arioch took Daniel to the king at once and said, "I have found a man among the exiles from Judah who can tell the king what his dream means."

The king asked Daniel (also called Belteshazzar), "Are you able to tell me what I saw in my dream and interpret it?"

Daniel replied, "No wise man, enchanter, magician or diviner can explain to the king the mystery he has asked about. But there is a GOD in heaven who reveals mysteries. He has shown king Nebuchadnezzar what will happen in days to come. Your dream and the vision that passed through your mind as you lay on your bed are these:

"As you were lying there, O king, your mind turned to things to come, and the revealer of mysteries showed you what is going to happen. As for me, this mystery has been revealed to me not because I have greater wisdom than other living men, but so that you, O king, may know the interpretation and that you may understand what went through your mind.

"You looked, O king, and there before you stood a large statue—an enormous, dazzling statue, awesome in appearance. The head of the statue was made of pure gold, its chest and arms of silver, its belly and thighs of bronze, its legs of iron, its feet partly of iron and partly of baked clay. While you were watching, a rock was cut out, but not by human hands. It struck the statue on its feet of iron and clay and smashed them. Then the iron, the clay, the bronze, the silver and the gold were broken to pieces at the same time and became like chaff on a threshing floor in the summer. The wind swept them away without leaving a trace. But the rock that struck the statue became a huge mountain and filled the whole earth.

"This was the dream, and now we will interpret it to the king. You, O king, are the king of kings. The GOD of heaven has given you dominion and power and might and glory; in your hands he has placed mankind and the beasts of the field and the birds of the air. Wherever they live, he has made you ruler over them all. You are that head of gold. After you, another kingdom will rise, inferior to yours. Next, a third kingdom, one of bronze, will rule over the whole earth. Finally, there will be a fourth kingdom, strong as iron—for iron breaks and smashes everything—and as iron breaks things to pieces, so it will crush and break all the others. Just as you saw that the feet and toes were partly of baked clay and partly of iron, so this will be a divided kingdom; yet it will have some of the strength of iron in it, even as you saw iron mixed with clay. As the toes were partly iron and partly clay, so this kingdom will be partly strong and partly brittle. And just as you saw the iron mixed with baked clay, so the people will be mixture and will not remain united, any more than iron mixes with clay. In the time of those kings, the GOD of heaven will set up a kingdom that will never be destroyed, nor will it be left to another people. It will crush all those kingdoms and bring them to an end, but it will itself endure forever. This is the meaning of the vision or the rock cut out of a mountain, but not by human hands—a rock that broke the iron, the bronze, the clay, the silver and the gold to pieces. The great GOD has shown the king what will take place in the future. The dream is true and the interpretation is trustworthy."

The king Nebuchadnezzar fell prostrate before Daniel and paid him honor and ordered that an offering and incense be presented to him. The king said to Daniel, "Surely your GOD is the GOD of gods and the LORD of kings and a revealer of mysteries, for you were able to reveal this mystery." Then the king placed Daniel in a high position and lavished many gifts on him. He made him ruler over the entire province of Babylon and placed him in charge of all its wise men. Moreover, at Daniel's request the king appointed Shadrach, Meshach and Abednego administrators over the province of Babylon, while Daniel himself remained at the royal court.

Second year of Nebuchadnezzar. 604 BC.

2:4—*Aramaic.* Since the astrologers were of various racial backgrounds, they communicated in Aramaic, the language everyone understood. From here to the end of chapter 7, the entire narrative is in Aramaic. These six chapters deal with matters of importance to the Gentile nations of the Near East and were written in a language understandable to all. But the last five chapters (8–12) revert to Hebrew since they deal with special concerns of the people.

Daniel 2:11—*do not live among men.* Are not readily accessible. The astrologers answered to king Nebuchadnezzar that their gods do not live among men; of course, they do not live among men because they do not exist. The GOD that exist is the GOD of the four Jews, who king Nebuchadnezzar brought with ruin after he besieged Jerusalem and ordered Ashpenaz, chief of the court officials, to bring some of the Israelites from the royal family.

2:14—*Arioch*. Meaning uncertain. It is also the name of a Mesopotamian king who lived centuries earlier (Ge 14:1, 9). In Genesis 14:1–9,

At this time AMRAPHEL king of Shinar, Arioch king of ELLASAR, KEDORLAOMER king of ELAM and Tidal king of GOIIM went to war against BERA king of Sodom, BIRSHA king of Gomorrah, SHINAB king of ADMAH, SHEMEBER king or ZEBOIIM, and the king of BELA (that is, ZOAR). All these latter kings joined forces in the Valley of SIDDIM (the salt sea). 4 For twelve years they had been subject to KEDORLAOMER, but in the thirteenth year they rebelled. In the fourteenth year, KEDORLAOMER and the kings allied with him, went out and defeated the REPHAITES in ASHTEROTH KARNAIM, the ZUSITES in Ham, the EMITES in SHAYEH KIRIATHAIM and the HORITES in the hill country of SEIR, as far as ELPARAN near the desert. Then they turned back and went to ENMISHPAT (that is, KADESH), and they conquered the whole territory of the AMELEKITES, as well as the AMORITES who were living in HAZAZON TAMAR.

Then the king Of SODOM, the king of GOMORRAH, the king of ADMAH, the king of ZEBOIIM and the king of BELA [that is, ZOAR] marched out and drew up their battle lines in the Valley of SIDDIM against KEDORLAOMER king of ELAM, TIDALE king of GOIIM, AMRAPHEL king of SHINAR and ARIOCH king of ELLASAR—four kings against five.

2:18—*God of heaven*. See note on Ezra 1:2. *Mystery*. A key word in Daniel (2:19, 27–30, 47; 4:9). It also appears often in the writings (Dead Sea Scrolls) of the Qumran sect (see "The Time between the Testaments," p. 1431). The Greek equivalent is used in the NT to refer to the secret purposes of GOD that he reveals only to his chosen prophets and apostles (see note on Ro 11:25).

In Ezra 1:2, "This is what Cyrus king of Persia says: 'The LORD, the GOD of heaven, has given me all the kingdoms of the earth and he has appointed me to build a temple for him at Jerusalem in Judah.'" In Romans 11:25, "I do not want you to be ignorant of this mystery, brothers, so that you may not be conceited: Israel has experienced a hardening in part until the full number of the Gentiles has come in. And so all Israel will be saved, as it is written: 'The deliverer will come from Zion: he will turn godlessness away from Jacob. And this is my covenant with them when I take away their sins.'"

2:22—*light dwells with him.* See Psalm 36:9: "For with you is the fountain of life; in your light we see light."

2:23–43—See map no. 7b and map no. 13 at the end of the Study BIBLE. The gold head represents the Neo-Babylonian empire (v. 38; see Jer 51:7); the silver chest and arms, the Medo-Persian empire established by Cyrus in 539 BC.

Daniel 2:32–43—The date of the fall of BABYLON; the bronze belly and thighs, the Greek empire established by Alexander the Great, c. 330; the iron legs and feet, the Roman empire. The toes (v. 41) are understood by some to represent a later confederation of states occupying the territory formerly by the Roman empire. The diminishing value of the metals from gold to silver to bronze to iron represent the decreasing power and grandeur (v. 39) of the rulers of the successive empires, from the absolute despotism of Nebuchadnezzar to the democratic system of checks and balances that characterized the Roman senates and assemblies. The metals also symbolize a growing degree of thoughts and endurance, with each successive empire lasting longer than the preceding one.

broken to pieces. See Matthew 21:44: "He who falls on this stone will be broken to pieces, but he on whom it falls will be crushed."

Daniel chapter 2 verse 44. "In the time of those kings, the God of heaven will set up a kingdom that will never be destroyed, nor will it be left to another people. It will crush all those kingdoms and bring them to an end, but it will itself endure forever." Revelation 21:1, "Then I saw a new heaven and a new earth, for the first heaven and the first earth had passed away, and there was no longer any sea."

2:48—Cf. the story of Joseph (Ge 41:41–43). In Genesis 41:41–43, "So Pharao said to Joseph, 'I hereby put you in charge of the whole land of Egypt.' Then Pharao took his signet ring from his finger and put it on Joseph's finger. He dressed him in robes of fine linen. He had him ride in a chariot as his second-in-command, and men shouted before him, 'Make way!' Thus he put him in charge of the whole land of Egypt."

Nebuchadnezzar's Dream of a Tree

DANIEL chapter 4:1–37—"To the people, nations and men of every language, who live in all the world: May you prosper greatly! It is my pleasure to tell you about the miraculous signs and wonders that the Most High GOD has performed for me. How great are his signs, how mighty his wonders! High kingdom is an eternal kingdom: his dominion endures from generation to generation.

"I, Nebuchadnezzar, was at home in my palace, contented and prosperous. I had a dream that made me afraid. As I was lying in my bed, the images and visions that passed through my mind terrified me. So I commanded that all the wise men of Babylon be brought before me to interpret the dream for me. When the magicians, enchanters, astrologers and diviners came, I told them the dream but they could not interpret it for me. Finally Daniel came into my presence and I told him the dream. (He is called Belteshazzar, after the name of my god, and the spirit of the holy gods is in him.) I said, 'Belteshazzar, chief of the magicians. I know that the spirit of the holy gods is in you, and no mystery is too difficult for you. Here is my dream; interpret it for me.

"'These are the visions I saw while lying in my bed: I looked, and there before me stood a tree in the middle of the land. Its height was enormous. The tree grew large and strong and its top touched the sky: it was visible to the ends of the earth. Its leaves were beautiful, its fruit abundant, and on it was food for all. Under it the beasts of the field found shelter, and the birds of the air lived in its branches: from it every creature was fed.

"'In the visions I saw while lying in my bed, I looked, and there before me was a messenger, a holy one, coming down from heaven. He called in a loud voice: "Cut down the tree and trim off its branches: strip off its leaves and scatter its fruit. Let the animals flee from under it and the birds from its branches. But let the stump and its roots, bound with iron and bronze, remain in the ground, in the grass of the field.

"'"Let him be drenched with the dew of heaven, and let him live with the animals among the plants of the earth. Let his mind be changed from that of a man and let him be given the mind of an animal, till seven times pass by for him. The decision is announced by messengers, the holy ones declare the verdict, so that the living may know that the Most High is sovereign over the kingdom of men and gives them to anyone he wishes and sets over them the lowliest of men."

"'This is the dream that I, King Nebuchadnezzar, had. Now, Belteshazzar, tell me what it means, for none of the wise men in my kingdom can interpret it for me. But you can, because the spirit of the holy gods is in you.'"

Then Daniel (also called Belteshazzar) was greatly perplexed for a time, and his thoughts terrified him. So the king said, "Belteshazzar, so do not let the dream or its meaning alarm you,"

Belteshazzar answered, "My lord, if only the dream applied to your enemies and its meaning to your adversaries! The tree you saw, which grew large and strong with its top touching the sky, visible to the whole earth, with beautiful leaves and abundant fruit, providing food for all, giving shelter to the beast of the field, and having nesting places in its branches for the birds of the air.

"You, O king, are that tree! You have become great and strong; your greatness has grown until it reaches the sky, and your dominion extends to distant parts of the earth. You, O king, saw a messenger, a holy one, coming down from heaven and saying, 'Cut down the tree and destroy it, but leave the stump, bound with iron and bronze, in the grass of the field, while its roots remain in the ground. Let him be drenched with the dew of heaven; let him live like the wild animals, until seven times pass by for him.'

"This is the interpretation, O king, and this is the decree the Most High has issued my lord the king: You will be driven away from people and will live with the wild animals; you will eat grass like cattle and be drenched with the dew of heaven. Seven times will pass by for you until acknowledge that the Most High is sovereign over the kingdoms of men and gives them to anyone he wishes. The command to leave the stump of the tree with its roots means that your kingdom will be restored to you when you acknowledge that heaven rules. Therefore, O king be pleased to accept my advice: Renounce your sins by doing what is right, and your wickedness by being kind to the oppressed. It may be that then your prosperity will continue."

The Dream Is Fulfilled

All this happened to king Nebuchadnezzar. Twelve months later, as the king was walking on the roof of the royal palace of Babylon, he said, "Is not this the great Babylon I have built as the royal residence, by my mighty power and for the glory of my majesty?"

The words were still on his lips when a voice came from heaven, "This is what is decreed for you, king Nebuchadnezzar: Your royal authority has been taken from you. You will be driven away from the people and will live with the wild animals; you will eat grass like cattle. Seven times will pass by for you until you acknowledge that the Most High is sovereign over the kingdoms of men and gives them to anyone he wishes."

Immediately what had been said about Nebuchadnezzar was fulfilled. He was driven away from people and ate grass like cattle. His body was drenched with the dew of heaven until his hair grew like the feathers of an eagle and his nails like claws of a bird.

"At the end of that time, I, Nebuchadnezzar, raised my eyes toward heaven, and my sanity restored. Then I praised the Most High; I honored and glorified him who lives forever. His dominion is an eternal dominion: his kingdom endures from generation to generation. All the peoples of the earth are regarded as nothing. He does as he pleases with the powers of heaven and the peoples of the earth. No one can hold back his hand or say to him: 'What have you done?'

"At the same time that my sanity was restored, my honor and splendor were returned to me for the glory of my kingdom. My advisers and nobles sought me out, and I was restored to my throne and became even greater than before.

"Now I, Nebuchadnezzar, praise and exalt and glorify the King of heaven, because everything he does is right and all his ways are just. And those who walk in pride he is able to humble."

Daniel 4:1–3—Nebuchadnezzar reached this conclusion after the experiences of vv. 4–37. The language of his confession may reflect Daniel's influence.

4:11—*grew large and strong.* In one of Nebuchadnezzar's building inscriptions, Babylon is compared to a spreading tree (4:22). *Its top touched the sky.* A phrase often used of Mesopotamian temple or towers (see also note on Ge 11:4). In Genesis 11:4, "Then they said, 'Come, let us build ourselves a city, with a tower that reaches to the heavens, so that we may make a name for ourselves and not be scattered over the face of the whole earth.'"

4:15—*let the stump Remain.* Implies that the tree will be revived later (see v. 26).

4:17—*messengers.* The agents of GOD, who are the ultimate source (see v. 24)

4:19—*Daniel was greatly perplexed.* Possibly over how to state the interpretation in an appropriate way.

4:25—*acknowledge that the Most High is sovereign.* He learned the lesson (compare v. 4:30 with v. 4:37).

4:26—*Heaven.* A Jewish title for GOD, later reflected in the NT expression "kingdom of heaven" (compare Mt 5:3 with Lk 6:20). In Matthew 5:3, "'Blessed are the poor in spirit, for theirs is the kingdom of heaven.'" In Luke 6:20, "'Blessed are you who are poor, for yours is the kingdom of GOD.'" All this happened but only because Nebuchadnezzar did not follow Daniel's advice.

4:33—*what had been said...was fulfilled.* See Proverbs 16:18. *Driven away.* Possibly into the palace gardens. His counselors, perhaps led by Daniel (see 2:48–49), could have administered the kingdom efficiently. In Proverbs 16:18, "Pride goes before destruction, a haughty spirit before a fall."

4:36—See Job 42:10, 12.

4:37—*those who walk in pride he is able to humble* (see Pr 3:34: Jas 4:10: 1 Pe 5:5–6). In Proverbs 3:34, "He mocks proud mockers. But gives grace to the humble." In James 4:10, "Humble yourselves before the LORD, and he will lift you up." In 1 Peter 5:5–6, "Young men, in the same way be submissive to those who are older. All of you, clothe yourselves with humility toward one another because GOD opposes the proud but gives grace to the humble. Humble yourselves, therefore, under GOD'S mighty hand, that he may lift you up in due time."

> DANIEL 5:1–31—King Belshazzar gave a great banquet for a thousand of his nobles and drank wine with them. While Belshazzar was drinking his wine, he gave orders to bring in the gold and silver goblets that Nebuchadnezzar his father had taken from the temple in Jerusalem, so that the king and his nobles, his wives and his concubines might drink from them. So they brought in the gold goblets that had been taken from the temple of GOD in Jerusalem, and the king and his nobles, his wives and his concubines drank from them. As they drank the wine, they praised the gods of gold and silver, of bronze, iron, wood and stone.
>
> Suddenly the fingers of a human hand appeared and wrote on the plaster of the wall, near the lampstand in the royal palace. The king watched the hand as it wrote. His face turned pale

and he was so frightened that his knees knocked together and his legs gave away. The king called out for the enchanters, astrologers and diviners to be brought and said to these wise men of Babylon, "Whoever reads this writing and tells me what it means will be clothed in purple and have a gold chain placed around his neck, and will be made the third highest ruler in the kingdom." Then all the king's wise men came in, but they could not read the writing or tell the king what it meant. So king Belshazzar became even more terrified and his face grew more pale. His nobles were baffled.

The queen, hearing the voices of the king and his nobles, came into the banquet hall. "O king, live forever!" she said. "Don' t be alarmed! Don't look so pale! There is a man in your kingdom who has the spirit of the holy gods in him. In the time of your father he was found to have insight and intelligence and wisdom like that of the gods. King Nebuchadnezzar your father—your father the king, I say—appointed him chief of the magicians, enchanters, astrologers and the diviners. This man Daniel, whom the king called Belteshazzar, was found to have a keen mind and knowledge and understanding, and also the ability to interpret dreams, explain riddles and solve difficult problems. Call for Daniel, and he will tell you what the writing means."

So Daniel was brought before the king, and the king said to him, "Are you Daniel, one of the exiles my father the king brought from Judah? I have heard that the spirit of the gods is in you and you have insight, intelligence and outstanding wisdom. The wise men and enchanters were brought before me to read this writing and tell me what it means, but they could not explain it.

Now I have heard that you are able to give interpretations and to solve difficult problems. If you can read this writing and tell me what it means, you will be clothed in purple and have a gold chain placed around your neck, and you will be made the third highest ruler in the kingdom."

Then Daniel answered the king, "You may keep your gifts for yourself and give your rewards to someone else. Nevertheless, I will read the writing for the king and tell him what it means.

"O king, the Most high GOD gave your father Nebuchadnezzar sovereignty and greatness and glory and splendor. Because of the high position he gave him, all the peoples and nations and men of every language dreaded and feared him. Those the king wanted to put to death, he put to death; those he wanted to spare, he spared: those he wanted to promote, he promoted: and those he wanted to humble, he humbled. But when his heart became arrogant and hardened with pride, he was deposed from his royal throne and stripped of his glory. He was driven away from people and given the mind of an animal; he lived with the wild donkeys and ate grass like cattle; and his body was drenched with the dew of heaven, until he acknowledged that the Most High GOD is sovereign over the kingdoms of men and sets over anyone he wishes.

"But you his son, O Belshazzar, have not humbled yourself, though you knew all this. Instead, you have set yourself up against the LORD of heaven. You had the goblets from his temple brought to you, and you and your nobles, your wives and your concubines drank wine from them. You praised the gods of silver and gold, of bronze, iron, wood and stone, which cannot see or hear or understand. But you did not honor the GOD who holds in his hand your life and all your ways. Therefore he sent the hand that wrote the inscription.

"This is the inscription that was written: MENE, MENE, TEKEL, PARSIN. This is what these words mean: MENE: GOD has numbered the days of your reign and brought it to an end. TEKEL: You have been weighed on the scales and found wanting. PERES: Your kingdom is divided and given to the Medes and Persians."

Then at Belshazzar's command, Daniel was clothed in purple, a gold chain was placed around his neck, and he was proclaimed the third highest ruler in the kingdom. That very night Belshazzar, king of the Babylonians, was slain, and Darius the Mede took over the kingdom at the age of sixty-two.

5:1—*king*. Belshazzar (meaning "Bel, protect the king!") was the son and viceroy of Nabonidus. He is called the "son" of Nebuchadnezzar (v. 22), but the Aramaic term could also mean "grandson" or "descendant" or even "successor" (see NIV text note on v. 22). See also note on v. 10 and NIV text note on v. 2.

5:7—*third highest ruler in the kingdom*. Nabonidus was first, Belshazzar second.

5:10—*queen*. See NIV text note. She could have been (1) the wife of Nebuchadnezzar or (2) the daughter of Nebuchadnezzar and wife of Nabonidus or (3) the wife of Nabonidus but not the daughter of Nebuchadnezzar.

5:11—*the time of your father*. Nebuchadnezzar died in 562 BC; the year is now 539.

5:17—*keep your gifts for yourself*. See Genesis 14:23 and note.

5:22–23—Three chargers were brought against Belshazzar: (1) He sinned not through ignorance but through disobedience and pride (v. 22); (2) he defiled GOD by desecrating the sacred vessels (v. 23a); and (3) he praised idols and so did not honor GOD (v. 23b).

5:26–28—See NIV text notes. Three weights (mina, shekel, and half mina or shekel) may be intended, symbolizing three rulers, respectively: (1) Nebuchadnezzar; (2) either Evilmerodach (2 King 25:27; Jeremiah 52:31) or Nabonidus; and (3) Belshazzar.

In 2 Kings 25:27, "In the thirty-seventh year of the exile of Jehoiachin king of Judah, in the year Evilmerodach became king of Babylon, he released Jehoiachin from prison on the twenty-seventh day of the twelfth month." In Jeremiah 52:31, "In the thirty-seventh year of the exile of Jehoiachin king of Judah, in the year Evilmerodach became king of Babylon, he released Jehoiachin king of Judah and freed him from prison on the twenty-fifth day of the twelfth month."

Daniel 5:28—*Medes and Persians*. The second kingdom of the series of four predicted in ch. 2 (see "Introduction: Author, Date, and Authenticity").

5:31—*Darius the Mede*. Perhaps another name for Gubaru, referred to in Babylonian inscriptions as the governor that Cyrus put in charge of the newly conquered Babylonian territories. Or "Darius the Mede" may have been Cyrus's throne name in Babylon (see NIV text note on 6:28; see also 1 Ch 5:26 for a similar phenomenon). Took over the kingdom. The head of gold is now no more, as predicted in 2:39.

Daniel in the Den of Lions

6:1–28—It pleased Darius to appoint 120 satraps to the throughout the kingdom, with three administrators over them, one of whom was Daniel. The satraps were made accountable to them so that the king might not suffer loss. Now Daniel so distinguished himself among the administrators and the satraps by his exceptional qualities that the king planned to set him over the whole kingdom. At this, the administrators and the satraps tried to find grounds for charges against Daniel in his conduct of government affairs, but they were unable to do so. They could find no corruption in him, because he was trustworthy and neither corrupt nor negligent. Finally these men said, "We will never find any basis for charges against this man Daniel unless it has something to do with the law of his GOD."

So the administrators and the satraps went as a group to the king and said: "O King Darius, live forever! The royal administrators, prefects, satraps, advisers and governors have all agreed that the king should issue an edict and enforce the decree that anyone who prays to any god or man during the next thirty days, except to you, O king, shall be thrown into the lions' den. Now, O king, issue the decree and put it in writing so that it cannot be altered—in accordance with the laws of the Medes and Persians, which cannot be repealed." So King Darius put the decree in writing. Now when Daniel learned that the decree had been published, he went home to his upstairs room where the windows opened toward Jerusalem. Three times a day he got down on his knees and prayed, giving thanks to his GOD, just as he had done before.

Then these men went as a group and found Daniel praying and asking GOD for help. So they went to the king and spoke to him about his royal decree: "Did you not publish a decree that during the next thirty days anyone who prays to any god or man except to you, O king, would be thrown into the lions' den?"

The king answered, "The decree stands— in accordance with the laws of the Medes and Persians, which cannot be repealed."

Then they said to the king, "Daniel, who is one of the exiles from Judah, pays no attention to you, O king, or to the decree you put in writing. He still prays three times a day."

When the king heard this, he was greatly distressed: he was determined to rescue Daniel and made every effort until sundown to save him. Then the men went as a group to the king and said to him, "Remember, O king, that according to the law of the Medes and Persians no decree or edict that the king issues can be changed."

So the king gave the order, and they brought Daniel and threw him into the lions' den. The king said to Daniel, "May your GOD, whom you serve continually, rescue you!" A stone was brought and placed over the mouth of the den, and the king sealed it with his own signet ring and with the rings of his nobles, so that Daniel's situation might not be changed. Then the king returned to his palace and spent the night without eating and without any entertainment being brought to him. And he could not sleep.

At the first light of dawn, the king got up and hurried to the lions' den. When he came near the den, he called to Daniel in an anguished voice, "Daniel, servant of the living GOD, whom you serve continually, been able to rescue you from the lions?"

Daniel answered, "O king, live forever! My GOD sent his angel, and he shut the mouths of the lions. They have not hurt me, because I was found innocent in his sight. Nor have I ever done any wrong before you, O king."

The king was overjoyed and gave orders to lift Daniel out of the den. And when Daniel was lifted from the den, no wound was found on him, because he had trusted in his GOD. At the king's command, the men who had falsely accused Daniel were brought in and thrown into the lions' den, along with their wives and children. And before they reached the floor of the den, the lions overpowered them and crushed all their bones.

Then King Darius wrote to all the peoples, nations and men of every language throughout the land:

"May you prosper greatly! I issue a decree that in every part of my kingdom people must fear and revere the GOD of Daniel. For he is the living GOD and he endures forever; his kingdom will not be destroyed, his dominion will never end. He rescues and he saves: he performs signs and wonders in the heavens and on the earth. He has rescued Daniel from the power of the lions."

So Daniel prospered during the reign of Darius and the reign of Cyrus the Persian.

6:7—The conspirators lied in stating that *all* the royal administrators supported the proposed decree since they knew that Daniel (totally unaware of the proposal) was the foremost of the three administrators.

6:10—*toward Jerusalem.* See 2 Chronicles 6:38–39. *Three times a day.* See Psalm 55:17. In 2 Chronicles 6:38–39, "And if they turn back to you with all their heart and soul in the land of their captivity where they were taken, and pray toward the land you gave their fathers, toward the city you have chosen and toward the temple I have built for your name; then from heaven, your dwelling place, hear their prayer and their pleas, and uphold their cause. And forgive your people, who have sinned against you." In Psalm 55:17, "Evening, morning and noon I cry out in distress, and he hears my voice."

6:16—*serve continually.* See 1 Corinthians 15:58: "Therefore, my dear brothers, stand firm. Let nothing move you. Always give yourselves fully to the work of the LORD, because you know that your labor in the LORD is not in vain."

6:23—*he...trusted in his GOD.* That the lions were ravenously hungry (v. 24) was no obstacle to the LORD'S rewarding Daniel's faith by saving his life.

6:24—*along with their wives and children.* In accordance with Persian custom.

Daniel, The End Times

12:1–13—"At that time Michael, the great prince who protects your people, will arise. There will be a time of distress such as has not happened from the beginning of nations until then. But at that time your people—everyone whose name is found written in the book—will be delivered. Multitudes who sleep in the dust of the earth will awake: some to everlasting life, others to shame and everlasting contempt. Those who are wise will shine like the brightness of the heavens, and those who lead many to righteousness, like the stars for ever and ever.

"But you, Daniel, close up and seal the words of the scroll until the time of the end. Many will go here and there to increase knowledge."

Then I, Daniel, looked, and there before me stood two others, one on this bank of the river and one on the opposite bank. One of them said to the man clothed in linen, who was above the waters of the river, "How long will it be before these astonishing things are fulfilled?"

The man clothed in linen, who was above the waters of the river, lifted his right hand and his left hand toward heaven, and I heard him swear by him who lives forever, saying, "It will be for a time, times and half a time. When the power of the holy people has been finally broken, all these things will be completed."

I heard, but I did not understand. So I asked, "My lord, what will the outcome of all this be?"

He replied, "Go your way, Daniel, because the words are closed up and sealed until the time of the end. Many will be purified, made spotless and refined, but the wicked will continue to be wicked. None of the wicked will understand, but those who are wise will understand.

"From the time that the daily sacrifice is abolished and the abomination that causes desolation is set up, there will be 1,290 days. Blessed is the one who waits for and reaches the end of the 1,335 days.

"As for you, go your way till the end. You will rest and then at the end of the days you will rise to receive your allotted inheritance."

12:1—*Michael.* See note on 10:13. *Time of distress.* See Jeremiah 30:7 and Matthew 24:21 and note; cf. Revelation 16:18. *Book.* See 10:21; see also notes on Psalm 9:5; 51:1; 69:28.

In Daniel 10:13, "'But the prince of the Persian kingdom resisted me twenty-one days. Then Michael, one of the chief princes, came to help me, because I was detained there with the king of Persia.'"

In Jeremiah 30:7, "'How awful that day will be! None will be like it. It will be a time of trouble for Jacob, but he will be saved out of it.'" In Matthew 24:21, "'For then there will be great distress, unequaled from the beginning of the world until now—and never to be equaled again.'" In Revelation 16:18, "Then there came flashes of lightning, rumblings, peals of thunder and a severe earthquake. No earthquake like it has ever occurred since man has been on earth, so tremendous was the quake."

In Daniel 10:21, "'But first I will tell you what is written in the Book of the Truth. No one supports me against them except

Michael, your prince. And in the first year of Darius the Mede, I took my stand to support and protest him.'" In Psalm 9:5; 51:1; and 69:28, "You have rebuked the nations and destroyed the wicked: you have blotted out their name for ever and ever... Have mercy on me, O GOD, according to your great compassion blot out my transgressions... May they be blotted out of the book of life and not be listed with the righteous.

12:2—The first clear reference to a resurrection of both the righteous and the wicked. Cf. John 5:24–30. *Everlasting life.* The phrase occurs only here in the OT.

> "I tell you the truth, whoever hears my word and believes him who sent me has eternal life and will not be condemned; he has crossed over from death to life. I tell you the truth, a time is coming and has now come when the dead will hear the voice of the Son of GOD and those who hear will live. For as the Father has life in himself so he has granted the Son to have life in himself. And he has given him authority to judge because he is the Son of man. Do not be amazed at this, for a time is coming when all who are in their graves will hear his voice and come out—those who have done good will rise to live, and those who have done evil will rise to be condemned.
>
> By myself I can do nothing: I judge only as I hear my judgment is just, for I seek not to please myself but him who sent me."

12:5—*two others.* Two was the minimum number of witnesses to an oath (see v. 7; Dt 19:15). In Deuteronomy 19:15, "'One witness is not enough to convict a man accused of any crime or offence he may have committed. A matter must be established by testimony of two or three witnesses.'"

12:7—*time, times and half a time.* See NIV text note; cf. 7:25". He will speak against the Most High and oppress his saints and try to change the set times and the laws. The saints will be handed over to him for a time times and half a time."

12:11–12—Apparently representing either (1) further calculations relating to the persecutions of Antiochus Epiphanes (see 8:14, 11:28 and notes) or (2) end-time calculations. In Daniel 8:14, "He said to me, 'It will take 2300 evenings and mornings; then the sanctuary will be reconsecrated.'" In 11:28, "'The king of the North will return to his own country with great wealth, but his heart will be set against the holy covenant. He will take action against it and then return to his own country.'"

12:13—*rest*. Die (see Job 3:17: "There the wicked cease from turmoil, and there the weary are at rest").

The book of Daniel tells us what will happen when we obey GOD and what will happen when we disobey GOD! When Nebuchadnezzar, king of Babylon, came and besieged Jerusalem, GOD delivered Jehoiakim, king of Judah, into his hand with some articles from the temple of GOD and carried them off to put in the treasure house of his god. They also brought some of the Israelites from the royal family and the nobility; among them were Daniel, Shadrach, Meshach, and Abednego.

To these four men, GOD blessed them with knowledge and understanding of all kinds. All the four young Israelites were assigned to serve in the king's palace after going through a daily routine training and certain amounts of food and wine to make them healthy to fit the standard service of the king. But Daniel resolved not to defile himself with the royal food. He asked the chief official for permission not to defile himself this way. It was impossible for the chief official to grant any person that request, but GOD had caused the chief official to show favor and sympathy to Daniel.

Royal food and wine. The Israelites considered food from Nebuchadnezzar's table to be contaminated because the first portion of it was offered to idols. Likewise, a portion of the wine was poured out on a pagan other. Ceremonially unclean were used neither slaughtered nor prepared according to the regulation of the law.

Daniel, Shadrach, Meshach, and Abednego obeyed the law of GOD. Let us read their story with King Nebuchadnezzar. The king had a dreams, and he was troubled and could not sleep. He summoned the magicians, enchanters, sorcerers, and astrologers to tell them what he had dreamed. He said to them, "I have had a dream that troubles me, and I want to know what it means." Then the astrologers asked the king to tell them the dream. The king replied, "I have decided: If you do not tell me what my dream was and interpret it, I will have you killed! But if you tell me the dream and interpreted it, you will receive from me gifts and rewards and great power."

The astrologers answered the king, "There is no man on earth who can do what the king asks!"

This made the king so angry and furious that he ordered the execution of all the wise men in Babylon. The decree was issued to put the wise men to death, and some were sent to look for Daniel and his friends to be put to death. When Arioch, the commander of the king's guard, had gone out to put to death the wise men of Babylon, Daniel spoke to him with wisdom and tact. Daniel went to the king and asked for time so that he might interpret the dream for the king.

Daniel, faithful and obedient to GOD, went and asked his friends—Shadrach, Meshach, and Abednego—urging them to plead for mercy from the GOD of heaven concerning this mystery so that he and his friends might not be executed with the rest of the wise men of Babylon. When GOD'S children obey his law, GOD knows their heart, and when they ask GOD for anything, GOD will answer their prayers.

During the night, the mystery was revealed to Daniel in a vision, then Daniel praised the GOD of heaven and said, "Praise be to the name of GOD for ever and ever. Wisdom and power are his." GOD changes times and seasons. GOD sets up kings and deposes kings. GOD gives wisdom to the wise and knowledge to the discerning. GOD reveals deep and hidden things. GOD knows what lies in darkness, and light dwells with him. Daniel thanked and praised GOD. "O GOD of my fathers, GOD has given me wisdom and power. GOD has made known to me what we asked of him. GOD has made known to us the dream of the king."

Daniel interpreted the dream for the king. When Daniel was brought to the king, the king asked Daniel, "Are you able to tell me what I saw in my dream and interpret it?"

Daniel replied, "No wise man, enchanter, magician, or diviner can explain to the king the mystery he has asked about. But there is a GOD in heaven who reveals mysteries." GOD has shown king Nebuchadnezzar what will happen in days to come. Please read, or maybe you already read Daniel chapter 2:1–49.

The whole world lived and experienced the interpretation of King Nebuchadnezzar's dream, and the fifth kingdom was the eternal kingdom of GOD, built on the ruins of the sinful empires of man. Its authority will extend to the whole earth and ultimately over a new heaven and a new earth.

My beloved, let us also read what happened to Shadrach, Meshach, and Abednego when they did not obey the king's command to fall down and worship the image of gold because they only fall down and worship their GOD, the creator of heaven and earth, and obey his law.

Shadrach, Meshach, and Abednego were brought in front of the king; and he said to them, "Is that true what I have heard that you don't pay attention to my command?"

They replied, "O King, we do not serve your gods nor worship the image of gold you have set up."

Immediately, the king commanded the three Jews to be put into the blazing furnace. Then the king leaped to his feet in amazement and asked his advisors, "Were not three men that we tied up and threw into the fire?"

They replied, "Certainly, O King."

He said, "Look! I see four men walking around in the fire, unbound and unharmed, and the fourth looks like a son of God."

Nebuchadnezzar then approached the opening of the blazing furnace and shouted, "Shadrach, Meshach, and Abednego, servants of the most high GOD, come out! Come here!" They all came out of the fire, and all the royal advisors crowded around them. They saw that the fire had not harmed their bodies nor was a hair on their heads singed; and there was no smell of fire on them. Then Nebuchadnezzar said, "Praise be to the GOD of Shadrach, Meshach, and Abednego, who has sent his angels and rescued his servants! They trusted in him and defied the king's command and were willing to give up their lives rather than serve or worship any god except their own GOD."

"Daniel in the Lions' Den." During the reign of King Darius, Daniel distinguished himself among the administrators and the satraps by his exceptional qualities that the king planned to set him over the whole kingdom. The administrators and the satraps were jealous of this outsider Jew and tried to finds charges against him. But they could not find any corruption in Daniel because he was trustworthy.

Finally, they said, "We will not find any basis for chargers against him unless it has to do with the law of his GOD." So the administrators and the satraps came with ungodly idea to kill the godly man Daniel! They went to King Darius and asked him to issue an edict and enforce the decree that anyone who prays to any god or man during the next thirty days, "except to you, O King," shall be thrown into the lions' den.

The king did as they requested and made it into law. Daniel learned that the decree had been published. Daniel, as usual, went home to his upstairs room where the window was opened toward Jerusalem. Three times a day, he got on his knees and prayed, giving thanks to his GOD. Just as he had done before, Daniel was caught by the administrators on his knees, praying and asking GOD for help.

The group went to the king and told him about Daniel's crime against the king and reminded him of the decree he had issued. The king answered, "The decree stands in accordance with the law of the Medes and Persians, which cannot be repealed." So the king gave the order, and they brought Daniel and threw him into the lions' den. The king loved Daniel and said to him, "May your GOD, whom you serve continually, rescue you!"

At the first light of dawn, the king got up and hurried to the lions' den. When he came near the den, he called to Daniel in an anguished voice, "Daniel, servant of the living GOD, has your GOD, whom you serve continually, been able to rescue you from the lions?"

Daniel answered, "O King, live forever! My GOD sent his angel, and he shut the mouth of the lions. They have not hurt me because I was found innocent in his sight. Nor have I ever done any wrong before you, O King."

Now let us read the book of Daniel, where it tells us what will happen when we disobey GOD. Judah was exiled to Babylon because she disobeyed GOD'S Word regarding covenant-keeping, the Sabbath years, and idolatry.

The LORD GOD spoke to Moses in Leviticus 25:1–7: "The LORD said to Moses on Mount Sinai. 'Speak to the Israelites and say to them: When you enter the land I am going to give you, the land itself must observe a sabbath to the LORD. For six years sow your fields and for six years prune your vineyards and gather their crops. But in the seventh year the land is to have a sabbath of rest, a sabbath to the LORD. Do not sow your fields or prune your vineyards. Do not reap what grows of itself or harvest the grapes of your untended vines. The land is to have a year of rest. Whatever the land yields during the sabbath year will be food for you—for yourself, your manservant and maidservant, and the hired worker and temporary resident who live among you, as well as for your livestock and the wild animals in your land. Whatever the land produces may be eaten.'"

In Leviticus 26:27–35, "'If in spite of this you still do not listen to me but continue to be hostile toward me then in my anger I will be hostile toward you, and I myself will punish you for your sins seven times over. You will eat the flesh of your daughters. I will destroy your high places, cut down your incense altars and pile your dead bodies on the lifeless forms of your idols. I will abhor you. I will turn your cities into ruins and lay waste your sanctuaries, and I will take no delight in the pleasing aroma of your offerings. I will waste the land, so that your enemies who live there will be appalled. I will scatter you among the nations and will draw out my sword and pursue you. Your land will be laid waste, and your cities will lie in ruins. Then the land will enjoy its sabbath years all the time that it lies desolate and you are in the country of your enemies; then the land will rest and enjoy its sabbaths. All the time that it lies desolate, the land will have the rest it did not have during the sabbaths you lived in it."

In 2 Chronicles 36:14–21,

> Furthermore, all the leaders of the priests and the people became more and more unfaithful, following all the detestable practices of the nations and defiling the temple of the LORD, which he had consecrated in Jerusalem. The LORD, the GOD of their fathers, sent word to them through his messengers again and again, because he had pity on his people and on his dwelling place. But they mocked GOD'S messengers, despised his words and scoffed at his prophets until the wrath of the LORD was aroused against his people and there was no remedy.
>
> He brought up against them the king of the Babylonians who killed their young men with the sword in the sanctuary, and spared neither young man nor young woman, old man or aged. GOD handed all of them over to Nebuchadnezzar. He carried to Babylon all the articles from the temple of GOD. Both large and small. And the treasures of the LORD'S temple and the treasures of the king and his officials. They set fire to GOD'S temple and broke down the wall of Jerusalem; they burned all the palaces and destroyed everything of value there. He carried into exile to Babylon the remnant, who escaped from the sword and they became servants to him and his sons until the kingdom of Persia came to power. The land enjoyed its sabbath rests; all the time of its desolation it rested until the seventy years were completed in fulfillment of the word of the LORD spoken by Jeremiah.

2 Chronicles 36:20–21—The conclusion of the two biblical histories is interestingly different: The writer[s] of Samuel and Kings had sought to show why the exile occurred and had traced the sad history of Israel's disobedience to the exile, the time in which the writer[s] of those books lived. With the state at an end, he could still show GOD'S faithfulness to his promises to David (2 Ki 25:27–30) by reporting the favor bestowed on his descendants. The chronicler, whose vantage point was after the exile, was able to look back to the exile not only as judgment but also as containing hope for the future. For him, the purified remnant had returned to a purified land (vv. 22–23), and a new age was beginning. The exile was not judgment alone but also blessing for it allowed the land to catch up on its Sabbath rests (Lev 26:40–45). And GOD had remembered his covenant and restored his people to the land.

In 2 King 25:27–30, "In the thirty-seventh year of the exile of Jehoiachin king of Judah, in the year Evilmerodach became king of Babylon, he released Jehoiachin from prison on the twenty-seventh day of the twelfth month. He spoke kindly to him and gave him a seat of honor higher than those of the other kings who were with him in Babylon. So Jehoiachin put aside his prison clothes and for the rest of his life ate regularly at the king's table. Day by day they gave Jehoiachin a regular allowance as long as he lived."

In 2 Chronicles 36:22–23, "In the first year of Cyrus king of Persia, in order to fulfill the word of the LORD spoken by Jeremiah, the LORD moved the heart of Cyrus king of Persia to make a proclamation throughout his realm and to put it in writing: 'This is what Cyrus king of Persia says: "The LORD, the GOD of heaven, has given me all the kingdoms of the earth and he has appointed me to build a temple for him at Jerusalem in Judah. Anyone of his people among you—may the LORD his GOD be with him, and let him go up."'"

In Leviticus 26:40–45, "'But if they will confess their sins and the sins of their fathers their treachery against me and their hostility toward me. 41 which made me hostile toward them so that I sent them into the land of their enemies—then when their uncircumcised hearts are humbled and they pay for their sin. I will remember my covenant with Jacob and my covenant with Abraham, and I will remember the land. For the land will be deserted by them and will enjoy its sabbaths while it lies desolate without them. They will pay for their sins because they rejected my laws and abhorred my decrees. Yet in spite of this, when they are in the land of their enemies, I will not reject them or abhor them so as to destroy them completely, breaking my covenant with them. I am the LORD their GOD. But for their sake I will remember the covenant with their ancestors whom I brought out of Egypt in the sight of the nations to be their GOD. I am the LORD.'"

This is the part of what will happen when we disobey GOD! When the Israelites sinned against GOD, GOD made them pay for their sins, but GOD always reminded them with the covenant he made with their fathers. Only the remnant of the Israelites, who were obedient to GOD, saw and lived in the land GOD promised to their fathers. GOD is love, and he loves us all. GOD wants us to be with him in heaven, but we have to obey his Word. It is that simple!

I am the perfect example; I am now living a life where GOD comes first, and I overcame all my fleshly desires! As I walk on the street going to work, people ask me, "You are so happy all the time. What is your secret?" I always reply: "I live according to GOD'S laws. It is so easy. I study the BIBLE every day. I am on my knees when I wake up in the morning and when I am ready to go to bed at night. And now that I am diligently serving GOD, I see his hand in my life."

Any time we come to GOD, he always opens his arms for us and gives us the same wages as anyone who served GOD from a young age! What a loving GOD we have, but we have to recognize him first and do all that GOD says, not only part of what GOD says. And we have seen all the examples since Adam and Eve up to Noah, and then all through Abraham, Moses, David, and Job—when GOD said about him, "There is no one on earth like Job." Until our LORD JESUS, who died for us so we could live forever with him in heaven and on earth. Glory be to GOD. I am all in for GOD. Amen. And amen.

The day is Saturday, May 11th at 12:12 p.m. I had strong thoughts for the first time; it came to me to reveal it to the world about the Jehovah's Witnesses. After 1,850 years, my false teacher claimed that GOD has chosen this brood of people to be his saints! And they are directed by the Holy Spirit! And they do accordingly! Until something happens between us, I promised I will not mention. I said to him, "How could the Holy Spirit direct you and you behave that way?" There was no response from him until another study, then he explained to me that nobody is perfect! But I said, "You claim to be a perfect group chosen by GOD!" His response was, "But when we make a mistake, we admit it!"

Before I do my perfect illustration about the deceivers, let us read Romans 16:17–18: "I urge you, brothers, to watch out for those who cause divisions and put obstacles in your way that are contrary to the teaching you have learned. Keep away from them. For such people are not serving our LORD CHRIST, but their own appetites. By smooth talk and flattery they deceive the minds of naive people."

In 2 Peter 2:1, "But there were also false prophets among the people, just as there will be false teachers among you. They will secretly introduce destructive heresies, even denying the sovereign LORD who bought them—bringing swift destruction on themselves."

My perfect illustration about the deceivers is this: as a professional tailor, I make handmade suits, which consist of lots of hidden handmade not visible to the eve. In the inside of the jacket, the well-constructed jacket, it's comprised of a hundred wool canvas and another canvas, calle, from the horse's tail hair. It is stiff, and it will not bend easy. When you try to fold it, the tailors put two layers of it against the wool canvas, and they sew it by hand. But if the tailor sews it by the machine, it will show bubbles on the fabric.

There are other hidden handmade stitches on the collar and on the lapel, also unseen to the naked eye, besides the handmade on the shoulders and the sleeve heads not visible to the naked eye. The visible hand stitch that is visible to the eye is on the outside of the jacket on the lapel, the collar, and the flaps of the pockets and the breast pocket.

The deception is when a dishonest tailor once told me this by bragging about how smart he is. He buys an already made suit for less than one hundred dollars, and he makes the hand stitches on the lapel, the collar, and the flaps of the jacket that are visible to the eye, but of course, there is no wool canvas on the inside to do the handmade on. The already made suit is done with a fuse fabric and glued to the fabric, but when you send your suit to the cleaner, it comes out looking like a very inexpensive suit.

I said to the dishonest tailor, "But you are deceiving the people and charging them lots of money for a suit that is only less than one hundred dollars." His response was: "I show them the handmade stitches on the outside, and the label says *handmade*! But the people are not tailors to know the difference."

My beloved, you have to be a tailor to be able to know the true handmade suit from the false handmade suit. My recommendation is to study the Word of GOD, the BIBLE, to be able to discern between a true BIBLE teacher and false BIBLE teacher! I was able to discern between the true and false BIBLE teaching when I studied the BIBLE for one year and a half with the so-called Jehovah's Witnesses. By my experience with them, I realized that I am the true witness to Jehovah among them, Assaf Sawaya.

When I was writing the story of the prophet Daniel, I came to chapter 5:1, about King Belshazzar, son of King Nebuchadnezzar. King Belshazzar saw something in Daniel 5:5–6: "Suddenly the fingers of a human hand appeared and wrote on the plaster of the wall, near the lampstand in the royal palace. The King watched the hand as it wrote. His face turned pale and he was so frightened that his knees knocked together and his legs gave way."

None of the enchanters, astrologers, diviners or the king could read the writing on the wall, except Daniel. And he was brought to the king to interpret the inscription. The king said to Daniel, "If you can read this writing and tell me what it means, you will be rewarded by being made the third ruler in my kingdom." Daniel answered, "O King, live forever. Yes, I can; but you did not honor the GOD who holds in his hand your life and all your ways.

Therefore he sent the hand that wrote the inscription: MENE, MENE, TEKEL, PARSIN. This is what these words means: MENE: GOD has numbered the days of your reign and brought it to an end. TEKEL: You have been weighed on the scales and found wanting. PERES: Your kingdom is divided and given to the Medes and Persians."

Daniel was rewarded by King Belshazzar. That very night, Belshazzar, king of the Babylonians, was slain; and Darius the Mede took over the kingdom.

I could relate to that mystery. When I was having a severe pain in my stomach, I went to my bedroom to relax on my bed, holding my stomach with my two hands and crying out to GOD to heal me by saying, "Dear LORD, if I am having this pain, I will not be able to work, and if I don't work, I will not be able to eat!" And as I was crying out my heart to GOD, suddenly, I saw a hand come out of the wall of my bedroom, traveling into my stomach, and it pulled the pain out of my stomach completely that very second! I was healed and kept scratching my stomach for about ten minutes! That miracle happened to me on Sunday afternoon at 2:00 p.m. And I was totally awake! Glory to GOD. GOD always showed me his love at my lowest points throughout my life, but GOD kept me in the valley and did not get me to the mountaintop until now, when I am devoting my entire life to GOD. Even at this late time of my age, seventy years old, GOD welcomes us at any time we come to him, and GOD will give us the same wages as if we served him since our childhood. What a loving GOD.

When I told my false former teacher about the miracle GOD has done in my life, he dismissed it as a satanic power and did not give credit to GOD! To me, that was another evidence that my false teacher does not believe in the GOD I believe in since my childhood when my loving mother always taught it to me. That is why I left this organization and their kingdom hall, but until now, I do not know who their god is.

On another occasion, GOD manifested himself into my presence and filled my heart with love, overflowing love into my heart for about twenty minutes until I could not take that overflow of love for my heart was about to burst out of my chest, telling me to go and hug my coworker after I told that coworker not to talk to me to avoid further confrontation with him and to avoid something drastic I may inflict on myself as a Christian.

The moment my coworker walked into my area to get his coffee, I saw myself walking toward him, surprising him by hugging him and telling him that GOD had directed me to hug him and "show you love instead of hate, like what we did to each other for the last year or more." My coworker welcomed my initiative, and I said to him that "GOD has manifested into my presence and filled my heart with love, directing me to give you a hug, and I obeyed GOD even if I had initiated not to speak to each other." My coworker was pleased with my loving gesture, and we became good friends. But it was all GOD'S plan because GOD saw that I was studying his Word, the BIBLE, every day and read in my heart that I am finally returning his love that he showed me throughout my life, saying, "Welcome back home, my child."

By obeying GOD, the result came so fast: our company did not renew their lease, and we have to move to another location that already exists. And they don't need another tailor in that location, but my coworker insisted that I come along because he explained to the corporate people that they have lots of clients that favor me as their tailor.

The moral of my story is that when we obey our loving Father, GOD, he always rewards us and lets us know that he is with us. We have to show GOD and let him know that we recognize his hand in our life. Now I am serving GOD, and he got me to the mountaintop instead of keeping me in the valley. But it took me a long time to realize all that. Praise be to GOD and his love for us.

When I told all that happened to me to my former false teacher, he did not make any comments. But later on when I said to him, "By obeying GOD, the result was I saved my job," then he said, "Oh yeah, that worked for you." As a teacher for the Word of GOD for fifty years, he never gives GOD any credit; I was wondering again, *Who is his god?*

If anyone mentioned in my book has harbored hate in his heart for me, I forgive you all, and I have love for you because JESUS showed me so much love and told me to love you all. And I am obeying all that JESUS said so I could inherit the forever-lasting life with him in heaven, where there is no sickness and there is forever youth and pleasure a million times over what we experience on earth.

My beloved, to have all the promises GOD has for us, it is simple: you have to obey all that GOD says and believe that GOD the Father has sent his Son to die for us all, and when you believe in that, you will be saved. JESUS, our LORD, was born as a human through the Virgin Mary and died for our sins because GOD knows we cannot do it on ourselves. JESUS took our sins to save us by the grace of GOD. JESUS took the sins of the living and the sins who are to live. JESUS died for all of us and was risen on the third day. JESUS was born again so we could be born again with him when JESUS comes back the second time to judge all of us. Righteous or unrighteous, we all will be raised from death to be judged. The righteous will be born again and be with him in heaven, living forever. But the unrighteous will be cast down to hell with their master, Satan, and that is life forever tormented with Satan in hell.

The second coming of JESUS is near, probably in our lifetime. We have to be ready by believing and obeying our LORD JESUS, our Savior, and he is our Savior, JESUS, who has shown me his power, his love, and what heaven is like! Now I am doing everything JESUS said so I could be with him in heaven instead of following the deceiver Satan and be with him in hell. I am among the smartest people.

It's the third time I go to see Chris to give me a one-hour lesson on the computer at the Clark County Library in Las Vegas. From the beginning, Chris walked me through the steps of the computer, as you hold a toddler by the hand and walk him step by step—from how to use the mouse and click on the line you intend to use until I was able to write on my own. Otherwise, I wouldn't be able to write my book that you are reading at the moment.

I asked Chris if I could get him a present or a compensation for his effort. Chris declined the gesture and said to me, the only gift he will accept is a good recommendation. A good recommendation it is, Chris, and you will read about it in my book when I sign the first page of my book and hand it to you, Chris.

I also recommend to all of us in this great country of the USA to help and support all the libraries in this country. When some elder person like me needs help in using the computer, they can go to any library in this great country and ask for Chris to help him or her how to use the computer and say to Chris that Assaf recommended him.

I keep going to Chris for more technical assistance, and without his assistance, I would not be able to start writing my book and probably I would have given up the idea to write it. Again, I thank you, Chris, for your help, and this great country for the caring heart they have for the unable man.

What a country the USA is. Thank you, America.

Assaf Sawaya

G OD uses all his children to preach his Word, the BIBLE. Men and women, our LORD JESUS has compassion and loves us all.

When JESUS was thirsty, he came to the well to have a drink of water. It was the sixth hour, noon time, in the midst of the heat. A Samaritan woman came to draw water at that time to avoid her townspeople so they don't point their fingers at her and say, "She is that sinner woman."

The thirsty JESUS asked her, "Will you give me a drink?"

The Samaritan woman said to JESUS, "You are a Jew, and I am a Samaritan woman. How can you ask me for a drink?" (For the Jews do not associate with the Samaritans.)

"If you knew the gift of GOD and who it is that asks you for a drink, you would have asked him and he would have given you living water."

The Samaritan woman said to JESUS, "You have nothing to draw water with. Where can you get this living water?"

JESUS answered her in John 4:13,

> "Everyone who drinks this water will be thirsty again but whoever drinks the water I give him will never thirst. Indeed, the water I give him will become in him a spring of water welling up to eternal life."

> The Samaritan woman said to JESUS, "Sir, give me this water so I won't be thirsty and keep coming here in the day to draw water, to avoid the humiliation and the hatred my people keep showing me.

JESUS told her, "Go. Call your husband and come back."

"I have no husband," she replied.

JESUS said to her, "You are right when you say you have no husband. The fact is, you have had five husbands, and the man you now have is not your husband. What you have just said is quite true."

"Sir," the Samaritan woman said, "I can see that you are a prophet. I know that the Messiah [called CHRIST] is coming. When he comes, he will explain everything to us."

Then JESUS declared, "I who speak to you am he."

Then, leaving her water jar, the woman went back to the town and said to the people, "Come, see a man who told me everything I ever did. Could this be the CHRIST?" They came out of the town and made their way toward him.

Many of the Samaritans from that town believed in him because of the woman' s testimony, "He told me everything I ever did." So when the Samaritans came to him, they urged him to stay with them, and he stayed two days. And because of his words many more became believers.

They said to the woman, "We no longer believe just because of what you said; now we have heard for ourselves, and we know that this man really is the Savior of the world."

JESUS used the Samaritan woman to preach to her townspeople that she saw JESUS and to believe her, and then they saw and heard JESUS themselves. That sinner woman preached the Word of GOD to the people who shamed her and showed her hate!

I am a sinner as well; and GOD is using me to preach his Word, and I am obeying GOD. My actions and behavior show that what I am doing what is pleasing to GOD because GOD has transformed me and he knows my loving heart. That is why GOD lifted me from the slimy pit I had put myself into to satisfy my selfish fleshly desires.

We were about twenty inmates in the math class. Our math teacher was also an inmate but with a PhD degree in math. He also gave me a one-hour private lesson to improve my math; and both of us attended the class of Toastmasters to be able to speak to an audience. One of his speeches was about the importance of math because everything in this life contains math, and he gave an example about me, stating, "When Sawaya came to his class, he did not know how to add or subtract fractions! But look at him now. He just finished trigonometry and is now studying the big-boy calculus." I was so proud about his comment, for what I accomplished in a short time during my incarceration. By the way, we both graduated from the Toastmasters class with a diploma, and also I got my GED certificate before I was released! Yeah.

Our PhD teacher is a funny guy, so I took advantage of the situation during the class, asking our teacher, "Mr. A? You are a PhD in math, and you ended up here with us all criminals. Didn't you do the math first?" He was laughing so hard that the class even stopped laughing before him, and he said to me, "I want to chalk one for you on the board, Sawaya," and he did!

I am going to start from the beginning. Who did not do the math? Lucifer, one of the three archangels—Michael, Gabriel, and Lucifer—was the leader of the angels in charge of praising and worshiping GOD. Lucifer, who became Satan, wanted to be worshiped himself, so he rebelled against GOD by not doing the math!

The second one who did not do the math was Adam. He allowed Satan to deceive him by doing what GOD told him not to do: to eat from the fruit of the forbidden tree of life. GOD made it clear to Adam, "The day you eat the fruit from the forbidden tree, you will die." Adam did not bother to do the math! And that is why we are all being condemned because of the sin of one man!

Adam's first son, Cain, also did not do the math by killing his own brother, Abel. The first murder happened on earth, and it was between two brothers. The motive was jealousy. Satan was jealous of his Creator, GOD, so did Adam who wanted to have more than what GOD blessed him with! Cain, in the same way, wanted more; he wanted what his brother had. We are not satisfied with what GOD has blessed us with!

But of course, there is an exception, like Noah. All generations from Adam to Noah did not do the math, except ten people: Abel, Enoch, and Noah and his family—a total of eight people.

GOD'S anger came on that hostile generation, and he brought the flood to destroy the earth and all that lived in it, except Noah and his family because they were righteous. GOD told Noah to build an ark. By faith, he did as GOD told him and built an ark that took him 120 years to build! Now that is doing the math, and we all know the flood came and destroyed the earth! The first man after the flood did not do the math. It was Ham, one of Noah's sons; let us read his story in Genesis.

> GENESIS 9:18–29—The sons of Noah who came out of the ark were Shem, Ham and Japheth. (Ham was the father of Canaan.) These were the three sons of Noah, and from them came the people who were scattered over the earth.
>
> Noah, a man of the soil, proceeded to plant a vineyard. When he drank some of its wine, he became drunk and lay uncovered inside his tent. Ham, the father of Canaan, saw his father's nakedness and told his two brothers outside. But Shem and Japheth took a garment and laid it across their shoulders; then they walked in backward and covered their father's nakedness. Their faces were turned the other way so that they would not see their father's nakedness.
>
> When Noah awoke from his wine and found out what his youngest son had done to

him, he said, "Cursed be Canaan! The lowest of slaves will he be to his brothers." He also said, "Blessed be the LORD, the GOD of Shem! May Canaan be the slave of Shem. May GOD extend the territory of Japheth: May Japheth live in the tents of Shem, and may Canaan be his slave."

After the flood Noah lived 350 years. Altogether, Noah lived 950 years, and then he died.

Ham did not do the math by broadcasting, rather than covering, his father's immodesty. After I read this story of Noah and that his son, by accident, saw his father's nakedness; now my own story is worth telling.

I had a guy working for me in my residence at one time for about more than one year. As I got into the bathroom to take a shower, for about two weeks, he comes at my door to ask me a question related to work. I had a feeling of what he had in mind. Finally, he succeeded and saw my nakedness, after two weeks of trying to open my bathroom door. I did not think much about it that time until some of our friends told me about that guy, that he was broadcasting about my nakedness! A year after that, two people attacked him in his house and left him to die! I felt sorry for the guy until I started studying the BIBLE and knew the importance of the Word of GOD.

Another example is when GOD said to the Israelites to observe the Sabbath of the land, and they disobeyed GOD. Then GOD allowed their enemies to conquer their land, and they were taken prisoners to Babylon for seventy years. We should not ever question GOD'S commands and obey him because GOD said so.

Generations of people did not do the math when they tried to build the tower of Babel. Let us read this story about Babel.

GENESIS 11:1–9—Now the whole world had one language and a common speech. As men moved eastward, they found a plain in Shinar and settled there. They said to each other, "Come, let's make bricks and bake them thoroughly." They used brick instead of stone, and tar for mortar. Then they said, "Come, let us build ourselves a city, with a tower that reaches to heaven, so that we may make a name for ourselves and not be scattered over the face of the whole earth."

But the LORD came down to see the city and the tower that the men were building. The LORD said, "If as one people speaking the same language they have begun to do this, then nothing they plan to do will be impossible for them. Come, let us go down and confuse their language so they will not understand each other." SO the LORD scattered them from there over all the earth, and they stopped building the city. That is why it was called Babel—because there the LORD confused the language of the whole world. From there the LORD scattered them over the face of the whole earth.

Why did GOD interfere? If the whole human race remained united in the proud attempt to take its destiny into its own hands and by its man-centered efforts to seize the reins of history, there would be no limit to its unrestrained rebellion against GOD. The kingdom of man would displace and exclude the kingdom of GOD.

Another righteous man who did the math was Abraham. When GOD said to him to leave his country and his family and go to the land that GOD will show him, Abraham did that by faith as GOD said to him and told him, "I will make you into a great nation." And GOD made him into a great nation through his son, Isaac. And Isaac did the math and walked with GOD. And after him, his son, Jacob, also did the math and became a great nation as GOD had promised their father, Abraham. After Jacob, his son, Joseph also did the math and obeyed GOD. When Potiphar's wife tried to seduce him, he ran from her to not fall into sin and later became Pharaoh, second-in-command. That is what will happen when we do the math and obey GOD.

Another man of GOD did the math, and it was Moses. He left the house of the Pharaoh and led the Israelites through the Sinai desert and then to the promised land.

Then the young man Joshua did the math with his friend Caleb when GOD said in Numbers 14:30, "'Not one of you will enter the land. I swore with uplifted hand to make your home, except Caleb son of Jephunneh and Joshua son of Nun.'"

In Joshua 1:1, "After the death of Moses the servant of the LORD, the LORD said to Joshua son of Nun, Moses' aide: "Moses my servant is dead. Now then, you and all these people, get ready to cross the Jordan river into the land I am about to give to them to the Israelites." After Joshua crossed the Jordan river, the LORD said to him, "Today I will begin to exalt you in the eyes of all Israel, so they may know that I am with you as I was with Moses."

Joshua was going to war against the five kings from Gilgal with his entire army, and the LORD said to him, "Do not be afraid of them. I have given them into your hand. Not one of them will be able to withstand you." Joshua took them by surprise. The LORD threw them into confusion before the Israelites. Again when we obey GOD, we will be victorious in all what we do! Glory to our loving GOD and Savior.

Rahab the prostitute did the math and saved herself and her family. GOD uses the sinners for his plan; and look at Rahab now! In the book of Hebrews 11:13, by faith, the prostitute Rahab, because she welcomed the spies, was not killed with those who were disobedient.

Joshua 2:1–24—Rahab and the Spies

Then JOSHUA son of NUN secretly sent two spies from Shittim. "Go look over the land," he said, "especially Jericho." SO they went and entered the house of a prostitute named RAHAB and stayed there.

The king of Jericho was told, "Look! Some of the Israelites have come here tonight to spy out the land." So the king of Jericho sent this message to RAHAB: "Bring out the men who came to you and entered your house. They have come to spy out the whole land."

But the woman had taken the two men and hidden them. She said, "Yes the men came to me, but I did not know where they had come from. At dusk, when it was time to close the city gate, the men left. I don't know which way they went. Go after them quickly. You may catch up with them." (But she had taken them up to the roof and hidden them under the stalks of flax she had laid out on the roof.) So the men set out in pursuit of the spies on the road that leads to the fords of the Jordan, and as soon as the pursuers had gone out, the gate was shut.

Before the spies lay down for the night, she went up on the roof and said to them, "I know that the LORD has given this land to you and that a great fear of you has fallen on us, so that all who live in this country arc melting in fear because of you. We have heard how the LORD dried up the water of the Red Sea for you when you came out of Egypt, and what you did to SIHON and OG, the two kings of the Amorites east of the Jordan, whom you completely destroyed. When we heard of it, our hearts melted and everyone's courage failed because of you, for the LORD your GOD is GOD of heaven above and on the earth below. Now then, please swear to me by the LORD that you will show kindness to my family, because I have shown kindness to you. Give me a sure sign that you will spare the lives of my father and mother, my brothers and sisters, and all who belong to them."

"Our lives for your lives!' the men assured her. "If you don't tell what we are doing, we will treat you kindly and faithfully when the LORD gives us the land."

So she let them down by a rope through the window, for the house she lived in was part of the city wall. Now she had said to them, "Go to the hills so the pursuers will not find you. Hide yourselves there three days until they return, and then go on your way."

The men said to her, "This oath you made us swear will not be binding on us unless, when we enter the land, you have tied this scarlet cord in the window through which you let us down, and unless you have brought your father and mother, your brothers and all your family into your house. If anyone goes outside your house into the street, his blood will be on his own head: we will not be responsible. As for anyone who is in the house with you, his blood will be on our head if a hand is laid on him. But if you tell what we are doing, we will be released from the oath you made us swear."

"Agreed," she replied. "Let it be as you say." So she sent them away and they departed. And she tied the scarlet cord in the window.

When they left, they went into the hills and stayed there three days, until the pursuers had searched all along the road and returned without finding them. Then the two men started back. They went down out of the hills, forded the river and came to JOSHUA son of NUN and told him everything that had happened to them. They said to JOSHUA, "The LORD has surely given the whole land into our hands: all the people are melting in fear because of us."

And now I say to the people who point at me, saying, "He is the bad guy": well, GOD has saved me from all the sins I committed for his plan and purpose. And I say to all of you who pointed their fingers and said, "Assaf is the bad guy." I say to all of you: look at me now! And read Matthew 7:1–5: "Do not judge, or you too will be judged. For in the same way you judge others, you will be judged, and with the measure you use, it will be measured to you. Why do you look at the speck of sawdust in your brother's eye and pay no attention to the plank in your own eye? How can you say to your brother, 'Let me take the speck out of your eye,' when all the time there is a plank in your own eye?"

Saul Did the Math
and Became Paul

Saul of Tarsus, Paul of Tarsus, Saul the Pharisee, the philosopher and the preacher of the Word of GOD, the BIBLE. Saul
thought serving God was by persecuting the Christians, and
he watched his people stone the Prophet Stephen to death until he
became Paul; Stephen, a man of God. Saul also destroyed the church.
Going from house to house, he dragged off men and women and put
them in prison. In Acts 9:1–19,

> Meanwhile, Saul was still breathing out murder-
> ous threats against the Lord's disciples. He went
> to the high priest and asked him for letters to the
> synagogues in Damascus, so that if he found any
> there who belonged to the Way, whether men
> or women, he might take them as prisoners to
> Jerusalem. As he neared Damascus on his jour-
> ney, suddenly a light from heaven flashed around
> him. He fell to the ground and heard a voice say
> to him, "Saul, Saul, why do you persecute me?"
> "Who are you, LORD?" Saul asked.
> "I am JESUS, whom you are persecuting,"
> he replied. "Now get up and go into the city, and
> you will be told what you must do."
> The men traveling with Saul stood there
> speechless; they heard the sound but did not
> see anyone. Saul got up from the ground, but

when he opened his eyes he could see nothing. So they led him by the hand into Damascus. For three days he was blind, and did not eat or drink anything.

In Damascus there was a disciple named Ananias. The Lord called to him in a vision, "Ananias!"

"Yes, Lord," he answered.

The Lord told him, "Go to the house of Judas on Straight Street and ask for a man from Tarsus named Saul, for he is praying. In a vision he has seen a man named Ananias come and place his hands on him to restore his sight."

"Lord," Ananias answered, "I have heard many reports about this man and all the harm he has done to your holy people in Jerusalem. And he has come here with authority from the chief priests to arrest all who call on your name."

But the Lord said to Ananias, "Go! This man is my chosen instrument to proclaim my name to the Gentiles and their kings and to the people of Israel. I will show him how much he must suffer for my name."

Then Ananias went to the house and entered it. Placing his hands on Saul, he said, "Brother Saul, the Lord—JESUS, who appeared to you on the road as you were coming here—has sent me so that you may see again and be filled with the Holy Spirit." Immediately, something like scales fell from Saul's eyes, and he could see again. He got up and was baptized, and after taking some food, he regained his strength.

Saul was on his way to Damascus to persecute the Christians. He thought he was serving GOD as a Pharisee, but when our LORD JESUS appeared to him on his way to Damascus to persecute the

Christians again, "Why do you persecute me?" JESUS blinded Saul for three days and then healed him. After Saul was healed, he did the math and realized the power of our LORD JESUS. Saul obeyed JESUS and started to preach in the synagogues that JESUS is the Son of GOD and the Savior of the world.

> ACTS 13:4–12. Saul and Barnabas, sent on their way by the Holy Spirit, went down to Seleucia and sailed from there to Cyprus. When they arrived at Salamis, they proclaimed the word of GOD in the Jewish synagogues.
>
> They traveled through the whole island until they came to PAPHOS. There they met a Jewish sorcerer and false prophet named Bar-JESUS, who was an attendant of the proconsul, Sergius Paulus. The proconsul, an intelligent man, sent for Barnabas and Saul because he wanted to hear the word of GOD. But Elymas the sorcerer (for that is what his name means) opposed them and tried to turn the proconsul from the faith.
>
> Then Saul, who was also called Paul, filled with the HOLY SPIRJT, looked straight at Elymas and said, "You are a child of the devil and an enemy of everything that is right! You are full of all kinds of deceit and trickery. Will you never stop perverting the right ways of the LORD? Now the hand of the LORD is against you. You are going to be blind, and for a time you will be unable to see the light of the sun."
>
> Immediately mist and darkness came over him, and he groped about, seeking someone to lead him by the hand. When the proconsul saw what had happened, he believed, for he was amazed at the teaching about the LORD.

Proconsul. Since Cyprus was a Roman senatorial province, a proconsul was assigned to it.

Saul, also called Paul. The names mean "asked [of GOD]" and "little," respectively. It was customary to have a given name (in this case, Paul [Hebrew, Jewish background]), and later name (in this case, Paul [Roman, Hellenistic background]). From now on, Saul is called Paul in Acts. This may be due to Saul's success in preaching to Paulus or to the fact that he is now entering the Gentile phase of his ministry. The order in which they are mentioned now change from "Barnabas and Saul" to "Paul and Barnabas." Upon their return to the Jerusalem church, however, the order reverts to "Barnabas and Paul."

JESUS blinded Saul, and JESUS healed Saul; and after three days, Saul was baptized and became Paul to serve JESUS, whom he was persecuting. Paul now is serving JESUS; after he saw the light through his eyes and his heart, then he became the preacher of the Word of GOD.

When Paul met Elymas the sorcerer, Paul said to him, "You are a child of devil. You are going to be blind." The LORD blinded Elymas, like he blinded Saul. The LORD could paralyze him or cut his tongue so he could not speak; but darkness came over him, and he was blinded. The message is powerful. Paul was blinded, and he saw the light in his eyes and in his heart and gave his life to LORD JESUS by believing in him and preaching his Word. When will Elymas see the light? "Because," Paul said to him, "for a time you will be able to see the light of the sun."

It took Paul three days to see the light, that JESUS is the Savior of this world. JESUS said in John 14:6, "'I am the way and the truth and the life. No one comes to the Father except through me. If you really knew me, you would know my Father as well. From now on, you do know him and have seen him.'"

Me…my Father. Once more, JESUS stresses the intimate connection between the Father and himself. JESUS brought a full revelation of the Father (cf. 1:18) so that the apostles had real knowledge of him. In John 1:18, "No one has ever seen GOD but GOD the One and Only who is at the Father's side has made him known."

Paul believed that JESUS is the way, and as soon as Paul realized that way, he was on his way to heaven where the Father GOD is. The question is, for Elymas, how much time will it take him to see the light? Paul did not specify the time it will take Elymas to see the light, but he left it up to him. Our LORD GOD also will leave it up to us to realize that JESUS is the way, the truth, and the life.

There is no other way to GOD except through his Son JESUS, and GOD the Father said that about JESUS. We all died for the sin of one man, Adam, and we will live by the sacrifice of one man, JESUS. In Romans 5:8, "But GOD demonstrates his own love for us in this: While we were still sinners, CHRIST died for us." GOD the Father said this about JESUS, "You are my Son, whom I love; with you I am well pleased."

The moment JESUS opened Saul's eyes, Saul's heart was open to JESUS, and he was saved that moment. Anyone who will open his heart to JESUS and confess that JESUS is LORD and preach to others about JESUS will be saved and on his way to heaven to live forever.

Will Elymas do what Simon the sorcerer did? When the people of Samaria accepted the Word of GOD by the preaching of Philip about the good news of the kingdom of GOD and the name of JESUS CHRIST, they were baptized. Simon the sorcerer believed and was baptized and followed Philip everywhere, astonished by the great signs and miracles he saw.

> ACTS 8:18—When Simon saw that the Spirit was given at the laying on of the apostles hands, he offered them money and said, "Give me also this ability so that everyone on whom I lay my hands may receive the Holy Spirit."
>
> Peter answered: "May your money perish with you, because you thought you could buy the gift of GOD with money! You have no part or share in this ministry, because your heart is not right before GOD. Repent of this wickedness and pray to the LORD. Perhaps he will forgive you for

having such a thought in your heart. For I see that
you are full of bitterness and captive to sin."

Is Elymas going to open his heart to JESUS and serve him, or
he is going to keep harboring bitterness in his heart and be captive to
sin? Well, his heart will determine when his eyes will be open.

I have an illustration to share. When I reached the gate to enter
to my home, there was a car in front of me trying to open the gate, so
I opened the gate for him to be able to get home. But the driver did
not see the gate was already open, so I pressed on the horn slightly
to get his attention. But he still was trying to get the combination.
Again, I pressed my horn louder. By then, he lost his temper and got
out of his car and used a bad language. I laughed at him and said,
"What you are trying to do? I did that for you. Just listen and open
your eyes. I am trying to show you that the gate is open. When you
listen, you will see. Don't be occupied by your thoughts only."

The gate is open, and I am helping you to go through it! How many
of us are trying to get through the gate and it is wide open, but we are
blinded by our hearts and eyes? We see that every day in our lives. If
we only listen and pay attention and not only depend on our intelligence because of our pride.

Our LORD JESUS came to earth and shed his blood for us and
opened the gate of heaven because of the love he has for us; but we
are still blinded with our occupied minds, and we don't see that the
gate is wide open. Only a few of us pay attention to where we going,
and the gate is open for us.

Our LORD JESUS died for us and was in the tomb for three
days. And then he was resurrected from death and lifted up to heaven
to be at the side of the Father. The prophet Jonah was three days in
the belly of the big fish, and from the belly of the fish, Jonah cried
out to GOD, and GOD saved him by commanding the fish to vomit
him onto dry land. Then Jonah obeyed GOD and went to Nineveh
and to proclaim in the city. Saul was blinded for three days, and our
LORD JESUS opened his eyes and became the apostle Paul, the servant of our LORD JESUS, our Savior.

The number three is used 467 times in the BIBLE. It pictures completeness, though to a lesser degree than the number seven. In Acts 19:8, "Paul entered the Synagogue and spoke boldly there for three months, arguing persuasively about the Kingdom of GOD." Three is the number of the Holy Trinity of Father, Son and Holy Ghost. JESUS spread Christianity for three years. Three wise men came to JESUS bearing three gifts: gold, frankincense, and myrrh. The three righteous patriarchs before the flood were Abel, Enoch, and Noah.

When Paul realized the power of our LORD JESUS, Paul did the math and became a follower of JESUS. In his letter to the Romans 1:1–7, "Paul, a servant of CHRIST JESUS, called to be an apostle and set part for the gospel of GOD—the gospel he promised beforehand through his prophets in the HOLY Scriptures regarding his Son, who as to his human nature was a descendant of David, and who through the Spirit of holiness was declared with power to be the Son of GOD by his resurrection from the dead: JESUS CHRIST our LORD. Through him and for his name's sake, we received grace and apostleship to call people from among all the Gentiles to the obedience that comes from faith. And you also are among those who are called to belong to JESUS CHRIST. To all in Rome who are loved by GOD and called to be saints: Grace and peace to you from GOD our Father and from the LORD JESUS CHRIST."

Prophets. Not just the writers of the prophetic books for the whole OT prophesied about JESUS coming.

Saints. The basic idea of the Greek for this word is "holiness." All Christians are saints in that they are positionally "set apart" to GOD and are experientially being made increasingly "holy" by the Holy Spirit.

Grace. In Ephesians 1:2, "Grace and peace to you from GOD our Father and the LORD JESUS CHRIST."

Peace. In John 14:27, "'Peace I leave with you; my peace I give you. I do not give to you as the world gives. Do not let your hearts be troubled and do not be afraid.'"

GOD has condemned all men as the result of the trespass of one man, Adam, when he was deceived by Satan because Adam did not do the math as GOD commanded him not to eat from the tree of knowledge of good and bad. Adam did not obey GOD and ate from the tree that GOD commanded him not to eat from! Adam was deceived by Satan; and Satan deceived himself by thinking he could disobey GOD, who created him. Satan did not do the math either. The conclusion of the deceived Adam and the deceiver Satan is eternal death, without the possibility of redemption! Let us read Romans 5:18–19: "Consequently, just as the result of one trespass was condemnation for all men, so also the result of one act of righteousness was justification that brings life for all men. For just as through the disobedience of the one man the many were made sinners, so also through the obedience of the one man the many will be made righteous."

Life for all men. Does not mean that everyone eventually will be saved but that salvation is available to all. To be effective, GOD'S gracious gift must be received (see v. 17). For if, by the trespass of the one man, death reigned through that one man, how much more will those who receive GOD'S abundant provision of grace and of the gift of righteousness reign in life through the one man, JESUS CHRIST?

At this point, I was struggling how to finish this chapter in an intelligent closing; so as usual, when I find myself at a stumbling block, I pray to GOD to help me to end what I am doing to an intelligent conclusion.

The time is close to 10:00 p.m., Monday, June 17th. A few hours before my seventy-second years for my birthday, a revelation came to me to write about Adam and how he was deceived by Satan. GOD has given us commandments and gave us the free will to obey his commandments or not to obey. GOD left all that to us to decide. Satan and Adam both were deceived; Satan deceived Adam, and Satan was deceived himself. At the beginning of my book, I stated that I was furious with Adam with how he was deceived and how we all were condemned to death because of one man's sin.

Satan and Adam were created not to fail GOD'S commands, but when they fail GOD'S commands, they both were sentenced to death without the possibility of redemption because JESUS did not die for them but for us who were sentenced to death because of the disobedience of one man, Adam.

GOD gave the free will to all of us because of his love to all, and GOD did not create us not to fail him because GOD knows we are weak and all of us could not obey his commands. GOD knows none of us is righteous. We cannot make it on our own. We need his grace and mercy; that is why GOD sent his Son to die for us because we all are sinners and sentenced to death for the sin of one man, Adam.

Through the sacrifice that our LORD JESUS did by shedding his blood on the cross, we were redeemed from our sins. That was the grace of the loving GOD for us. But if we were created not to fail GOD'S commandments and then failed his commandments, we will be sentenced to death like Satan and Adam without the possibility of redemption. That means that JESUS would not die for us to redeem us because we were born not to fail GOD'S commandments, so GOD would not send his Son to die for us.

GOD created JESUS not to fail him, and JESUS did not fail GOD and went through the suffering on the cross and took our sins—he who did not sin. And while JESUS was suffering on the cross, JESUS asked his Father to pass that cup JESUS was about to endure, but then he said, "It is not my will but your will." JESUS asked the Father to pass that cup because it was so difficult to go through what JESUS was about to go through—the pain—to take our sins because JESUS did not sin.

JESUS also was telling us that we, the sinners, ought to remember what JESUS did for us because of the love he has for us. No one could do what JESUS did, unless he is GOD himself! My brothers and sisters, I urge you to do the math to have an everlasting life in heaven or on earth by studying the Word of GOD, the BIBLE.

The end of age is near. It could happen in our lifetime, so be ready. There is no pleasure in this life to compensate the pleasure in heaven or on earth, where we will have an eternal life and the pleasure is a million times over what we experience in this lifetime. I hope to all to be there with me! I say that with confidence because I am doing what pleases GOD, and if I fail him, I am covered with our LORD'S blood, JESUS CHRIST. If I don't make a career of my sin, I am covered. Glory to GOD our Savior.

GOD loves his children; and when we accept, acknowledge, and return his love, GOD will manifest himself and give birth of faith in our hearts. When we reach that love and faith, GOD will bless us in peace of mind in our lives on this earth and will remove every stumbling block out of our ways, even mountains! In Matthew 17:20, "JESUS said to his disciples, 'I tell you the truth, if you have faith as small as a mustard seed, you can say to this mountain, "Move from here to there," and it will move. Nothing will be impossible for you.'"

When we focus on GOD and the faith we have in him, then the mountain will be like a gravel, and we will be able to move that mountain as we move the gravel! No matter how big is the stumbling block in our lives, by the faith we have in our GOD, we will be able to remove anything and be free from it because JESUS said to his disciples, "Every one of you, when you reach that faith GOD has blessed with and obey all his commandments, will be his servants and perform miracles."

"JESUS Heals a Paralytic" (Mark 2:3–12) tells us the story of a paralytic man and his four friends who carried him to see JESUS to heal him, but they could not get to him to JESUS because of the crowd; they went to the staircase to the side of the house that has a flat roof accessible by means of an outside staircase. The roof is made out of dirt, supported by mats of wood and also by wood beams. I lived in a house like this house described by the book of Mark in Lebanon during my childhood, and I remember in the winter, we used to shuffle off the snow to protect the roof from caving in and also the dripping of the water.

That was the only way for those four men to get to JESUS: by making an opening in the roof above JESUS. After digging through the roof, they lowered the mat the paralyzed man was lying on, but when JESUS saw their faith, he said to the paralytic, "Son, your sins are forgiven." So are our sins will also be forgiven by JESUS when we have that faith.

Those five men had their focus on JESUS and how to get the paralytic to him. They did not consider the property damage they caused to the owner of the house or the dust falling on the crowd; and the crowd themselves did not bother to complain when they noticed the five men and their faith.

Another story of faith is about a dead girl and a sick woman. A synagogue ruler named Jairus seeking JESUS fell at his feet and pleaded with JESUS, "My little daughter is dying. Please come and put your hands on her so that she will be healed and live."

So JESUS went with him. A large crowed followed and pressed around JESUS, and a woman was there who had been subject to bleeding for twelve years. When she heard about JESUS, she came up behind him in the crowed and touched his cloak because she thought, *If I just touch JESUS's clothes, I will be healed.* Immediately, her bleeding stopped.

At once, JESUS realized that power had gone out from him. JESUS turned around in the crowed and asked, "Who touched my clothes?"

His disciples answered, "There are lots of people pressing against you, and you ask, 'Who touched me'?"

Then the woman came and fell at his feet and, trembling with fear, told JESUS the whole truth. JESUS said to her, "Daughter, your faith has healed you. Go in peace and be freed from your suffering." The mountain was moved from that woman's life by the faith she has in our LORD JESUS when he said to us, "If you have faith, as a mustard seed, you could move mountains."

While JESUS was still speaking, some men came from the house of Jairus. "Your daughter is dead," they said.

Ignoring what they said, JESUS told Jairus, "Don't be afraid. Just believe." JESUS went with his disciples to the home of Jairus.

People crying and wailing loudly, JESUS said to them, "Why all this commotion and wailing? The child is not dead but asleep." JESUS took the child's father and mother and his disciples where the child was. JESUS took her by the hand and said to her, "Talitha koum! [Little girl, I say to you, get up!]"

Immediately, the girl stood up and walked around. She was twelve years old. JESUS gave a strict order not to let anyone know about that miracle! Because in the vicinity of Galilee, JESUS often cautioned people whom he healed not to spread the story of the miracle. His great popularity with the people, coupled with the growing opposition from the religious leaders, could have precipitated a crisis before JESUS's ministry was completed. You could also see the strict orders in Mark (1:44; 5:19; same 7:36; 8:26). JESUS sent him away at once with a strong warning: "See that you don't tell this to anyone. But go, show yourself to the priest and offer the sacrifices that Moses commanded for your cleansing, as a testimony to them."

The Healing of a Demon-Possessed Man

MARK 5:1–20—When JESUS got out of the boat, a man with an evil spirit came from the tombs to meet him. This man lived in the tombs, and no one could bind him anymore, not even with a chain. For he had often been chained hand and foot, but he tore the chains apart and broke the irons on his feet. No one was strong enough to subdue him. Night and day among the tombs and in the hills he would cry out and cut himself with stones.

When he saw JESUS from a distance, he ran and fell on his knees in front of him. He shouted at the top of his voice, "What do you want with me, JESUS, Son of the Most High GOD? Swear to GOD that you won't torture me!" For JESUS had said to him, "Come out of this man, you evil spirit!"

The JESUS asked him, "What is your name?"

"My name is Legion," he replied, "For we are many." And he begged JESUS again and again not to send them out of the area. A large herd of pigs feeding on the nearby hillside. The demon begged JESUS, "Send us among the pigs; allow us to go into them." He gave them permission, and the evil spirits came out and went into the pigs. The herd, about two thousand in number, rushed down the steep bank into the lake and were drowned.

Those tending the pigs ran off and reported this in the town and countryside, and the people went out to see what had happened. When they came to JESUS, they saw the man who had been possessed by the legion of demons, sitting there, dressed and in his right mind; and they were afraid. Those who had seen it told the people what had happened to the demon-possessed man—and told about the pigs as well. Then the people began to plead with JESUS to leave their region.

As JESUS was getting into the boat, the man who had been demon-possessed begged to go with him. JESUS did not let him but said, "Go home to your family and tell them how much the LORD has done for you, and how he has had mercy on you."

So the man went away and began to tell in the Decapolis how much JESUS had done for him. And all the people were amazed.

Across the lake. The east side of the lake, a territory largely by Gentiles, as indicated by the presence of the large herd of pigs—animals Jews considered "unclean" and therefore unfit to eat.

Lived in the tombs. It was not unusual for the same cave to provide burial for the dead and shelter for the living. Very poor people often lived in such caves.

He had often been chained. Though the villagers no doubt chained him partly for their own protection, this harsh treatment added to his humiliation.

He would cry out and cut himself with stones. Every word in the story emphasizes the man's pathetic condition as well as the purpose of demonic possession—to torment and destroy the divine likeness with which man was created. No matter how much Satan will succeed in tormenting some people for the short time he has on earth, GOD already gave him a life sentence in hell where he will be tormented himself for eternity. And Satan will not be able to destroy the divine likeness with which man was created.

What do you want with me…? A way of saying, "What do we have in common?" "Mind your own business!" The demon was speaking using the voice of the possessed man. *Son of the Most High GOD. Swear to GOD that you won't torture me!* The demon sensed that he was to be punished and used the strongest basis for an oath that he knew, though his appeal to GOD was strangely ironic.

My name is Legion for we are many. A Roman legion was made up of six thousand men. Here the term suggests that the man was possessed by numerous demons and perhaps also represents the many powers opposed to JESUS, who embodies the power of GOD.

Not to send them out of the area. The demons were fearful of being sent into eternal punishment, i.e., "into the Abyss." We don't actually know the real name of the possessed man with two thousand demons, which got him the nickname of Legion. The demons are the fallen angels. They also were deceived by Satan. They follow a loser, and they are obligated to oppose JESUS because they did not obey their creator, GOD. I hope we do learn from the mistakes of others so we don't have to pay the big price the deceived ones had to pay.

The proof came out of the mouth of the demons by asking JESUS to keep them in the area they're in and not send them into eternal punishment, into the Abyss, but eventually they are on their way to where they belong because they were created not to fail GOD.

But we here on earth have the chance to live for eternity by acknowledging that our LORD JESUS became a human and died for us, whoever believes in him. Glory to our Savior and LORD JESUS the CHRIST. Amen to that.

He gave them permission. See note on Matthew 8:32: "He said to them, 'Go!' So they came out and went into the pigs, and the whole herd rushed down the steep bank into the lake and died in the water.

And told about the pigs as well. In addition to the remarkable change in the demon-possessed man, the drowning of the pigs seemed to be a major concern, no doubt because it was so dramatic and brought considerable financial loss to the owners.

Plead with Jesus to leave their region. Fear of further loss may have motivated this response, but also the fact that a powerful force was at work in their midst that they could not comprehend.

Tell them how much the Lord has done for you. This is in marked contrast to JESUS's exhortation to silence in the case of the man cleansed of leprosy, perhaps because the healing of the demonic was in Gentile territory where there was little danger that Messianic ideas about JESUS might be circulated.

JESUS said to Jairus, the father of the little girl "Don't be afraid. Just believe," after some people came and said to Jairus, "Your daughter is dead. Why bother the teacher anymore?" But JESUS said to the father of the little girl, "Just believe." When we believe and have faith in GOD, mountains will be moved no matter how magnificent the mountain is in our lives; GOD will move it when we believe in him, but not when we depend on our strength and ability and what resources we might have. Peace of mind comes not by what we've accomplished or by authority but by what we know about the love of GOD for us and our faith in him.

Here is another faith story about a powerful man, the centurion (Matthew 8:5–13).

> The Centurion man is a Roman military officer, in charge of 100 soldiers; he came to JESUS asking for help. "LORD" he said, "my servant lies at home paralyzed and in terrible suffering."

JESUS said to him, "I will go and heal him."

The Centurion replied, "LORD, I do not deserve to have you come under my roof. But just say the word and my servant will be healed." [The Greek for *healed* actually means "saved" or "be freed from your suffering."] The Centurion said to JESUS, "You don't have to come to my home. For I am a man under authority with soldiers under me. I tell this one, 'Go,' and he goes; and that one, 'Come,' and he comes. I say to my servant, 'Do this,' and he does."

When JESUS heard this, he was astonished and said to those following him, "I tell you the truth, I have not found anyone in Israel with such great faith." Then JESUS said to the Centurion, "GO! It will be done just as you believed it would." And his servant was healed at that very hour.

The centurion is a Roman officer. He never met JESUS, but he heard about the miracles that JESUS did and believed in what he heard. He went to JESUS, believing that JESUS will heal his servant. Jairus as well. His little girl was dead, but JESUS said to him, "Don't be afraid. Just believe. Just believe." And JESUS brought his little girl back to life! Just believe.

The message to all of us is what JESUS said two thousand years ago: just believe and it will be done to you. Just believe. Also JESUS said to all of us in John 14:6: Just believe that "I am the way and the truth and the life. No one comes to the Father except through me." Just believe.

In conclusion, I wrote this book to share with everyone on this earth my testimony about the love of GOD for us and GOD'S purpose for all his children to be saved and live forever as GOD intended for Adam and Eve.

Adam disobeyed GOD when he ate the first fruit of the tree that GOD commanded him not to eat from, and that is how we are all condemned to death, because of the sin of the man Adam. But because of the love of GOD for this world, GOD has sent his first fruit and without any blemish, his only Son JESUS, to redeem us from sin. And whoever believes that JESUS took our sin, he who did not sin, and suffered and died on the cross will have everlasting life with JESUS in heaven.

GOD loved Abraham because he had faith in GOD and was ready to sacrifice his first fruit and only son, Isaac, by the promise of GOD. But GOD prepared the sacrifice for Abraham, and GOD said to Abraham, "Do not slay the boy," because Abraham was going all in for GOD. GOD wanted all of us to be like Abraham and the other prophets like Jonah, Job, Daniel, and others.

For the prophet Jonah, I wrote about him because of my mother. She told me his story throughout my childhood, about how GOD saved him from the belly of the big fish after three days; but my false preacher said to me that Jonah survived by being in the belly of the fish because the big belly of the fish contains lots of volumes of air! And that is how Jonah survived for three days in the belly of the big fish; and that is how I left the kingdom hall of my false preacher. He, they, all of them ignored the power of GOD. When Jonah was thrown overboard the ship, GOD has provided for him the big fish to swallow him and then to vomit Jonah on dry land.

GOD defeated Satan by Job when GOD allowed Satan to inflict a severe suffering on Job, but Job did not allow Satan to deceive him like Adam did! And GOD said about Job, "There is no one on earth like Job," of course, until the coming of our LORD JESUS CHRIST.

My mother also told me about how GOD saved Daniel from the mouth of the lions when he was put there to be eaten by the hungry lions because of his faith in his GOD. My mother also new the names of Shadrach, Meshach, and Abednego and how GOD saved them from the blazing furnace because they did not bow to the image of gold that King Nebuchadnezzar has set up on the plains of Babylon. But GOD was with them and delivered them from the blazing furnace without the burning of one hair on their heads because they believed in their GOD, the creator of heaven and earth.

My beloved, brothers and sisters, do not be deceived by the enemy of GOD. The way to be in heaven is to study the Word of GOD, the BIBLE, like what I am doing now. I study the BIBLE every day to be able to serve our LORD GOD, the way GOD wanted us to be to serve his purpose and return his love for us; then we will please him and GOD will bless us with our heart's desires and we will enjoy our time here on earth until our LORD JESUS comes back and will be resurrected from death to be with him in heaven. That is, of course, if we believed in him, that JESUS died for our sins because of his love for us; and I am living his love, and I am dedicating my life to serve him until I breath my last. Glory to GOD. Amen to that.

JESUS said to us, "Just believe." And I do believe.

I have finished the tuxedo for David, my son, to wear on his wedding day and shipped it to him. I was living in San Diego at that time. His mother called me to thank me for the beautiful tuxedo I made for David, and I sent her the airline ticket to fly to San Diego from Las Vegas. She stayed with me a few days to drive to San Francisco and to where the wedding was taking place.

The day before the wedding, I said to Maureen, "I am not be able to make it to the wedding!"

"Are you out of your mind?"

"I just don't have the money to go to the wedding."

"Do you think making your son a tuxedo is enough?"

"Oh, if I did not know that!"

I went to my room to cry myself to the shame I brought on myself because of my selfish habits; I built a bad reputation for myself by prioritizing my gambling habits. I don't have a credit card to use, and none of my friends trust me when it comes to money. I did not learn my lesson until I started studying the Word of GOD, the BIBLE, at a late age; but never it is late to come to GOD. He welcomes you at any time you come to him. GOD is love, and when we acknowledge that and obey GOD, he gives us our heart desires.

That is my purpose why I am sharing my testimony with you. I hope I am making a difference with all of my testimony, and I hope to forgive me like how our GOD has forgiven me for all my trespasses.

About the Author

Written by Majid Sawaya
Assaf Sawaya, Magister in Arabic Literature,
Lebanese University, 1967

Assaf Sawaya was born in a village in northern Lebanon called Douma, in a family compound of six brothers and three sisters. His father worked outside town and would come home every two months. His mother cared for all the children during his absence; she was a saint. Assaf was the tallest of all his brothers (six feet, four inches), with an expressive face and healthy body. He looks like a movie star; he was a playboy until he got married. Spiritually, he has a good, loving heart and is a humble, loyal, and straightforward person with virtue.

Before his teenage years, Assaf moved to the city of Antelias, a suburb of Beirut, with his oldest brother. He became a professional craftsman as a tailor, and after a few years, his older brother helped him open a tailor shop next to his business. Assaf became an instant success and after four years, expressed his desire to immigrate to the US because he heard the drumbeat of civil war. He was right; the civil war broke out a few years after.

Assaf moved to the US and opened the way for his entire family to move to the great country of the US. Assaf married when he came to the US; but the marriage ended in divorce, and his life changed. He became a dealer at a casino besides his own business as a tailor; but as a dealer, he created a gambling habit and was losing all the money he was earning in both of his jobs.

Sawaya was then imprisoned for seven months in Lebanon on drug charges, though he was supposed to serve seven years according to Lebanese law. After his release, he went back to the city of Las Vegas and continued to deal drugs through people he had met in the prison in Lebanon. He was again imprisoned but was released after only three years instead of serving a full life sentence.

Sawaya has confessed that God was with him all the time, and he relates that to his loving heart. He truly believes in God, and he is surrendering the rest of his life to God. Sawaya has said that every time he gets himself into deep trouble, God will lift him up no matter how deep he is! God has a purpose for his life, and the changes have been very noticeable.

When Sawaya came up with the idea to write a book about his life, his brother apologetically laughed. However, his determination to write was very impressive, and after one year, he was able to finish and publish his book. God has already begun to change lives through this book, starting with Sawaya's older brother who has started to change himself by studying the Bible and asking God to accept and transform him.